Decebal and Trajan

Book Two of the Roman - Dacian Wars
100 – 102 A.D.

Peter Jaksa

Attention Publishing

CHICAGO, ILLINOIS

Peter Jaksa/Attention Publishing
30 North Michigan Avenue, Suite 908
Chicago, IL 60602
www.addcenters.com

Publisher's Note: This is a work of fiction. Names, characters, places, and incidents are a product of the author's imagination. Locales and public names are sometimes used for atmospheric purposes. Any resemblance to actual people, living or dead, or to businesses, companies, events, institutions, or locales is completely coincidental.

Decebal and Trajan / Peter Jaksa. -- 1st ed.
ISBN 978-1-7349923-7-3

For Griffin and Reid

Freedom is a possession of inestimable value.

– MARCUS TULLIUS CICERO

Contents

> Chapter 1

Spring Flowers

Sarmizegetusa, Dacia, March 100 AD

Princess Adila led the small group of children into the woods. They were on a morning mission to gather spring flowers for the Queen's birthday celebration. As the snows slowly melted, daffodils, crocuses, and tulips of every color bloomed wildly in grassy patches of soil a short distance down the mountainside below the city walls.

Her mother, Queen Andrada, would be celebrating her birthday tomorrow. Adila's plan was to surprise and delight the Queen with large bouquets of each kind of flower. She could hardly wait for the festive city-wide celebration and the look on her mother's face when the children walked in with their bouquets.

The children often walked in these woods under the watch of a palace guard, but not this day. Adila felt completely safe leading the younger children on this secret mission. The dangerous animals such as the wild boars had long ago been hunted out of the area. No one had seen a bear in these woods for a long time. Sometimes there were wolves but wolves kept their distance from humans unless they were starving, and there were no starving wolves in the spring. No, Adila did not worry about wild beasts. But neither, unfortunately, did she think about Iazygis.

At fifteen Adila was the oldest of the group, which also made her the leader. She was a vocal and gregarious girl who showed natural leadership qualities even among people a few years older than her. On this sunny day she enlisted the help of her younger cousin Ana and their friend Lia to carry back the large wicker baskets of flowers. Adila's brother, ten year old Dorin, came along to offer his protection. He was accompanied as always by his dog Toma.

"Come on, you have enough flowers!" Dorin said to his sister after half an hour of flower picking. He was getting bored and hungry. Toma ran off in pursuit of a squirrel or some other small animal.

"We're almost done," Adila replied. She cut the stems of some red tulips with a small sharp knife and placed the flowers in Ana's basket. "Help me with these and then we can go."

"Dorin doesn't pick flowers, it's unmanly," Lia said teasingly. She and Dorin were born just one day apart and grew up treating each other as brother and sister. Lia was the daughter of two Christian refugees who fled from Rome to escape the persecutions of Emperor Domitian. Ana, the niece of King Decebal, was one year younger and also Lia's best friend.

Dorin ignored the teasing, which he was used to. He looked around for his dog but could not see or hear him. He gave a loud whistle. "Toma! Here, boy!"

"That's enough!" Ana cried to Adila. "The basket is getting heavy." She was a slim girl with light brown hair and amber-brown eyes.

"All right, all right," Adila said with a laugh. She looked at the three baskets piled high and nodded her approval. "Yes, I think we have enough flowers."

Lia looked around. "Where did Dorin go?"

"Wherever Toma went, as usual," Adila replied. She picked up her basket. "Let's go home, he will follow us."

The way back to the city was an uphill climb. The girls walked slowly, making their way between the trees and thick shrubbery. They did not walk very far when Ana stopped, a startled look on her face. The two others stopped with her.

"What is it?" Adila asked, more curious than concerned.

"I heard something," Ana whispered. Her expression was anxious and her heart beat fast.

"Don't be afraid, there are no bears around here," Adila said with a smile. "Come on, follow me."

She turned to walk uphill, making her way through the trees and bushes. The younger girls followed. Ana looked back, fearful again.

"There is someone following us, Adila."

"It is probably Dorin. Stop imagining --"

Adila's voice was cut off abruptly when a man stepped out of the bushes behind her and clasped a rough hand over her mouth to keep her silent. His other hand placed a knife at her throat.

"Ebem, no!" a low voice from the bushes growled a warning, but the warning was too late to stop the attack. Someone hissed a furious curse, then three more men stepped out and surrounded the girls. They were young men, warriors. They were not Dacians.

The man called Ebem held Adila tightly and she froze in his grasp. The man did not look at her but directed himself to Lia and Ana. "Shhh! Do not make sound!"

Lia was petrified, still as a statue. Ana dropped her basket and squirmed against the hand that had grabbed her upper left arm to hold her in place. These strange men were armed with knives and swords. There was no escape.

Ebem took a step backwards. Adila planted her feet on the ground, desperately shook her head free and gave a very loud and piercing scream. Ana turned her head sideways and bit viciously into the thumb of the man holding her arm. The man yelped with pain and let go. She dashed off between the trees, running frantically downhill.

"Dorin! Dorin! Help!"

The man whose thumb Ana bit was right behind her. He was now angry and closing on her fast. He never saw the furry blur of a figure flying through the air, fangs going for his throat, knocking him down to the ground. Toma was a Dacian shepherd breed, a large and very powerful dog built like a wolf.

As he fell the warrior hit his head against a fallen log and was momentarily dazed. He struggled furiously to keep the dog away from his throat, but was severely clawed and bitten on his hands and arms. He tried to roll away and Toma jumped back on him.

Dorin ran up to them, face flushed and in a panic.

"Adila go help Adila!" Ana cried, pointing back in the direction from which she had come. Dorin ran after her back up the mountain.

What they found at the spot of the first attack came as a complete surprise. Two of the enemy warriors were dead on the ground, one with an arrow in the middle of his back and the other with a throat cut by a sword. Tarbus, a tall and strongly built Dacian warrior, had Adila's attacker on the ground and his foot planted firmly on the man's chest. Ebem had a deep slash across the left side of his face that was bleeding down his cheek and neck. Adila stood nearby, holding the small flower knife she had used to defend herself. Lia was holding Adila in a tight hug. Ana ran to join them.

"Dorin, are you all right?" a nearby voice asked. Dorin turned to see Cotiso, his adult half-brother, holding a sword stained red. He and Tarbus had been hunting nearby when they heard Adila's scream.

"Yes! But there's another one down there!" Dorin said, pointing downhill. "Toma attacked him!"

He ran back towards the spot, Cotiso following. They found Toma standing and still growling over the dead body of the enemy soldier. The man's windpipe was ripped open and a pool of blood gathered around his head. He was badly bitten and mauled, and never had a chance to draw his sword.

Dorin shouted happily and bent down to stroke the dog's neck.

"Good boy, Toma! Good dog!"

"It looks like you trained your dog well," Cotiso said with a grin.

"Toma knows what to do, he doesn't need much training." Dorin looked down at the dead man. "Who are these people?"

"They look like Iazygis," Cotiso said and spat on the ground. "What they are doing this close to Sarmizegetusa I don't know. Most likely spying on the allies' meetings with Father, I suppose." Their father, King Decebal, had called for a summit of Dacia's allies. The envoys were still gathering in the city.

"Ana said they attacked Adila," Dorin said angrily.

"They did. Adila fought off one of them for a short while but she was very lucky that we were nearby." Cotiso frowned at the thought of the tragedy that could have been. "Let's go, Brother. We must take our prisoner to the King."

When they got back to the group they found Tarbus smiling and the Iazygi prisoner with bruises on his face and holding his side.

"Good, you're back!" Tarbus said. "I got tired of beating up on this pig." He reached down and pulled up the prisoner by his shirt. "Let's go, you dirty swine. King Decebal will want to have a word about you attacking his daughter."

They led the unhappy prisoner up the mountain slope towards the road and the city gate, dragging him when he slowed down due to his broken ribs. Ana, Lia, and Adila followed, each carrying a basket of spring flowers. Dorin and Toma brought up the rear, keeping a sharp lookout just in case.

King Decebal was not happy. He had just met with an envoy from the Marcomanni tribe, and the man brought bad news. Chief Attalu of the Marcomanni had been replaced by one of his rivals. This new chief was more inclined to avoid conflict with Rome rather than to ally with Dacia against Rome. The Marcomanni were one of the most powerful of the Germanic Suebi tribes. This was a significant political and military setback for Dacia.

Representatives from the Sarmatians, Bastarnae, Celts, and Scythians were still arriving in Sarmizegetusa for the summit. As the richest nation and most powerful military power in the region, Dacia was the center of anti-Roman resistance. Many of Dacia's neighbors were worried about Rome's military expansion, and for good reason. Rome had an appetite for plunder, slaves, and new lands to occupy.

Emperor Trajan built many new Roman colonies in Moesia and Pannonia, and along the Ister River which the Romans called the Danubius. Roman legionnaires were promised a generous plot of land when they retired. There was no more land for settling in Italia, so new colonies had to be built in newly conquered territories. Trajan himself came from a family that lived in such a colony in Hispania, founded by retired army veterans. The Emperor was generous with his soldiers, which earned him the loyalty and love of his legions.

For the past decade King Decebal had worked to build political and military alliances with Dacia's neighbors. Some were not in favor of working with Dacia, such as the Iazygi tribes that lived to the west of Dacia. The Iazygis were old enemies of Dacia who often allied themselves with Roman armies. King Decebal kept them in check by forming pacts with all of the Iazygis' neighbors, so that they found themselves surrounded by Dacian allies.

Now, sitting on his throne, Decebal watched impatiently as his son Cotiso, along with his friend Tarbus, brought a Iazygi prisoner before him. Standing beside the King's throne was the old and very wise Vezina, High Priest of Zamolxis and chief advisor to the Dacian king. Standing beside Vezina was Diegis, younger brother to King Decebal and the father of Ana.

The prisoner limped as he approached. His bloodied face was cut and bruised from the rough treatment he received. The three men stopped a distance from the throne.

"Kneel before the King," Cotiso ordered. When Ebem hesitated Tarbus pushed down hard on his shoulder and the prisoner went down to his knees.

"Who are you? And what are you doing here on Dacian land?" King Decebal asked in a sharp voice.

Ebem knew that he was a doomed man and he was resigned to his fate. Still he was determined to maintain pride and honor before his captors. To his astonishment he found himself face to face with King Decebal and the High Priest Vezina, two names universally known and hated by all Iazygis. The King looked to be about forty years old, his black hair graying at the temples, but he was still fit and built like a warrior. Vezina was a tall and thin man, with a long white beard flowing down his chest. No one quite knew how old Vezina was.

Tarbus slapped Ebem across the back of the head. “Answer promptly when the King asks a question.”

The prisoner cleared his throat before speaking. His throat felt very dry. “I am Ebem of the Iazygi. I am here on a scouting mission.”

“You mean a spying mission,” Vezina corrected him.

“A scouting mission,” Ebem repeated.

“And what are you scouting, Ebem?” Decebal asked.

“Our mission is to scout the city. To see who arrives and leaves.”

“In other words, to spy on Dacia’s allies and see who meets with King Decebal. Speak plainly, man," Vezina said.

Ebem gave a small shrug. “It does not matter what we call it.”

“How did you manage to travel from your home lands all the way to my city walls undetected?” Decebal asked. This irked him the most, not the spying mission. He expected Iazygis to spy.

“Fast horses travelling in the night. That brought us close to the city, then we walked the rest of the way. Dacia is a big country with big open spaces where few people live, as you know, King.”

“And not nearly enough cavalry patrolling around Sarmizegetusa,” Decebal said. “We shall have to fix that. You do us a favor by making our problem clear, Iazygi.”

General Diegis, Ana’s father, spoke up. “Why did you attack the girls? My daughter was among them. Was that part of your mission?”

The prisoner lowered his eyes. “No, that was a mistake.”

“A fatal mistake,” Diegis said through gritted teeth.

“How could you be so stupid?” Vezina asked, honestly curious.

Ebem knew he deserved the scorn. He gave a small shrug. “I acted without thinking.”

Decebal gave him a cold stare. "The oldest girl is my daughter."

"I beg for mercy," the prisoner pleaded, bowing low. "I know that you must kill me, King Decebal, but give me a warrior's death."

Decebal shook his head. "You attacked children. Children! That is an act of a coward, and you deserve the death of a coward." He turned to the palace guards standing nearby. "Take him away. Give him to the women."

Every Dacian woman capable of handling a weapon was expected to train and fight alongside the men. They had equal responsibility for protecting their children, their families, and their homes. Many trained as archers. Some learned to fight with a spear. Very few were strong enough to fight male warriors with a sword. Killing was best learned from experience, and so they sometimes participated in the executions of captured enemy.

Ebem the child attacker was taken out to an open grassy field. Women were asked to volunteer for the execution squad. About ten came forward, young women in the early stages of their training.

The prisoner was led to the center of the group, forced to his knees once again, and left there. His hands were tied in front of him and he was powerless to fight back. This was not a battle but an execution. His shame was so great that he could only stare at the ground, not meeting the eyes of his executioners. This was an ignoble manner for a Iazygi warrior to die.

The women were not armed with spears or swords. Each carried a long stick, about the length of a spear, with a sharply pointed end. These were commonly used in spear training.

One woman began the ritual by stepping forward and plunging her sharp stick into the prisoner's thigh. Ebem did not make a sound then, and not for the next woman who stabbed him in his side, and not for the one after that. He toppled on his side, suffered and bled in silence, and eventually he died.

"Sending scouts to the very walls of Sarmizegetusa was a very brazen act," King Decebal declared in his council meeting. "We will retaliate against the Iazygis and punish this behavior."

"I will plan a raid, Sire, and see that it is carried out," General Sinna said. He was in charge of the Dacian cavalry. Most small raids were carried out by hit and run cavalry attacks. These inflicted some casualties and sent a message to the enemy. A large scale attack would also involve the infantry.

"Good, see to it today," Decebal said. "Now let's address the bigger problems."

Besides King Decebal and General Sinna there were seven other men seated around the large table in the throne room. Vezina was Decebal's closest advisor. General Drilgisa was in charge of infantry, and also Dacia's best and most lethal warrior. Diegis, the King's younger brother by five years, was also a general of infantry. Buri was a big and fierce warrior, and Decebal's bodyguard and close friend.

Visiting allies included Prince Davi of the Roxolani Sarmatians, Dacia's closest ally. He was also related by marriage, the husband of Decebal's younger sister Tanidela. Chief Ailen of the Celts was a handsome young warrior sporting a neatly trimmed beard. Chief Fynn of the Bastarnae tribe was a big and gregarious man.

Chief Fynn turned to Vezina. "What news of developments in Rome, Vezina? I know that you are better informed than most of the senators of Rome."

Vezina acknowledged the compliment with a nod. "Indeed I should be better informed, I pay more for information than any ten senators combined."

"And all of it money well spent!" Diegis chuckled.

"To answer your question, Chief," Vezina continued, "Emperor Trajan is acting true to character. He is making preparations for a very large campaign."

"He began preparations last year while he toured Banat and Moesia, even before returning to Rome as the new Caesar," said Davi of the Roxolani. "His visits earned him the loyalty of the legions in those provinces. He also strengthened their forts and improved their mobility via both road and river travel."

"And now he adds more legions to those forts along the Ister," the King said. He turned to Vezina. "Which makes eight legions, total?"

"Yes, Sire. Eight legions so far."

"Soon to be nine legions when you add the troops travelling east from Germania," said Chief Ailen of the Celts. "They are moving by road and by river. Their artillery is being moved by river."

"That's smart," Diegis said. "Boats travel much faster than oxen pulling wheeled artillery."

"The bastards are preparing for a full invasion," General Drilgisa said. He had been a slave in Rome as a child and harbored a lifetime hatred for all things Roman. "Tettius Julianus attacked Dacia with nine legions. Is Trajan assembling a larger army than Julianus?"

"Yes, that is exactly what he is doing," King Decebal answered evenly. "Everything we're seeing points to that."

"Indeed, Sire," Vezina agreed. "By all accounts Emperor Trajan is putting together a larger invasion force than Rome has ever seen."

"That would be something to see," Chief Fynn said.

"Not only to see, Chief Fynn," the King said. "We'll also have to fight it and kill it."

"Of course. Which is why, my friends, we must all stick together," Fynn said. "King Decebal, you have the strongest army among our allies but you could not hope to defeat the Romans by yourself."

Diegis' jaw tightened. "Ask Cornelius Fuscus and Tettius Julianus about that, Chief."

Fynn smiled. "I am not insulting you, my friend. I am only saying that Emperor Trajan will come with a much bigger army. We should not compare this to the armies of Fuscus or Julianus."

"No offense taken, Fynn," Diegis replied. "And you are right."

"Also know this," Fynn continued. "Trajan is a far superior general to Cornelius Fuscus and Julianus. Ask the Chatti or the Marcomanni about that."

Everyone present knew what he meant. Emperor Trajan earned his military reputation by defeating those powerful Germanic tribes during his wars in Germania and Pannonia.

"You are right, Fynn," Decebal agreed. "Dacia could hold off the Romans for a time. We would inflict heavy losses on their armies. But as you say, it would be difficult to defeat them. We simply do not have the numbers." He looked at the faces of his allies around the table. "Which is why we are all gathered here today."

Prince Davi nodded. "We stay together. We fight together. We are a match for Rome, together."

"On that we all agree," Vezina said. "And so does Trajan. Why else do you think he is planning such a massive army for invasion?"

"Because he fears us!" Drilgisa said. "He sees us as a threat to Rome's authority."

"And he is not mistaken," Decebal said. "We are a threat to Rome's authority. Emperor Domitian feared the threat and paid us to keep the peace. Emperor Trajan seems determined to remove the threat. That makes him dangerous to our security, much more dangerous than Domitian."

"Rome is always dangerous to our security, King Decebal," said Chief Ailen. "That was also true for my father's generation, and his father's generation, and the generations before them. Rome's empire always expands, it never shrinks. Our only choice is to determine when and how to fight them."

"Well said, young man," Vezina agreed. "And sometimes our choices are forced upon us. That time is coming soon, I think."

That night, after the evening meal, King Decebal and Queen Andrada retired to their sleeping quarters. That quiet time in the evening was usually the only time they could relax and talk with each other. He trusted and valued her wisdom and her common sense. She trusted him in the same way.

"Today was a very crazy day," Andrada said, sinking her head down onto a large soft pillow. Her long black hair spread out and framed her beautiful face. "I am glad that it's over."

"Yes, it was," he agreed. "How is Adila? I did not have time to speak with her yet."

"She is fine. She is strong," the Queen said. "A little shook up. Do you know that she fought off her attacker with a flower knife?"

"A flower knife?"

"Yes! She used the little knife for cutting flowers to slash the Iazygi's face. Thank the gods that Cotiso was very close by and killed the Iazygis."

Decebal nodded. "Zamolxis was watching over the children today. He sent Cotiso and Tarbus to rescue them."

Andrada smiled but kept silent. She was not as confident as her husband that the gods were always so attentive or helpful.

"The Iazygi met with justice," Decebal said. "Did Adila participate in the execution?"

"No, she did not wish to take part in that. She was angry with the man, but can you guess why?"

"Because he attacked her, obviously."

"No," the Queen explained with an amused smile. "She was angry because the man ruined her surprise for me."

"What surprise?" he asked, puzzled.

"The reason Adila went into the woods, and took the girls with her, was to pick flowers and surprise me tomorrow during my birthday celebration. Now her surprise is ruined."

That made Decebal chuckle. "She has your sentimental nature, Wife. Now she needs more of your common sense. It was foolish to go into the forest without guards to accompany them."

"Thankfully she has your killer nature with a blade, Husband," the Queen teased. "But yes, it was foolish. She has learned her lesson."

"She can still present you with the flowers tomorrow. Perhaps you can pretend to be surprised?"

"No need to pretend about anything. It was a lovely thought, and I told her so. My gift was that the girls were returned unharmed. Dorin as well. He played the rescuer, along with his dog."

"Yes. I will talk to him and let him know that he acted bravely."

She turned to look into his eyes, no longer in a teasing mood. "Our children must be brave, or else they will never survive."

"They are brave. And they will continue to be so, come what may."

"Do you know why I love spring flowers?" Andrada asked.

The question took him by surprise. "No. Why?"

"Because they are beautiful. And because they are fragile, and do not last for very long." A shadow of sadness crossed her face. "I do not want our children to be like spring flowers."

Decebal reached out to softly touch her cheek. "You worry too much. Dacia's children are not spring flowers." His lips widened into a smile. "They shall bloom in the summer and have their full season in the sun. This I swear to you, upon my soul."

"Will Trajan attack us?" she asked. This was the uppermost worry on her mind.

"Yes," Decebal answered without pause.

"This year, do you think?"

"We cannot know when, my dear. Not all of Vezina's spies can tell us yet when he will invade. This emperor is a planner, I am told, but he takes it to extremes." He gave a small shrug. "He takes action when he feels ready. And we must also be ready."

"Trajan is not the only planner," the Queen said. "We'll be ready."

The celebration for Queen Andrada's thirty-eight birthday included a public feast, a mid-day festival of song and dance, and several very large bouquets of spring flowers that genuinely delighted the Queen. After the music and dance performances she spent the next two hours greeting well-wishers. Mothers brought their young children to see their Queen and sing her a birthday song.

The Queen was loved by many for her kindly nature and generous spirit. Andrada ran the free medical clinic that was located near the royal palace. She worked directly with people as a healer and doctor of herbal medicine. Her main assistant at the clinic was Zelma, the Christian refugee and mother of Lia. Eleven years earlier, on a state visit to Rome, Diegis rescued Zelma and her husband from arrest and execution that Christians were subjected to by Emperor Domitian.

Andrada's two daughters, Adila and Zia, stood by their mother and helped greet the guests. They both had long shiny black hair, like their mother, and also their mother's big blue eyes. Zia was two years older and the more quiet and thoughtful of the sisters.

Adila gave her sister a nudge. "Oh look, here comes Tarbus."

Zia was already looking in that direction, which made her sister smile knowingly. Zia's eyes always grew brighter when Tarbus was around. The three of them grew up as friends, but Zia was now old enough to think about young men and marriage.

"Hello, Tarbus," Andrada greeted him with a warm smile. "Thank you for saving the girls. Gallantry runs in the family, so it appears?"

Tarbus greeted her with a small bow and accepted the compliment graciously. He was the son of Buri, King Decebal's bodyguard and friend. Buri had protected Decebal's life for many years and fought at his side in countless battles.

"Happy birthday, My Queen," Tarbus said. "I wish you good health and much happiness in the coming year." His eyes strayed to the two princesses. "Hello Adila. Hello Zia."

"I also want to thank you," Adila said. "You saved our lives."

"My life as always is at your service, Princess Adila," Tarbus said humbly. He spoke to Adila but his eyes strayed to Zia. Zia looked like she was feeling shy.

"Zia is also thankful," Adila said casually. "Perhaps she will walk with you and tell you herself?"

Zia blushed and gave her sister an annoyed look. "I can speak for myself, thank you!"

"Of course you can," the Queen said. "But perhaps a walk would be a nice break from standing around and greeting my well-wishers? I'm sure Tarbus would be happy to escort you."

"Yes, My Queen," Tarbus agreed happily. He turned to Zia with a smile. "I would be honored, my lady."

Zia took him by the upper arm and led him away down the garden path. "Let's go then, before we start getting lectured about what a fine day this is for a walk!"

Tarbus looked back over his shoulder. "Farewell!"

"They are growing fond of each other," Andrada said mildly. "When did that start to happen?"

Adila sighed. "For almost a year, Mother. Zia hides it well but she has no secrets from me."

"Ah, I see," Andrada said wistfully. "I have been too preoccupied with other matters to notice."

"Too preoccupied to notice what?" King Decebal asked, having just arrived. He took the seat next to the Queen. Buri was with him, and remained standing beside the King.

"That our eldest daughter might be thinking of starting her own family soon."

"Well, my dear, she is old enough," Decebal said. "Many young women her age are already mothers."

"Yes, I know that," the Queen patiently replied. "I am simply not prepared to lose her just yet."

"You will not lose her, My Queen," Buri said. "Girls never abandon their mothers, even when they have children of their own. Boys, on the other hand," he paused and shrugged. "Sons are different."

Andrada looked up at the small giant of a man. Although a holy terror on the battlefield, the big warrior had a kind disposition when he was not in battle. Buri's joy in life was to tend to his orchards of apples and pears. He preferred to grow things, not kill them.

"Tarbus will always remain loyal to you," Andrada said.

"You are right, My Queen," Buri said pleasantly. "In any case my son is a warrior and in no hurry to get married. I am certain that Princess Zia will find a good man of noble birth to make her happy."

Andrada shot a quick glance at her daughter. Adila giggled, then quickly looked away.

"Buri, Drilgisa believes that Tarbus is ready for some light officer duties," the King said. "He has a sharp mind and good judgment. He is brave and honest and earns the men's respect."

That got Buri's full attention. "I am happy to hear that. General Drilgisa is a good judge of men."

"Yes he is, and I agree with him. I have known Tarbus since he was a little boy. He is mature enough now to lead a company of infantry."

Buri grinned. "Yes, Sire. Should I tell him?"

"No, let Drilgisa tell him. Tarbus will be responsible to the General and it is best that promotions come from one's superior officer."

Buri nodded. "Of course, Sire. You are right."

"Your pride is well founded, Buri," Andrada said. "Tarbus will serve Dacia well. We need more like him."

"Yes, I wish we had more like him," Decebal agreed. "Many more."

> Chapter 2

The Good Ruler

Rome, April 100 AD

The family of Emperor Marcus Trajan was a family of three generations of women. Since their move to Rome all lived together amicably in the imperial palace. The Empress Pompeia Plotina shared equal responsibility in running the household with Trajan's older sister, Marciana. Both were very intelligent, level headed, and responsible, and got along well without jealousy or disagreements. They set the tone for the rest of the household and that made it a happy household.

Marciana's only daughter, Salonia Matidia, moved in with the Trajanus family after her second husband died. Her two young daughters came with her. That was almost fifteen years ago. She was Trajan's only niece and the Emperor, who had no children of his own, treated her like a daughter.

Salonia's two daughters were now teenagers. They were raised as part of the Trajanus family since they were babies. Vibia Sabina was sixteen years old. Her half-sister, Mindia Matidia, was one year older. Each had their mother's elegant looks and gentle nature.

Over the years Trajan spent much of his time with the army. He was gone for months and sometimes years at a time, first in Spain and later on campaign in Germania and Pannonia. Pompeia and Marciana managed the family's vast wealth, which included large farms worked by very large numbers of slaves, various factories, and other businesses. Both were wealthy in their own right apart from Trajan's property and wealth. Both were fierce defenders of Trajan and supported his career advancements through their financial and political influence.

When he was home Trajan took pride and joy in his family. He and Plotina were similar in character and temperament. They were proud but unassuming and put on no airs of divinity. Plotina had a good political mind, and many credited her for the Emperor's ability to win favor with all groups. Trajan wanted to present himself to the public as the good ruler, a Caesar who championed the old traditional Roman values. Plotina was an important part of that political image.

The Emperor joined his wife at her breakfast. She was sitting on a dining couch, a low serving table in front of her. Across the table was another couch where Salonia, Vibia, and Mindia were seated and having their breakfast. Three people to a dining couch was the usual custom in Rome.

"Good morning, my lovelies," Trajan greeted them pleasantly. He sat down besides Plotina.

"Good morning, Husband," the Empress said. "Do eat something before you run off. The lictors are waiting outside but let them wait a while longer." She reclined back on the couch, sipping warmed lemon water flavored with honey.

"You look dressed for a Senate meeting today, Uncle," Salonia said casually.

Trajan wore a toga that was bleached a very bright white, folded to drape perfectly over his tall and athletic body. The Senate of Rome was waiting to hear from Caesar this morning on important matters of state.

"I am indeed," Trajan said. "Caesar's work with the Senate never ends. And why is everyone up so early?"

"We have riding lessons this morning, Great-Uncle," said Vibia. Among the family, at home in the royal palace, formal titles such as Caesar were not used.

"I wish I could go riding with you," Trajan said lightly. "That would be more interesting than listening to senators give long and boring speeches all day, eh?"

"I would like to see a Senate meeting," Mindia spoke up.

"Hush, now," her mother chided gently. "You know that women are not allowed inside the Senate House. It is a man's place."

"That is true," the Empress said. "But what you can do one day, Mindia, is stand outside the Senate House door and listen to the speeches inside."

"That only works when it's a hot day and the doors are kept open to get fresh air," Trajan said. He turned to his great-niece who had a disappointed look on her face. "Mindia, ask Cotta to bring you to the Senate House after your riding lesson. I will order the doors to be kept opened for you, hot day or cold."

"Oh, thank you!" Mindia said brightly. She often listened to her grandmother Marciana and her great-aunt Pompeia discuss politics, and found that she was curious to see the Senate meetings in person.

"You are welcome," said the Emperor. "Vibia, would you like to come also?"

The girl rolled her eyes. "No, thank you. No Senate speeches for me. I will read poetry instead."

Breakfast was finished and Salonia stood up to leave. "Come, my daughters. You mustn't be tardy for your lessons."

The girls stood and said their farewells, and followed their mother outside. Obedience and politeness were both valued and demanded in the Trajanus household.

"Such bright girls," Trajan said after they left. "Mindia shows some interest in politics, is she taking after you?"

Plotina laughed. "More likely she takes after her grandmother, I would think."

"Ah! And Vibia is as fond of poetry as ever. That, my dear, sounds like your influence." Pompeia loved Greek culture, particularly poetry and philosophy.

"On that count you are right, Husband. Oh, which reminds me, Marciana and I need to discuss a matter with you regarding Vibia."

"Of course."

"But in the meantime, what message for the Senate today?"

Trajan leaned back on the couch. "The usual promises. A few still worry that I will turn into Domitian."

The Empress scoffed. "Such foolishness. You are no Domitian."

Trajan leaned over and gave her a kiss on the cheek. "And you, my dear, are no Domitia Longina!" It was meant as a compliment. The former Empress Domitia was known as a flamboyant lover of luxury and special privilege, the exact opposite of Plotina's modest image.

"Nor would I wish to be," Plotina said. "Although I am told the poor woman quite enjoys her new public role as the tragic widow of Emperor Domitian. How sad."

Trajan shrugged. "Domitia was always loved by the people. Now, that is all she has left. I do not begrudge her some happiness."

"Nor do I, Marcus. She suffered enough under the thumb of her mad husband." Plotina paused briefly, lost in thought. "I hear more rumors that she was complicit in the conspiracy to assassinate that mad husband. Could that be true?"

"Ah! That is a complicated question," Trajan said. "The conspiracy against Domitian was wide and included some of the most powerful people in Rome. Towards the end of his rule Domitian went mad and suspected that everyone was plotting against him. People lived in fear for their lives. Some took action out of fear for their lives."

"One of those people being the Empress Domitia herself?"

"Perhaps. We may never know for certain, my dear. Of the people associated with her who would know, all are dead. Her steward Stephanus, the man who initiated the attack on Domitian, was killed by servants during the attack. Parthenius and the Praetorian prefect Petronius Secundus were later executed by supporters of Domitian."

"The dead tell no tales," Pompeia said. "So the conspirators were members of Domitian's personal staff, also the Praetorian Guard, very likely members of the Senate of Rome, and perhaps the Empress Domitia herself."

"No one dares accuse members of the Senate. Perhaps that is for the best," Trajan said. "Emperor Nerva worked hard to undo the damage done to the Senate by Domitian's reign of terror. There is still damage left to undo. I still have to persuade some of Domitian's former enemies to not take their revenge on his former supporters."

"What a mess!" Pompeia exclaimed.

"It is indeed," Trajan said. "That is why it is best to not concern ourselves with rumors regarding Domitia Longina or anyone else. The sooner these rumors fade away the better."

"I understand, and agree," Pompeia said. "But tell me, are there complaints in the Senate still? What else do they want from you?"

"They always want more. It never ends."

"You promised not to kill senators, and kept your promise," the Empress said with a wry smile. "You kept your hands off their money and their properties. You treat them with dignity. So what else?"

"There are always some who wish to restore the Senate of Rome to the power it had when Rome was a Republic."

"More foolishness!"

"Foolishness, indeed," Trajan said dismissively. "Julius Caesar showed us the way, and the Divine Augustus after him. Caesar must rule, not some motley collection of nobles."

"A good Caesar must rule, Marcus," the Empress said. "A strong Caesar, but not a tyrant. Domitian was arrogant and severe. Emperor Nerva was benevolent but did not have a strong hand. You are neither of those things."

"Wise words as ever, my dear," Trajan said with a smile. "I should have you talk to my critics and convince them that our way is the right way."

"Pah! Your critics are like flies buzzing around a stallion."

A sleepy voice entering the room got their attention. "What flies? What stallion?"

"Senate flies, Sister," Trajan said as Marciana came to join them. His older sister looked tired and sleepy eyed.

"Pests, all of them," Marciana proclaimed. "They irritate but do no real harm." She was a woman of strong political opinion.

"You did not sleep well, Marciana?" Plotina asked.

"I did not," she answered. A woman of fifty-one, of medium height and build, Marciana was beginning to show some signs of age. These included gray hairs and trouble sleeping.

"Well, I shall leave and let you two talk," Trajan said, standing. "The Senate of Rome awaits."

"Wait, before you leave," Plotina said. She caught Marciana's eye. "We want to discuss the matter of Vibia."

Trajan paused. "What of Vibia?"

"She is almost sixteen," Marciana said. "A young noblewoman of her age should think of marriage."

Trajan had to agree. Roman men of noble birth married when they were in their middle to late twenties. Roman women of noble birth married about ten years younger.

"I see," Trajan said. "And you agree that she should marry now?"

"Yes," Plotina said. "Her mother is also of a like mind."

"And who do you have in mind for a husband?"

The Empress gave him a bright smile. "Hadrianus."

"Hadrian?" The choice took Trajan by surprise.

Publius Aelius Hadrianus, who everyone called Hadrian, had also been raised as part of the Trajanus family. Hadrian's father, who was Trajan's cousin, had died when the boy was ten years old. Trajan was appointed as one of the boy's guardians. Hadrian then joined and was brought up in the Trajanus household.

Since Trajan was gone with the army the majority of the time, it was more accurate to say that the boy was raised by Pompeia Plotina and the women of the household. Hadrian shared Pompeia's strong interest in Greek culture including poetry, art, and philosophy. To Trajan's displeasure, some people were calling the young man "the little Greek." Coming from another Roman male that was not at all a compliment. It seemed clear however that the adult women of the household all adored Hadrian.

The reason for Trajan's surprise was simple. In Rome marriages among the nobility were arranged for financial and political reasons. Marrying Vibia to Hadrian would bring Hadrian into the Trajanus inner circle, which would raise his status considerably. This was a tremendous boon for Hadrian.

On the other hand, Trajan could see no obvious advantages for Vibia. The only thing Hadrian had in his favor was that all the adult women of the Trajanus family thought highly of him. Trajan did not know how Vibia felt about the marriage, but that was not a concern in the decision. The adults responsible for her made all decisions, with the final say belonging to Trajan.

"Brother? Does Vibia have your blessing to marry Hadrian?" his sister asked impatiently.

"Well, since you all agree, it appears that I am outvoted," Trajan said jokingly. As the male head of the household it was his decision to make, but he always took into account the wishes of his wife and his sister. "Yes, Vibia has my blessing."

"Wonderful!" Pompeia said. Marciana looked pleased as well.

Trajan walked briskly outside to join the squad of twelve lictors who would escort him to the Senate House. His mind was not on Senate meetings, but on family matters. At the age of twenty-four, through his marriage to Vibia Sabina, Hadrian was about to become very closely aligned with Emperor Trajan. It would shape the future for both men, although what that future held was not yet clear.

Gaius Plinius Secundus was known as a firebrand in the Senate of Rome, a politician who admired and styled himself after the great Cicero. In later times he would become known as Pliny the Younger, to distinguish him from his famed uncle Pliny the Elder who was killed in the eruption of Vesuvius. On this day Pliny, who was blessed with the speaking talents of a natural politician, addressed the Senate in order to praise Caesar and his family.

Emperor Trajan looked on, resting comfortably in his chair which was placed to face the assembly. On directions from Caesar the doors of the Senate House were kept open to let in the fresh air, and also to satisfy the curiosity of a grand-niece who wished to listen in.

"Some men are embarrassed by their choice of wives," Pliny said with complete sincerity, "and for good reason! They bring shame and grief to men of noble family and noble character. Our great Caesar, on the other hand, has trained his women well."

This was a great compliment to a Roman man's ability to manage a household. Trajan was pleased. He continued to listen patiently.

"The Empress Pompeia Plotina is the very model of traditional Roman virtue. All women of Rome admire her and wish to emulate her. She is modest, as is Caesar. She walks on foot among her fellow citizens of Rome, as does Caesar. She seeks no greater glory than obedience and devotion to her husband, as do all virtuous women of Rome. She is morally pure."

Pliny did not say so directly, however it was clear to all that his praise of the current Empress, Pompeia, painted a sharp contrast with the previous Empress, Domitia. In doing so Pliny also painted a contrast between the character and family of the current Emperor, Trajan, to the former Emperor, Domitian. Most senators hated the very memory of Domitian and his destructive reign.

Pliny continued his passionate oratory. "Let us praise also Ulpia Marciana, honored sister of noble Caesar. Her behavior is similarly above reproach. She is a woman of humility, honesty, and candor. She is of good heart and gentle disposition, and shares a household with the Empress Pompeia without any jealousy or rancor. We must credit this family harmony to the wise and firm guiding hand of our noble Caesar. As he rules his family, so he rules Rome!"

Pliny paused briefly to let his message be absorbed. He was almost finished and wished to end on a strong note. Every male Roman of noble family was trained in oratory from the time he was a child, to use those skills precisely in moments like this.

"Hercules, as we all know, was sent to Earth to bring justice and virtue to humankind. Noble Caesar, with the body and the strength of Hercules, was sent to us from Hispania for the same godly purpose!" Pliny boomed in a loud and clear voice. "And glorious Jupiter brings wisdom and justice to the affairs of men. Yet Jupiter rests today. He rests because he has given those divine tasks of spreading wisdom and justice to noble Caesar. Let us thank Caesar and praise Caesar for his boundless devotion to doing the work of the gods here on Earth!"

The senators applauded and shouted their approval. Pliny gave a curt bow in the direction of the Emperor, then took his seat among the other senators. Trajan walked to the center of the floor. After a period of basking in the applause he raised his hand for silence.

"Fathers of the nation! We should all act to promote virtue, and wisdom, and justice!" Trajan spoke in a strong and clear voice. He was not as polished as Pliny but made up for it with authority.

"Show reverence for the gods by embracing virtue and rejecting vice. Be fair and just, and you will make no enemies. Reward your friends but also work with those who would be your rivals, and do this for the benefit of the people of Rome. This I have done and will do. I wish to appoint only the best, whether they be allies or rivals. This is what a good ruler must do."

That earned more loud applause from the assembly. The Emperor had indeed kept his promises to treat senators justly and reward those who merited high rank.

"Seek harmony and peace, but always be prepared for war," Trajan continued. "To that end Rome must address the wolf on our northern frontier. Some in the north grow overly proud, arrogant, and bold. They bribe our allies to form alliances with them. They bribe our own engineers, our skilled craftsmen, and even our soldiers to join their side. This is an outrage against Rome's dignity and honor. I tell you now that this outrage will end."

All the senators cheered loudly. It was clear to everyone assembled what wolf the Emperor was talking about. Dacia and King Decebalus had been a thorn in Rome's side for the past fifteen years. They beat back two failed invasions into Dacia and inflicted heavy casualties on Roman armies. They killed the Roman governor of Moesia, killed a Roman general in battle and destroyed his legion, and captured the Eagle standards of defeated Roman legions.

The Emperor Domitian signed a peace treaty with King Decebalus that was heavily in Dacia's favor. He paid Decebalus large sums of money every year to keep the peace. For over a decade Domitian's ignoble treaty was viewed by the Roman nobility as a humiliation and a stain on Rome's honor.

"We are favored by Jupiter and all the gods," Trajan continued, "yet every year Rome pays treasure to a proud and arrogant barbarian king. The barbarian's power and pride grows and grows. This too is an outrage, a stench in the nostrils of the gods. I tell you now, Rome will wage war on this pride and arrogance!"

The cheering erupted loudly and senators rose to their feet. Trajan had just promised to go to war with Dacia. This was the news they waited to hear for many years. Emperor Trajan was the Caesar who would finally put Decebalus in his place. He would restore Rome's damaged pride. This Caesar was indeed doing the work of the gods!

Trajan stood tall in the center of the floor, strong and serene, and accepted their enthusiastic affirmation of his rule. He had the army on his side, and the people, and the Senate. He was the master of Rome, which made him the master of the world.

In the afternoon the Emperor went from the Senate House to visit his closest friend, Licinius Sura. Like Trajan, he was also from Hispania. He was a decade older than the Emperor, and had been a long-time friend and mentor since Trajan was a young man. He had been a key figure over the years in Trajan's rise to power. Among the friends he influenced was Senator Nerva, who would eventually become the

Emperor Nerva. This Emperor Nerva would later adopt Trajan as his son and set him on the path to become the next Caesar.

Trajan liked to surprise his friend with random visits. He always left his guards outside so that he could talk in confidence with his friend. He never feared for his safety in the house of Sura.

Sura was already entertaining a guest, another native of Hispania. Marcus Valerius Martialis, more commonly known as Martial, had been the court poet for Emperor Domitian and Emperor Nerva. His books of epigrams were widely read by the educated classes in Rome because they were often scandalous and always entertaining. Martial catered to wealthy patrons and served them well, praising those in favor and skewering those in disfavor. He was very pleased to offer his loyalty and his talents to the new Caesar.

"Ah, the Trajan sun has risen!" Martial cried as Trajan entered the room. He had no sense of modesty and took pride in his talent for flattery. "Bask, you mortals, in the brilliance that is Caesar!"

"I need no flattery, Marcus," Trajan told him with a relaxed grin. "In the Senate House today Gaius Plinius compared me to Hercules and Jupiter! That is flattery enough."

Words of modesty aside, the smile on Trajan's face showed that he was pleased. Beneath the Emperor's common-man exterior burned a fierce pride. His fellow Hispanics, Sura and Martial, understood his desire to show the arrogant Roman nobility that he, a so-called new man from the provinces, was a better man than them. The same pride drove them as well.

Sura filled a silver goblet with wine for Trajan, and re-filled his own. "Marcus' flattery is so sincere that many people take it for truth. A poet for the ages, come to Rome from Hispania!"

"Rome praises and quotes my little books of epigrams. They love me," Martial said with a smile. "Sincerity is a sharp and powerful weapon, Licinius."

"Your wit is a sharp and powerful weapon, Marcus," the Emperor said. Trajan was not a lover of poetry and took soldierly pride in that fact, but it was easy to like Martial.

"I thank you for that high compliment, Caesar."

"Your poetry has caused more scandals in Rome than a hundred gossips," Sura teased him. "Have you no sense of shame?"

"None!" Martial said with a straight face. "None at all, Licinius. My poems are naughty, but my life is pure."

"Your poetry made enemies for Domitian," Sura continued. "You sang his praises, shall we say, a touch too highly?"

"Not fair, Sura," Martial replied. "Domitian needed no help from me to make enemies."

Trajan laughed. "That is true. Simply write what you will, when you will. Be yourself, Marcus. Nothing more."

"I have now discovered, in my old age, that is one of the secrets to living a happy life," Martial replied. The poet was nearing sixty years old. "And speaking of age, I must leave you fine gentlemen and retire for the day."

Trajan clasped him on the shoulder. "Rest well, my friend. Let the poetry wait for another day."

Martial nodded a farewell to both men and was escorted out by a servant. Although his mind was as sharp as ever he was feeling his wine more as he got older. Both Sura and Trajan were heavy drinkers and Martial long ago stopped trying to keep up with them.

Sura turned to Trajan. "To what do I owe the honor of this visit?"

"Since when do I need a reason to visit a friend?"

"You do not, Marcus Ulpius. So tell me, how was your meeting with the Senate? I was too occupied with business to attend."

"They worship me," Trajan chuckled. "By the gods, Licinius. Pliny gave a speech and told them that I am doing Jupiter's work on Earth!"

"That fellow has a golden tongue, he will go far," Sura said. "What is important to understand, Caesar, is that it is not empty flattery. The Senate and the people of Rome view you as the good ruler."

"They view me so because I am a good ruler," Trajan said.

Sura nodded. "You are that, Marcus. We've had conversations on the subject over the years. Now that you are Caesar you bring those conversations to life, no longer just ideas but actions."

Trajan poured himself more wine. He took a sip and savored the taste. It was an excellent wine. The Emperor loved and collected the best wines from all over Italia, and from points more distant.

Trajan raised an eyebrow. "Tiburtine?"

"Yes, Tiburtine. A new arrival from an excellent vintage. If you like I shall have some delivered to the palace."

"Yes, do," Trajan said. He paused briefly in thought. "Do you know what is surprising to me, Licinius?"

"What is that?"

"It is not as difficult being the good ruler as I once feared."

That took Sura by surprise. "How do you mean?"

"I tell the Senators that I will not kill them or exile them, or steal their wealth, and they praise me for it. But you see, I had no wish to kill them or rob them in the first place. It is not such a difficult thing to treat them respectfully and provide fair justice."

"Ah, I see. Those things are natural to you because they come from your character. But think, Marcus," Sura paused to look him in the eye, "why did Domitian not do those things? Or Nero?"

"I suppose you will tell me that it was not in their character?"

"Precisely. Men of strong character are rare. By that I mean true character, honest character that is not a ploy. And that is why good rulers are rare."

The Emperor paused to sip his wine. Sura was a friend he could trust completely, and he often ran ideas by him to get his opinion.

"I must make a decision soon regarding a man's character."

"Oh? Whose character?"

"Lusius Quietus."

"Ah!" Sura exclaimed, surprised again. Lusius Quietus had been a general of the Moorish cavalry with an impressive record of military victories, and also a tarnished reputation. He was removed from command by the Roman Senate due to his unnecessary and savage massacres of the civilian populations in conquered territories.

"Are you thinking of appointing him to your staff, Marcus?"

"I am. I want his military career rehabilitated. And I want him in command of cavalry for the Dacian invasion."

"The Senate will not be pleased. They regard the man as little more than a savage and a criminal."

Trajan waved his hand dismissively. "I don't want wealthy nobles or politicians for battle commanders, Licinius. I need killers."

"I see. The character of Lusius Quietus will never change, Marcus. If you rehabilitate his career and give him command again, will that reflect poorly on your character?"

The Emperor shrugged. "That is no matter. I must do what a good ruler should do."

"And what should a good ruler do in this instance?"

Trajan answered without hesitation. "Make certain that Rome succeeds in the invasion of Dacia."

Sura nodded. "Woe to the women and children and old men of Dacia then, shivering with fear in their beds."

> Chapter 3

Storm Clouds

Sarmizegetusa, March 101 AD

Collecting and interpreting information was the chief duty of the High Priest of Zamolxis. In addition to supervising the training of the priest class, and performing religious rites during the major Dacian holidays, the High Priest was the closest and most trusted advisor to the Dacian king. Vezina had been the chief counselor to King Scorilo, then King Duras, and now King Decebal. Scorilo had been Decebal's father, Duras his uncle.

The High Priest gathered information from a large number of sources. He bribed informers from many foreign capitals, including Rome. Traders and other travelers who came through Dacia knew that an audience with the High Priest would be profitable for them if they had good information to share. Even rumors, when properly pieced together and interpreted by Vezina, could provide valuable information and insights. Vezina did not rely on superstition and reading tea leaves, he relied on information to understand what was currently happening and to predict what might happen in the future.

The most frequent source of information for Vezina and Decebal came from the small army of Dacian cavalry scouts. These riders were the King's eyes and ears throughout the kingdom of Dacia and all along Dacia's borders. They often ventured across borders into the territory of Dacia's neighbors. In particular they made a point of crossing the Ister River into Rome's near provinces. Their missions were exploratory, not hostile. King Decebal needed to know what was happening within his kingdom and along its borders.

The very capable veteran Tsiru was commander of the cavalry scouts. He was getting older now and no longer looked forward to riding on scouting missions that meant being in the saddle for weeks on end. For that reason he was relying more and more on Dadas, his young assistant. Dadas was built like Tsiru, short and slim, but was fifteen years younger.

Tsiru and Dadas were giving a report to King Decebal's senior council, seated around a table in the throne room. Besides Vezina the council also included the King, Queen Andrada, generals Diegis and Drilgisa of the infantry, and general of the cavalry Sinna.

"My King, My Queen, and Your Holiness," Tsiru addressed the head of the table. "Dadas has just returned from a mission to Moesia and Banat. We have scouting reports on the major Roman forts and army camps."

Vezina gave a nod to greet both scouts. "Trajan has built up his armies along the Ister for two years now. Are more troops arriving?"

"Yes, Your Holiness," Dadas replied. "More legionnaires arrive from the south and also from the eastern provinces, along with equal numbers of auxiliary infantry. The Roman troops are equipped with full complements of artillery and cavalry. Auxiliary troops are armed in the custom of their tribes."

"How many legions are camped beyond the Ister?" Decebal asked.

"Nine full legions, Sire," Tsiru answered. "Five legions are camped in Moesia and four legions in Pannonia, including the ones that marched in from Germania. That comes to fifty thousand fighting men. We count thirty thousand auxiliary troops, a mix of infantry and cavalry. Gauls, Iazygi, and German cavalry make up the largest part of their horse."

Diegis frowned. "With eighty thousand they already outnumber us two to one."

"Rome will always outnumber us, Diegis," the King said. "Trajan is gathering legions from Macedonia and Germania. He can bring in troops from as far away as Spain and Syria if he so chooses. We do not have that option."

Tsiru cleared his throat. "Dadas has something to show you that you will find interesting."

Vezina raised an eyebrow. "What is it?"

Dadas walked up to where Vezina was seated, reached into a pocket in his sheepskin vest, and brought out a leather coin pouch. He emptied three silver coins on the table in front of the High Priest.

"Your Holiness, these are newly minted coins being distributed to the legions in Moesia and Banat. They are a bonus gift from Emperor Trajan to his legionnaires."

Vezina picked up one of the coins and took a close look, front and back. The front was a strong face in profile of a Roman god, a wreath of laurel leaves wrapped around a thick head of curly hair. On the back of the coin was a Roman temple with an inscription.

"Mars Ultor," Vezina said, sliding one of the coins to Decebal. The King picked up the coin and examined it closely, admiring its fine detail. It was beautifully designed and crafted, as were all the coins minted in Rome.

"Is the Emperor sending a message?" the King asked Vezina with a wry smile.

"I would think so, Sire," Vezina replied. "This is a message to the troops. Its purpose is to inspire the troops."

"Who is Mars Ultor?" Queen Andrada asked curiously.

"He is Mars the Avenger," Vezina replied. "Mars the god of war takes the form of Mars Ultor when Roman armies seek revenge for wrongs done to them. He is the Roman god who restores lost pride and honor."

"And whom," Andrada continued, "will Mars Ultor seek revenge against?"

Decebal gave her a half smile. "Why, against those who have done the greatest harm to Rome's pride and prestige of course."

"Us, My Queen," General Drilgisa agreed. "Good! Let the bastards come, we knew they would sooner or later."

Vezina gave a solemn nod. "Indeed, Drilgisa. But Trajan will come with a very large and well equipped army. I would not be too eager to clash with him."

"It makes no difference whether or not I am eager!" Drilgisa said. "Rome will invade just the same. And we have to beat them back just the same."

"Drilgisa is right," Decebal said. "This is not a fight we choose but it is a fight that we must win." He paused for a heartbeat. "It is a fight we will win, no matter which Roman god Trajan puts on silver coins."

Diegis spoke up. "It is not Mars Ultor we have to fight but the nine legions camped across the Ister."

"Ah!" Vezina said. "I think that we will have to defeat both, their legions and their god. Mars Ultor is a powerful symbol for them."

"A symbol for what?" Diegis asked.

"The Mars Ultor on these coins," Vezina explained, "is nothing more than a symbol for Emperor Trajan himself."

Decebal casually tossed back the coin back so that it landed in front of Vezina. "Now he compares himself to a god, eh? So much for that rubbish that the Emperor is a humble man."

Drilgisa laughed. "There is no such thing as a humble Emperor! They all pretend to be gods. Some of them even believe it to be true. It drives them mad, like Nero and Domitian."

"Emperor Nerva was a humble man," Vezina said. "It did not serve him well when he was named Caesar."

Decebal waved his hand dismissively. "I was only talking in jest, Trajan is highly ambitious of course. And we, my people, stand in the way of his ambitions."

"We do not stand alone," said Vezina.

"No, we do not." Decebal looked to the general of cavalry. "Sinna, send out messengers today to all allies. Tell them to be ready on short notice. Spring is almost here and that means marching season for the Roman armies."

"Yes, Sire. I will see to it immediately."

"So," Queen Andrada wondered, "does Emperor Trajan finally feel ready to wage war against us?"

Decebal gave a nod. "I think so. He must have planned it for this year all along."

"Ah, I was getting used to peace," she said. "But peace never lasts."

"No, My Queen, peace does not last," Vezina said. "Not in this world."

Cotiso dedicated two hours each day for archery practice. On some days it stretched out to three or four hours or more. He practiced on foot and also from horseback, in every kind of weather. After years of practice his arrows found their target nine times out of ten. At a hundred paces he could hit a target the size of a man. At twenty paces his target was the size of a man's palm, small enough to find a spot not protected by armor. As a horse archer he could close in to within fifteen paces, hit an open face or neck, then quickly ride away.

As a youngster Cotiso had been tall for his age but very thin. Reed thin, his father called him. His archery made him physically strong, with a broad chest and shoulders and muscular arms. He did not have the sword skills to be a superior swordsman, but no matter. He was very lethal with a bow.

Cotiso was on foot, hitting arrow after arrow into the middle of a straw filled target fifty paces away, when his sister Adila walked up to him. They shared King Decebal as a father. Cotiso's mother was Tyra, Decebal's first wife. He was thinking of her when Adila interrupted his thoughts.

Cotiso often thought of his mother during the seemingly endless hours of archery practice. Tyra had died when the boy was six years old. He took her loss very hard for many years. Now, twenty years later, he remembered her in a more positive way. She had been slim, very pretty, and very kind. He was a serious boy and she tried to make him laugh. Besides her wiry build Cotiso inherited her light brown hair. He had his father's dark brown eyes.

Adila, daughter of Decebal and Andrada, was born when Cotiso was already eleven years old. He grew up very protective of his younger sisters, and due to the age difference he treated them almost like a parent. When he rescued Adila from the Iazygi scouts he felt very much like a protective parent. Afterwards he even scolded her for being careless and placing herself in danger.

"Hello, Brother," Adila greeted him. She was carrying a hunting bow. A leather quiver of arrows was slung over her shoulder.

"Hello, Sister," he replied with a smile, glancing at the bow in her hand. "Are you going to do some hunting with that?"

Adila was in a serious mood. She nodded her head towards the target, bristling with arrows like a porcupine. "I want to learn how to do that. Will you teach me?"

"Of course I will, if you are serious about it. Are you sure that you want to kill Iazygis now instead of rabbits and deer?"

"Yes! I am sure. Iazygis and Romans and anyone else who tries to hurt me. And please don't treat me like a child, Cotiso."

"I am sorry for that, I did not mean it to sound that way. You are not a child and you should be able to defend yourself."

"Good!" Adila held up her bow. "I know how to shoot rabbits, but that is not good enough."

"To start with, that bow is not good enough. If you want to kill human enemies, from a distance and with accuracy, then you need a soldier's bow."

"I don't have one," Adila said, frustrated.

Cotiso walked over to where he kept his spare bow and an extra quiver of arrows. The weapon was a compound bow, three feet long, beautifully carved so that it was both light and strong. He handed it to his sister.

"This is a soldier's bow, Adila. It is made from the wood of a yew tree, so that it bends easily but does not break. That gives it power."

"Thank you," she said. "Can I borrow it?"

"No, not borrow. You can have it. You will learn to take care of it properly and to use it properly. Take it with you everywhere so that you get a feel for it, so it feels like a part of you. Do you understand?"

"Yes, I think so. It should feel natural to me."

"Exactly. It must feel like part of your arm, then shooting will feel natural. With practice you will shoot smoothly and accurately, time after time, without thinking about the steps you have to follow. When you can do that, then you will be an archer."

"I understand, and I will work at it even if it takes a long time."

"Good." Cotiso turned her toward the target. "Now let's try it. Hit that."

Adila notched an arrow and took aim. Pulling back the bowstring was much harder than what she was used to with her hunting bow.

"Don't aim too much," Cotiso said. "Don't look at the arrow tip, just look directly at the spot you wish to hit and let the arrow fly."

Adila loosed the bowstring. The arrow flew off with a twang, in a straight line for the target, but fell just short.

"This is harder than it looks!" she exclaimed. "It is much harder to draw than my hunting bow."

"Of course it is, but that gives you range and power. You're not hunting rabbits any more, remember? Here, watch me do it."

Cotiso took an arrow, notched it, pulled the bowstring back to his ear, shot, and watched the arrow sink into the center of the target. It was all one smooth motion that took only two heartbeats.

"It is so easy for you!" Adila said. "You didn't even have to aim."

"You aim with your mind, not with your eye, Adila. Look directly at what you want to hit and your mind and your bow arm will guide the arrow exactly there." He paused and gave her a grin. "Of course that skill comes with experience."

She groaned. "How much experience?"

"Well, considering that I have been practicing daily since before you were born, I would say a great deal of experience."

"I will never be as good as you," she said dejectedly.

He turned and caught her eye. "Listen to me now. With practice you will get stronger and better. You don't need to be as good as me, only good enough to put an arrow into a Roman at thirty paces. You do that, then if the Roman is still moving you run like hell. Do you understand?"

"Yes, I can do that," Adila said with a grin.

"Good. Starting today you will practice with me for one hour every day. Every day, outside practice unless there is heavy rain and then we practice in a barn. If I am not available then you will practice with either Tarbus or Osan."

"Thank you, Brother. I want to be good at this. I want…" Adila paused, searching for the right words.

"What?"

"I want to be a warrior," she said with firm conviction. "I want to protect myself. I never want to feel helpless again."

"Spoken like a true warrior, Adila. Now let's get to work."

"Yes, teacher. Where do we begin?"

He handed her the leather quiver with twenty arrows. "For a start, you will shoot these arrows at the target and learn how to do it properly. I will give you guidance when I see a need. Then you will do it again. And again. And again. And tomorrow, we'll do the same."

Zia entered the medical clinic half walking and half running. People stepped out of her way, not because she was royalty but because the look on her face said that she was on a mission and willing to run through anything or anyone in her way. She made her way straight for the long table in the back where her mother Queen Andrada and her assistant Zelma were examining several jars of herbal medicines.

The Queen was a doctor of herbal medicine, and she insisted on spending time every day supervising operation of the public clinic. After some persuasion from the King she finally agreed to delegate the training of assistant healers to Zelma.

Zelma had been a healer even before she came to Sarmizegetusa. After years of training with Andrada and Vezina, and doing daily work with the city's large population, she was highly knowledgeable and also experienced enough to be a trainer of other doctors.

"Mama!" Zia called when she reached them, slightly out of breath. "Aunt Dochia sends for you. She says that it's time."

"Ah, good," Andrada said. "Tanidela has been sounding impatient the past few days."

"You had better go now," Zelma said with a smile. "Sometimes babies get impatient too."

"As we both know from experience! She has Dochia and also a midwife, but I will go and be with her."

Zelma turned to the princess, whose face was still flushed from her run from the palace. "Zia, will you stay here and help me with these medicines? We can continue your lessons now, if you wish."

"Yes, I would like that," Zia said. "Or do you wish me to go back with you, Mama?"

"No, stay and help Zelma," Andrada said. "You will be a doctor one day, my daughter, and the lessons you learn now will save lives."

"I will see you tomorrow, Your Highness," Zelma said pleasantly. She was a Christian refugee from Rome who was saved from death by Diegis. Over the past twelve years she became not only Andrada's top assistant but also a close friend. Their children, Dorin and Lia, grew up together.

Andrada bid a quick farewell and headed for the door at a brisk walk. The two bodyguards who always accompanied her outside the palace hurried to catch up. The Queen did not fear for her safety from her own people but precautions had to be taken against Dacia's enemies.

The medical clinic was located within an easy walk from the royal palace. Andrada walked through a side entrance into the palace, then turned and hurried down a hallway leading to Tanidela's rooms in the royal living quarters.

Tanidela was the younger sister of the King. The people called her the beautiful rose with thorns, a compliment to her beauty and her sometimes fiery character. For the past several weeks she had been a guest at Sarmizegetusa while her husband, Prince Davi, was visiting allies of the Roxolani.

The Roxolani were a large Sarmatian tribe to the east of Dacia. It would be better for her to be with her sister and her brothers in Dacia when her first child was born, Tanidela had argued. Davi was very devoted to his wife and did not require much convincing.

Andrada's deerskin shoes barely made a whisper as she walked down the stone floors of the palace hallway. She turned a corner to Tanidela's rooms and broke into a smile. The faint sound of a baby's cries came through the doorway from the room just ahead.

Tanidela was lying on the bed, propped up by a large pillow. She looked tired and somewhat pale but was happily looking down at the infant held in her arms, wrapped in a soft blanket. Her sister Dochia stood beside her. Servants were already tidying up the room. The midwife had done her job well, and after one more look at the baby and mother the woman took her leave.

"This one was in a hurry it seems," Andrada said as she greeted the women. "I came as soon as Zia told me."

"Your timing is good," Tanidela said wearily. "Come and see my beautiful daughter."

"Ah, she is beautiful," the Queen said, peering down at the small swaddled bundle. "I could hear her from outside in the hallway so we know her lungs are healthy!"

"It was a very easy birth," Dochia said. "The baby is healthy. And Tanidela is a little tired but otherwise fine."

Andrada took a clean cloth and wiped a bit of perspiration from the new mother's brow. "Yes? You are feeling well?"

"As well as can be expected, Sister," Tanidela replied with a weary smile.

"Of course. In a few days it gets easier," Andrada said. "In a few weeks, when Davi returns, you will be ready to travel if you wish."

"I don't think I will be in a hurry to travel for a while!" Tanidela said with a soft laugh.

"It would be wise to put off travel for some time in any case," the Queen said. "Better for you and better for the baby. Also Davi might be needed here for military reasons."

"Just as well then," Tanidela sighed. "I need a rest."

"When Davi returns," Dochia wondered, "will he be disappointed that you did not give birth to a new prince of the Roxolani?"

"He will be happy," Tanidela said. She glanced down at the infant who was already falling asleep. "How can he not be happy?"

"Oh, you know how men are," Dochia said.

"How are they, Sister?" asked King Decebal in a teasing tone. He entered the room with Cotiso walking by his side.

"You know exactly what I mean!" Dochia said with a laugh. "Sons! Give us sons!"

"Oh? I forgot to make those cries when my daughters were born," Decebal said lightly. "How careless of me."

"That's only because you already had Cotiso," his sister argued stubbornly.

"That is not fair," Andrada protested. "Decebal was very happy to see both our daughters. As soon as he returned from his military campaigns, I mean," she added.

Cotiso walked up to Dochia and gave her a kiss on the cheek. "Auntie, I always wondered how men are. Will you teach me?" he teased with a grin.

“Stop, you two!” Dochia cried, trying not to laugh. “You know that I’m right.”

Decebal walked to the bedside and took Tanidela’s hand. “I am happy for you, Sister.”

“Thank you, Brother,” she said. “I am glad that you are here. And Cotiso, I am happy that you are here. I have something that I wish to tell you."

Cotiso drew closer. “What is it, Aunt Tanidela?”

“I have chosen a name for my daughter, and I want you both to hear it first.”

Decebal, Cotiso, and Dochia knew instantly what she meant. It took Andrada a heartbeat to understand, and that drew a smile.

“I shall name her in memory of my sister in law, who I loved and who I still miss dearly. My daughter’s name shall be Tyra.”

Decebal looked at his sister and thanked her with a solemn nod. Cotiso walked up to the bedside. He gazed in wonder at the face of the sleeping infant, then took his aunt Tanidela’s hand and kissed it softly. His eyes thanked her because somehow in that moment his mind was blank for words.

> Chapter 4

Mars Ultor

Viminacium, Banat, April 101 AD

Emperor Trajan departed Rome at the head of his legions in late March, after the winter snows melted. Sacrifices were made by priests in the temples of Rome to ensure the safety of the Emperor and the success of the army. The invasion of Dacia had been hoped for and anticipated for many years, and it was understood by all that this was a historic occasion. The mood in Rome was happy and optimistic.

The Emperor arrived in Viminacium, located to the east of the large trade center of Singidunum, in late April. This location on the Danubius River was equally distant from Moesia and Pannonia and thus provided a convenient place for the army to gather. A bridge of boats was being constructed to cross the river, following the practices many years earlier of Cornelius Fuscus and Tettius Julianus.

Emperor Trajan had an army of fourteen legions prepared and eager to begin this invasion of Dacia. In addition to his legionnaires he had fifty thousand auxiliary troops from Rome's allies including Gauls, Thracians, Iazygis, and Celtic and Germanic tribes. His cavalry troops were mostly Gauls, Iazygis, and Germans, along with his Moorish cavalry from Africa.

Nine legions had been stationed along the northern frontier for years, and the rest were marched in for this campaign. The Emperor also had the Praetorian Guard troops for his personal protection. In total this was the largest single army ever assembled in the history of the Roman Empire.

The legions were fully equipped with artillery, cavalry, and the vast stores of supplies needed for a long campaign. The armor worn by legionnaires had been modified with vambraces to protect against the Dacian falx, which had proved so deadly in past battles. It was modified based on armor worn by gladiators in the Roman arenas.

Emperor Trajan set the stage for the greatest invasion campaign in the history of Rome. Preparations were fully and painstakingly completed over the past three years. Strategy and planning was worked out in detail. Men and weapons were in place. It was almost May, the ideal time to march and initiate a campaign. All that was left now was to execute the plan.

Trajan's army crossed the Danubius over the boat bridge. It was a slow process considering the vast amount of men and supplies that had to be moved from one river bank to the other over the narrow bridge. Horses had to be led across in single file with a cover over their heads so they would not panic and bolt. Field artillery were pulled across slowly and carefully, the smaller pieces by mules and the larger pieces by oxen. The larger supply wagons also needed to be pulled by oxen. Oxen were slow, stubborn, and ponderous animals, and so everything took longer than the army officers hoped for.

Once the army was on the Dacian side of the river the Emperor made the ritual sacrifices to Mars. A boar, a ram, and a white bull were slaughtered following sacred religious rites. The sacrifices were then burned on the altar as an offering to Mars. No Roman army commander would start a military campaign without first asking for the blessings of the gods.

Following the religious rites the Emperor held a meeting of his war council. With him were his most trusted generals, all men of proven ability who could be counted on to carry out Trajan's strategy. The Prefect of the Praetorian Guard, Tiberius Claudius Livianus, was also a close friend. Gnaeus Pompeius Longinus, now in his middle fifties, was a longtime friend and mentor. Gnaeus had been Trajan's successor in Pannonia, a prime reward for a friend. General Laberius Maximus was the governor of Moesia. Trajan counted on him to be one of his top two commanders.

Trajan's closest friend and confidant was Lucius Licinius Sura. Most recently serving as governor of Germania Inferior, he was being given an opportunity for military glory before he returned to politics in Rome. Trajan's lifetime habit of gaining loyalty by rewarding his friends was raised to great new heights now that he had the power and the privileges of Caesar.

The young Publius Hadrianus, called Hadrian, was groomed by the Emperor for higher leadership positions. Hadrian's marriage last year to Trajan's great-niece Vibia Sabina strengthened his position in the Emperor's inner circle. To Trajan's dismay, however, Hadrian seemed to lack the passion for military leadership and conquest that was so prominent in his other army commanders.

The commanders gathered around a large map laid out on a table in Trajan's command tent. The Danubius frontier was drawn out in detail. Above that was Dacia, drawn in less detail because Roman forces had never been active that far north.

"Gentlemen, tomorrow we march to battle. First we take Lederata, here, which is closest and will not be difficult. We drive any Dacian forces in our way north towards the fort of Arcidava, here. After we take Arcidava we march east towards Tapae," Trajan said, stabbing a finger at each point on the map as he went along.

The Emperor moved his finger along the Danubius to a distance approximately one hundred miles to the southeast. "General Lusius Quietus is crossing the Danubius here, and will march northwest into Dacia. He will do what Lusius does best, which is to terrorize and pacify the countryside. He will drive any Dacian forces to the west, towards Tapae."

"Tapae is the key," Laberius Maximus declared. "Just as it was for Fuscus and for Julianus."

"Yes it is, Laberius," Trajan agreed. "Tapae guards the way into the heart of Dacia. Decebalus will give us a fight there, as he did with Fuscus and Julianus."

Trajan paused and his face turned grim. "Decebalus slaughtered Fuscus and his legions. He fought and then retreated before Julianus because he was badly outmanned. Julianus took heavy losses fighting in the mountains of Dacia, and his invasion stalled because he had to retreat for the winter. Our invasion, gentlemen, will not stall."

All the generals were familiar with the history of Rome's Dacian wars under Emperor Domitian. All were determined to put Dacia in its place and to assert Rome's authority. The most passionate and committed of them all was Caesar himself.

"Once we reach Tapae we shall combine our forces with the army of Quietus coming in from the east. Decebalus will put up a fight but he cannot stop us. Between our legions and auxiliary forces we have near one hundred and fifty thousand men. We have Dacia at great disadvantage."

"We have a clear advantage in numbers, Caesar," General Gnaeus Longinus said. "But let us also consider, Decebalus has three things in his favor that provide him some advantage. I say some advantage, but by no means a decisive advantage."

"Expand your thinking, Gnaeus" the Emperor said. Although he had the superior military mind, which all recognized and respected, Trajan invited and even welcomed ideas from those serving under him. It was a rare quality for a Roman commander, and it earned him even greater loyalty from his men.

"First, the mountain roads to Sarmizegetusa are guarded by a string of very strong and well defended forts. The walls are made with stone, in the murus dacicus fashion. They are made thick and sturdy and our siege artillery will not be enough to bring them down. Decebalus has spent the past ten years building up his defenses. We can take these forts, but our losses will be heavy."

Trajan nodded. "We are prepared for that. True, Decebalus has built up his defenses, and what makes it worse is that he is doing so with Roman engineers supplied to him by Emperor Domitian! Now he bribes and buys engineers anytime he wishes. His reserves of gold are said to be vast, unfortunately."

"All the more reason to stop him now before he grows even stronger, Caesar," said Maximus.

"Quite so. Continue, General Longinus."

"Second, Decebalus has narrowed the gap in field artillery. Our engineers have trained his engineers to build more scorpions and carrobalistae, and to use them effectively. We have a big advantage still but Dacian artillery is now significantly better compared to our previous wars with them."

"I am not afraid of Dacian artillery," Maximus scoffed. "We will have them overwhelmed still."

Longinus gave a nod. "Agreed. We should expect higher casualties from artillery than in previous conflicts, however."

"And third?" Trajan asked.

"Third, Caesar, is an advantage the Dacians have that is as old as Dacia. Because of the worship of their god Zamolxis and their belief in immortality, they are not afraid to die. Some even welcome it and die happily in battle, because when they die they immediately join their god Zamolxis. This makes them fight with a fanatical passion. In combat they become demons."

"Your point is well taken, Gnaeus." Trajan gave an indifferent shrug. "We cannot change their beliefs, so we will simply have to kill the demons, eh?"

"Yes, Marcus," Longinus agreed. "And yes, we have the advantage. I am simply stating that we should understand the strengths of this enemy and not underestimate them again."

"We are not underestimating Dacia," Trajan said in an even tone. "That is why it took us three years to prepare for this war."

Lederata, Dacia, May 101 AD

Across the Danubius River, and one day's march east of Viminacium, was the Dacian city of Lederata. This was a border outpost rather than a well defended fortress. Some Dacian cavalry skirmished with the vanguard troops of the Roman army, then rode off to the north.

Hadrian rode besides Emperor Trajan, along with the Praetorian Prefect Tiberius Livianus and Licinius Sura. Although Hadrian was not yet given any important military tasks, he was involved in the council meetings and discussions of the top military leaders. His job was to listen and, when necessary, to deliver messages from Trajan to the other commanders. In later years this treatment would become a source of resentment for Hadrian towards his childhood guardian Trajan. He would never fully escape the feeling, while Trajan was still alive, that he was being treated as Trajan's messenger boy.

As the Emperor approached Lederata at the head of his army a group of Roman cavalry scouts rode to meet them from underneath the city walls. They were in no hurry and rode at a leisurely pace.

"Hail Caesar!" the lead scout saluted.

"Report," Trajan ordered. "Did you meet resistance?"

"No, Caesar. The city appears deserted."

Trajan was mildly surprised. He did not expect to meet any major Dacian forces this far south, but he anticipated some battle from the city's defenders.

"Very well," the Emperor said. He turned to Hadrian. "Take one cohort of infantry and search the city. Then report back to me."

"Immediately, Caesar," Hadrian replied and rode off.

"Are they not going to fight us?" Sura asked.

"Decebalus will not fight us on the plains, Licinius. He wants to draw us into his mountains and his forests. That has always been his fighting strategy."

"Not a bad strategy," said Livianus.

"It's the strategy I would use if I was in his position," Trajan agreed. "He knows that he can't match us on open ground. We will have to fight him in the mountains."

An hour later, as evening approached, the army began setting up camp around the city. Hadrian rode back through the city gates with the expected news.

"Not a Dacian in sight, Caesar. Also nothing worth looting, not even a chicken coop. They even took all the chicken eggs with them."

Emperor Trajan was an old school soldier. He loved the military life, the campaigns, the marching, even the day to day routines of military camp. He marched on the ground with his soldiers and ate his meals with them in the mess tents. He was, in his eyes, both the soldiers' commander and also their comrade in arms.

Trajan and two personal guards joined a mess table of six soldiers. One older man, an experienced veteran with an air of authority, was speaking to five younger men who were in their early twenties. The soldiers were not surprised when Trajan joined them for the meal. This was common behavior for their commander.

"Good day, my fellow soldiers," the Emperor greeted his men. A servant quickly brought him a plate of food. In deference to his title this food had been selected ahead of time, and tasted by his official taster to make certain that it contained no poison.

The older man in the group gave a respectful nod in greeting. He had a deep scar across the left side of his forehead. "Good day. You honor us with your company, Caesar."

"It is always my honor to talk with Roman citizens," Trajan said pleasantly, "and particularly so with legionnaires. Are these young officers listening and learning well, Prefect Capito?"

"They are, Caesar. And if not, I bring out the lash," the man replied with a grin. Some of the men laughed at his joke. They respected his knowledge and liked the man as a fair officer.

Sextus Capito was a camp prefect. Although each legion was commanded by a legate, usually a Roman noble of senatorial rank, responsibility for ground operations fell to the camp prefect. He was typically an older and experienced soldier, often a former centurion with extensive battlefield experience. The legion's younger officers looked to him as the voice of experience and reason.

Trajan knew the names and histories of each of his legions' camp prefects because these experienced men were indispensable to his army functioning well. The aides gathered around Capito were junior tribunes, young nobles who were there to watch and learn before they were advanced to higher positions.

"The lash motivates quickly," Trajan admitted, also with a grin, "although I prefer to motivate capable men by rewarding them with money and promotions."

The Emperor started his meal, hungrily. As he ate he looked around as the eager faces of the young tribunes. "How goes your training, men?"

One of the tribunes took the lead. "Very well, Caesar. We train in battlefield tactics every day. The auxilia are training with us because we must coordinate their efforts with the legion."

"Excellent," Trajan said. He paused his eating and looked around the table. "Tell me, men, what makes the Roman army the finest army in the world?"

"Roman leadership," replied a tribune without hesitation.

Trajan nodded. "Leadership is important, yes. But leadership alone does not win a battle or a war."

"A Roman legion has the best equipment in the world," declared another tribune. "We have the best weapons, the best armor, and the best artillery."

"Indeed we do, Tribune. Superior equipment is an advantage, but better equipped armies often lose battles." Trajan turned to Capito. "And what do you say, Prefect?"

"Training," Sextus replied immediately. "Superior training gives a Roman legion our biggest advantage."

"Exactly right." Trajan looked around at the tribunes. "Listen to every word this man tells you, remember it, and obey. Most of all, obey. When you are faced with a horde of screaming Dacians or Celts what will save your lives and the lives of your men, and allow you to win the battle, is your training."

"Yes, Caesar." Coming from the Emperor himself, this was advice these men would remember for the rest of their lives.

"Now I wish to speak with Prefect Capito, so you men will excuse us," Trajan said pleasantly.

The young men moved briskly, gathering their belongings and leaving quickly. Caesar's time was more valuable than gold and should never be wasted.

"Good men?" Trajan asked

Sextus nodded. "The lads are fine. They come from noble families and are used to a soft life, so I have to drive them hard."

"Good. Drive them as hard as you need to, things will only get more difficult and challenging for them."

"Yes, Caesar."

"Sextus, you campaigned with Cornelius Fuscus," Trajan said, coming to the point. "You fought at the first battle of Tapae."

"I did, Caesar. I led the assault on the city walls. However I did not join General Fuscus in his drive north through the mountain pass where he was attacked by Decebalus and the Dacian army."

"It is just as well that you did not join him, or else we would not be sitting here having this conversation," Trajan said glumly.

"Yes, Caesar. Is there anything you wish to know about that time?" Capito asked cautiously.

Trajan shook his head. "What's done cannot be undone. We learn from the mistakes of others and make sure to not repeat them. I am interested only in the battles that lie ahead, Capito."

"Of course, Caesar."

"I am interested in your opinion about the readiness of our army. How are the men's spirits?"

"The men are in very good spirits. They are eager to advance and engage the Dacians."

Trajan gave a nod. "Good. And what is your opinion of the changes in armor?"

Capito replied with a smile. "An excellent improvement, Caesar, and a very necessary one. It will save many of our boys from losing their arms and legs to the Dacian falx."

"I think so too, Sextus. They are modifications based on armor worn by gladiators to protect the knee, forearm, elbow, and neck. If these are effective for gladiators, why not for legionnaires?"

"And yet," Capito shook his head sadly, "nobody thought of these changes before you, Caesar. The soldiers in the armies of Generals Fuscus and Julianus learned to dread fighting against the damn falx."

"Learn from the mistakes of others and move on, Sextus. It is our sacred duty as commanders to provide the best for our men. This we have done. Now let us look ahead. Always look ahead."

"Yes, Caesar. Decebalus will find that Roman soldiers are harder to kill this time around."

"Indeed. We will be more difficult to kill. Train your men hard, Sextus. We have many hard battles ahead."

The Roman army marched north towards Arcidava following a river valley. In this matter they had very little choice. One of the essential requirements for moving a large army was to find enough grass, shrubbery, and other forage for the animals. In addition to the large numbers of cavalry horses, the pack animals had to be fed and kept healthy and alive or the army would be paralyzed.

Most of the army's food and supplies were carried by mules. Oxen pulled the heavy baggage carts and the wheeled artillery. Emperor Trajan scheduled his invasion to begin in late spring because that is when there would be ample new grass and foliage to feed his animals.

For the same reason he followed the river valley, where vegetation grew more plentiful.

The army moved slowly because on a good day oxen travelled at a speed of two miles per hour. On good, paved Roman roads a legion could travel perhaps twenty miles in a day. On the dirt roads and tracks of Dacia the army was making perhaps ten miles a day. At times there were no roads at all. In some woodsy areas the Roman engineers had to take axes and chop their way through a section of forest to create a path.

Legionnaires marched in columns, six men abreast. Their day started early in the pre-dawn light when tents were taken down. The lead parties were sent ahead to find ground for the next camp. At the new location the lead party staked out locations for tents, grazing areas, supply wagons, and so on. In the late afternoon the baggage wagons arrived and were unloaded, tents were set up, and cooking fires were lit. Animals were unharnessed and set to pasture. Dinner rations were then handed out before night fell, because nightfall meant going to sleep after a long and exhausting day.

For Trajan's army each day required taking apart a small city in the early morning, moving it down the road ten miles or so, and then setting up the city again before nightfall. This was army life during campaign season, day after day, for weeks and months on end.

Peladea, Dacia, May 101 AD

The army of General Lusius Quietus crossed the Danubius River on a second boat bridge southeast of Emperor Trajan's main army. The cavalry general also commanded twenty thousand infantry, which were used primarily as a mop up force and for short sieges of walled cities. His main attacking force consisted of four thousand cavalry that appeared out of nowhere and struck with fast and lethal fury.

The farming village of Peladea was half empty. The young men of fighting age had left weeks ago to join their units in the Dacian army, which were camped in the mountains to the west. Their wives and children went with them, as did many other women and children of the village. In times of war the safest place for them to be was in the mountains.

The people who stayed behind were the older people who cared for the livestock and other farm animals, and looked after the villagers who were too old or too sick to travel. The crops had already been planted, but the animals could not be abandoned.

If the enemy came to Peladea, the people believed, they would likely take their food supplies. That was acceptable because they had food hidden away in the nearby hills to last until the new crops were ripe for harvesting. Peladea was not a fort and had no military value whatsoever. The villagers expected that they were not worth the bother of an invading army. They were mistaken.

The Roman cavalry attacked in early morning from the west, north, and east, to block off routes of escape. Those panicked few who tried escaping towards the south came face to face with General Quietus and the main body of his army. Villagers were killed where they stood, pierced with spears and slashed with swords. The old and the sick were killed in their beds. Children were cut down with their parents. Village dogs barked, howled, and attacked the intruders, and were quickly put to death. Farm animals were killed in their pens.

This Roman army was not an army of military conquest, but an army of terror. Their only mission was to kill and burn and destroy everything in their path. Theses tactics were meant to frighten the Dacian people into submission and crush their will to resist. As later years would show, these barbaric tactics failed and only strengthened the resistance of the Dacian people. That unfortunately would be no comfort to the slaughtered villagers of Peladea.

> Chapter 5

Arcidava

Fort of Arcidava, Dacia, May 101 AD

King Decebal called his war council meeting in the dining hall of the fort of Arcidava. This fort was located in the western part of Dacia, at least a week's march west of Tapae. The council meeting had a feel of urgency because the main Roman army, led by Emperor Trajan himself, was marching towards this location.

As usual the High Priest Vezina, befitting his role as chief advisor, had the seat of honor at the King's right hand. General Diegis was representing the Dacian infantry at this meeting, while General Drilgisa was in the field positioning the main body of the army in the woods south of the fort. General Sinna represented the cavalry.

Dacians made up the largest part of King Decebal's army, however this was an army of allies. Prince Davi of the Sarmatians brought five thousand elite cavalry with him. Chief Fynn led the Bastarnae tribes and was in charge of their infantry. Chief Ailen of the Celts brought eight thousand fierce warriors with him from their homelands west of Dacia. The Celts and Sarmatians in particular felt as threatened by Rome as did the Dacians.

Vezina gave them a briefing. "Our scouts count ten legions plus another forty thousand auxilia. This gives Emperor Trajan around ninety thousand fighting men. The cavalry are Gauls and Iazygis."

"This is Trajan's main force," Davi added. "My cavalry scouts are keeping track of a smaller army in the east, led by Lusius Quietus and his Moorish cavalry. As you know, King Decebal, he is laying waste to the countryside there."

"Is that the same Lusius Quietus they call the Butcher of Parthia?" Fynn asked.

"The same," Decebal said grimly. "And for now at least he is the butcher of Dacia. He kills civilians and burns down villages and farms, and we don't have enough troops to go after him."

"Why is Trajan dividing his army?" wondered Ailen. He was the youngest officer there and respectful of the knowledge of his elders.

"I can think of several reasons," Vezina replied. "Most of all he wants us to divide our army. After all, the usual Roman strategy is to divide and conquer, is it not?"

"The bastards brag about it," said Diegis with a laugh. "They even stamp it on their coins."

"They will not divide us," Decebal said. "We fight as one unified army. If we don't, then their numbers will overwhelm our armies."

"Trajan might also wish to trap us between his two armies," Fynn added. "We can't have that either."

Decebal shook his head. "No, we will not allow that. We will give this Roman army a fight here and bloody them. Then we retreat to Tapae. When Quietus comes west he will combine his army with that of Trajan, but they will not trap us between them."

"My men are ready," Prince Davi said. "You men fight them in the forest with your infantry, and my cavalry will chew up their flanks."

"You all know the battle plan," Decebal said. "Stay coordinated and fight as one army."

"Of course," the Sarmatian agreed. "My men are simply impatient and eager to fight the enemy. They have trained for years for this."

General Sinna gave him a grin. "My cavalry feels the same. Then again, horsemen are always impatient."

"Will you defend the fort?" Fynn asked Decebal.

"No, Fynn, we will not. The better strategy is to keep the entire army together for this battle, and also for the march east afterwards."

"Trajan already outnumbers us two to one, we cannot sacrifice a portion of our army to defend the city," Vezina explained. "Arcidava cannot be defended against this Roman army, and in any case the fort has no strategic importance for the battles still ahead."

"Let's get to work then," Diegis said. "I want to run the artillery units through more drills before the Romans get here."

"Dacian infantry units with artillery," Ailen said with a smile. "That should give the Romans a surprise, eh?"

"They know that we have it," Diegis replied. "Their surprise will be that we know how to use it as well as they do."

"Indeed, Brother," Decebal said. "Train your men well. All of you chiefs, prepare your men well for the fight. We face a powerful enemy that expects to crush us. Let's make them pay a bloody price for their arrogance."

The Roman army camped on the edge of a narrow valley south of Arcidava. The Dacians and their allies were positioned in the woods across the valley, and Emperor Trajan expected them to put up a fight there. As always he wanted his army organized and fully deployed when he marched on the enemy position. Nothing his army did was ever rushed or unplanned.

Trajan reviewed the battle plan with his top generals. Gnaeus Longinus would direct the auxiliary troops, which were always the first units to be committed to battle. There was no military advantage to placing auxiliaries in front, rather it was a practical tactic to save the lives of Roman legionnaires. Legionnaires were Roman citizens. Auxiliary troops were barbarians who were expendable.

Laberius Maximus would command the legions that would follow the auxiliary's attack, if needed. Trajan himself had command of the general strategy and overall attack. He also directed the wing cavalry, which played a critical role in plans of attack and the outcome of the battle. Hadrian joined the group but mostly watched and listened.

"The enemy is staying sheltered in the forest," Longinus said. "They will not attack us in the open, so we have to go to them."

"A smart tactic," Trajan said. "They conceal their numbers and their positions. No matter, in the morning we advance and drive them out."

"How many men are we facing, Caesar?" asked Maximus.

"We cannot know until they show themselves. Decebalus is fighting a delaying action. He will not commit to a major battle here."

"Is Decebalus here?" Hadrian wondered.

"We shall see, Hadrianus," the Emperor replied. "I hope that he is. After all these years I want to finally see him, face to face."

"And take his head off," Longinus said with a laugh.

"And take his head off," Trajan said with a wry smile.

"Ah! Speaking of meeting face to face, here is someone who has actually met with Decebalus," Laberius Maximus said, turning to a Roman soldier who had just entered the tent.

The newcomer was a man in his early forties, of medium height and athletic build, with black hair and pale gray eyes. He walked with the formal and somewhat stiff gait of a lifelong Roman army officer.

"Welcome, Titus!" Maximus greeted him. "Caesar, this is my aide, Titus Lucullus."

Lucullus gave Trajan a smart Roman salute, standing very straight and fully extending his right arm. "Hail, Caesar!"

"Welcome, Lucullus," Trajan said. "I know your name. You were stationed in Moesia?"

"Yes, Caesar. I was serving with the Governor in Moesia. General Maximus now gives me the honor of serving on his staff here."

"We need you here, Titus, not in Moesia," Maximus said. "You know the Dacians better than any of us."

"I am at Caesar's service, and yours too, General."

"And you arrived just in time," Trajan said. "King Decebalus is waiting on the other side of this valley. Perhaps you can re-new your acquaintance with him, eh?"

"Or perhaps you can convince him to surrender and save us all a lot of trouble?" Longinus asked.

Titus smiled at the joke. "One thing we can count on for certain, King Decebalus will never surrender."

"I expect not," Trajan said. "You will tell me more about him later. Join me for the evening meal, Titus."

"Of course, Caesar, I would be honored. I must tell you that I only spoke with King Decebalus briefly. I know his brother Diegis, and his general Drilgisa, much better."

"Good, you can tell me about them too. I make it a point to know my enemy."

On the edge of the woods opposite the Roman line an artillery battery of ten Dacian scorpions were being positioned to face the enemy. These deadly torsion weapons were capable of hurling iron bolts and hitting targets with some accuracy from three hundred yards away. Each wheeled artillery piece was operated by eight engineers.

This artillery battery was protected by a troop of sixty infantry armed with spears and swords, led by a young captain named Tarbus. Positioned behind the infantry was a group of thirty archers led by Cotiso, the son of King Decebal. The biggest threat to the artillery group was from a fast cavalry strike that did not allow them time to retreat. The job of the infantry spearmen and archery troops was to fight off any such attack.

The Roman army emerged at a slow walk from the woods on their side of the valley. They were in a very long line and formed a thick mass of soldiers, going twenty or thirty rows deep. These were not legionnaires, Cotiso saw, but auxilia infantry. All were barbarians, as the Romans called them, most of them prisoners of war or volunteers from Rome's allies.

The auxiliary troops wore whatever clothing was traditional for their tribes. They did not wear metal armor, but the much inferior leather armor or no armor at all. They did not carry a scutum, the heavy and sturdy Roman shield, but a variety of shields of different shapes and sizes. They were poorly armed compared to the Roman legions, carrying whatever weapons they brought with them from their home tribes.

What the auxila lacked in quality, however, they made up for in numbers. Often they won a battle all by themselves by overwhelming a weaker enemy. By taking the lead in every battle, and taking the casualties, they reduced the loss of life of Roman citizens in the army.

"Fire!" the captain of artillery shouted to his men. Ten scorpions fired their large iron bolts, were quickly and efficiently re-armed, and fired again. The bolts travelled so fast that the enemy soldiers never saw them coming. Some bolts killed or injured two or three men. The enemy lines slowed and faltered in the sections targeted by artillery.

"Stay sharp!" Tarbus shouted to his men as the artillery barrage continued and the Roman army drew closer. "Expect an attack!"

"You are right, look over there," Cotiso said to him, pointing to a break in the Roman line. Infantry troops moved aside to open a gap. Through the gap streamed a row of Roman auxiliary cavalry, riding straight for their artillery position.

"Form up!" Tarbus shouted the order. "Stand fast! Do not let them through!"

The Dacian infantry formed a line in front of their artillery, two men deep. The soldiers in the front row went down on one knee and planted the ends of their long spears into the ground, the spear blades angled out to meet the chest of a charging horse. They knew that no horse would charge into a row of spear points. The men in the second row were armed with long spears for fighting off riders and also with shorter throwing spears. Cotiso and his archers lined up behind the infantry wall.

"Let them come in range!" Cotiso shouted. "When they get close target the horses!"

Groups of Dacian infantry emerged out of the woods on each side of the artillery position. Their mission was to fight the approaching Roman infantry. The mission of protecting the artillery and its crews belonged to Tarbus' spearmen and Cotiso's archers.

"Now!" Cotiso shouted and sent an arrow flying in the direction of the charging Roman cavalry. All the other archers did the same. Some arrows found targets and riders and horses fell. The mission of the archers was to put a wall of shafts in the path of approaching cavalry. As the Roman riders closed within range the infantry with throwing spears added to the missile barrage.

"Hold steady!" Tarbus yelled. The cavalry closed with frightening speed. The horses in front veered away from the wall of spears and became easy targets for arrows. The animals panicked and screamed in pain, bolting away from the Dacian lines. A rider approached close enough to throw his lance and hit one of the kneeling spearmen in the face. Cotiso put an arrow into his side just below the ribcage. The rider slumped down, then fell sideways to the ground.

Another Dacian spearman fell dead to a thrown lance. He was quickly dragged back out of the line and replaced by the spearman behind him. More riders got near and threw their lances. Small gaps in the defensive wall appeared where spearmen fell.

"Close the line!" Tarbus shouted.

A Roman rider shouted a fierce Iazygi battle cry and charged at the end of the spear line from an outside angle. Arrows hit his horse in the shoulder and the side, and the enraged and panicked animal charged blindly ahead. It took a spear in the chest but crashed into the Dacian line, falling sideways and taking out three spearmen. The Iazygi rider flew over the spear line and crashed hard at the feet of Tarbus. Before the man could gather himself Tarbus speared him in the neck, and was met with a spray of blood that covered his lower legs. A neck shot was a fast and easy kill.

Cotiso put an arrow into the chest of another approaching rider. He was suddenly alarmed to hear loud hoof beats coming from his left, which told him that a large group of riders was approaching fast. The very next moment his alarm turned to joy and excitement. The new riders were Prince Davi and Sarmatian cavalry, who smashed into the Roman cavalry like a storm. The Dacian artillery crews cheered the Sarmatians with gusto.

Sarmatian riders and their horses were covered in armor. They fought with lances, swords, and bows. The Roman auxiliary cavalry were no match for them in either equipment or fighting skills and were swiftly overwhelmed. Those who were not quickly killed or wounded rode off to escape from their attackers.

The fierce battle with the Roman cavalry had only taken a few minutes. The captain of the artillery crews looked up to see that the Roman auxiliary infantry were closing in on them, and Dacian and Bastarnae infantry were walking out to meet them. The strategy now called for the artillery units to retreat and let the infantry fight the battle. Preserving the artillery was more important than killing a few more Romans.

"Pack it up! Let's go!" the captain called out. His crews were well trained and sprang into action. The scorpions would be hitched to mules and wheeled to the back of the lines. Their role in this battle was over.

Cotiso walked over to Tarbus, whose white woolen pants, shirt, and even neck and face were splashed with blood. Tarbus would go and escort the artillery crews to the rear, while the archers would stay and support the infantry in battle.

"Well done, Tarbus," Cotiso told him, his voice filled with pride. "Your men fought well."

Tarbus acknowledged with a nod. "You too, my friend. Now I must go with these crews and and make sure no harm befalls them."

"Go, then. And Zamolxis go with you."

By mid-day the infantry battle was still being fought fiercely, mostly by the edge of the woods on the Dacian side of the valley. Decebal was outnumbered and would not risk committing his full army to the fight. At the same time the Dacian infantry and cavalry was getting the best of the Roman auxiliaries. The battlefield was covered with the bodies of the dead and the moans and screams of the wounded.

Emperor Trajan watched the battle from horseback from behind the Roman lines. His generals Longinus and Laberius Maximus were alongside, along with Tiberius Livianus who was in charge of the Praetorian Guard. The Praetorian Guard, Caesar's personal guard, surrounded the Emperor's command post.

Trajan was not happy but neither was he discouraged. He turned to address Maximus.

"Well, Laberius, we have learned one thing today."

"What is that, Caesar?"

"Dacian infantry is superior to our auxiliaries, even when they are outnumbered."

Maximus grunted. "That much seems true, Caesar. They are better equipped and have superior fighting ability."

Longinus brought his horse nearer. "But are they a fighting match for our legionnaires? There is one way to find out."

"They are not better than our legions," Trajan declared. "However now we will find find out, because our auxiliaries are getting killed. Laberius?"

"Yes, Caesar?"

"Commit your troops. Send in two legions to relieve the auxilia and end the slaughter."

"Immediately, Caesar. We'll show these barbarians how Romans fight." Maximus turned his horse and rode off.

Off to one side Titus Lucullus cleared his throat. He was startled to find that it caught the Emperor's attention.

"Do you have something you wish to say, Lucullus?" Trajan asked calmly.

"It is of no significance, Caesar," Titus replied, feeling somewhat embarrassed.

"No, tell us, I insist," Trajan continued. "I find that men are often most honest in moments of spontaneous expression, in spite of themselves."

"The statement from General Maximus about showing barbarians how Romans fight. It simply reminded me of a similar statement made about Decebalus. A long time ago, Caesar."

"Oh? Explain yourself, Titus."

"Was that a statement from Tettius Julianus perhaps?" asked Gnaeus Longinus, genuinely curious. "He fought against Decebalus, with you ably by his side."

Lucullus shook his head. "Not General Julianus. I meant Governor Sabinus."

Longinus chuckled. "That was indeed a long time ago! You have an interesting history, Lucullus."

The Emperor was not as amused as Longinus. "That was a failure in leadership and foolish overconfidence, Titus. But never hesitate to be honest with me whatever your concerns might be."

"Yes, Caesar. In truth my reaction was not a concern, but simply a bad memory I think."

That made Trajan smile. "Bad memories teach us not to forget bad experiences, so that we may learn from them. We shall not forget the example of Oppius Sabinus."

"No, Caesar."

"I grow wiser as I grow older, Lucullus. And do you know what contributes so greatly to my wisdom?"

"Yes, Caesar?"

"Learning from the mistakes of others," Trajan said in a solemn voice, and turned his attention back to the battlefield. "And under no circumstances repeating them."

On the other side of the valley Decebal was also watching the battle from horseback from the edge of the woods. Vezina, Chief Fynn of the Bastarnae, and Chief Ailen of the Celts were with him.

"Trajan is committing his legions finally," Fynn pointed out. This was the moment they had been waiting for.

"He is indeed," the King said. "Now he knows that he needs to spill legionnaire blood if he plans on victory."

"A great deal of legionnaire blood, I hope," Vezina said grimly.

"Should we call our troops back and begin the march to Tapae?" asked Chief Ailen.

"No, not yet," Decebal replied. "Give our troops a chance to prove to themselves that they can stand up against Roman legions."

Fynn nodded towards the small group of mounted figures on the other side of the valley, the obvious Roman command post. "And prove it to him, too?"

"I only care about what our troops believe, Chief Fynn," Decebal said. "What Trajan believes makes no difference to what we do or don't do."

"True enough," Fynn replied. "We should get our wounded and our supply wagons on the road east, at least. There is no good reason to delay their march."

"Of course," Decebal agreed. He turned to a Dacian cavalry officer. "Message to General Diegis. Begin the withdrawal now, with priority for our wounded and the artillery."

"Yes, Sire! Immediately."

Vezina had a question. "Arcidava is evacuated, Sire. Do we leave it for the Romans, or put it to the torch?"

"Leave it be," the King answered. "At this time it is of no use to us or to the Romans. When the war is over we'll want it back."

The retreat of the Dacian army and their allies was organized and orderly, Emperor Trajan noted. They took the road east to Tapae as he expected they would. Their army was smaller and lighter and thus could travel faster than his Roman army. He would follow Decebalus but it was not strategically necessary to give immediate chase. There was no place for the Dacian army to go where the Roman army could not follow. He would fight this war in an orderly way, his way.

It was sobering for the Emperor to consider that although he drove the Dacians out of Arcidava, the enemy inflicted considerable losses on the Roman army as well. His auxiliary infantry and cavalry both took a beating. The battle was won when Maximus attacked with his legions, however the Dacians and their allies put up a fierce resistance even then. They showed that they were not afraid of the Roman army.

They found the fort of Arcidava deserted. Trajan noted the thick walls made with stone, the large water towers, and the very large granaries that were left empty. The fort was built to withstand a long siege, although this time Decebalus had chosen not to defend it. Ahead for his army, Trajan knew, were dozens of other forts just like this one.

> Chapter 6

Gathering Forces

Sarmizegetusa, June 101 AD

Recently the Princess Adila found herself feeling trapped and stifled, like a bird in a cage desperate to spread its wings and fly away. She was insufferably impatient with waiting around in Sarmizegetusa for news about the war with Rome. Her father the King was leading the army. Her brother Cotiso was a captain of archers. Adila continued her archery practice as Cotiso had taught her, shooting a hundred arrows a day, every day. She was getting stronger and more accurate. She was also getting impatient to shoot at more than targets filled with straw.

One afternoon she went to talk about this with her mother the Queen. Andrada was not in her quarters, a servant told her. She had gone to visit her sister in law, Tanidela. Tanidela and her infant daughter were staying with Decebal's family while her husband Davi was fighting against Rome.

Why was it that the men were so involved in life while the women of the royal family were expected to stay home and wait for them, Adila wondered? She did not know the answer to that question. In the end she decided that she had no patience for sitting around and waiting. There were Dacian women who travelled with the army in support roles, and even some who fought with the army. Dacian women were free to make their own choices.

Adila found the Queen and both her aunts, Dochia and Tanidela, talking softly because the infant Tyra was asleep in her rocking crib. After looking in on her baby cousin she went to sit in a chair next to her mother.

"What is it?" Andrada asked. "You look like you have something on your mind."

"I wish to go and join Tata and our army," Adila said calmly. Being clear and direct was always the best way to make a point, her father always said. He was the king so he should know.

The three women looked at her with complete surprise. In one of those rare moments, Andrada was at a loss for words.

Dochia broke the silence. "It seems that you gave your mother a shock, Adila dear, so let me ask you instead. Why do you wish to join the army?"

"Because I feel helpless just waiting here, Auntie. I want to be with Tata and Cotiso. I want to see what is happening."

Andrada took a patient tone with her daughter. "Your father and brother are fighting the Romans precisely so that you can wait here, where you are safe, until the war is over."

"I don't want to be safe!" Adila said, then reminded herself to tone down her voice because the baby was sleeping. "I mean of course I want to be safe, Mama, but I want more than that. I want to be there and be involved so that I know what is going on. And if I am needed, I want to fight for Dacia."

"You are only sixteen years old," the Queen said, trying to reason with her headstrong daughter.

"So? There are boys no older than me fighting as soldiers. Tata fought in the army when he was sixteen, he told us so."

Tanidela spoke up in support of the Queen. "Some boys your age are big enough and strong enough to fight, but many are not. And girls are not. It is too dangerous for you to join the fighting."

"I would not fight hand to hand, Auntie. Cotiso taught me how to use an army bow months ago. I have been practicing every day. I am getting very good at it."

Dochia shook her head slowly. "It takes many years of practice for a warrior to become an archer, dear girl. A few months of practice is not enough."

"I have watched you practice," Andrada said, "and I know that you take it seriously. But shooting at straw men targets is not the same as shooting at soldiers who want to kill you. You know this."

Adila's face hardened with determination. "I have made a decision to go. I am no longer a child and don't require anyone's permission."

The Queen was no longer feeling patient. "If you don't wish my permission, then what are you asking for?"

"I just want your blessing, Mama."

Andrada looked at Tanidela and Dochia. "What am I going to do with these children of mine?"

Dochia looked sad and remained silent. She was thinking of the death of her only child, the son who died many years ago. The thought of Adila placing her life in danger was painful to her.

Tanidela gave a half smile. "It seems to me that you can either give her your blessing, or your ill feelings."

Andrada sighed. She turned to look her daughter in the eye. "I am the Queen. I can order you not to go."

"Yes, Your Highness, you have that power," Adila said with a polite smile. "But you will not give that order because you know it would not be right. It would be a very selfish order and given only because I am your daughter."

Andrada paused in thought for a moment. She strived to teach her children to be strong and independent. Now she faced the results of her teachings. "I will not give you that order, Adila. But I will ask one thing of you."

"What is it, Mama?"

"In two days Osan and a new detachment of archers are leaving for Tapae to join the city garrison. Until then I want you to think about your decision very carefully," the Queen said. "If after that time you feel as certain about your decision as you do now, then you have my blessing to go with them."

Osan was a servant of Diegis, and also an excellent horse archer. He was someone the Queen trusted with her daughter's life.

"Thank you, Mama," Adila said with gratitude. Her mother's trust and approval would never cease to be important to her.

"Have you talked to your sister about this?" Andrada asked.

Adila shook her head. "No."

"Perhaps you should," Dochia suggested. "It will come as much of a surprise to her as it was for us, I think."

"You are right. I will go talk to her now." Adila said her goodbyes and left.

The baby Tyra was stirring. Tanidela walked over to the crib.

Andrada smiled. "Enjoy your sweet baby while you can, Sister. They get more complicated later on."

Tanidela looked back over her shoulder. "Complicated?"

"Yes," said the Queen. "They grow up and think for themselves."

The Dacian army was still a day's march from Tapae and slowed by a river crossing. The river was not swift and was shallow enough in some places to be forded by infantry soldiers and horses. The army still required river barges to transport the wheeled artillery, supply wagons, and other materials that could not be allowed to get wet. Loading and unloading the barges was tiresome and slow work in hot weather, even with a very large supply of manpower.

King Decebal assigned the job of coordinating the river crossing to his brother, General Diegis. Diegis in turn gave orders to officers of the Dacian armies. The chiefs of the allied tribes each led their own armies. Scouts rode back and forth with messages and instructions.

Prince Davi and his guards rode up to join Decebal and the cavalry of the Royal Guard, who had not yet crossed the river. The Sarmatian heavy cavalry, easy to identify because both men and horses were covered in armor, were protecting the rear of the army column and supply train. They would be among the last troops to cross the river.

Decebal greeted his closest ally warmly. "Greetings, Davi. What do your scouts tell you?"

"The Roman vanguard is two days march behind us. Trajan is in no hurry to catch up."

"No, he is not in a hurry," Decebal agreed. "There is no point in exhausting his army in pursuit. We will not give him a fight here in any case, and Trajan know that. Any attacks from their cavalry on our column?"

"No. The Roman legion cavalry are scouts and observers, they don't want a fight. Some of their Gallic cavalry picked off a few of our stragglers who foolishly wandered off to forage, but the Gauls don't want to face my men."

"Very smart Gauls," Decebal said. "I would not want to fight your cavalry either."

The Sarmatian paused to wipe perspiration from his brow. It was a hot day, and hotter still under his armor. He watched a column of infantry wadding across the river, holding their clothes and weapons on top of their shields which they held high up over their heads. The water came up to chest level for the shorter men. The water looked cool and inviting and Davi envied them.

"Tomorrow we camp at Tapae," Decebal said. "General Drilgisa went on ahead to plan our positions and to reinforce the city guard. Forward elements of General Quietus' army will reach Tapae soon."

"Ah, so the Butcher is done killing civilians and will join forces with Trajan's army?"

Decebal nodded. "Yes. I am certain that was Trajan's plan all along. We will fight his combined army at Tapae."

"Good!" Prince Davi said with a grin. "That will save us the trouble of having to chase after Quietus later."

"Indeed," Decebal agreed. "Now look after your men, Davi. Be the rearguard for the rest of today. I want the entire army across the river by nightfall."

"Our pleasure," Davi said. "I shall see you tonight on the far bank."

Decebal watched the Sarmatians ride off, their horses' hooves kicking up dust to leave in their wake. They were perhaps the finest cavalry in the world, and he wished he had an army of them. He would need each and every one of them in the battle to come.

When Emperor Trajan combined his forces with that of General Quietus the Romans would have an army of close to one hundred and fifty thousand fighting men. His Dacian army and their allies would be outnumbered by two to one. Yet they had to put up a fight, and once again the main battleground would be at Tapae. Tapae, the gateway to Dacia. Bloody Tapae.

Tapae, June 101 AD

The High Priest Vezina stood on top of the ramparts of the walls of Tapae and watched the approaching columns coming in from the west. He knew that one column would be the Bastarnae army, and another the Celts. The larger column, stretching out into the distance as far as the eye could see, would be the Dacian army. The Sarmatian army of cavalry, he expected, would be guarding the rear units against any pursuing enemy forces.

The massive gate of Tapae faced west. The city walls were built high and thick, made with limestone and andesite. An outer stone wall was reinforced with an inner wall of pounded earth and gravel, followed by an inner stone wall. The walls could not be burned, and they could withstand a pounding from battering rams, catapults, and other siege artillery. Ramparts built atop the walls provided fighting platforms for archers and spearmen guarding against a direct assault on the walls.

The northern side of the city was built against the steep mountain side. Northwest of the city was the mountain pass, approximately eight miles long, that cut through the mountain range and led into the interior of Dacia. This was the invasion route favored by those who tried to attack Dacia from the south. It had destroyed the large Roman army of Cornelius Fuscus and damaged the even larger army of Tettius Julianus.

The previous day Vezina noticed riders approaching from the east. They did not ride to the city walls, but either camped within sight of the city or rode back towards the east. These were no doubt cavalry in the vanguard of the Roman army that had been pillaging eastern Dacia. Vezina was glad and very relieved to see the Dacian army approaching from the opposite direction.

"Our King has a great sense of timing," Drilgisa said as he walked up to stand beside the old and wizened priest. He looked at Vezina's resplendent blue robe, trimmed with gold and silver thread, the robe of the High Priest of Zamolxis. "Two more days, Vezina, and you would have had to exchange the holy robe for a suit of mail armor to fight Lusius Quietus and his army coming from the east."

"Yes, he does indeed," said the priest. "Decebal always had a great sense of timing even before he became king. It is part of what makes him a great general."

"Yes, unlike me," Drilgisa said with a grin. "I depend on sheer stubbornness and pure dumb luck."

Vezina was used to the general's good-natured bantering. Drilgisa was a proud and fierce fighter who inspired his men to great efforts. He had never lost a battle.

"Do you remember the last time we fought the Romans here?" Vezina asked. "That was thirteen years ago. It's funny, but it surely does not seem like that long ago."

"Of course I remember," Drilgisa replied. "Julianus put the city to the sword because they refused to surrender, you barely escaped with your life, and I got a Roman arrow through my shoulder."

"Yes, those poor people," Vezina said with sadness. The soldiers defending the city and the civilian population were massacred. He only escaped capture or death by pretending to be dead and hiding among the freshly killed corpses.

"This is a different time," Drilgisa said in a somber tone. "The last time we had to leave the city to its own defenses because our army was not yet fully assembled. This time we have our armies in place, and we have our neighbors as allies fighting with us."

Vezina gave a nod. "All this is true, General. We face a much larger army, but they are driven by greed and pride. We are a united army fighting for our freedom and survival. As long as we stick together we can fight them off."

"We will stick together. No one is afraid of Rome, and to Hades with their numbers!" Drilgisa said forcefully. "Think of this, Vezina. The youngest of our men, and those from the Bastarnae, or the Celts, or the Sarmatians, they do not remember a time when Dacia lost a war to Rome. So why should they fear Rome?"

Vezina chuckled. "That is one way to look at it, I'll admit. It is only us old goats who understand the threat of Rome."

Drilgisa spat out over the edge of the wall. "I see no threat, only Romans that we need to kill. Kill the Romans and the threat is gone." He grinned again and gave Vezina a friendly slap on the back. "See how simple life is?"

"Yes, I do see your point," Vezina replied with a smile. "Now let's get to work, Drilgisa. Before the killing comes the planning and the preparation. We have a great deal of preparing to do."

In the Roman camp Emperor Trajan had a great deal of his own planning to attend to. Stretched out over a table in his command tent was a large, newly drawn map of Tapae and surrounding territory. He expected to be here for a while, so camps with fortifications had to be laid out and built up for his massive army. Centuries of dealing with surprise attacks, many of them leading to catastrophic losses, had taught Roman armies to never set up camp without also building defensive fortifications. Even while only marching on maneuvers the Emperor's armies put up fortifications every evening and took them down every morning.

Circling the table with the Emperor were his generals Laberius Maximus, Gnaeus Longinus, and Licinius Sura. In addition to laying out territory for the camps they had to plan out areas for assembling various formations of troops. They also needed to plan out attack strategies based on the terrain and the location of enemy troops. No one had any doubts that King Decebalus would make a stand here, and that he would fight a defensive battle. They would have to attack him and kill his army.

"Gnaeus, you will position the auxilia infantry here, here, and here," Trajan pointed out locations on the map. As the commander in chief he was in charge of overall strategy.

"Yes, Caesar," Longinus agreed. "I can cover a wide front and still have enough troops in reserve."

"Are your men in good spirits?" the Emperor asked. One could never be fully certain of the loyalty and fighting spirit of auxiliary troops. None were Roman citizens, and for all practical purposes they either fought under duress or fought as mercenaries.

"Good enough," said Longinus. "If you mean will they fight, then the answer is yes. They took a beating at Arcidava, but now they want another shot at the Dacians."

That was the answer Trajan wanted to hear. "Good. We will give them that chance." He turned to Maximus. "Laberius, you command six legions. Place them behind the auxila, here, here, and here."

"Yes, Caesar," Maximus said. "Let the auxiliaries soften them up, then my legions will cut through them like a knife."

"Let's see how the fighting goes, Laberius. Always keep in mind the second objective."

"Of course, Caesar," Maximus replied in a firm voice. "I have not forgotten." The first objective on Trajan's staff was of course to win the battle. The second objective was to keep the loss of legionnaires to a minimum. They had a duty to protect the lives of Roman citizens, and legionnaires were all Roman citizens.

A sentry opened the tent flaps and Hadrian walked in. He nodded to the generals and saluted the Emperor. "You sent for me, Caesar?"

"Yes, Hadrianus. I have a mission for you."

"Command and I obey, Caesar," Hadrian said. As the youngest member on Trajan's staff he still looked for opportunities to prove his worth to the older men.

"We need you to go and kill a lion with your bare hands, Young Hercules," Longinus said jokingly. He enjoyed teasing Hadrian about his Greek looks and mannerisms. Hadrian was used to it and took it in good spirits.

"There are four cavalry messengers from General Lusius Quietus waiting outside," Trajan informed the young man. "You will return with them to their army, with orders for General Quietus."

"Yes, Caesar."

Trajan beckoned for him to come closer and pointed to an area on the map. "In two days' time, no later, General Quietus will bring his entire army to this location. You will guide him there. He will then report to me as soon as he arrives."

"Yes, Caesar. Do you have written orders for me to carry?"

Trajan shook his head. "No. These orders come directly from me, and will be relayed directly to him by you." The Emperor gave him a half smile. "He will find you sufficiently persuasive, I think. Go now, Hadrian. We have no time to waste."

"At once, Caesar." Hadrian bid the generals farewell with a nod and walked briskly outside to find the Moorish cavalry messengers.

"A test for Quietus?" asked Maximus.

"Yes," Longinus said. "And for Hadrian, unless I am mistaken."

"More for Lusius than for Hadrian," Trajan told them in a matter of fact tone. "He has been running around on his own for many weeks now, it is time to pull in the reins."

Vezina and Diegis were watching the maneuvers of the Roman army in the far distance. They had the best observation post available, the ramparts on top of the wall above the gate of Tapae. The ramparts were built high and wide to serve as a fighting platform for archers and light artillery positioned to defend against an attack on the gate.

"Trajan's army moves like a snail," Diegis observed. "All those men and beasts. How does he feed them all?"

"Half the army is made up of civilians whose job is to support the fighting men," Vezina replied. "And their beasts, of course. The army would be paralyzed without their beasts of burden."

"That is an advantage we still have, Vezina. Our army is becoming more like the Romans, but we will never be like the Romans. We are lighter and travel faster."

"Yes. Your brother the King has always used that advantage well. I trust that will continue."

The sound of many and heavy approaching footsteps on the wooden platform made them turn around. King Decebal was leading a small entourage in their direction. Cotiso walked beside him, and four members of the Royal Guard followed.

"Greetings, Sire," Vezina said. Diegis gave his brother a nod.

Decebal looked at the army in the distance. "How long will they take to settle in, Vezina? In your estimate."

"Two days at most I would think, Sire. They are in no hurry but are still very efficient under Trajan."

"I agree," Decebal said. "He will be in no hurry to attack, but we must be ready in any case."

"We are ready now, Brother," Diegis told him. "Drilgisa has the men ready. So do Fynn, Ailen, and Davi. There will be no surprises."

Cotiso was the youngest among them and had eyes like a hawk. He was staring at a column of fifty Dacian horse archers approaching the city gate. The look on his face was one of astonishment.

Decebal noticed his son's reaction. "What is it?"

"That is Osan bringing in the new archers," Diegis said.

Cotiso started laughing. "So it is. But look behind Osan, Uncle." Then he turned his head to look at the King, watching his reaction.

As archers drew closer Decebal noticed that riding right behind Osan was a young woman with long black hair, dressed in the simple uniform of an archer. She was looking up at the ramparts just above the gate, watching Decebal and his companions. Then she raised her right arm and waved at them with enthusiasm.

"Adila! What is she doing here?" the King posed the question to no one in particular. He turned to Cotiso. "Go fetch your sister. Bring her here. Now!"

Cotiso grinned and hurried to the steps leading down from the ramparts. He took the steps down two at a time.

Decebal turned to his brother. "No surprises, you said?"

"I meant the Romans, Brother. I cannot account for the actions of our children."

It took only a short while before Cotiso returned, Adila walking up the steps right behind. She looked tired and dusty from the long trip, but otherwise in good spirits. She walked up to the King and, not knowing what the situation called for, gave him a small bow.

"Hello, Tata."

"I am happy to see you, Daughter. But tell me, why are you here? Is there bad news from home?"

Adila was surprised by his question. She shook her head. "No bad news, Tata. Everyone is well. I came to join you and the army."

"You came to join me? And the army? That is not possible!"

Adila expected this reaction. "The Queen said the same thing at first. But then she gave me her blessing."

Decebal shook his head, not sure what to believe. "Gave you her blessing? Truthfully?"

"I would not lie to you. All I ask for is to be allowed to serve Dacia, as would any citizen of Dacia." Her tone was serious, not the tone of a child. It took them all by surprise except for Cotiso. He had seen her determination when she first asked for training with a war bow.

"This is a war zone, Adila! It is no place to play soldier."

"I am not playing soldier. Cotiso taught me to shoot a soldier's bow, and I am getting good at archery. Osan will vouch for me," she said, nodding towards the warrior standing nearby.

Decebal had not noticed that Osan came up with them. He was a young warrior, about the same age as Cotiso. The young man stood quietly, half expecting a royal blast of anger directed in his direction.

Instead Decebal turned his attention to Cotiso. "You taught her to be an archer? Why?"

Cotiso stood his ground. "Because she asked me to. Because she wanted fighting skills to defend herself if necessary. There is nothing wrong with that. I admire her for it."

"Very well," the King pronounced. He looked at his daughter and his son. "Adila, you have a right to volunteer to serve in the army the same as any other citizen. Cotiso," he gave his son a stern look, "as long as she is here she is your responsibility. You taught her martial skills, now you will look after her and teach her how to stay alive."

"I will," Cotiso said.

"Thank you, Tata," Adila said with gratitude.

Vezina gave her a kind smile. "Young lady, on military campaign he is not your Tata. You will address the King as Sire, or My King."

Adila returned his smile. "Thank you for the lesson, Your Holiness." She turned back to her father. "Thank you, Sire."

"You are welcome," said Decebal. "And one more thing, Adila. As long as the army is here you are not to go outside the walls of Tapae. That is an order. Do you understand?"

Adila nodded. "I understand."

"Good. You might have some archery skills but you do not yet have the necessary survival skills."

"You will stick with me," Cotiso said to his sister. He motioned to the stairs leading down to ground level. "Come on, let me show you to your quarters. You must be tired, thirsty, and hungry."

"How did you guess?" Adila asked with a grin.

Decebal watched them walk away, then turned to face the young man named Osan. He knew him from his years as a servant of Diegis and his family. "Thank you for bringing my daughter safely to me."

"I am honored to do so, My King," Osan said with a bow. "Also, Sire, I bring letters from the Queen and from your sisters." He reached inside his tunic and brought out a long pouch made from thin leather. Inside were three letter scrolls. He handed the pouch to the King with another curt bow, then took his leave.

"That should be the last of the surprises, I think," Diegis said.

"I hope you are right," Decebal said. "The last thing I expected to see today was my youngest daughter riding up to the city gate in the uniform of an archer."

"She has a fighting spirit, Sire," Vezina said. "One must appreciate that in a young person."

Decebal took one last look at the Roman army in the distance, then turned to leave. "I will be very happy to appreciate her fighting spirit, Vezina, perhaps in five or ten years from now. At this moment I fear that she is much too young."

"Then I shall pray to Zamolxis to protect her, Sire."

Decebal clasped him on the shoulder as he walked by. "Pray hard, Vezina. Pray with all your heart."

> Chapter 7

Third Battle of Tapae

Tapae, July 101 AD

The Dacian battle plan that early morning, designed by King Decebal and agreed to by all the officers, was to separate their infantry into two major battle groups. The slightly larger forward group, directly across from the Roman lines, was led by General Drilgisa. They had strong support from field artillery and from the Sarmatian armored cavalry. This group had the most power and flexibility, and could be positioned for defense to absorb a Roman attack or for offense to launch an attack of their own.

The second and slightly smaller Dacian infantry group, led by General Diegis, was positioned behind the first group. Their mission was more defensive in nature, situated to protect the mountain pass and the walls of Tapae. They could also maneuver quickly to support and reinforce the first infantry group as needed.

The infantry of the Bastarnae tribes, led by Chief Fynn, was on Drilgisa's right side. So was the Sarmatian cavalry. This was the side that would hammer the Roman army the hardest should the King decide to attack.

The infantry of the Celtic tribes, led by the young Chief Ailen, was positioned on Drilgisa's left side. So was the Dacian cavalry of horse archers, led by General Sinna. Although not as strong as the armored

Sarmatian horsemen, Sinna and his Dacian riders were the equal or better of their Iazygi and Gallic cavalry foes.

Vezina and Cotiso had responsibility for defending the Tapae city walls. They had a thousand troops manning the walls, a combination of Dacian archers and spearmen. Most of the civilian population had been evacuated and sent to the forts in the north. Those civilians who remained were in support roles for the city defenders.

King Decebal, accompanied by Buri and the Royal Guards cavalry, placed his mobile command post between the armies of Drilgisa and Diegis. This allowed him to gage the flow of battle directly without being in harm's way, and to direct troop deployments quickly. He also relied on Vezina and Cotiso to be his eyes on the city walls and to send him information of their observations via messengers on fast horses.

In his younger days King Decebal had been a strong and skilled warrior who fought on the front lines to lead and inspire his men. That bravery in battle and brilliant military leadership earned him the respect of Dacian soldiers and the Dacian people. The King was still fit as a soldier, however his days of fighting on a battlefield were long past. He was more valuable as a military strategist and leader of his nation. He was simply too important to risk his life in battle.

"Will the Romans attack today?" Buri wondered as they surveyed the field. The big warrior, who had fought beside Decebal in so many battles, now served only as the King's bodyguard. He would defend the command post ably, but otherwise his days on the battlefield were over as well.

Decebal looked up at the ramparts on top of the city walls. "Vezina thinks so, and he is in the best position to observe the enemy. They have been positioning their army for battle since yesterday."

"Our men grow impatient," Buri said. "They want to kill Romans."

"Young men are always impatient. We were like that once."

Buri grunted. "I was always more impatient for the war to end, not to begin. I am impatient to go home to my farm and my family."

"That's because you have more sense than most men, Buri," the King said with a smile. "Now be patient for a little while longer. The Romans are forming their battle lines."

Emperor Trajan sat tall and regal in the saddle as he surveyed his troops deploying for battle. He was taller than most men, and sitting astride a big war horse gave him a clear view of the ground ahead that would soon become a bloody battlefield. Trajan's command post was guarded by a cohort of Praetorian Guards and access to Caesar was very strictly limited.

Licinius Sura was in the command post with Trajan, along with General Laberius Maximus and his aide Titus Lucullus. Sura was there for company, more as a friend than a military aide. His role, and his value to Trajan, was political and financial. General Gnaeus Longinus was in the field directing the auxiliary troops that would launch the attack. Laberius would command the legions that would join in the attack after the auxiliaries bloodied the enemy. Titus had been summoned to receive instructions for a special assignment.

"Lucullus, you directed the siege on Tapae when you served with General Julianus? Is that correct?"

"Yes, Caesar," Titus replied.

"You stormed the walls and took the city in three days, that was quite impressive," Trajan said. He gave Lucullus a sour look. "But Roman casualties were very high."

"Yes, Caesar, they were," Titus said calmly. "General Julianus was impatient to attack Decebalus and wanted the city taken in a hurry."

"You will find, Lucullus, that I do nothing impatiently or in much of a hurry. Be that as it may, we will not siege the city walls today. But you know the city's defenses better than anyone else on staff. I have a different assignment for you that you will carry out today."

"Yes, Caesar," Titus said "As you command."

"You are given command of one cohort of cavalry and two cohorts of legionnaires." Trajan looked at Maximus. "Laberius will select the troops and instruct them to follow your orders."

Maximus gave a quick nod to acknowledge the order. Titus was surprised to be given such a large command, being so new to the staff. A cohort of cavalry was two hundred and forty fighting men. Two cohorts of legionnaire infantry were close to one thousand men. This was obviously a big assignment.

"As the battle develops, sometime this afternoon you will make an approach to the walls of Tapae from the east and make a quick strike attack with your cavalry on the city gates." Trajan paused to gauge Titus' reaction and was pleased to see the man maintain perfect composure. The mission was not above him.

"I understand, Caesar," Titus acknowledged. "A surprise attack to capture the gates will save us the trouble of a siege. Will Caesar send the order to attack?"

"No, Lucullus, I am trusting you with that decision. Use your judgment on when to press the attack based on your observations of the city defense. With the blessings of Mars you will catch the enemy by surprise and capture the gates before they can react in force. The infantry will follow immediately on the heels of the cavalry and hold the gates until I send you more reinforcements."

"An excellent plan, Caesar," Maximus said.

"I will not fail you, Caesar," Titus said. "It is an excellent plan and I will execute it."

"Very good," the Emperor said. "Laberius, see to your men. You as well Lucullus."

The two men saluted, then turned their horses and rode away.

Sura watched them leave, then surveyed the armies in the field. "A fine day for a battle, Marcus," he observed in a calm and casual voice.

It was a clear and sunny day, the sun beating down from a bright blue sky. It was already warm in early morning, which promised to become a very hot day in the afternoon.

"It is that," Trajan replied. The look in his eyes was hard as iron, burning with intensity. "Today we make history, Licinius. We right the wrongs done against Rome for the past fifteen years."

"Indeed, Marcus. This is the day we have prepared for since you took the crown of Caesar."

They sat quietly and watched the field artillery being pulled into place by mules and horses. The scorpions and ballistae would begin the battle with a barrage of bolts and large oversized arrows against the massed Dacian troops. General Longinus was directing infantry into position in the front lines. He had command of twenty thousand swordsmen, spearmen, and archers, a massive strike force to throw against the Dacians and their allies.

Three riders approached the command post and were allowed to pass by the Praetorian Guard. Moorish cavalry often drew attention because most of the common soldiers had never seen African men. The city of Rome was home to a wide variety of people from all over the world, Africa included, but few people from Africa travelled to the Danubius frontier.

General Lusius Quietus pulled up and saluted the Emperor from horseback. "Hail, Caesar!" He was a tall man, with the trim build of a lifetime cavalry soldier. His piercing brown eyes and hooked nose gave him a fierce and predatory appearance. Quietus also knew that he owed his rehabilitated military career to Emperor Trajan, and that made him both grateful and loyal.

"Greetings, Lusius. Are your men ready to fight for Rome today?"

"For Caesar and for Rome! Which is why I come to make a request of Caesar."

"What is it you ask for, General?" Trajan kept his voice even. This general sometimes tried men's patience, but most importantly he got results on the battlefield. His demanding manner sometimes had to be accommodated.

"My men request the honor to lead the attack against the Dacian command post, Caesar," Lusius said. He paused to allow Trajan to entertain the idea. "I have scouted the enemy's position and see their weaknesses. Send in the infantry to engage their lines, Caesar, then allow me to attack their left flank and drive a wedge between their two battle groups." He paused again and gave the Emperor a small respectful bow, bending forward slightly from the waist. "I will bring you the head of Decebalus, Caesar."

"That is a bold plan, Lusius," Trajan replied. "Boldness coupled with good judgment often turns the tide of battles and wins wars." He paused for a moment before offering his decision, reminding Quietus of the rank of authority. "I cannot grant you that authority in the field, however. You will follow the general battle plan."

Quietus gave a nod. "I understand, Caesar. It is a strategy worth considering, surely."

"I will consider it, Lusius. Wait for my orders before making any such attack. Understood?"

"Yes, Caesar," Quietus said.

"Now see to your men, Lusius. I need your cavalry to excel in your mission today."

"We will not fail you, Caesar." Quietus saluted again, turned his horse, and rode away followed by his two guards.

"That one is used to being left to his own devices," Sura observed, watching the riders depart.

"He has an independent streak. I do not mind. Most of all I need him to carry out orders successfully, and he does that very well."

"Hold the reins tight, Caesar," Sura advised.

"Ah, stop worrying, Licinius," the Emperor said. "I have yet to meet a horse or a man I could not control."

From their high ramparts above the city gates Vezina and Cotiso had been closely watching enemy deployments since sunrise. The enemy was massing their army south of the city. The Romans never rushed but they were still fast and efficient. Auxiliary infantry lined up front. Artillery and cavalry positioned on the wings.

"They will launch their attack within the hour," Vezina said. "Two at the most."

Cotiso turned his head left to look towards the east. It was still early morning and the sun was not yet high in the sky. Soon it would be, and the day would quickly grow hotter.

"I would not wish to be standing on that field for long in the hot sun," Cotiso said. "I would attack now."

Vezina smiled patiently. "That's a fair point. And no doubt Trajan has considered that, and a hundred other things besides."

Adila walked up to join them. She seemed surprised to find Cotiso with a stern frown on his face. Her orders were to be no more than twenty paces away from Cotiso at all times, and she had wandered off down the ramparts for a look at the Dacian army to the west.

"Adila, you must stay with me if you want to stay on the wall. Do you understand?"

"Yes, Brother."

"I am not your brother here, I am your commanding officer. Now obey your orders or I will send you down to the women's quarters and there you will stay."

"Yes, sir," Adila replied respectfully. "It will not happen again. I will do as you say."

Vezina beckoned her to come closer. He pointed to some Roman troops in the distance. "Do you see that cart there, drawn by the two mules?"

Her gaze followed his finger to a wheeled cart, far away. It had a boxy looking weapon on it, with what looked like a giant slingshot or bow in front. A crew of six men was positioning the weapon to face the Dacian infantry while two other men tended the mules. "Yes, I see it. That's Roman artillery."

"That is a carrobalistae," Vezina explained. "It can fire a very large arrow at a distance of over eight hundred feet."

Adila nodded to show that she understood. She felt confused and awed by everything going on around her, but did not want to show her confusion or fear. This was what she had asked for.

"When the fighting begins they will be shooting at our army," Vezina continued. "When they wish to they will aim at us. When they do, and later in the battle they will, they can reach the top of the city walls and the men on it."

"That means us," Cotiso said. "One of those arrows can take your head completely off, and you will never see it coming."

"I understand," Adila said, her voice dry.

Cotiso looked her in the eye. "This is an order, Adila. When we are attacked by artillery or by archers, you will go down to ground level and stay there."

"I can fight back against archers," she said, sounding hopeful.

Cotiso remained silent but gave her a stern, sharp look.

"Yes, sir," she relented. "I will obey orders and go down to ground level."

"What does Father call soldiers who don't obey orders?" he asked. "You must remember, he said it many times."

"Dead soldiers," Adila said grimly.

"Yes. Dead soldiers. And you will not be one of them."

Vezina turned to Cotiso. "I believe that you have made your point clear and the young lady understands. She will follow your orders." He turned his attention to the field. "Now let's focus on the enemy, Cotiso."

"Yes, Your Holiness. It looks like the frontline troops are starting to advance."

"And here they come," Vezina said.

The Roman field artillery opened fire first. Scorpions, the light bolt shooting ballistae, sent a shower of iron bolts into the massed Dacian infantry. They could target specific sections of the enemy formations with accuracy and deadly force. The sharply pointed metal bolts could penetrate shields and any form of armor. Carrobalistae fired their large arrows in the same manner and with the same lethal effect. Each Roman cohort of five hundred men was given ten carrobalistae, and so General Gnaeus Longinus opened fire with over four hundred of these mobile artillery.

"Hold steady!" Drilgisa shouted from the front line of the Dacian infantry. He gave the order not because his men needed instructions, but because men needed encouragement. They needed to hear from their officers. There was no defense against artillery, so some men would die and the others would endure. None would consider the cowardly option of running away.

To the left of Drilgisa was Tarbus, tall, strong, and unyielding in the face of the enemy. Like most Dacian soldiers he had a shield and helmet but no other armor. The men fought in ordinary clothing, loose fitting woolen trousers and tunics that went down to the knee. The Dacian shield was round, made of tough oak wood and covered with a copper sheath. Tarbus was armed with a sica, the razor sharp sword with a curved tip. The men around him wielded falxes, swords, spears, and battle axes.

The Roman auxiliaries advanced at a quick pace. Germans and Gauls formed the front ranks because Trajan considered them his strongest and fiercest warriors. Men were grouped with their fellow native tribesmen, which made them fight with maximum pride and unity. When Dacian artillery hit their ranks, with the same deadly effect as the Roman artillery, they did not flinch.

The Dacians did not have as many artillery pieces as the Romans, but they had many more archers. When the Roman infantry closed to within two hundred paces of the Dacian lines, Dacian foot archers loosed a swarm of arrows at them. When they approached within a hundred and fifty paces, Dacian horse archers joined in to rain more devastation on the poorly armored auxiliary infantry. The two lines had not yet met face to face, but on both sides the ground was already littered with bloody, screaming, and dying men.

"Hold your ground! Kill the bastards!" General Drilgisa shouted fiercely at the top of his lungs.

The Roman infantry covered the last twenty paces at a run, screaming their blood curdling battle cries in their own languages. A heavily bearded warrior rushed straight for Drilgisa, shield in front and sword raised to strike down at him. The Dacian general had no shield because he was fighting with a falx, the two handed sword with a long blade and long handle and the wicked curved tip shaped like a scythe.

From many years of bloody experience Roman legionnaires knew to fear and dread fighting against the falx. This Gallic soldier was not as wise, and now he rushed to his doom. Drilgisa was anything but an easy target. He had a long reach advantage and would never allow the soldier to get within sword striking distance. Quick as a blink he swept the falx blade low, underneath the Gaul's shield, and found an unprotected knee. The falx sliced through muscle and bone and hacked off the lower leg in one slashing blow. The Gaul gasped with shock and pain and fell like a cut stalk of corn. His life bled out from his severed leg even as the men behind him stepped over him.

Tarbus met a warrior head on and pushed forward with his shield. Each struggled to gain their footing and push the other away. Tarbus had a height and strength advantage and slowly gained leverage against his foe. Dacians trained relentlessly in hand to hand combat, and indeed preferred it. Tarbus angled his shield and his feet, pushed hard to move the soldier's shield slightly to the left, and lunged with the sica to stab upwards into the man's abdomen. He drew back just as quickly so the sword would not get stuck in the soldier's guts. Blood gushed over his sword hand and his lower legs.

A Roman spearman rushed Tarbus and lunged with his weapon towards the Dacian's exposed neck. Tarbus raised his shield to block the spear blade. He fought instinctively and moved by reflex, skills that came naturally from years and years of training. As he knocked the spear blade aside he took a quick step forward and slashed his sica across the unprotected spearman's neck.

A young Dacian soldier from behind Tarbus rushed forward, too eager to reach the enemy. He traded sword blows with a Roman, frantic to find an opening for a killing blow. A Roman spearman joined the fight and drove his spear into the young man's upper leg. He staggered backwards, then fell on his side as his leg gave away.

"Stay in line!" Drilgisa shouted to his men. He stepped up and thrust the falx forward in very quick short moves to drive back the two Romans. "Tarbus!" he yelled.

Tarbus knew what Drilgisa intended. He stepped up, but instead of attacking he grabbed the wounded Dacian by the collar of his tunic and dragged him roughly back into the Dacian formation. He gave the young man an angry and disgusted look.

"Never break formation!" Tarbus yelled at him. "General Drilgisa just saved your life, you fool!"

Before the dazed young warrior could say anything in reply two men who served as medics picked him up and carried him away. At the far back of the Dacian lines surgeons were already busy treating the wounded. The morning was still young, and it promised to be a very long day.

Three hours into the battle King Decebal surveyed the battlefield from the saddle of his big war horse. The sun was now overhead and beat down mercilessly on the masses of soldiers struggling to kill their enemies before their enemies killed them. The day turned very hot, the hottest day of the summer thus far. Exhaustion and lack of water became enemies in addition to the Romans advancing on his army.

General Drilgisa rode up to the command post on a tired and sweaty horse, with two guards riding alongside him. One of them was Tarbus. The infantry troops of General Diegis had moved to the front to relieve Drilgisa's men and give them a much needed rest. Men became fatigued quickly in battle, and tired men were easy to kill. The heat and thirst made the fatigue worse.

Drilgisa and his guards dismounted wearily.

"Have some water then give me your report," Decebal said to the three riders.

Buri brought them a bucket of water along with drinking cups. He looked at his son Tarbus with a mix of concern and pride. Tarbus looked like a bloody horror, his tunic and trousers stained with blood.

"Here, drink," Buri said. He caught his son's eye, his expression full of pride "You look like you had a busy morning, Son."

Tarbus took the cup and drained it thirstily. "There's a lot more fighting ahead, Father. We are just getting started."

"We are losing many men, Sire." Drilgisa reported. "The men are holding their own however. We're killing more of them than they're killing us."

"This is what we saw in Arcidava," the King said. "Our men are better than their auxiliary. However Trajan has not committed his legions yet."

Drilgisa nodded. "Which he will do, of that we can be sure." He glanced up towards the sun overhead. "For the next four or five hours we will be fighting in the afternoon heat. Do you think he is saving the legions until the heat cools off?"

"Possibly," Decebal answered. "Our men should be tired then and his legionnaires will be fresh."

"Cavalry!" one of the Royal Guards shouted the alarm. The Guards formed a tight circle around the command post, half the men on horse and half on foot. Buri picked up a spear with a long shaft and moved to stand beside the King. The others picked up their shields and drew their swords.

An alae of eighty Roman auxiliary cavalry was riding furiously around the Dacian left flank, kicking up a cloud of dust between the infantry and the city walls. They carried lances and screamed war cries to terrify any enemy in their way. They skirted around the edges of the Dacian infantry and aimed straight for the command post.

"Moors!" Drilgisa said. "Form a line of spears, here!" he shouted to the troop of spearmen. The men were already forming up. The enemy cavalry would never reach the King, but they could still kill him from a distance.

Dacian foot archers fired a volley of arrows in the path of the charging riders. Some horses and men were hit, some fell or were slowed down, but the rest charged ahead heedlessly. In their lead was a tall rider with a hooked nose and fierce brown eyes who shouted to his men to kill Decebalus.

The fifty cavalry of the Royal Guard charged forward to intercept the attackers. They threw their lances at the Moorish cavalry while at full gallop, then drew their swords. The Moors did the same. Some threw their lances at the Dacian cavalry, but others kept riding at full gallop until they were in range to hurl their spears at the men in the command post. It only took seconds for them to close the distance.

A wall of shields formed in front of King Decebal, the imposing large figure of Buri among them. A few thrown lances reached their position and were knocked down harmlessly. The Moors could not advance past the wall of spears, and now became easy targets for the Dacian archers.

The Moorish cavalry were lightly armored. Their horses were not. Archers killed the horses, and their downed riders were quickly hacked and killed by Dacian swordsmen and spearmen. Their leader's horse became skittish, an arrow lodged in its left rump.

Decebal took a step forward for a closer look at the man, his shield on his left arm and holding a sica in his right hand. These were the moments when he still craved the excitement of battle.

"Sire, stay behind cover!" Buri urged him.

"That is Quietus," Decebal said. He recognized the man's look of authority and knew enough about the infamous general to place him.

"Brazen bastard, isn't he?" Drilgisa growled.

King Decebal turned his head towards him, a half smile on his face. "Most top generals are, Drilgisa. You know that."

More Dacian cavalry closed in from the north. Quietus saw them, shouted an order to his men, and led them in retreat at full gallop. His bold strategy did not succeed but it was worth trying. He would explain later to Emperor Trajan that he saw an opportunity he could not pass by.

The infantry of the Bastarnae tribes fought on the right flank, beside the Dacian infantry of General Diegis. They were a Germanic people who, over the centuries, had migrated far to the east of their German tribal relatives to settle in the territory northeast of Dacia. Although their neighbors were now Dacians, Sarmatians, and Scythians, they still worshipped Odin and carried on many German traditions.

Chief Fynn was dressed for battle like most of his men, bare chested and wearing baggy trousers. He was a big, burly warrior with a bushy red beard. Unlike his German cousins on the Roman side of the field, Fynn was armed with a falx. Many of the Bastarnae warriors learned happily that this two-handed long handled Dacian weapon was devastatingly effective even against Roman legionary armor.

The falx gave Fynn and his warriors a great reach advantage over the much shorter Roman gladius. It could slice off arms, legs, and necks in one swift cutting blow. Because of its extra length and curved blade, in the hands of a powerful warrior the falx had enough striking power to split a shield and maim or kill the man behind it.

Fynn and his men already beat back three attacks from auxiliary troops of Gauls and Spaniards. His men were tired and sweaty in the heat of the afternoon. They were proud and fierce warriors however who expected to endure anything that came their way. Teenage boys brought up water skins to the front lines for the soldiers to drink from, but there were never enough of them and never enough water.

There was a lull in the fighting and General Diegis took time to walk along the line with some of his men to inspect and encourage the men. Like Fynn, Diegis was pleased with the success of their combined troops against the enemy attackers. The field in front of them was thickly littered with dead bodies, both Roman attackers and Dacian defenders, but their men would not back down.

Fynn greeted Diegis with a wolfish grin. The Dacian's face was drenched in sweat and his clothes were red with bloodstains. He had a small cut on his left thigh that was bleeding but not too badly. "Well fought, General," Fynn greeted him. "We're giving Trajan more than he bargained for."

"We are," Diegis agreed. "Your men are fighting well."

"We are killing Gauls and Spaniards mostly, also some Germans. Trajan must send his legionnaires against us soon, I think."

"Yes," Diegis said, looking at the Roman formations on the other side of the field. "I think so too. Be prepared for a legion attack. The legionnaires are armored and fight with more discipline."

"My men know how to fight Romans, Diegis. Let the bastards come."

"They will have their chance soon enough. So will mine," Diegis said. "We must continue to fight as one army, Fynn. King Decebal will most likely send orders to change tactics when the legions attack, so be alert."

"Of course. I expect that Decebal will change tactics when Trajan changes tactics. The Romans may outnumber us but they will not outsmart us."

"No, my friend, they will not. And neither will they outfight us as long as we stick together."

In the middle of the afternoon Emperor Trajan and General Maximus sent four legions to the attack. The Roman strategy was always to commit the auxiliaries first. Sometimes they were good enough to win the battle on their own, although certainly not this battle. They were always good enough to inflict large numbers of casualties and soften up the enemy forces. The legionnaires would then follow up to overwhelm and rout the tired and weakened enemy.

It was widely accepted as fact that a Roman legion was the finest military unit in the world. Legionnaires wore quality metal armor, had superior weapons, and had much superior training compared to the auxiliary troops. Each legionnaire was armed with a pilus, the six foot long weighted throwing spear that could penetrate a shield at twenty paces and kill the man behind it. Each carried a scutum, the large rectangular shield that covered a man from the neck to below the knee. Fighting in tight formation, behind their wall of shields, a Roman legionnaire was a difficult soldier to kill.

A fierce barrage of field artillery fire preceded the advance from the legions. Dacian artillery answered with their own barrage. Units of Dacian archers moved closer to the front to meet the new attack. Dacian and Sarmatian cavalry hung back in the wings, waiting for an opportunity to attack later in the battle. Cavalry were not successful against tight formations of heavy infantry.

"Save your arrows!" Diegis shouted to the units of archers standing just behind his front line. "Wait for them to open up!"

The legionnaires approached at a slow walk in densely packed squares, protected on all sides and overhead by overlapping shields. They sacrificed speed for protection. This was the testudo formation, much practiced and loved by every legion because it was almost near impenetrable against enemy archers and thrown spears. The shield walls would have to open up when the legionnaires made contact with enemy soldiers, to allow them to use their weapons. Until then they felt as secure as the tortoise for which the formation was named.

When they were within pilus throwing range of the Dacian lines the legionnaires came out of their testudo formations and formed a battle line. Now the Dacian foot and horse archers loosed swarms of arrows in their direction. The Romans threw their spears and killed hundreds of Dacians, Celts, and Bastarnae infantry. They drew their swords and charged the enemy lines, shouting their piercing battle cries. Often the opposing lines panicked and scattered in the face of this fierce armored attack.

"Hold steady!" Fynn shouted to his warriors, although he knew that none would even think of retreating. Like all Germans the Bastarnae took great pride in being fearless in battle. And if they died on the battlefield, they would dine with other heroes in Odin's great hall that very night.

Fynn and his men met the Romans head on, using falxes and spears to find openings between the legionnaires' wall of shields. The Romans were better protected but their foes could move quicker and had weapons that gave them a reach advantage.

The tall bare-chested warrior next to Fynn swung a big battle axe at the shield of the Roman in front of him. The axe made a dent but the shield absorbed the blow and made it harmless. The legionnaire brought his gladius up and stabbed towards the axe man's abdomen, his blow falling just short when the man took a quick step back. The gladius was a short stabbing weapon and the quick lunge upwards was a legionnaire's preferred kill move.

Fynn stabbed with his falx at the Roman's neck. The soldier raised his shield and easily blocked the blow. He staggered back as the man with the axe rushed him and struck another powerful blow to the top of his shield. The Roman lunged again with the gladius and this time the other man was not quick enough to escape. The sword plunged into the warrior's exposed belly, bringing a loud grunt of pain and shock from the Bastarnae. Fynn slashed down with the falx and sliced off the Roman's exposed sword hand at the wrist. The legionnaire fell back, his lower arm gushing blood over the dying Bastarnae axe man.

"Kill them!" Chief Fynn shouted to his men, caught up in the madness of battle frenzy. "Kill every last bastard one of them!"

The Bastarnae joined him with their own battle cries and attacked the Roman line. More men fell, screamed, and died, and soon the dusty ground was slick with blood from the bodies of the dead and dying.

General Sinna led two hundred Dacian horse archers towards the right flank of the Roman infantry. Earlier his men had slaughtered the crews of two dozen artillery pieces and the squads of spearmen guarding them. His horse archers rode in and killed the spearmen without getting within range of their spears. The artillery crews were left defenseless. After their quick strike the Dacian cavalry was driven away by Roman cavalry with support from a squad of Roman archers and a unit of legionnaire heavy infantry.

Now Sinna was looking for an opening to attack legionnaires. He was not foolish enough to attack fixed legionary positions directly or expect to break them. His horse archers were most effective against enemy cavalry, archers, and artillery units. Against infantry they were only effective when the legionnaire units broke down. They could also inflict some casualties by nibbling away at the infantry formations from the flanks or, if they were lucky and could gain position, from the rear.

The Roman right flank was faced off against the Dacian left flank, where Chief Ailen and his army of Celts were putting up a fierce fight as usual. No warriors fought with more passion and pure reckless aggression than the Celts. Before they left their tribal lands their priests, who called themselves druids, burned sacred herbs and chanted ancient chants to cast spells of invincibility on the soldiers. Like the Dacians and the Bastarnae they also believed strongly in an afterlife and did not fear death.

Chief Ailen had a cut on his scalp. The streaky mix of blood, sweat, and dirt on the left side of his face looked like war paint, which made him look even more savage than usual. He shouted curses at the Romans as he fought them with a heavy long shafted spear. The legionnaires were heavily armored, fought as a highly disciplined unit, and were slowly pushing his men backwards on the battlefield.

Ailen heard the Dacian horse archers before he saw them, first the hoof beats of hundreds of horses beating on the dry dusty ground and then their shrill battle cries. They attacked the Roman right flank in waves, riding to within twenty paces and shooting with accuracy to find faces, necks, and exposed legs. Centurions shouted sharp commands and legionnaire units turned to face the cavalry attacks and find cover behind their shields.

The hit and run cavalry attacks on their flank stopped the Roman attack cold. It also gave the Celtic infantry an opening to attack. "Kill them!" Chief Ailen cried and rushed forward to drive his spear at a legionnaire who was now under attack from two sides.

Vezina looked at the sun in the western sky and judged it to be the middle of the afternoon. Some clouds were drifting in on the western winds but the sun was still beating down harshly. It was hot on top of the walls, simply standing and watching the battle as he was. He did not like to think what the conditions were like down on the battlefield below where men struggled to kill and to stay alive.

The Dacian army and their allies were being slowly pushed back since Emperor Trajan committed his armored legions. The losses were heavy on both sides, however. The Dacian army would not break. This battle would not be settled today, Vezina decided. It would most likely stop at sunset. Two great armies were caught in a death struggle and neither was willing to back down.

"Vezina!" Cotiso called to get his attention. The young man had eyes like a hawk, better than those of the High Priest. "Their artillery is being re-positioned."

"They are aiming at us!" Adila said with more surprise than fear in her voice. "As you said they would, Your Holiness."

Vezina took a quick look at the Roman artillery positions to the south, on the right flank of Trajan's army. Many of the scorpions and carrobalistae had been turned towards the city walls, and their crews were busily loading the bolts and arrows that would very soon be hurled at them.

"What are they doing?" Cotiso asked, puzzled. "I see no infantry being sent against the city walls."

"They want to give us something to worry out, kill some of our city defenders," Vezina said. "It has been too peaceful up here."

Cotiso turned to Adila. "Time for you to go to ground level. Stay there until I summon you again."

"Yes, sir," she said, sounding disappointed.

A missile from a carrobalistae struck the wall with a loud noise several feet below where they were standing. The wall was made of stone and too thick to be damaged by light artillery, but the missile sent dust and chips of rock flying outwards.

"Get down!" Cotiso shouted and swiftly crouched down to one knee, pulling Adila down with him. Vezina did the same. Metal bolts and arrows were now flying at the defenders on the walls. The men crouched down or fell flat on their stomachs. Inside the walls men and women who had been carrying supplies to the army stopped in their tracks. Those who were caught just outside the gates returned quickly to take cover behind the walls. The only protection against the artillery fire was the stone city walls.

"Adila, go," Cotiso instructed her. "Stay low, belly to the floor, and take those stairs to the ground. This is no place for you."

She nodded swiftly and silently. A metal bolt flew overhead and made a whistling sound, but it was moving much too fast for her to see it. All of the projectiles were flying too fast to see. Adila crawled to the wooden stairs built against the inside wall in the eastern corner of the wall. She hated being treated like a child. On the other hand, she thought, better that than being cut in half by a giant arrow from a ballista.

Adila reached down with her foot for the first step when she heard the sound of galloping horses. Many horses, their riders in a hurry and approaching fast. That was not right. They were approaching from the east of the city, and there was no army, Dacian or Roman, to the east of the city. These horses were very out of place. What were they doing here?

Adila swallowed hard and made a decision to take a risk. She raised her head above the parapet and took a quick look towards the approaching sound of hoof beats. In the distance, but closing rapidly, was a very large group of cavalry. Even her untrained eye could tell it was Roman cavalry. Behind the cavalry and moving at a very brisk pace was an even larger group of infantry who were clearly Roman legionnaires.

She knew instantly that the cavalry would ride around the eastern wall, turn the corner, and make a dash for the city gate. The gate that was open and still allowing Dacians to come back inside the city walls to escape the artillery fire.

"Cotiso!" Adila shouted to her brother at the top of her lungs. "Cavalry! Roman cavalry!"

He looked in her direction. She pointed over the wall, to the east. "Cavalry! Romans!"

Vezina was already on his feet and running to the inside edge of the wall, shouting down to the guards below. "Close the gates! Close the gates now! Now!"

No Dacian soldier ever hesitated for an instant to obey a command from the High Priest. The guards scrambled to move the heavy, massive gates and shut them. They ignored the cries of the people still trapped outside. The city was in peril and they had no choice.

Cotiso could now hear the cavalry also. He stood up and watched as the first riders turned the corner and galloped towards the gate. "Bastards!" he muttered. In a heartbeat he notched an arrow on his bowstring and shot at the nearest approaching cavalryman. Cavalry did not wear metal armor as did Roman infantry, and a well-placed arrow at close range often went through their leather armor. Cotiso's arrow found an unprotected right shoulder and the rider yelped with pain and dropped the lance he was carrying in his hand.

Other archers on the wall joined Cotiso in shooting at the Roman riders. They were in a fight now and could not worry about Roman artillery fire. The city was under attack. A number of men were hit by incoming bolts and arrows, one being knocked clean off the wall and sent tumbling to the ground below. The fallen men were ignored. The enemy had to be repulsed.

The leading Roman rider saw the city gates closing with only a small gap remaining between them. He made an audacious effort to drive his horse straight into that gap, but the terrified animal balked and stopped short. The Roman shouted a curse. He was silenced by arrows that pierced his chest and his throat. The man tumbled to the ground and his spooked horse galloped off.

More cavalry milled around the gate, but quickly understood that they were too late. The heavy gates were closed shut and bolted from the inside. They had no means to attack the gate or the men on top of the walls. The infantry trailing behind had no ladders or other siege equipment to get over the walls. Their mission had failed.

Standing on top of the wall just above the gate, Vezina noticed that one particular rider towards the back of the group was staring up intensely at him. Something about the man's build and his posture struck him as familiar. Memories flooded back of this Roman figure on a horse, before the gates of Tapae, when the city was under siege many years ago. He stared back towards the figure and raised his right arm in greeting.

Titus Lucullus was astonished that Vezina would recognize him in the crowd of riders. He urged his horse to move and not present an easy target for the Dacian archers who kept shooting at his men.

"Retreat!" Titus shouted. He waved farewell to the tall, thin figure on the city wall, then turned his horse and urged him into a gallop heading south. We shall meet again, old man, he wanted to say, but there was no time and no way to say it now.

"Did you know that Roman officer?" Cotiso asked Vezina as they watched the cavalry ride away. The Roman infantry marched after the cavalry. Even the Roman artillery stopped firing at the defenders on the walls and were again being pointed towards the Dacian army. All had been part of a mission, and the mission failed.

"Yes," Vezina answered. "I knew him a long time ago, when you were just a boy. He got the better of me then and he sacked Tapae."

Cotiso paused for a short moment. "Was that Titus Lucullus?"

"Yes," Vezina said, looking at him with surprise. "How do you know his name?"

"Uncle Diegis told me stories about him. Of his visit to Rome, and his talks with Lucullus during the war with General Julianus."

"Well, well," Vezina chuckled. "It seems that Titus has quite the reputation."

Adila walked up to join them. She had her bow strapped on her back and a sheepish look on her face.

"I am sorry that I wasn't much help," she said, looking from Cotiso to Vezina to catch their reactions.

"What do you mean?" Cotiso asked.

"I shot six arrows at the Romans. Every one of them missed."

Cotiso looked like he was going to lose his temper again. "Why were you shooting at the Romans? I told you to go down to ground level and stay there!"

"The city was under attack!" Adila said. "I had to do something."

Before Cotiso could speak again Vezina held up a hand to stop him. "No more scolding for today, please."

Cotiso calmed down. "Yes, Your Holiness."

Vezina turned to Adila. "The blessings of Zamolxis be upon you, my dear brave girl. If not for your alertness and your warning we might all be fighting for our very lives right now."

Adila blushed. "I could have done more."

Vezina shook his head. "No. You did more than any man on this wall today. You saved the city gates."

Emperor Trajan watched the dark clouds on the horizon, not happy with the situation. The time was late afternoon. The heat had cooled off considerably, and now storm clouds were moving rapidly across the sky. It had the look of a quickly developing summer storm.

"We are pushing them back, Marcus," Licinius observed, looking out over the battlefield. "You will have your victory."

"Yes, but at heavy cost," Trajan said. He looked again towards the west and frowned. "And by the looks of those storm clouds I will not have my victory today. If nightfall does not stop the battle first, then the storm will."

Sura gave a dismissive shrug. "So then you will have your victory tomorrow. What difference does one day make?"

"On a practical level, none," The Emperor said sourly. "But you see, Licinius, I do not simply wish to defeat Decebalus. I want to crush Decebalus. Our victory must be overwhelming."

"Of course, Caesar," Sura agreed, his tone turned somber. "You are right as usual."

Generals Maximus and Longinus approached the command post, riding side by side. Their guards trailed behind them. They pulled up beside Trajan and Sura.

"We are beating the enemy, Caesar, but nightfall approaches," Maximus said. "As does this damn storm that is about to hit us."

"What are your thoughts?" Trajan asked Maximus and Longinus. He was open minded about hearing the opinions of his men, a quality that earned him strong loyalty and even affection from his officers.

"Get the men inside their tents and give them a meal before the storm hits," Longinus offered. "We can resume the battle tomorrow."

"And your opinion, Laberius?"

"I agree with Gnaeus, Caesar. The men are fighting hard, but I think this is enough fighting for one day."

"I see," the Emperor said. He turned to Sura. "And what of this storm? Will it be a problem tomorrow, do you think?"

"You know how these summer storms go, Caesar," Sura replied casually. "They last for half a day, one full day at the most. I expect this one will pass us by before sunrise tomorrow."

"Very well, gentlemen, we are in agreement then," Trajan said. "Pull your troops back to camp. Set up fortifications along the entire perimeter, as usual. I want no surprise attacks. We shelter for the night and resume battle in the morning."

Trumpets from the Roman signal corps signaled an end to the fighting for the Roman troops. The men gratefully lowered their weapons and retreated slowly, each unit intact and always staying in the proper formation that the situation called for.

The Dacian soldiers and their allies were just as glad for the break from fighting. They carried their wounded to the surgeons' tents, then retired to their respective camps. The men were exhausted from the fighting and the heat, and wished for nothing more than a meal and a few hours of sleep.

The chiefs and generals of the allied armies gathered to meet at King Decebal's command post in the field. Every army lost many men, however the battle went as well as they could expect. They all understood that the Romans' superiority in numbers would take a toll. None was willing to give up the battle.

"The Romans have learned a few lessons about fighting a man armed with a falx," Drilgisa said to King Decebal. "Many legionnaires now wear armor like gladiators to protect their forearms and knees, not to mention their necks."

"Yes, that is one of Emperor Trajan's innovations for this war," Decebal explained. "What works for gladiators in the arena works just as well for his legionnaires in the field."

"My men killed enough of the legionnaire bastards today," Fynn said with a growl. "I only wish that we had more falxes, Decebal."

The King nodded in acknowledgement. "We'll make more falxes. We will supply you with all you need, Fynn."

Chief Ailen of the Celts gave a nod to Sinna. "The cavalry support was outstanding today, General Sinna. More of the same tomorrow?"

"Of course, my friend," Sinna replied. "Prince Davi will chase the Moorish cavalry all over the battlefield and we'll take out artillery and infantry. Is that a fair exchange, Davi?"

"That sounds good to me," Davi said. "The Moors rush at us and throw their lances, then turn and ride away. Their one advantage is speed over our armored horses."

Large raindrops began to fall from the dark and heavy clouds. They all knew that a heavy downpour would follow. Rolling thunder rumbled in the distance. Buri groaned loudly at the sound of it.

"You Dacians do not like thunder and lightning?" Ailen asked.

"We dislike the gods being in a foul mood," Decebal said. "That is what the storm means to us."

"Odin loves a good storm," Fynn said. "Thunder and lightning, they are like music to us!"

"And what do your Celtic gods say?" Drilgisa asked.

Ailen grinned. "We worship over two hundred gods, Drilgisa. Some love a storm, some don't. Only our druids can interpret the signs that the gods send to us."

The rain suddenly became a heavy downpour and all the men were quickly soaked.

"To your men," Decebal said. "We meet here again at first light. We gave Trajan a hard battle today. We'll do the same tomorrow."

Davi, Fynn, and Ailen headed for their camps. King Decebal and the Dacian officers headed for the city of Tapae. They were all glad to get out of the rain.

> Chapter 8

Omen From Zamolxis

Tapae, July 101 AD

None of the men and women in King Decebal's dining room inside Tapae could fully enjoy their evening meal. The food was good and plentiful, breads, cheeses, ripe plums and pears and other fruits. Their appetites were dulled however by the sounds of the rainstorm raging outside. Dark clouds and stormy weather was a sign of Zalmoxis' anger. What Zalmoxis might be displeased about exactly they did not know. Their religion and beliefs simply told them that their god was angry.

Adila sat at a table next to her father and her brother Cotiso. Today had been her first experience with the violence of war. She knew what it felt like to place her life at risk. She had seen people being killed, and she had listened to the screams of the wounded and dying. She had much to think about.

"Adila," the King said to get her attention. "Cotiso tells me that you were very brave on the wall today."

She picked at a piece of bread, finding that her appetite deserted her. "I tried. I did not kill any Romans. Cotiso killed two, I think."

Decebal shook his head, patiently. "Your duty here is not to kill Romans."

"What is my duty, then?"

"To stay out of trouble," Cotiso answered with a grin.

"You were curious to see what war looked like," the King said. "Very well, since you are here, your duty is to watch and learn. And help out in small ways when you can."

She nodded her head respectfully. "Yes, Tata. I just wanted to help instead of sitting around the palace day after day."

Vezina gave her a proud smile. "You helped already. We just barely had time to shut the gates, thanks to your warning."

A peal of very loud thunder seemed to vibrate the walls of the house. It drowned out all conversation.

Decebal looked from Vezina to Cotiso. "Who is in charge of the sentries tonight?"

"I am, Sire," Cotiso replied. "The men were grumbling because of the heavy rain but they will do their duty."

"Keep them on their toes, Cotiso," Vezina advised. "They think the Romans will not attack in this weather, so they might get careless. But trouble comes when you least expect it."

"Yes, Your Holiness," Cotiso said. "I will make my rounds as soon as I finish my meal. I will make sure no one is falling asleep."

Drilgisa gave him a grim smile. "If you find any sentry asleep, throw him over the wall."

Cotiso glanced at the King and raised an eyebrow.

"Yes," Decebal said in a serious tone. "General Drilgisa is right. A sleeping sentry endangers everyone. Over the wall, head first, and don't think twice about it."

"Yes, Sire." Cotiso pushed his plate away and got to his feet. "I will go and make my rounds now."

"Do that," Decebal said, "then get some sleep. You will be on the wall again on sentry duty before sunrise."

"Yes, Sire. I shall see you in the morning."

"Can I come with you?" Adila asked her brother, sounding hopeful. She was restless and wanted to walk.

"Sure, but it's raining buckets and you will get soaked," he said. "And besides you have eaten nothing."

"I'm not hungry," she said and stood up to join him. "I want to see the sentries do their duties. One day I might be one of them."

Decebal frowned. "Patience, Adila. You may yet be a warrior one day, but not this day and not in this war."

"Yes, Sire," Adila said, imitating her brother but with a smile on her face.

Beneath the heavy overcast skies the night was completely dark. There was no moon and no stars shining any light through the heavy clouds. The darkness was interrupted only for the brief moments when lightning flashed across the sky and lit the ground beneath. Lightning flashed in the distance, followed by rolling thunder. At times it flashed closer by, followed by loud booming thunder.

Cotiso and Adila checked on the guard detachment by the city gates. No guards were asleep, but they were doing their best to find what little shelter they could. There would be no movement of people or animals in or out of the city during the night so the gates were kept shut and bolted.

Cotiso climbed up the wooden stairs leading to the ramparts on top of the city walls. Adila followed closely behind him. The rain was too heavy for burning torches so they moved slowly and carefully in the darkness, the floors and walls around them lit only by the brief flashes of lightning.

At the top of the wall they stopped to get their bearings.

"Aren't you glad you came with me?" Cotiso asked with a laugh. They were both thoroughly wet and the night air was surprisingly chilly.

"Yes!" she cried. "A little rain and darkness don't scare me. If the sentries can do this then so can I."

"All right, but be careful where you go. And watch your step!"

The first sentry post was just past the stairs built against the wall. Two spearmen stood guard, looking out over the ground between the city walls and the Roman army in the distance. When lightning flashed it showed only empty barren ground. In places the heavy rain gathered in large puddles and rivulets.

"Staying awake, men?" Cotiso asked them jokingly.

"Yes, sir," one of the soldiers replied. They recognized the visitors as the King's son and daughter and were instantly on alert.

"Nothing moving out there, sir," the other sentry added, "not even a chipmunk."

"Good. Stay alert, men. If the Romans send an attack party they will do so under cover of darkness. And if they are determined they will find a way to get over the wall."

"Don't worry, sir, nothing will get past us."

"I hunted chipmunks in the woods," Adila said. "They are good at hiding themselves, so be careful!"

The spearmen laughed at her joke and even Cotiso had to smile.

"Adila, this is as far as you go. You will stay here and talk to these soldiers if you wish. I will check on the other posts and come back here. I won't take very long."

"But why?" she asked, surprised and disappointed.

"Because the floor is wet and slippery and dangerous to walk in the dark. It is too dark anyway and nothing for you to see. You will wait for me here, that's an order," Cotiso explained.

"Yes, sir," Adila said. She was getting used to military authority and her place in it.

Cotiso moved carefully towards the next sentry position that was perhaps thirty paces away. Adila caught brief glimpses of him when lightning flashed. She looked out over the open fields, along with the two sentries. She found that she had nothing to talk about. The men were being careful to not say anything foolish to the King's daughter. They stood and watched in silence, getting soaked to the skin by the pouring rain.

The flash of light was extremely bright but so brief that Adila's eyes almost did not register it. There was a simultaneous deafening loud noise that left her stunned, and a physical force like a blow that knocked her off her feet. For a moment she lay on the ground, too stunned to think. One of the guards was also down on the ground next to her, moving slowly as if in a daze.

The other guard was somehow still on his feet, leaning on his spear to maintain his balance. He was looking in the direction where Cotiso had gone, about thirty paces away, where something made of wood was burning.

Adila got to her feet slowly, feeling unsteady. She seemed to be unhurt but felt like she was in a dream. She started to walk towards the small wood fire. The guard who was on his feet reached out a hand to restrain her but she shook his hand away. As she approached the fire she could make out three bodies sprawled on the ground. None was moving.

She was oblivious to the rain that was running down her face and blurring her vision. In the dim light of the fire she saw that the first body was that of a soldier she had never seen before. The man's face was marked with a strange red pattern that looked something like a spider web but was not a spider web. His eyes were open and glassy looking, lifeless and staring at nothing.

The second body was Cotiso, sprawled on his back, his arms splayed out to the sides. His eyes were closed and his face looked peaceful. Adila dropped down to her knees beside him. She tried to see if he was breathing but she could not tell. Her vision was blurry with rainwater. She bent down from the waist and placed her head on her brother's chest, her left ear pressed against the wet woolen shirt at the center of his chest. She tried hard to listen for a heartbeat. Listen, she told herself, her tears mixing with the pouring rain. Listen hard. Listen for a heartbeat.

But there was no heartbeat.

They summoned King Decebal up to the ramparts and he arrived within a minute, Buri trailing behind him, guards carrying covered torches right behind him. The sentries at the top of the stairs looked terrified as they pointed the King towards the spot where lightning had struck. Adila was standing near three bodies, with one guard who was brave enough to stand with her.

As Decebal walked briskly towards them Adila turned and walked towards him. She seemed in a daze. Decebal took her in his arms and held her tight for a moment.

"Are you all right?"

"Yes, Tata. Cotiso…" Adila stopped and broke into sobs.

"Yes, they told me," he said gently. "I will take care of Cotiso. Now I want you to go inside and wait for me there."

"Come with me, Adila," Buri said. He led her patiently down the wet stairs and back to the dining hall, accompanied by one guard with a torch.

Decebal went down on one knee beside the body of his oldest son. His brave and noble son who had suffered and endured so much in life. Who had worked and fought and turned himself into a warrior and a leader. The King could not comprehend this loss. He always accepted the possibility that his son might die in battle someday, which was a risk they all shared as warriors. To die in battle fighting for the freedom of his people was a noble thing. But not like this. Not like this.

Decebal felt a profound sadness and shed tears for his son. Soon the sadness turned to anger, then the anger turned to rage. He rose to his feet and turned his head up towards the dark sky, the rain heavy on his face. He balled his hands into fists and raised them up towards the sky.

"What do you want from me?" the King bellowed at the stormy heavens. "Have I not served you well enough? Have I not sacrificed enough for you? What more do you want? Damn you! Damn you!"

Rain pelted, lightning flashed, and thunder boomed. Zamolxis was silent.

The Dacian soldiers began to leave Tapae at daybreak. They did so without orders, and in many cases against direct orders. First in small groups, then larger groups, and finally entire units of the army started the march north through the mountain pass of Tapae. In some cases they disobeyed their officers, but in more and more cases their officers went willingly with them. The Dacian army was leaving the site of battle.

The storm passed by during the night and the sun was shining again. Soon the day's heat would dry up the muddy battlefield and the paths leading north from the city.

Drilgisa reacted with fury. He did not draw his sword because he well knew that would lead to him spilling Dacian blood. No matter his furious anger, he would not kill his countrymen for following their religious beliefs. He made an effort to persuade them at least.

"Cowards!" he yelled at the men marching away. "You cannot leave your King like this! You cannot run away in the face of our enemy!"

One of the older warriors stopped and faced him. He served under Drilgisa's command for many years and fought with him in many battles. His face was calm but determined.

"We are not cowards, General," the man said. "I fear no enemy and neither do the rest of these men." He paused and shook his head sadly. "Zamolxis sent a terrible storm last night to show his anger. He took the life of the King's son. Can there be a more clear and terrible omen?"

"We must fight the Romans!" Drilgisa insisted. "King Decebal led us here for this fight. Our allies are here to fight with us. We cannot give up the fight now!"

The soldier shook his head again, reluctant to say what he had to say next. "We cannot disobey an omen from the gods. Zamolxis does not wish for us to fight this battle. King Decebal himself would not wish for us to disobey our god."

Drilgisa knew the simple truth that this old warrior was right. These soldiers were not running away from the Romans. They were turning away from what they saw as the clear and terrible displeasure of their god. Zamolxis had sent a great storm before the battle was complete. He took the life of a prince of Dacia. The only way for the soldiers to interpret this omen was that they must abandon the fight.

"Go, then," Drilgisa said, waving the man down the road. "I will not stop you."

"I shall see you again, General. We will fight together again." The soldier turned and walked away. Supply wagons joined the streams of men. These soldiers had seen the last of the battle of Tapae.

Inside the city walls King Decebal and his family and closest advisors held vigil over the body of Cotiso. He was laid out on top of a table, a blanket underneath his body and a burial shroud waiting nearby for him to be wrapped in. He looked peaceful in death, as if asleep.

Adila stood by her father, her face devoid of feeling. She wished to wake up from this bad dream, but knew it was not a dream. Diegis was grim faced as well, as was Buri. They had both watched Cotiso grow up since he was born. Prince Davi of the Roxolani had known Cotiso since he was a young boy. Vezina gave him the blessings of Zamolxis, however the funeral rites would come much later.

King Decebal knew that much of his army was leaving. Neither he nor anyone else could stop them. The power of the King of Dacia could not rule over the power of the god of Dacia. In truth, the King's own religious beliefs made him question the wisdom of going against a sign from Zamolxis.

Chief Fynn of the Bastarnae and Chief Ailen of the Celts entered the room together. They paid their respects to Decebal and Adila. Both had armies that expected to fight a major battle today, but now those plans were up in the air. The matter had to be settled because the Roman army was camped nearby and would soon be mustering for battle.

Chief Fynn spoke up first and voiced what they all were thinking. "We cannot fight the Romans if our armies are not united."

"No," Decebal said. "We cannot."

"My people watch your soldiers leave and they lose heart," Ailen said. "The Dacian army is the main force of this army. We cannot fight the Romans on our own."

The King nodded in agreement. "No one expects that, Chief Ailen. None of us can fight Rome alone."

"We can fight skirmishes against Roman units," said Prince Davi, frustrated, "but cavalry skirmishes cannot defeat an army."

Chief Fynn frowned. "Can you not convince your men to stay and fight?" He shifted his gaze between Decebal and Vezina.

"We cannot," Decebal said in a somber voice.

"The soldiers fear the anger of the gods," Vezina offered. "It is what they learn from the time they are born. Indeed, it is what they fear most."

"So they believe your god Zamolxis told them not to fight?" Ailen asked.

"Yes, Ailen," Vezina said. "No one will convince them otherwise."

"Then this battle is over," Fynn said with finality.

No one disagreed with the Bastarnae chief. The Romans had a big advantage even when the allies were united. Without the Dacian troops their situation was hopeless.

"What are your plans?" Ailen asked the King.

Decebal paused in thought for a moment. "We shall retreat north for now. There is no better choice."

"Trajan will follow you, for certain," Fynn said.

"No doubt," Decebal agreed. "We will fight him in the mountains. It is the Dacian way."

Diegis, who had been silent, finally spoke up. "We are in a very dangerous position here, Brother. We have to retreat north now, this morning, before the Romans attack. We shall re-form and organize our army in the mountains."

"You are right, Diegis," the King agreed. "Go and take command of the retreat immediately. The supply wagons are already positioned in the mountain pass, give the order for them to go."

"Immediately," Diegis said, and turned for the door.

"I will take my men home," Fynn said. "They will be disappointed, but if we stay here we are slaughtered."

"Of course, Chief Fynn," Decebal said. He looked at Ailen. "You will do the same?"

"Yes, King Decebal," Ailen said, also disappointed. "We must."

Decebal looked to Davi. "And you, Prince Davi?"

"My men will remain with your troops for a time. Our combined cavalries will cover the retreat. Emperor Trajan will be slow to catch up with his infantry, but we should keep General Quietus away from the rear units and the supply wagons."

"Thank you, Davi." Decebal turned to Fynn and Ailen. "See to your armies, then, my friends. We shall fight together again, I promise you. Just not today."

The allies bid their farewells and left, leaving Decebal with Adila and Vezina.

"What of Cotiso, Tata?" Adila asked in a soft voice.

The King looked at his dead son and allowed his grief to return. "We shall take Cotiso home. His burial will be in Sarmizegetusa, his home, not here." He turned and caught Vezina's eye. "Would you take him home, Vezina? Take a unit of infantry and cavalry along with whatever supply wagons you need. Go now."

"Of course, Sire," Vezina replied.

Decebal put an arm around Adila's shoulders. "You must go with them, Adila. It is time you went home also."

"Yes, Tata. When will you be there?"

"In time, Daughter. I must see to the army first. But I will see you there, in time."

"The Dacians are leaving!" Hadrian announced as he entered the Emperor's command tent. He had been out early with the cavalry to scout the enemy positions.

Trajan looked up from his breakfast plate. Licinius Sura was with him, along with the generals Longinus, Maximus, and Quietus. The troops were already in the field but they would wait until the high officers finished their meal.

"Who is leaving, and where are they going?" Trajan asked. "Be specific, Hadrianus."

"The entire army is retreating, Caesar! Infantry, artillery, cavalry. All of them are moving north, and wasting no time about it."

Now Hadrian had everyone's full attention. He grinned at their surprised reactions. "They don't want to give us a fight today."

Trajan looked around at his officers with a questioning look. "What is Decebalus planning? Any ideas?"

Each of them shook his head no. "This is a complete surprise to me, Caesar," Maximus offered. "Lucullus tells me that Decebalus is unpredictable, but this stratagem follows no logic."

"Perhaps he wants to draw us into the mountain pass and fight us there," Quietus wondered.

The Emperor gave a nod. "He prefers to fight us in the mountains, it makes the most sense for his army and it's worked for him in the past. But why retreat now, when he offered battle yesterday?"

"It makes no sense," Longinus said again.

"Perhaps we should pursue them while they are in retreat?" asked Lusius Quietus.

"No. They have a good head start on our infantry, we cannot chase them and catch them now," Trajan said. "See what your cavalry can do, Lusius. Nothing reckless, but scout them well and attack where you have an advantage."

"Understood, Caesar."

"Bring me back prisoners, Lusius. Dacian prisoners are preferable. I need information on what Decebalus is up to, and we have none."

"Are the city defenders still defending the walls?" Longinus asked Hadrian.

"No, General. From what I could see the walls are not manned. They are clearing out Tapae as well."

"Very curious," Trajan said. "I fully expected that Decebalus would force us to siege the city. He is making it too easy for us. "

"They lost thousands of men yesterday," Licinius Sura pointed out. "It may be that he is simply saving the forces he has left."

Trajan frowned. "We lost thousands of men yesterday as well. The losses are heavy on both sides. It may be that Decebalus needs to pause the fighting and replace his losses, but so do we."

"All the more reason not to rush after them now," said Longinus.

"I agree, Gnaeus."

The generals fell silent. All their carefully laid plans were suddenly no longer relevant. No one would have predicted Decebalus simply marching away. They waited for Trajan to make the next decision. He made it quickly.

"Gnaeus, move the auxiliary troops north as far as the mountain pass. Guard against any return of Dacian troops or their allies."

"Yes, Caesar."

"Laberius, move the legionnaire camp to the open ground west of the city. We will rest and re-fit our units there until we are ready to march again."

Maximus gave a nod. "Yes, Caesar."

"Hadrian? Find suitable accommodations for me in Tapae. We shall be here for a short time, I think. Decebalus will not go very far, and we will go after him when we are ready."

> Chapter 9

Casualties of War

Tapae, August 101 AD

Caesar Trajan summoned Titus Lucullus to the large and comfortable dining room at command quarters in Tapae. The large house was conveniently close to the city gates, and was most recently occupied by King Decebalus of Dacia. It was the best place for the Emperor to meet with his staff.

Lucullus was escorted into the room, approached the Emperor's table, and saluted smartly in the Roman fashion. "Hail, Caesar!"

Trajan looked up from the letter he was writing on a letter scroll. There was a pile of letters on the table in front of him.

"Come Titus, join me. Have some wine?"

Although it was only late morning the Emperor had already had several cups of wine. Trajan had a strong passion for war and for wine, it was said. He indulged his passion for wine on a daily basis.

"I will Caesar, thank you," Titus replied. He was not a big drinker and did not drink in the morning, but it would be poor form to refuse Caesar's invitation. Men who liked to drink usually liked to drink in the company of others.

Lucullus poured himself a cup of wine from a silver pitcher at the end of the table. He paused to take a sip. Romans usually drank their wine mixed in equal parts with water, but this wine was full strength and undiluted.

"How may I be of service, Caesar?" Titus asked respectfully.

"Sit, Lucullus, sit!" Trajan gestured to a bench on the opposite side of the table. "I wish to talk honestly so let's drop formalities. Do you like the wine?"

"The wine is excellent, Caesar," Titus replied as he took a seat. "I am not as knowledgeable as you of course, however even I can tell this is an excellent vintage."

"Good! Choose a Falernian red or a Picine white and you can't go wrong."

"I shall remember that, Caesar."

Trajan smiled. He paused to take a long sip of his own wine. "Tell me about the Dacian fortresses on the roads to Sarmizegetusa. You are one of only a few Romans who travelled those roads. You were inside the walls of Sarmizegetusa. You were a guest at the Dacian court. You spoke with Decebalus and his High Priest."

"I have. What does Caesar wish to know?"

"Last time you went as a visitor, now you go as an invader," Trajan said. "You have a military mind, Titus. Tell me what I need to know as the invader."

"I understand, Caesar. The road to Sarmizegetusa will be difficult and full of obstacles. The Dacians have a long string of forts, which they call davas. The walls are made of stone, not wood. They cannot be burned down. The Dacians build their walls in the maurus dacicus style, which cannot be brought down by battering rams, catapults, or other siege machines."

"If we cannot go through walls we will go over them," the Emperor said. "We will lose more men doing so but it must be done."

"Yes, Caesar. The mountain roads between the davas are hilly and go through thick woods and forest. It is perfect terrain for ambushes and hit and run raids. We should count on the Dacians to hit us along the roads, every day. General Julianus found this to be a very vexing problem."

"Understood. We cannot prevent those attacks, but we can fight them off." The Emperor stopped to re-fill his wine cup. "And when we reach Sarmizegetusa? How would you attack the city, Titus?"

Lucullus paused to gather his thoughts. It was a difficult question and he knew the Emperor would not be pleased with his answer. "The city is strongly defended, too well defended to be attacked head on, Caesar. It is built into the side of a mountain. The city walls are thirty feet tall and nine feet thick, made with large blocks of stone. The ramparts will be swarming with archers, spearmen, and artillery, all well protected from our artillery. Such was my view during my visit, many years ago. Decebalus has strengthened the city defenses even more since then."

"Any city can be attacked, Lucullus!" Trajan chided him. "Even Rome was attacked and sacked by barbarians, once."

"That is true, Caesar. You asked me to speak truthfully, so I will. In truth the Dacian holy city is better defended than Rome or any other city I have seen with my own eyes."

"I shall expect you to speak truthfully at all times, Titus. That is why I summoned you here. I have no patience for liars or fools, or for those who tell me what they think I want to hear."

"Yes, Caesar. I understand."

"When we reach Sarmizegetusa you will be by my side. I repeat, any city can be attacked successfully. If a long siege is necessary then we will starve them out."

Lucullus gave a nod. "I think that a long siege will be necessary. The city grounds are vast. They grow much of their own food inside the walls. They have their own water supply, enough for drinking and also enough for bathing and to run a sewer system underneath the city. It will be difficult."

Trajan gave him a patient smile. "Nothing worthwhile comes easy, Titus."

"Indeed so, Caesar," Lucullus acknowledged. "When we reach Sarmizegetusa I will be honored to be at your side."

"Good. Tomorrow we march north through the Tapae pass. I will command the bulk of our forces and pursue Decebalus and his army. You will continue to assist General Maximus. Once through these mountains he will take two legions and attack the cities and forts in Banat. We will deny Decebalus troops and supplies to replace those he has lost."

"An excellent plan, Caesar."

"Provide Maximus with your knowledge of the Dacians, Titus. I want Decebalus defeated before winter comes. We will not repeat the mistake of Tettius Julianus and have our attack stalled in these mountains when the snows and freezing weather hits."

"I understand, Caesar. King Decebalus will try exactly that, to stall our attack before the harsh winter cold arrives."

"I know how the man thinks," Trajan said. "But tell me, strategies aside, what do you actually expect Decebalus to do?"

Titus answered without any hesitation. "The unexpected, Caesar."

Sarmizegetusa, August 101 AD

Vezina and the funeral procession bringing back Cotiso were greeted by a grief stricken city. Many thousands of Dacians died at the battle of Tapae, and many of them were from Sarmizegetusa. News of the battle had been brought to the city by cavalry messengers who rode ahead of the funeral procession and arrived two days earlier.

Queen Andrada embraced her daughter Adila with relief. She greeted the body of her step-son Cotiso with grief. By the time they arrived in the city she already made funeral plans and arrangements. King Decebal was still away, leading the Dacian army in the war with Rome, and the Queen was ruler of the city.

After being greeted by the Queen outside the palace entrance, Vezina had the body of Cotiso taken straight to the High Temple of Zamolxis. The priests there would prepare it for the funeral rites and burial that would take place the next day. The body would be washed, wrapped in a burial shroud, and purified through prayers.

Adila found herself embraced on her return by her entire family, standing and waiting outside the palace doors. She embraced her mother, and then found herself smothered in the fierce embraces of her aunts Dochia and Tanidela. They were followed by her sister Zia, her cousin Ana, and her younger brother Dorin. It was a reunion mixed with joy and sorrow, but she was glad to be home.

"I was worried for you every day that you were gone," Zia said to her sister when they were resting in their rooms inside the royal living quarters. "You're not planning on leaving again, are you?"

"I don't know," Adila replied in a quiet voice. "Right now I honestly don't know what I will do."

"The army is no place for you, Adila! Look at what happened to our brother."

Adila shook her head. "Cotiso was killed by a lightning strike. That could have happened here, or anywhere else." She felt a shudder go through her at the memory of seeing his body on the walls of Tapae. That terrible image was burned into her memory forever.

"You know what I mean," Zia continued. "He would still be alive if he had stayed here with us."

"Nobody is safe, Zia!" Adila said in a sad tone. "If the Romans are not stopped they will come here. Will I be safe then? Will you?"

Zia had no reply. There was a hard edge to her sister that had not been there before.

"Cotiso was a true warrior," Adila said. "When the Romans came to attack the city he stood on top of the walls and killed them with his bow. He did not fear death. He did not worry about keeping safe. He cared only about defending the people inside the city."

"I understand. He always tried to protect us, since we were born." Zia paused to wipe away a tear. "He was doing what Tata always does. Uncle Diegis. Buri. Tarbus. All of them."

"It is what we all must do, if we can," Adila said.

"Some of us are better suited for it than others, Sister. Some are natural warriors, and others are more suited to be healers. I will let you guess which one of us is which."

That made Adila smile. "You are a natural healer. I don't know yet if I will ever be a warrior, but I will try."

Zia reached out with a finger and tapped Adila twice in the center of her chest. "Cotiso once told me that being a great warrior starts in here. It is in the heart."

"Yes? Do you think he was right?"

"Without a doubt," Zia said, "I am sure that he was right. You have the heart of a warrior. You need only to get stronger and gain more experience."

"Thank you for saying that. The next time I see a Roman soldier I will be better prepared."

"May I ask you a question?" Zia said, sounding mildly anxious.

Adila gave her a half smile. "I know what the question is, but go ahead and ask."

"Did you see Tarbus there? Is he well?"

"Yes, I saw him, although we did not have time to talk. He is well. He fights at the side of General Drilgisa."

"Good," Zia said, relieved.

"I wish this terrible war wound end," Adila said grimly. But she knew that it would not end any time soon, and knew that her part in it was not over.

Funeral rites for Cotiso and the Dacian soldiers killed at the battle of Tapae were performed by the High Priest of Zamolxis. A very large crowd gathered in front of the royal palace to hear the prayers given by Vezina. People were dressed in funeral black to mourn their sons, brothers, fathers, and their young Prince.

By ancient Dacian tradition Cotiso was buried in a plain grave, without a gravestone or other statuary. He was laid to rest near his relative, King Duras. Like the former king he was buried wrapped in a shroud, face up, with his head pointing to the east. He was dressed in his finest clothes. His war bow was placed at his side.

A public funeral feast, or pomana, followed the burial ceremony. The funeral feast lasted all day and long into the night. The Dacians celebrated weddings and mourned funerals with equal reverence for the occasion.

Early the next morning Adila went to the open field that was used for archery practice. She carried two leather quivers, each filled with twenty arrows. She would shoot all her arrows at a target thirty paces away. She would then retrieve all the arrows, move back ten paces, and shoot all the arrows at the target again. She would then repeat the process. And again. And again. She would not be satisfied until, of the two hundred arrows, only twenty or fewer missed their mark.

She found that her strength and her aim improved steadily, day by day. Don't think, Cotiso told her, simply act in one smooth motion. Notch the arrow, pull back, loose. The same smooth motion every time. Allow the bow to become an extension of your arm. Don't aim the arrow head, simply look at the target and let your arm guide the arrow there. One smooth motion.

Adila was surprised by how much archery calmed her mind, an unexpected benefit. While she practiced she thought about many things. She thought about her past, and also about her future. She thought about her time in Tapae. She thought many times about that terrible night in the dark on the ramparts on the walls of Tapae.

She did not know if Zamolxis sent that bolt of lightning. She would never know the answer to that question. It would be a cruel god who took such action, a god she could never worship. But she did not know the will of the gods. What she knew was that the bolt of lightning took her brother and changed her life forever. She was a different person now. She could not bring her brother back, but she could honor him by following in his footsteps. In dedicating herself to that she would keep him alive, if only in some small way. Some small but meaningful way.

Buridava, Mountains of Dacia, September 101 AD

"How many raids this week on engineering units and supply camps?" King Decebal asked his commander of cavalry.

"Thirty, including Davi's big raid," General Sinna replied. "Trajan has his army marching in tight formations, but we hit them on their flanks in places of our choosing. Then we're gone before they know what hit them. The Romans don't have enough cavalry to protect their entire column."

"Good," Decebal acknowledged. "Hit their engineers hard, the bridge builders and road builders. We want to slow down Trajan's advance as much as we can."

"He doesn't seem to be in any particular rush," Diegis said. "Attack a fort here, burn a village there."

"Trajan does not do anything in a rush, Diegis. He is methodical. He builds his plan piece by piece."

"Bastard must be half beaver," Drilgisa muttered.

"Beavers can do a lot of damage, if you let them," Buri said.

"We're not talking about blocked streams flooding your orchards, Buri," Drilgisa chided him. "But this particular beaver needs a sword through his guts."

"I agree," the King said. "However at this time we don't have enough swords for that. Without our Celtic allies and the Bastarnae we are outnumbered three to one."

"We have fought wars of resistance before. And won them," Diegis said. "We can win again."

"Yes, Brother, we can win again," Decebal said. "We cannot kill this Roman army, it is too big, so we must outlast it. Trajan will not fight us in the winter, in the mountains."

"But how long can we slow them down?" Drilgisa asked. "Sooner or later we must fight them."

"Until next spring, Drilgisa. Perhaps summer. We will gather our allies again and re-group."

"You have much more patience than I do, Sire," Drilgisa said. "But then I have never been known for my patience."

"Generals can afford to be impatient at times, my friend," Decebal replied. "Sometimes it even works to their advantage. Kings do not have that luxury."

Just then Tarbus entered the room, a big smile on his face. The reason for his good mood was clear when they saw Vezina walking in right behind him. Just the presence of Vezina brightened everyone's mood.

"Sire," Vezina greeted the King first with a small bow.

"Welcome back, Your Holiness," Decebal said. "I trust that your journey was not too difficult?"

"No more than usual," he replied. In truth his bones ached from the long ride, but he would not complain. "I bring greetings from the Queen and from your children."

"Thank you, Vezina." Decebal was thinking only of the son who was now gone. "And Cotiso's funeral. You put him to rest?"

"Yes, Sire. Cotiso had a funeral fit for a prince. He was loved by all and now is mourned by all." Vezina was fond of the young man and the sadness in his voice was genuine.

Decebal gave him a solemn nod. He found that he had no voice at the moment.

"And Princess Adila?" Buri asked. "How is she?"

"Profoundly sad, however she is a strong young woman," Vezina replied. "Cotiso taught her how to use a war bow, because she asked him to." He paused to glance at Decebal. "She seems determined to master its use."

Decebal gave a small smile. "I do not mind. She has a strong mind, like her mother. And some day it may save her life."

"It may indeed," Diegis said. "We should train all our children to be warriors."

"And speaking of children, little Ana sends a letter for you," Vezina said. "It is in my mail pouch. I shall get it for you."

"Thank you, Vezina."

The High Priest turned back to the King. "And how goes the war here, Sire? I bring fifty archers and two hundred infantry with me, but we need many more I am sure."

"Ten thousand more, of each, would be a good start," Decebal said. "The situation is unchanged, Vezina. Our men are with us again, but most of our allies have left. The Sarmatian cavalry are with us still."

"The new infantry will help," Drilgisa said. He looked to Tarbus to get his attention. "Tarbus, they are assigned to you. We'll get them into shape, and you will learn how to be an officer."

"Yes, sir!" Tarbus replied. "I am deeply honored, sir."

"You will do well, Tarbus," Decebal told him. "And you could not ask for a better teacher."

"I agree, Sire," Buri said, happy for his son.

"Now let's get to work, gentlemen," Decebal said. "Set an example for your men. We lead by action, not words."

Mountains of Dacia, October 101 AD

On top of the walls of the Dacian fort, Emperor Trajan saw, was a row of spikes with severed heads impaled on them. The heads wore the helmets of legionnaires. These were very old trophies of war, from battles fought long ago. General Tettius Julianus last fought in these parts of Dacia some twelve or thirteen years ago. The legionnaires who lost their heads had most likely been his men.

From his vantage point on high ground Trajan could see that the fort was very well defended. The battlements were swarming with archers, spearmen, and more than a dozen pieces of artillery. A very large water tank could be seen in the background, along with several thin but tall buildings that were most likely full of grain and other foods. The fort was designed similar to Arcidava. Unlike Arcidava however, this fort was prepared for a long siege and the men inside would fight to the end.

There was a small village below the fort. To Trajan's disgust the first auxiliary troops on the scene, infuriated by the Roman severed heads on the walls, massacred most of the Dacian villagers and set fire to their houses. These were civilians, women, children, and old men, and the slaughter was senseless.

The Emperor turned to General Gnaeus Pompeius Longinus, who was also watching from horseback nearby. "Gnaeus?"

Longinus urged his horse a little closer. The Emperor was also surrounded by his friend Licinius Sura, the Prefect of the Praetorian Guard Tiberius Livianus, and young Hadrian.

"Yes, Caesar?" Longinus asked.

"Instill more discipline in these savages, our auxiliaries," Trajan said in a calm tone. "There will be no slaughter of civilian populations unless I order it."

"Yes, Caesar," Longinus agreed. "I will have a talk with the officers involved. Although, to be fair, looking at those Roman heads on the walls, I am not surprised they were provoked to violence."

Trajan turned to him sharply. "They will follow orders, damn them! It makes no difference whether they feel provoked, they fight under the command of a Roman officer. That officer is you, Gnaeus."

"Of course, Caesar," Longinus answered calmly. He and Trajan had been good friends for many years, and there was no animosity between them. Longinus also knew well that on a battlefield Trajan's word could never be doubted or questioned. "I will see to it that your orders are obeyed, Marcus."

"Do we attack this fort?" Licinius Sura asked. Lately the Emperor was becoming selective in attacking certain targets but not others. Attacking the Dacian forts was taking longer than expected, and it was costing more Roman casualties than originally expected. The battle of

Tapae took a heavy toll on Trajan's army as well as the army of Decebalus. The Roman casualties were still not replaced. They would not be replaced until the spring, most likely.

"No," Trajan said. "We will leave enough troops to siege the fort, and move on. Those men in there are not going anywhere and they will not trouble us. They are not worth the trouble of taking heavy losses and slowing our advance."

"I agree, Caesar," Sura replied.

Trajan turned to the other generals. "Gnaeus? Tiberius? What is your opinion?"

"I agree," said Longinus.

"As do I," replied Livianus.

"And Hadrian? What do you think?"

"I agree with your decision, Caesar," Hadrian said.

"Good!" Trajan said. "Because I am leaving you in charge of the siege, Hadrianus."

"Yes, Caesar."

Hadrian agreed, but was clearly not pleased. It seemed to him that he was always given the most minor assignments. Although he could not say so, he was starting to resent being the Emperor's errand boy.

"Put the siege in place, Hadrianus. Then delegate it to some junior officer and rejoin the main army. I would not waste your talents to keep you stuck here for weeks or months of time."

"I understand, Caesar. I will do as you command."

> Chapter 10

The Envoys

Mountains of Dacia, November 101 AD

Planning strategy from a position of weakness, Vezina knew, was completely different compared to planning from a position of equal or superior strength. With the loss of its most important allies Dacia was in a position of weakness. For the time being its best strategy was to fight a war of attrition and survival. It was a strategy that could not be continued for a very long time.

A second strategy, which could prove very tricky to achieve, was to make another peace treaty with Rome. This was not an option that King Decebal would be happy with. Emperor Trajan would hold all the advantages and would make things difficult for Dacia. It was worth considering however, and the High Priest brought up the idea for discussion during the council meeting in Decebal's tent. Generals Diegis and Drilgisa were also there with the King.

"Let us send an envoy to talk with Trajan," Vezina suggested. "Let's see what he thinks at least, Sire."

"It would be a show of weakness," Decebal replied in an even tone. "We are not defeated. Trajan knows this."

"No, we are not defeated, Sire," Vezina agreed. "But neither would sending an envoy be a sign of weakness. Kings often talk with each other, even during war."

"I went to meet with General Julianus during the last war," Diegis pointed out. "That worked out to our advantage."

Decebal gave a nod. "That is true, Diegis. However conditions were different then. We had Julianus at a disadvantage, his army was about to starve and freeze in our mountains."

"The same will be true for Trajan soon," Drilgisa offered. "Now he attacks Dacian forts and villages but in two months his army will be sheltering in winter camp."

"They most likely will," said Decebal. "Then when spring comes he will continue his invasion and we will fight him again."

"Fight, or make a treaty." Vezina gave a small shrug. "Those are the choices."

"The only choice is to fight the invader!" the King exclaimed hotly. He slammed his fist down on the table. "There will be no talks of peace treaties while we can still fight."

"As you wish, Sire," Vezina said. There would be no treaty talks now, not while Decebal's pride was unbending.

Roman camp, Dacian mountains, November 101 AD

Two Praetorian Guards escorted the two blood-stained men from the auxiliary cavalry. As they approached the Emperor's command tent it became clear that the blood was not their own, but that of their dead Dacian enemies. One soldier carried a severed head in each hand, holding them by the dead men's long hair. The second soldier also carried a cut off head in each hand, and also a third severed head carried by clenching the dead man's hair between his teeth.

Licinius Sura watched them approach with an amused smile. "More gifts for Caesar, I see."

Trajan was standing outside the tent, watching the army settle in for the night. Tiberius Livianus and Gnaeus Longinus stood nearby, along with Sura. They knew that soldiers took pride in presenting

Trajan with such bloody gifts, and knew that these barbarians should not be discouraged from showing their pride in killing.

The men stopped a short distance in front of Trajan."

"Gifts to honor Caesar!" one of the Praetorian's announced. "These are the heads of Dacian raiders who attacked a party of our road building engineers!"

Trajan acknowledged their offer with a nod. The auxiliary riders bowed to Caesar, then put the severed heads down at their feet.

"Well done, men," Trajan said. "You are Iazygi?"

"Yes, Caesar," one of them answered. "We are Iazygi cavalry. We take great joy in killing Dacians."

"Good," Trajan said. "It is a true joy to look upon the heads of your dead enemies. However there is one thing I want you to do for me."

"Your wish is our command, Caesar!"

"Bring me living heads, not dead," Trajan said. "Heads that can still talk. I want live prisoners that can provide information about the Dacian army. Do you understand?"

"Yes, Caesar, we understand. We will not kill them until after you talk to them."

Trajan laughed. "Very good. You are dismissed."

"We will see how that goes," Longinus said with a smile. "The Iazygi hate the Dacians with a passion. The animosity goes back for generations."

"All to our benefit, Gnaeus," Trajan said. "They make up some of our best fighting cavalry."

Another group of four Praetorians approached. They escorted three men dressed in civilian clothes, the simple kind worn by Dacian peasants. They had been searched and none carried any weapons.

"Speaking of Dacians, now what?" Tiberius Livianus asked.

"They look like a humble lot," Sura observed.

"They should feel humbled, we are destroying their lands," Trajan said. He held up his hand and the small group of men stopped.

"Kneel before Caesar!" one of the Praetorians commanded the frightened looking visitors. They went down on their knees, then looked up expectantly at the Roman officers.

"Who are you and what you do you want?" Sura asked.

"We live in the village of Giura, down in the valley," one of the men said. "We come to ask Caesar for clementia." Clementia was mercy that Caesar granted to prisoners and local tribes when he so decided.

"Who gives you authority to negotiate for peace?" Trajan asked. "Are you sent by your King Decebalus?"

"No, Caesar, we have not spoken with our king. We speak only for ourselves and our village."

Trajan frowned. "Then you waste your time, and you waste my time. Tell your king that if he wants peace he must humble himself and talk to me face to face." He motioned to the guards. "Take these people back from where they came."

"Yes, Caesar!" The guard beckoned to the visitors. "Come along, you."

"Not a good sign for Decebalus," Sura offered, watching the men leave. "First his allies leave him, now his peasants want to deal with Rome directly."

"If he sees himself in a weak enough position he might capitulate," Tiberius Livianus suggested.

Trajan frowned. "His position is not yet so weak. Also his pride will not allow him to capitulate so easily."

"Might it be worthwhile to send an envoy to talk with the Dacian King?" Sura asked.

Something in his friend's tone took Trajan by surprise. "You sound serious about that, Licinius. What is on your mind?"

"I have given the matter some thought," Sura began. "First, we have nothing to lose by talking to the Dacians simply to discover their expectations. If Decebalus refuses to surrender we proceed to kill him anyway. Second, if Decebalus capitulates we achieve victory at very little cost. It would save a great number of Roman casualties and not further weaken our army. And third," Sura looked at the men around him and gave them a smile, "it would save us the time and trouble of spending the winter in these godforsaken mountains."

"All very excellent points," Gnaeus Longinus said.

"Licinius, you will be returning to Rome next month in any case to run for election for consul," Trajan said with a wry smile. "So you at least will not spend the winter in these godforsaken mountains."

Sura gave a nod. "In truth, that is also part of my considerations. I have no role in the military victories here beyond serving on Caesar's staff. Let me return to Rome with a diplomatic victory, at least."

Trajan raised an eyebrow. "You wish to be the envoy?"

"Why not? The envoy must be someone in a high position who will be seen as speaking for Caesar."

"The idea has merit," Livianus said.

"Very well," the Emperor agreed. "You will go to the Dacian camp, Licinius, and ask for the surrender of Decebalus. He must submit to the authority of Rome." He turned to Livianus. "And you, Tiberius, will take a detachment of the Praetorian Guard and escort him. Enough men to deter aggression, but not so many as to put fear into the Dacians and invite aggression. Your title as Praetorian Prefect will further add gravitas to the delegation."

"Of course, Caesar," Livianus acknowledged. "I will be happy to provide protection. I would be even happier to meet Decebalus and spit in his eye."

"Spitting makes for poor diplomacy, Tiberius. Sura will do the talking, you job will be to support him. Leave as soon as your men are ready," Trajan ordered. "We will give Decebalus this one opportunity for diplomacy."

"Thank you, Marcus," Sura replied. "Even barbarian kings are open to listening to reason, are they not?"

General Longinus laughed. "You are about to find out, Sura. Come back and let us know, would you? I am eager to find that out myself."

"Anyone is open to reason," Trajan said, "but only if it serves their own interests. Decebalus will negotiate with you if he thinks it will serve his interests. Go, Licinius, and see what you can do."

Sarmizegetusa, November 101 AD

Queen Andrada insisted on her family being gathered around the royal dining room table for the evening meal. It was the only time they were all together. Sadly, she thought, the group gathered around her table was getting smaller. Decebal more often than not was away campaigning with the army. Cotiso was buried near the Holy Temple of Zamolxis, near King Duras and Mirela.

Tanidela and her infant daughter, Tyra, left the city one week ago to travel to the Dacian fort of Piatra Alba. They would spend two weeks there to see Prince Davi, then travel on to the Sarmatian lands east of Dacia. Tanidela was a princess of Dacia and would very likely soon become Queen of the Sarmatians. She had responsibilities to fulfill to her people there. Also, she and Davi had decided, their daughter would be safer from Roman attacks in Sarmatia than she would be by staying in Dacia. The Emperor Trajan invaded Dacia for revenge and for gold. He would not travel to attack as far east as the Sarmatian tribal lands.

Seated around the table was Dochia, who next to Andrada was the rock of the family. The sisters Zia and Adila had become even closer since Adila's return from her brief and unhappy stint with the Dacian army. Eleven year old Dorin found himself the only male present in the royal household, and was yet unsure what that meant for his role in the family. His younger cousin Ana, the daughter of Diegis, had been treated as part of the immediate family since she was very young.

Servants brought in trays of freshly baked bread and freshly made butter. Bread was a staple with every meal, always baked fresh for that meal. It was served this meal with a rich, thick vegetable soup that was flavored with cream.

"I saw that you brought back three rabbits this afternoon, Dorin," the Queen said to her son. He was hungrily spooning soup into his mouth between bites of bread and butter.

He looked up with a look of pride on his face. "Oh, yes. I have been teaching Toma how to herd rabbits out in the fields."

Dochia laughed. "How does a dog herd rabbits?"

"He's a Dacian sheepdog, Auntie! Herding comes naturally for them. He chases rabbits from the brush, and before they can run to their rabbit holes he herds them in my direction. Then I shoot them with my hunting bow." He paused and grinned. "It's easy."

"Good," Andrada said, sharing in his simple pride. "Tomorrow we will have rabbit stew."

"I don't like rabbit stew," Ana declared. "I like chicken better."

Dorin frowned. "Don't eat it then! No one is forcing you, you know."

"I did not say I was forced, you don't have to get mad about it," Ana said pleasantly. "I just said I don't like it. It tastes like, you know – rabbit!"

"Well, I like rabbit," Adila said. "Just keep hunting them, Dorin. It's also good practice for your archery skills."

"It really is," he said. "I learned how to lead them just right, no matter how fast they are running. Of course sometimes they change direction quickly and that makes it harder."

"If you can hit rabbits on the run, well then you can for certain hit Romans," Zia said. "They don't move nearly as fast and they don't change directions."

That made Adila laugh. "Yes, that is true. Just think of Romans as bigger and slower rabbits. Except these rabbits wear armor, and they shoot back at you."

Dorin held up his empty bowl to a servant. "More soup, please?" He turned back to Adila. "If I ever see Romans I will need more than my hunting bow."

She nodded in agreement. “Yes, you will. Is it time to pick up a soldier’s bow, do you think?”

“Yes!” he cried. “Will you teach me? I watch you practice and I can tell you are getting much better.”

Adila shot a quizzical glance at her mother.

“Yes, I think it’s a good idea,” Andrada said. “Cotiso was about your age, Dorin, when he started practice with a soldier’s bow.”

The mention of Cotiso’s name quieted the conversation around the table. His memory was still too fresh and sad in their minds.

“I miss Aunt Tanidela,” Ana finally said. “And little Tyra, too.”

“Oh, little Tyra will be a charmer,” Dochia said. “She was just learning how to smile and laugh and say a few baby words.”

“Do you think they are with Prince Davi now?” Zia wondered.

“Yes, they will have reached Piatra Alba by now,” Andrada said. “So they should be with Prince Davi now, I should think.”

“My poor sister, she was so looking forward to seeing him again,” Dochia said. “And Davi, the poor man has hardly seen his child at all since she was born!”

“He’s not so poor,” Ana said. “He’s a prince of the Roxolani!”

Dochia gave her a patient smile. “You can be rich in gold, land, and horses, but also be poor in love.”

“Oh, I see,” Ana said.

The Queen gave a sigh. “He is only poor in time, Dochia. Time to spend with those he loves. War makes us all poor in that way.”

“You are right,” Dochia said. She paused briefly in reflection. “Are you thinking of my brother, the King?”

“I was,” Andrada replied. She looked around the table and gave them a small, sad smile. “I was thinking of the King. The poorest man in Dacia.”

“He would never say so, Mama,” Zia said.

“No, never,” Adila agreed, shaking her head.

"No, he would never say so," the Queen acknowledged. "He would never even think so. But that is only because this life of war is the only life he knows."

"I hate war," Adila said. Her face hardened into something tough and unforgiving.

"Me too, Daughter."

"Do you think they will make peace, Mama?" Zia asked, trying to sound hopeful.

Dochia frowned. "Men only make peace when they are desperate."

"I don't know, Zia," the Queen answered. "Your Tata will do what is best for Dacia. Then we will see what happens."

Dacian mountains, November 101 AD

General Livianus led an escort composed of a centuria of Praetorian Guard infantry, roughly eighty men. They carried the banners of an official delegation up front and also in the rear of the column. Sura was a Senator of Rome, and so the banner of the Senate of Rome was prominently displayed. Drummers beat a marching tune, so as to announce their presence far in advance of running into any Dacian troops. They wanted to avoid surprising or alarming the enemy.

The first sign of the enemy was a troop of Dacian cavalry that met them on the road and blocked their path. Livianus gave the order for his Praetorians to halt. No sooner had they done so than two streams of Dacian infantry emerged from the wooded slope above them. One large group of Dacians formed in front of the Roman column, one to their rear, and more soldiers could be seen among the trees. The Praetorians were quickly surrounded. They were outnumbered by four or five to one.

"Hold steady unless attacked!" Livianus ordered. "We are not here to fight!"

Sura walked to the front of the column to confront the Dacian troops. "I am Lucius Licinius Sura! I am a Senator of Rome! I come as a peace envoy from Emperor Trajan and from the Senate and people of Rome! Who is in charge here?"

The Dacian infantry parted in the middle to allow several of the cavalry riders to ride to the front. Their leader was an older soldier in his late thirties, with the distinguished looks and bearing of a high ranking officer. He looked from Sura to Livianus, more curious than hostile.

"I am Tsiru, Captain of Scouts for King Decebal," the man said. "What do you want, Senator?"

"I am here to talk with King Decebalus and his advisors. This is a mission of diplomacy and peace."

"I see," Tsiru replied. He looked over the Roman column, the men standing in marching formation six men abreast. "I will escort you to see our leaders, Senator Sura. The rest of your men go no further. They will camp here, in place, and wait for your return."

Livianus stepped up to stand besides Sura. "I am General Tiberius Claudius Livianus, Prefect of the Praetorian Guard. I will accompany Senator Sura, along with ten of my men for escort."

"You may accompany Senator Sura, General. But only you," Tsiru decided. "You will not need an escort."

Livianus opened his mouth to protest, but Sura held up his hand to stop him. "That is acceptable, Tiberius. If they wish to kill us, ten men won't save us."

Tsiru gave them a smile. "That is true, Senator. Now give orders to your men, I will get you horses, and we'll be on our way."

King Decebal got word of the Roman delegation while meeting with Vezina and Diegis in his command tent. Tsiru left the Romans some distance away, down the mountain slope, and walked up to Decebal's headquarters to inform him of their mission.

"Very impressive," Vezina remarked as Tsiru finished his report. "Sura and Livianus are the highest ranking envoys Trajan could have sent, other than Trajan himself."

"It is meant to impress us that Trajan is serious," Decebal said. He turned back to Tsiru. "Did Senator Sura give indication of the peace terms he wants to discuss?"

"No, Sire. He will discuss terms only with you, he said."

"Oh, ho!" Vezina exclaimed. "That sounds like he means business."

"Or perhaps it's simple arrogance," Diegis said calmly. "I saw enough of that when I was in Rome. Most of them are like that."

Decebal frowned. "Roman arrogance does not concern me, but I am curious to find out what Trajan would propose."

"Nothing to our benefit," said Vezina.

"Most certainly not."

"Will you talk with them?" Tsiru asked.

"No, Tsiru. In times of war kings talk to kings." Decebal turned to Diegis. "You will be my envoy, Brother."

Diegis laughed. "Me, again? Well, why not I suppose."

"You are brother to the King," Vezina said. "That makes you a most suitable spokesman. And besides," Vezina paused and smiled, "under my guidance you have learned to behave more like a diplomat and less like a Dacian hothead."

"Ha!" Diegis bent at the waist and gave him a small bow. "Who can resist your tutoring in patience and wisdom, Vezina?"

"Find out what they want," the King said to Diegis. "Sura will want concessions and promises. You will not provide any at this time."

Diegis gave a nod. "Understood. Tsiru, lead the way."

"You will not remember me," Sura said, "but I remember you. I saw you once before, during the crown ceremony in the royal gardens of Emperor Domitian."

"Ah! You were among the crowd of Senators there?" Diegis asked.

"A crowd, indeed. The entire Senate of Rome was gathered there to watch Diegis, brother of Decebalus, accept the golden diadem from Emperor Domitian to make Dacia a client kingdom of Rome."

"I remember," Diegis said evenly. It was not a happy memory but it no longer irked him as much as it once did.

Sura noticed his cool reaction. "The Emperor did not treat you with the honor and decorum your position deserved, I'm afraid."

"No matter. Your Emperor Domitian was not a man of honor. Your own people stabbed him ten times, I hear?"

Sura grimaced. "He was stabbed seven times, as I understand."

"My uncle, the late King Duras, used to say that you Romans are overly fond of assassinating your leaders," Diegis said with a smile.

"Sadly there is some truth to that," Sura admitted. "However that is not what I came here to discuss, General Diegis."

"I was about to say the same," Livianus interjected, irritated by this Dacian's poor attitude and lack of deference towards Rome. "Shall we get to the point?"

"Of course, General Livianus," Diegis said pleasantly. "So what do you wish to discuss?"

Sura cleared his throat. "Emperor Trajan offers terms of peace. It will benefit both our nations to end this destruction."

"Continue," Diegis said. Tsiru was standing at his side, but Diegis was clearly the spokesman for Dacia.

"King Decebalus must become a true client king of Rome, not a pretend one," Sura began. "Dacia must become a true client kingdom of Rome, not a rogue power that always goes its own way. Too often Dacia has been openly hostile to Rome."

Diegis looked at them in silence for a few moments. "King Decebal will always act to protect Dacia's interests," he replied. "Emperor Domitian gave Dacia very favorable terms in our last peace treaty with Rome. Does Emperor Trajan now wish to change those terms?"

"What do you think?" Livianus replied with a sneer. He did not like and had no patience for the Dacian's insolent tone.

Sura turned to him with a mild frown. "We are here to seek an understanding, Tiberius. Not hostilities."

"What I think," Diegis said, giving Livianus a hard look, "is that you lost many men at Tapae and you are losing many more attacking our forts in the mountains. What I think is that this war is difficult for you, more difficult than you originally planned for." Diegis stopped and noted that neither Roman looked eager to contradict him. "And what I also know," Diegis continued, "is that in a month or two, when the heavy snows fall, your army will be cut off and starving and freezing in the mountains."

Livianus gave him a defiant look. Sura kept his composure.

"As I said, General Diegis," Sura continued, "an end to the fighting will benefit both our nations. Do you not agree?"

Diegis gave a nod. "On that we agree, Senator. Let us end the fighting. But on what terms?"

"Why, on the terms that I just stated! Dacia will conduct itself as a proper client kingdom to Rome, and accept the authority of Caesar and the Senate and people of Rome."

Diegis looked doubtful. "Those terms are overly broad, Senator. A treaty must be negotiated in some detail."

"Will Dacia accept Rome's authority? Speak clearly, yes or no," Livianus said impatiently.

Diegis gave a shrug. "Depends on terms, as I said. Here is one thing you may tell your Emperor, however. Dacia will never sacrifice its freedom. We will fight to the last man before that happens."

"Do you speak for King Decebalus?" Sura asked him.

Diegis gave him a wolfish grin. "I speak for all Dacians."

"So do I," Tsiru added, also with a grin.

Sura saw no benefit to challenge them. "Negotiations may happen at some time in the future. I'm afraid that none of us have authority to accomplish that here and now."

"I agree, Senator," Diegis said.

"And what happens in the meantime?" Sura wondered.

"That depends on Emperor Trajan," Diegis replied. "In truth, this reminds me of another conversation I had many years ago. General Tettius Julianus was asking himself the same questions."

"Emperor Trajan is no Julianus," Sura said dismissively.

"No, he is not," Diegis agreed, "but the situations are the same. Snow is snow. Freezing is freezing. Starvation is starvation. Ask your Emperor if he does not agree."

Sura had to laugh to himself. The discussion was at an end. He would have some stories to tell in the Senate House, but nothing else was gained from his mission.

"Very well," Sura said. "Will your King not talk to us directly?"

Diegis shook his head. "He will not. He will talk only to Caesar."

"Then perhaps one day they will talk," Sura said. He turned to Livianus. "Our work here is finished, Tiberius."

"Waste of time," Livianus said with a scowl. "Now we get back to fighting, eh?"

Diegis gave him a cold smile. "We shall meet again on the field of battle, perhaps."

Livianus returned the hostile look.

Sura stood up and motioned to Tsiru. "We should leave before we have bloodshed. Give my regards to your King, General Diegis."

"And also to your Emperor, Senator. Perhaps we shall talk again. Captain Tsiru will give you safe passage back to your men."

There would be no peace in Dacia just yet.

> Chapter 11

The Captive Princess

Piatra Alba, Dacia, November 101 AD

Waiting for Davi to arrive at the fort of Piatra Alba made Tanidela wish she had stayed with her sister and Queen Andrada in Sarmizegetusa. The fort was cold and drafty whenever the wind picked up. She had Tyra to keep her busy, and also the help of two servants. Lipa was a middle aged nursemaid. She was very helpful with the baby but not one for interesting conversation. Seba was a handmaiden who was livelier, but was barely fifteen years old and still learning how to do the basic tasks of her job. Tanidela missed adult company with whom she had some things in common.

Her little girl was picking up a few words, much of it from Seba who enjoyed playing with the child. Tyra was crawling energetically and would soon be walking. Her mother looked forward to getting her to Sarmatia, which had wide open fields of grass and wildflowers. It was good horse country. Good open country to run around in.

Davi should have arrived almost a week ago, and still they waited. He was engaged in some military conflict with the Romans. Strangely she did not worry about his physical safety, for he seemed unbeatable as a warrior. Sarmatians fought as heavy cavalry. Both riders and horses wore armor uniquely made in Sarmatia. It did not make them invincible, but it did make them hard to kill.

"Would you like more warmed milk, my lady?" Seba asked. She had warmed a pan of cow's milk over a small fire. Lightly sweetened with honey, it was a good drink to ward off the chills.

"No, thank you, Seba," Tanidela said. "If I have any more milk I will turn into a cow."

Seba giggled. She turned to the older woman. "Would you like more, Lipa?"

"Sure," the nursemaid said, holding out her cup. "I don't mind. I already am a cow."

That brought a laugh from both women.

"Lipa, you made a joke!" Tanidela exclaimed.

Seba filled the woman's outstretched cup with the hot milk. "Oh, don't let her fool you. She knows how to be funny, she's just shy. Isn't that right, Lipa?"

Before Lipa could reply they all turned towards the door, opened noisily and hurriedly by Loran. The Sarmatian warrior was captain of their cavalry escort and their chief protector until Davi arrived. Loran was tense, his eyes wild.

"Romans!" he announced in a rush. "We must leave immediately, my lady!"

Tanidela snapped quickly out of her bored stupor. "But, Davi! My husband is expecting –"

"No time, my lady!" Loran protested. "A Roman army is marching this way and will be here soon. If we don't ride away now we'll be trapped here."

Tanidela swung into action. "I will take Tyra. Lipa, you bring her things. Seba, take clothes, only those you can carry yourself. Now!"

They cleared the room in a minute and ran outside the small house. The courtyard was a mass of people moving in all directions, not chaotically but in an organized hurry. The fort's defenders, who numbered in the several hundreds, ran to their positions on the walls or other locations in the fort.

The twenty Sarmatian cavalry riders rushed to their horses. Some brought the horses around for Tanidela and her party. Her favorite horse, a chestnut mare, was bridled, saddled, and ready for her to mount. One of the men stepped forward to assist her.

Loran cursed very loudly, which startled the three women and made Tanidela pause. They turned to match his gaze and saw the massive gate of the fort close shut. Several men struggled to put the large iron reinforced crossbar in place, strong enough to resist the assault from a battering ram. Nobody would leave the fort now.

"What is happening?" Tanidela asked Loran, her eyes shining with anger and fear. "Why did we have no earlier warning?"

"You must return to the house, my lady," he said. "We cannot leave now so we must shelter in place."

"Yes, we must," she said. "You will come with me, Captain, because I need some answers."

When they were settled back inside the house the baby Tyra was crying loudly, upset by the agitation of the adults around her. The nursemaid took her from her mother to rock and comfort her.

Loran provided what little information he knew.

"The Romans surprised us, my lady. They attacked quickly with large numbers of cavalry. They must have killed our scouts before they could give warning."

"But are we not safer inside the fort than outside on the road?"

"Yes, my lady, we are safer for now." The man stopped to collect his thoughts. "We don't know yet how large this Roman army might be. They attack Dacian forts with a full legion or more. That is five thousand men, my lady, and will overwhelm the fort's defenses."

Tanidela sat down in a chair, suddenly tired. Davi would not reach them now. She might never see him again.

"So, we wait," she said.

"We wait," said Loran. "And we fight."

Titus Lucullus watched from horseback as the two legions of infantry moved towards the fort of Piatra Alba. As usual the auxiliary units were in front, the Roman legionnaires behind them. They would be positioned just outside the range of the Dacian archers on the walls. The large siege artillery and smaller field artillery were left clear lines of fire to the fort. The artillery bombardment would begin as soon as the legions were in place.

"If this weather holds up, Titus, I want the fort sacked within three days," said General Maximus, watching from his saddle.

"Yes, sir," Lucullus acknowledged. "We outnumber the defenders ten to one, perhaps fifteen to one. We have overwhelming advantage in artillery. It will be a short siege."

"And they have the advantage of stone walls," Maximus said, with a quick nod towards the fort. The walls were bristling with archers and spearmen. "That's not marble, is it?"

"No, General," Titus said. "It is granite, I believe. White marble would be much whiter, and also the cost would be absurd to make those fort walls."

"Ah, the cost," Maximus said casually. He had the much superior forces in this battle and no concerns about its outcome. "Decebalus has no cares about the cost. The streets of Sarmizegetusa are paved with gold, so I hear?"

Titus gave him an amused smile. "I can swear to the fact, based on personal experience walking on those streets, that the streets of gold of Sarmizegetusa are a myth, General."

Laberius Maximus gave a grunt and turned his eyes back to the walls of his enemy.

"Hit them with artillery as soon as ready. Build a large number of ladders, Titus. We shall need them."

"Assault the walls tomorrow, General?"

"Yes. We scale the walls at first light. As you said, let's make it a short siege."

"Yes, sir," Lucullus agreed. Scaling well defended stone walls was always costly, but results were achieved quickly.

The large and heavy boulders, launched from catapults positioned eight hundred feet away, started to fall on Piatra Alba one hour after the Roman army arrived. They could not break through the thick and sturdy outer walls of the fort, but smashed through buildings inside as if the roofs and walls of houses were children's toys. They caved in roofs and crushed those inside. Ballistae hurled rocks and iron bolts. The smaller field artillery pieces, scorpions and carrobalistae, added a barrage of arrows and sharp metal bolts.

Each legion was assigned thirty artillery pieces. The fort suddenly faced an onslaught from sixty of these machines of destruction. The defenders returned fire with eight carrobalistae from the ramparts on top of the walls, but these could not begin to match the combined firepower of two Roman legions.

"Oh!" Seba cried out, raising both hands above her head to shield from falling straw and dust from the thatched roof above them. Some projectile had hit a glancing blow off one of the outside walls of the house, but it was enough to shake the entire structure. Tanidela and Lipa lowered their heads to prevent the falling debris from getting into their eyes, the nursemaid bending over the baby to shield her with her body. Loran was in the room with them, and would stay by Tanidela's side to the end.

"Is there a safer place to move to?" Tanidela asked him.

"No, my lady," he replied. "The Roman artillery is firing at us from different directions. This house is as safe a place as any."

"I pray to Zamolxis to keep us safe," Lipa said. She was Dacian and would never abandon faith in the Dacian god.

"Yes," Tanidela agreed. "Pray hard."

Outside the house men readied themselves for the infantry assault yet to come. Supplies were put in place including very large numbers of arrows and spears for the defenders on the walls. Water buckets had to be filled and carried up, for there would be fire arrows and fires to put out.

Three hundred archers and four hundred spearmen defended the fort of Piatra Alba. They would defend their fort to the death. They would fight for Dacia, and for each other. Every warrior also knew that in this battle they were fighting for something more, something that put fire in their hearts and steel in their spines. They were fighting for a princess of Dacia. They were, each and every one, fighting to protect Tanidela sister of King Decebal.

In the early morning two cohorts of auxiliary infantry approached the fort at a steady walk. Some among the thousand men carried long ladders for scaling the walls. As soon as they were within range the defenders on the walls loosened a rain of arrows and spears on their formations. Now the battle was on.

Some of the auxilia soldiers carried their shields raised over their heads, in imitation of the Roman testudo formation. Unfortunately for them neither the quality of their shields, or their armor, or their training, was even close to the quality enjoyed by the legionnaires. Dacian arrows and spears found unprotected faces, necks, legs, and arms. They would not stop the attackers but would substantially thin out their ranks.

"The second units are in place and ready to advance, sir," Lucullus informed General Maximus.

"Good. After these units are bloodied send in the second units."

"Yes, General."

Auxiliary infantry always led the attack and suffered the most casualties. Once they weakened the fort's defenders, by inflicting casualties and wearing down the enemy through sheer exhaustion, Maximus would send in units of legionnaires. At that moment the legionnaires were not needed however.

The attacking infantry placed their ladders against the walls and began the dangerous climb. Only the bravest or most foolish were willing to be among the first because it was almost certain they wound end up dead or injured. Archers on the ramparts had a clear shot at them not only from above but also from the sides. They wore leather armor, not metal, and sometimes no armor at all. A Dacian archer shooting from close range could not miss such easy targets.

The attackers who reached the top of the ladders faced a swarm of angry defenders armed with spears, axes, and swords. Hundreds of attackers were dying in the assault. Almost none made it onto the ramparts, and those who did were quickly killed by spears or thrown back down over the wall.

"We are in for a difficult fight, Titus."

General Maximus made the observation in a casual tone. He had been in many battles in his military career, and knew well that some battles were more difficult than others.

"We are indeed, sir," Titus replied. "They are defending with a fierce passion."

"That they are, brave fools," Maximus said. "The outcome will still be the same. In the end, we crush them."

Lucullus glanced up at the sky, clear and blue except for a few white clouds. There was no sign of any dark clouds on the horizon. "The weather is holding up, General. Mars Ultor smiles on us."

"And well he should! Caesar sacrifices to Mars Ultor every day, as do I. We are the beloved of the gods, Titus."

"Yes, sir. As we should be," Lucullus said, and believed it utterly and completely.

Maximus glared towards the fort, a frown on his face. "The attack is losing its fire. Send in the second units."

"Immediately, General." Titus turned to a messenger with orders. It was important to keep pressure on the defenders, to wear them down. He did not want to give them rest or hope.

At sundown the Roman attack on the walls slowed down, then stopped altogether. The attackers pulled back out of bow range. Men drifted in small and large groups to their camps for the night. The battle was over for this day.

Large patches of the ground below the walls were littered with bodies and slick with blood. The dead soldiers would be cleared away in the night to prepare the ground for the next day's attack. The few high ranking officers who perished were given individual burials. The rest, in the hundreds, would be laid to rest in large graves.

Inside Piatra Alba most of the exhausted defenders on the wall walked down wooden steps to ground level for a meal and, later, a few hours of sleep. Sentries were posted to guard against an unlikely Roman night attack. Many of the Dacian defenders nursed minor wounds that surgeons would tend to. Those who had suffered major wounds were already dead or soon would be.

Loran returned to the women's house from a quick tour of the fort. He was grim faced and solemn but not dejected.

"Our soldiers fought well, my lady," he reported. "The Romans came in waves and we beat them back every time. They will attack again tomorrow, so we must do the same then."

"Our losses?" Tanidela asked.

"Perhaps two hundred," Loran guessed. "The enemy lost closer to three or four hundred."

"There are many more of them than us," she said.

Loran nodded. "That is true. By counting their flags we estimate two full legions."

"So, ten thousand Romans?"

Loran nodded again.

"Then how do we beat them?"

"We cannot beat them, my lady, they are simply too many. We can only survive. And the way to survive is to make their losses too heavy for them to accept."

"And hope they go away?"

"Yes, and hope they go away." Loran paused and gave her a half smile. "It has happened before, in other battles at other forts."

"If Zamolxis wills it, it shall be so," Tanidela said.

Loran gave her a look and paused, unsure if he should say what was on his mind.

Tanidela noticed. "What is it?"

"Our soldiers take strength from two sources," he said.

"Yes?"

"As ever, they take strength from Zamolxis. And now they also take strength from you, my lady."

That took her by surprise. "From me? How do you mean?"

"Every soldier in this fort, man and woman, feels a fierce pride to protect you. You are a princess of Dacia, my lady," Loran concluded, and gave her a small bow.

Tanidela sat back in her chair, gathering her thoughts.

"Captain Loran is right," Lipa said. "I feel that pride, also."

Tanidela gave her a grateful smile. "Thank you, Lipa." She stood up and turned to Loran. "I must see our soldiers and talk to them. You will escort me."

"Yes, my lady. I am honored to do so."

"Don't leave us!" Seba protested, sounding like a frightened child.

Tanidela turned to her with a firm smile. "You stay here with Lipa and Tyra. You will all be safe until I return." She turned and followed Loran out the door.

The Dacian soldiers were surprised but very pleased to see Tanidela walking among them to greet them. They all stood as she approached, even the wounded.

"No! Do not rise for me!" she said to a man with a wounded arm, placing a hand on his shoulder. "All of you! Tend your wounds, finish your meals. I only want to see you. And greet you. And thank you."

As she mingled among the soldiers Tanidela greeted their smiles of joy with her own bright smiles. Most of the soldiers were men, but more than a few were women. The women had fought with spears, and their faces were grimy with sweat and dust just as much as the men. Some wore bloody bandages, just as the men.

Tanidela made her way around the inner wall of the fort, stopping to talk here and there with individuals and small groups. These were her people, and for the first time in her life she understood fully the strong sense of pride that Loran described just a short while ago. She shared their pride, their passion for life, their fierce independence. These were her people, and she was one of them. Being born into a royal family was simply an accident of birth.

As she made her walk around the fort Tanidela heard a few people calling out her name.

"Tanidela! Tanidela!"

These were not calls for attention, but simple calls of greeting. Some turned into calls filled with joy and pride.

"Tanidela! Tanidela!"

She turned and waved back to the callers, her own heart filled with joy and pride. More people picked up the calls and their voices grew louder.

"Tanidela! Tanidela! Tanidela!"

"What are they shouting in the fort?" Laberius Maximus wondered. He was seated at a table outside his tent finishing his evening meal. At that distance the voices sounded distant and muffled.

"It sounds like they are calling someone's name," Titus guessed.

"Whose name?"

"I cannot say, sir." Lucullus turned to the general's young aide, standing nearby. "Castor, your ears are sharper. Do you make it out?"

The young man turned to hear the distant voices better. "It sounds like they are saying tani dela, sir. Those must be Dacian words."

"What is a tani dela?" Laberius asked.

Titus' eyes grew wider. He strained to hear again.

"Lucullus, you look like you've seen a ghost," Maximus said.

Titus looked him in the eye. "It is not a matter of what, sir, but of who. I believe they are chanting Tanidela."

"Explain?"

"If I am correct, General, they are chanting the name of Tanidela. She is the sister of King Decebalus."

Maximus slammed his cup down on the table. "Jupiter's nuts! Are you certain?"

"It makes the most sense. What other woman named Tanidela would earn such an honor?"

"You may be right, Titus," Maximus conceded. "This makes it even more important that we capture the fort and capture this princess with it."

"Caesar would no doubt greatly appreciate being handed the sister of Decebalus as a captive," Lucullus said.

"Caesar," Maximus growled, "will have our heads if we lose her."

"That is also a possibility, sir."

"This is not a joke, Lucullus. I make it your responsibility to get me this fort," Maximus ordered. "Capture Piatra Alba and bring me the sister of Decebalus. Alive and unharmed!"

"Yes, sir," Titus agreed. "I shall make it my personal mission to bring her out unharmed. Tanidela is a prize beyond measure."

On the third day of the siege the Roman attackers were able to get some men on top of a small section of the wall. They were quickly and easily killed, and their bodies were thrown down to the ground to scatter their fellow attackers assembling below. On the fourth and fifth days of the siege the Romans killed more defenders, but suffered heavy losses as well. The Dacian defenders were down to almost half their original number, and still they fought on the wall like demons.

"They are slow to replace their losses in all sections of the walls," Lucullus observed. "They are stretched too thin and have no reserves."

"Very well, Titus," Maximus said. "They are at the breaking point, so let's break them. This morning we will attack with two cohorts of legionnaires, then two more in the second wave."

"I agree, General. They will break today."

"Have you given the men their orders?"

"Yes, sir. I have given orders that no women are to be killed or abused when the men get inside the walls."

"Very good. As soon as the gates are opened, Titus, take a unit of legionnaires and go inside the fort yourself."

A heavy barrage of Roman artillery fire started the morning attack. The legionnaires approached slowly. They marched in tight squares, in the defensive testudo formation that was ideal for approaching the enemy in a siege attack. They had the right equipment and also the discipline to form a wall of shields, overlapping each other, that would protect them from arrow and spear attacks from overhead and from all sides.

By late morning the Dacian defenders realized they were losing the battle. The Roman troops attacked in force in too many places for the Dacians to defend. Legionnaires climbed over the walls and fought their way, as disciplined units, towards the gates. The Dacians on the ground were not equipped or trained well enough to fight Roman heavy infantry.

Once the gate guards were killed and the gates were pushed open, the battle was all but over. The last remaining Dacians on the walls retreated to a corner of the fort to consolidate their forces and fight on. Very few would be taken prisoner.

"Stay inside this house, my lady, until the Romans arrive," Loran said. He was resigned to his fate but determined to do what he could to protect the women. "Stay in place here. You will find only chaos and death outside the house."

"I understand," Tanidela said. "You cannot protect us any longer. Go and save yourself."

Loran gave her a fierce look. "When the Romans arrive do not fight them or they will kill you. Tell them, very loudly, that you are Dacian royalty. Do you understand?"

Loran turned his head towards the door because the sounds of fighting from outside were getting close. His men were still standing guard outside the door.

"Yes, I know what to do," Tanidela replied. "Now go. And thank you Loran for everything you have done for us."

"Farewell, my lady," Loran said. He gave a bow towards all three women, then turned quickly and went out the door.

Tanidela picked up Tyra in her arms and ushered the other two women to the far side of the room, as far from the door as possible. Tyra was asleep. Lipa stayed surprisingly calm. Sepa looked scared, her hands trembling. Roman voices shouted outside the house.

"Be brave, Seba," Tanidela told her. "You will be all right."

The door burst open, kicked in by a Roman soldier. The baby Tyra woke up and started crying loudly. A grizzled veteran legionnaire stepped into the room with a drawn and bloodstained gladius in his right hand. He was followed close behind by a younger soldier.

"Well, what is this?" the older soldier asked above the loud cries of the baby. The younger man stepped beside him, his sword in attack position. Both men stared intently at Tanidela, who was adorned with jewelry on both arms and around her neck.

"I am a princess of Dacia," she told them loudly. "I wish to speak with your superior officer."

Tanidela spoke to them in Dacian. The Dacian language and Latin were surprisingly similar however, and diplomats and tradespeople often communicated very well even without interpreters. She hoped they would understand the important key words.

"What did she say?" the young soldier asked.

"Something about our superior officer," the veteran soldier said with a scowl. He took two steps forward and used his sword to point at Tanidela's gold bracelets. "I won't hurt you. You give me some of your gold. You understand? Gold?" He took another step forward and pointed again with the tip of the gladius.

Lipa moved quickly and unexpectedly and stepped in front of Tanidela, shielding her.

"Lipa, no," Tanidela said calmly but forcefully. "Let me talk to them." In her arms Tyra wailed even louder.

"This pig will not touch you," Lipa said.

The young soldier laughed. "I think she called you a pig, Marcus!"

Marcus moved menacingly towards them, holding the gladius out in front. "Move aside, you sow, or I'll make you squeal like a pig."

"Stop!"

The loud and ferocious voice from the doorway made everyone freeze in place.

Titus Lucullus stormed into the room, four other legionnaires right behind. He stepped in front of Marcus and his companion and turned on them in a fury. "Touch these women and Caesar will have you skinned alive!"

"Yes, sir! Sorry, sir!" Marcus stumbled to get the words out.

"I will deal with you two later. Now get out. Out!"

Titus watched them rush out and quickly calmed down. When he turned to face the women he had the calm poise of a diplomat. Lipa stepped aside. Tyra, startled by the shouting and sensing her mother relax, stopped crying.

"You are the lady Tanidela?" Titus asked.

"Yes, I am. Thank you for your assistance. And who are you?"

"I am Titus Lucullus. I have spoken with your brother Diegis many times. Unfortunately," Titus added with a smile, "I have not had the same opportunity to know your other brother, Decebal,"

Tanidela smiled back. "Perhaps someday you will, in better times. Yes, Titus, I know your name. Diegis spoke well of you."

"And I think highly of him. Now, Lady Tanidela, I am happy to do a service for you. You will come with me, please?"

"What service is that, Titus? Am I now your prisoner? Guest?"

"Guest, my lady. But not my guest, I am not so highly ranked. For the present you are the guest of General Laberius Maximus. When we arrive at Caesar's camp you shall be the guest of Trajan Caesar."

"I see," Tanidela said. "This child is my daughter, Tyra. These women are my servants and under my protection. I ask that they also be given the same guest courtesies."

"Of course, Lady Tanidela," Titus agreed. "Your family and your household shall have the same protections. Now we must go, General Maximus is eager to see you."

"And the rest of the people in the fort?" Tanidela asked, but knew that it was a foolish question even as she asked it.

Titus shrugged. "If they surrender they might live. I am told that Dacian warriors very seldom surrender, however."

"No, they do not," Tanidela said. "They prefer for their souls to live a life of immortality in the kingdom of Zamolxis rather than live on this earth in a life of slavery."

"Such are the fortunes of war, my lady."

Tanidela found there was nothing more left to say. She gathered her daughter and her servants, and prepared herself for what she knew would be a long journey.

Two days later the army of General Laberius Maximus marched away from Piatra Alba. They suffered heavy casualties in a very difficult battle, but also destroyed the fort and its garrison. Just as importantly they captured a royal prisoner who was sister to King Decebalus of Dacia. The Emperor Trajan would decide her fate, because he alone best knew her worth.

Over two thousand died in the siege of Piatra Alba. Most were Roman auxiliary troops and legionnaires, however the entire Dacian garrison also perished. The Romans buried their dead in large graves. No one was left on their side to bury the Dacians. They were left for the beasts of the field and the carrion of the skies, because such were the fortunes of war.

Six days later Prince Davi of the Roxolani tribe of Sarmatians arrived with three hundred cavalry from a campaign to the west that had lasted much longer than planned. He found the fort of Piatra Alba in a wrecked condition and the Dacian garrison destroyed. If he had arrived sooner his troops would have made no difference against the two legions of General Maximus.

After searching for hours among the corpses, Davi finally decided that his wife and child were not among them. He had no idea what their fate was or where they might be.

Happily some answers came only hours later when old allies rode up to greet them. To Davi's great surprise their leader was Loran, the captain of Tanidela's former cavalry escort. After the fort of Piatra Alba fell and the gates were opened by the Romans, Loran and his men made a desperate charge on horseback to fight their way out through the open gates. Only six of the twenty riders survived.

Loran was certain that Tanidela, her daughter Tyra, and her two servants were taken captive by General Maximus. As a member of Dacian royalty she would be treated well. This was the best news Davi could have hoped for. Perhaps he could work with King Decebal to negotiate with the Romans. Perhaps. At least they were alive, and where there was life there was hope.

> Chapter 12

Decebal's Gambit

Sarmizegetusa, November 101 AD

News of the attack on Piatra Alba and the capture of Tanidela was delivered to the royal court of Dacia by Prince Davi. It was received by a grim and saddened King Decebal and Queen Andrada. They met with the King's Council in the throne room to hear the latest reports from the Dacian scouts who were following the Roman army of General Maximus.

The generals Diegis, Drilgisa, and Sinna were leading the Dacian troops in the mountains. They were keeping the Romans at bay and making raids on isolated Roman positions. Vezina as always was at Decebal's right hand. Tsiru collected and coordinated information from all the scouts.

"Maximus marches east at a good pace," Tsiru reported. "He will match up with the main army of Emperor Trajan in Banat, we think."

"We can be sure of that," Vezina added. "He is finished with his raids on Dacian forts in Banat. Also, his siege of Piatra Alba cost him heavily in Roman casualties."

"Upwards of a thousand casualties, Loran estimates," Davi said. He turned to look at King Decebal. "The city defenders put up a fierce resistance to protect Tanidela."

Decebal gave a grim nod. "Has anyone seen Tanidela travelling with Maximus, Tsiru?"

"No, Sire. Our scouts could not get that close. Also she would be travelling with the general's command staff and under heavy guard."

"Will she be treated well?" Queen Andrada asked, worried. Over the past twenty years she and Tanidela had been like sisters.

"Yes, Trajan will make certain of that," Decebal answered. "She is his most important prisoner."

Davi looked to Vezina and Decebal. "Might there be a way to trade for her freedom?"

Vezina shook his head, sadly.

"There is no one to exchange for her that Trajan would be willing to accept," Decebal said. "Except me."

"Or me," Andrada added.

"You are not going anywhere," Decebal said, stating the obvious. The Queen of Dacia would never be offered into captivity.

"I would exchange myself and gladly," Davi declared.

Decebal gave him a solemn nod. "I know you would, brother. However Trajan's fight is with me and Dacia. It is not with you and the Roxolani, even though you are allies of Dacia."

Davi sat back in his chair, utterly frustrated. He knew that Decebal was right. For the first time in his life he felt powerless.

"So what do we do?" Andrada asked.

"We continue to fight, My Queen," Vezina answered. "Emperor Trajan has discovered that we're a tough nut to crack, and winter is approaching."

"Will he attack us in the winter?" the Queen asked.

"No, he will not," Decebal said. "He will not risk having his army trapped and cut off in our mountains over the winter."

"I agree, Sire," Vezina added. "He will reach the same conclusion as General Julianus. A Roman army caught in the Dacian mountains in the heart of winter will perish."

"I don't wish to sit around until springtime!" Davi exclaimed. "I want to go after the Romans who took Tanidela and my daughter!"

"We are not going to sit here until springtime," the King declared in a forceful voice.

"What is your plan, Sire?" Vezina asked.

"We attack the bastards."

Roman camp, Dacian mountain valley, November 101 AD

General Laberius Maximus was the Emperor's most trusted military advisor. They knew each other for many years and agreed on military strategy. Most importantly to Trajan, General Maximus had a history of achieving results. Caesar Trajan himself had a well-known history of military victories, and he demanded the same from his generals.

General Maximus rejoined the Emperor's army with his troops bloodied, but still feeling victorious after their campaign against the Dacian forts. The Roman army was systematically reducing Dacian fortifications and decreasing the number of Dacian troops available to King Decebalus. Caesar already had Decebalus outnumbered, and he would continue to sap away the Dacian king's military strength.

The setting sun cast long shadows on Trajan's group of officers meeting outside his military tent. Wine was already flowing freely. Licinius Sura and Hadrian stood with the Emperor, reviewing a large map on the table. The main body of the army would be moving south in the next two weeks, which required a great deal of planning and coordination of men, animals, and equipment.

"Here he comes now," Sura announced, looking up from the map with a grin on his face. It was clear to all whom he meant. Maximus was the hero of the hour.

The hero's party included Titus Lucullus, and also three Dacian women escorted by four guards. The slim and still elegantly dressed woman walking in front of the other two was cradling a baby to her bosom. She walked with an attitude of quiet but strong dignity, the look of a woman who was used to being treated with deference.

"Welcome back, Laberius," the Emperor greeted his general. "I congratulate you on your victories."

Maximus replied with a small bow. "All for the greater glory of Rome, Caesar. I am happy to be back in Caesar's council."

"You bring a guest, General?" Trajan asked with a nod towards the women.

Lucullus led Tanidela gently forward. "Caesar, I present the lady Tanidela, Princess of Dacia and sister to King Decebalus."

"Welcome, lady," Trajan greeted her with a polite smile. "I have been waiting for your arrival so that I may speak with you."

Tanidela acknowledged his greeting with a polite smile of her own. "I would be honored to speak with you, Caesar."

"The child is your daughter? What is her name?"

"Her name is Tyra, Caesar. It means to flow…"

"Like a river," Trajan finished with a smile.

"Do you speak our language, Caesar?"

Trajan shook his head. "Our languages are similar enough. I can understand much of the Dacian language, and I seldom need the aid of an interpreter."

Tanidela nodded. "As I can understand many words in the Latin language, Cesar."

"We must speak freely," Trajan said. "Will you give your child to your servant, and join me in my tent?"

Lipa took half a step forward, looking alarmed. Tanidela turned to her and fixed her with her eyes. "It is all right, Lipa. Caesar and I shall talk. You will stay here and hold Tyra until I return."

"Yes, my lady," the older woman acknowledged, then reached out to take the baby.

"Maximus, Sura, Hadrian, you shall join me in my tent," Trajan said. "Lucullus, you will escort the Lady Tanidela to join us."

"Yes, Caesar," Titus replied. "This way, lady, please."

And so Tanidela, younger sister of King Decebal of Dacia, joined the Roman high military command to walk into the royal tent to be interviewed by Emperor Trajan of Rome.

Three hours later Trajan had a more detailed understanding of the Dacian royal family, their military command, and their nobility. He was polite and gracious, and had no need whatsoever for threats or coercion. For her part, Tanidela did not need to be coerced. She had no military knowledge that would endanger Dacian forces if it fell into Roman hands. She spoke freely of her family, including her brother the King. The Emperor held her life and the life of her child in his hands. She had no reason to lie and no desire to do so.

Trajan drained the last of his fourth cup of wine, sipped from a silver goblet with exquisite engravings on its sides. His thirst for wine was sated and, for the moment at least, so was his curiosity. The interview was nearing its end.

Tanidela sat quietly on a chair opposite the Emperor, sipping cool water from her own silver goblet. She did not drink wine. Hundreds of years ago Zamolxis taught the people of Dacia that wine dulls men's senses, and so they drank it sparingly and on special occasions. She watched politely and patiently as Trajan, Sura, and the young Hadrian drank cup after cup like thirsty travelers after a long day's journey. Maximus and Titus Lucullus drank more sparingly.

"What will convince your brother to submit to Rome and make peace?" Trajan asked, getting to his final point.

Tanidela took a moment to compose her answer to this crucial question, which she knew was the main purpose of this interview. "If you are asking, Caesar, what would make Decebal surrender?" She slowly shook her head. "The answer is, nothing and no one. He will never surrender Dacia."

The Emperor paused to pour himself more wine. "He signed a peace treaty with Rome before, as you know. That was with Emperor Domitian," he reminded her.

Licinius Sura snorted with derision. "He signed a treaty that was all in his favor! And that fool Domitianus agreed to it, which caused Rome many years of grief."

Trajan was annoyed by this undiplomatic outburst but gave his friend a patient smile. "I am well aware of that, Licinius. The reason we are here, after all, is to correct Domitian's mistake."

That statement took Tanidela by surprise. "Are you not here to conquer Dacia, Caesar?"

"I am here to bring glory to Rome, Lady Tanidela. If that requires me to conquer Dacia, then I shall conquer Dacia. If your brother the King submits to me and makes a just peace with Rome, then perhaps it will not be necessary to conquer Dacia."

"I see," Tanidela replied. "What Caesar considers a just peace King Decebal might consider surrender. My answer is as before, Caesar."

"Is there no one who can talk sense to your brother?" Maximus asked.

"Your brother Diegis, perhaps?" Titus suggested helpfully.

Tanidela gave him a half smile. "They are like two peas in a pod. Diegis is just as proud and stubborn as his brother."

Trajan put his empty cup on the table and stood up. The interview was over. "I thank you for your honesty and you graciousness, Lady Tanidela. Your reputation precedes you as the beautiful rose with thorns. I suspect the thorns part is exaggerated?"

"It is a silly reputation, Caesar, but the people seem to like it."

Trajan nodded. "Now I must see to my army. And you must begin your journey."

Tanidela was taken aback. "Journey, Caesar? Am I no longer your guest?"

"Oh, you are my honored guest, and shall remain so. But not," he paused and gestured outside, "not in these brutal army camps."

"Where do I journey to, Caesar?"

Trajan gave her a kind smile. "You and your child will travel, as my guests, to Rome."

Tanidela let the shock of his announcement sink in. She would never see Davi again, or her family, or Dacia. She pushed away her disappointment and dealt with the practical manners. "And what of my servants? Lipa is an excellent nursemaid, and Seba is growing into a very capable handmaiden."

Trajan laughed. "When we were outside your nursemaid would have stabbed me in the neck if she had a knife handy. No, I will assign you a new nursemaid and a new handmaiden. They will be Roman servants, loyal to me first. Surely you understand why?"

Tanidela nodded. "And what happens to Seba and Lipa?"

The Emperor shrugged. "They are prisoners of General Maximus, which makes them his property. He will do with them as he wishes."

Tanidela looked to Maximus but the general was already walking away. Titus Lucullus was more helpful.

"They will be sold into slavery, Lady Tanidela. That is the fate of women who become prisoners of war." He noted her look of worry and spoke to her more quietly. "I will have them placed with a good family in Moesia. You have my word."

Hadrian, who had kept very quiet, came to join them. As the youngest member of Trajan's staff his role was to listen, learn, and run errands as needed. He was about to run another errand, but a very important one.

"Lady Tanidela," Hadrian greeted her with a bright and charming smile. "I shall be travelling with you on our journey to Rome. I am made Caesar's imperial quaestor, his messenger as it were, to inform the Senate of Rome about Caesar's military campaign."

"I see," Tanidela said. Her world was changing too quickly and her mind was spinning.

"Hadrianus is an excellent travel companion," Titus said. "No shortage of poetry and Greek philosophy with him around!"

Hadrian ignored the tease. "That older and distinguished looking gentleman over there, as you have learned, is Licinius Sura. He will be travelling with us also. Once home he will run for election for consul of Rome."

"And win, no doubt," Titus said.

"And win, no doubt," Hadrian agreed. Trajan's chosen candidate for consul of Rome was guaranteed to win election.

"We should go now, Lady," Lucullus told her. "You will be leaving in the morning. You should make travel preparations for yourself and your daughter."

"Yes, you are right," Tanidela said and sat up quickly. There was no time for talk, she needed to take action.

"Until morning, then," Hadrian said with a gallant bow.

"Until morning," Tanidela said, then gave a last glance towards the Emperor. Trajan paused his conversation with Sura and gave her a nod in farewell.

Tanidela followed Titus Lucullus outside into the cool evening air. Her life was turned upside down. Decebal, Decebal, she thought to herself. What are your pride and stubbornness doing to us all?

Ister (Danubius) River, Moesia, January 102 AD

The ice of the frozen Ister River was thick enough to support the weight of the Dacian and Bastarnae soldiers marching across it. It was strong enough to support the weight of the Sarmatian cavalry leading their skittish horses across the ice. It was sturdy enough to support the supply wagons being pulled by mules and horses. Yes the ice was thick enough in many places to support the crush of men and animals moving across it. However in some places, the treacherous places, it was not.

The armies of Dacians, Bastarnae, and Sarmatians crossed the frozen river from north to south, Dacia into Moesia. King Decebal was waging war against the Roman forts and settlements there.

Emperor Trajan had his army camped hundreds of miles to the west along the Danubius in southern Dacia. Caesar was waiting for additional legions to arrive to replace the troops lost at Tapae and in the fighting in the Dacian mountains. He planned to shelter in camp and weather out the winter snow and cold. Decebal was going to spoil Caesar's plans.

"Somebody should build a bridge across this river," Chief Fynn said. He was on horseback, along with Decebal and Davi, watching the army crossing from the north bank of the river.

"Nobody can build a bridge that long!" Davi exclaimed. The Ister was a wide and mighty river that ran from Germania in the west all the way through Scythia in the east.

"Nobody has tried, perhaps," the Bastarnae chief continued. "Think of it! We could cross the Ister in all seasons, in summer as well as winter"

Decebal shrugged. "Dacians have been crossing the Ister in the wintertime for generations. So have the Bastarnae, Fynn."

"Indeed we have. Still, it would benefit –"

A loud cracking sound from the river instantly demanded all their attention. It was the gut wrenching sound of ice breaking, followed by the yelling of men and screaming of animals as they plunged into freezing water. One of the supply wagons broke through the ice and took several nearby men with it. The river flowed swiftly underneath the ice, and those who fell in were quickly swept away under the ice and would never be seen again. There was nothing to be done except to go wide around that patch of ice and pray to avoid hitting another weak spot of thin ice.

Chief Fynn cursed under his breath. "Poor devils. As I was saying, it would be a benefit to not lose men and horses in a winter crossing over the ice."

Decebal patted the neck of his horse, the animal acting spooked from the distressed cries of the animals that just perished. "I will not argue with you, Fynn. If you can find such a master bridge builder send him to me and I will shower him with gold."

Davi urged his horse forwards towards the frozen riverbank. "We should cross now, and damn the thin ice. There are Romans on the other side waiting to be killed."

They dismounted and led the horses across, slowly and carefully, keeping a good distance between themselves. The supply wagons were most at risk but there were thin spots where even a horse would prove too heavy. It was a risk that had to be taken because they were invading the Roman province of Moesia again.

Roman camp, southern Dacia, January 102 AD

Emperor Trajan was pleased to see two new legions arriving to his winter camp on the Danubius. The reinforcements for his army were Legio I Flavia Minerva and Legio XI Claudia, and both were placed under Trajan's personal command. They would replace the troops lost in the battle of Tapae the previous summer.

Trajan had to re-draw his plans again for the invasion of Dacia. The enemy was stronger and more determined than he originally thought. No matter. He had the advantages in men and resources, and time was on his side.

With Licinius Sura back in Rome, Trajan's closest friend on his staff was General Gnaeus Longinus. He was an old friend and former mentor to a young Trajan. With Sura gone, he was also the Emperor's new drinking partner.

"The news is that Licinius is newly elected as a consul of Rome. A happy day for him," Longinus said in a pleasant tone.

Trajan raised his wine goblet in a toast. "To the continued good health and happiness of Licinius! He has more than enough money, but serving as consul is good for his pride."

"Ah, his pride," Longinus chuckled. "Sura has arrogance, what need does he have for pride?"

"Unkind, Gnaeus!" Trajan exclaimed. "Every man worth his salt has pride. It drives us to excellence. Arrogance, on the other hand, is the bread of fools."

"You are not arrogant, Marcus, and certainly no fool."

"Sura is no fool either. He will manage the Senate well for me while we campaign."

A commotion outside the tent caught their attention. Trajan's young aide entered.

"A messenger from Moesia, Caesar. He seems in a rush."

"Well? Send him in then, never keep news waiting."

A moment later a tired looking captain of cavalry entered the tent. He stood stiffly and gave the Emperor a smart salute, right arm fully extended in front of him. "Hail, Caesar!"

"News from Moesia?" Trajan asked. "Speak up man. You look like you haven't slept for days."

"The Dacian army is attacking our camps in Moesia, Caesar. They caught us by surprise and overran our defenses."

"The Dacian army?" Trajan put down his wine. "Are you certain they are Dacian?"

"Yes, Caesar. Fifteen thousand men, we estimate. Dacian infantry, Sarmatian cavalry, and Bastarnae infantry included. They storm our forts and kill all inside."

"Is Decebalus leading them?" Longinus asked.

"I believe so, General. But I cannot say for certain."

Trajan gave a half smile. "This looks like something Decebalus would do. While we sit here he attacks our weakest positions. The man is full of surprises, eh?"

"Evidently so," Longinus agreed. "He is forcing our hand, Caesar. We cannot let him rampage while we wait here."

Trajan got to his feet, now fully alert and decisive. "At first light tomorrow I leave for Moesia with five legions. You will stay here with the remainder of the army, Gnaeus, and defend Banat. Decebalus might have more surprises for us."

"Of course, Caesar. Although if he took his army east, the main battle will be fought there."

"Stay on the alert here, Gnaeus. I will take the battle to Decebalus, and he will wish that he had stayed in Sarmizegetusa."

"Yes, Caesar," Longinus said. He knew that Emperor Trajan was on a mission now and that made him a terrible force. Decebalus had done something unforgivable. He made Trajan feel outmaneuvered, and that deeply stung Caesar's pride.

Sarmizegetusa, January 102 AD

Queen Andrada ruled the people of Sarmizegetusa more or less in the fashion of an indulgent parent. The people lived responsible and simple lives, and did not require much ruling. Their day to day lives centered on family life. With Dacian men serving in the army of King Decebal, family life was matriarchal. Andrada trusted the women of the city to be practical and use good judgement in running the lives of their families.

The High Priest Vezina no longer travelled on military campaigns. He stayed in the city to oversee the training of priests of Zamolxis, and also to serve as Andrada's advisor. The Queen had known Vezina her entire life. She learned to trust his judgment completely, as King Decebal trusted him.

On this day the High Priest was assisting the Queen in planning a mission for Dacian diplomats. Tsiru, the former chief of scouts but now an advisor to the Queen, joined them. So did Dochia, sister of Decebal and a princess of Dacia. The four of them met around a table in the throne room. With Decebal and Diegis fighting in Moesia, they were the highest ranking officials in Sarmizegetusa.

An envoy had arrived from Queen Orica of the Sakae tribe of Scythians. The envoy was sent to begin discussions for a treaty with Dacia, which they all knew could be of vital interest for Dacia. Dacia would now send a royal envoy for discussions with the Queen. The

Scythians, located to the east of Sarmatia, were a vast people of many tribes. They would make a powerful ally in the war against Rome.

"What do we know about the Queen?" Andrada asked. "And who should we send as an envoy to treat with her?"

"She is a fierce ruler," Vezina replied emphatically.

Andrada gave him a wry smile. "I imagine she would have to be, to rule as a woman over the horse lords."

"Yes, that is so," the High Priest agreed. "She worships Hestia, the goddess of earth. She uses steam to release vapors from hemp, which gives her visions of the past and the future. If her prophets are wrong she burns them in a bonfire."

"Her prophets do not grow to a ripe old age, I take it?" Dochia said with a laugh.

"Not as old as me, surely," Vezina replied. "I would have turned to smoke many years ago."

"That would have been a pity, Your Holiness," Tsiru said.

"I repeat myself, Vezina," Andrada said. "Who should we send as the King's envoy?"

He gave her an easy smile. "I have already spoken to her."

"Her?"

Vezina turned to Dochia. "Are you still willing to make the long journey, My Lady?"

"I certainly am," Dochia replied, then looked to Andrada. "By the Queen's order, of course."

The Queen was taken aback. Dochia had not left Sarmizegetusa for many years. She had been in mourning over the death of her young son.

"This is something you wish to do, Dochia? Forgive me, I am not opposed, just surprised."

Dochia gave a solemn nod. "I am a princess of Dacia. It is time I did my duty as a member of the royal family."

"Princess Dochia is the best possible representative to meet with Queen Orica," Vezina explained. "She is the King's sister. She is wise and has the calm temperament of an able diplomat. And she would be able to talk with the Scythian queen woman to woman."

"I see. All good reasons," Andrada said. "I question, will you be safe?"

"Who is safe these days, Sister? We must fight this war in every way we can. This is my way."

"Very well, you have my blessing then," the Queen said. She turned to Tsiru. "You will escort Dochia to Scythia and back. Take as many cavalry as we can spare."

"Yes, My Queen," Tsiru agreed. He paused for a moment in thought. "I will take forty cavalry as the escort. We will not venture far south and should avoid the Roman patrols."

"That is a good plan," Vezina said. "You will reach Scythia by the middle of March and meet with their Queen. Return here by April."

"How soon can you leave?" Andrada wondered.

"Tomorrow," Dochia said firmly. "There is no time to be lost. Dacia needs allies, and the Scythians will make formidable allies."

"Yes, tomorrow," Tsiru said. He stood up and gave the Queen a small bow. "I will go and make preparations immediately."

"Yes, Tsiru, go," Andrada said. As he walked away she called after him. "Protect her well, Tsiru! We lost one princess to Roman custody, we cannot lose another."

He looked back with a smile and gave her a wave.

Andrada turned to Dochia and Vezina. "Now let's discuss terms for a treaty. What do we need? What does Scythia want?"

> Chapter 13

Dochia

Rome, February 102 AD

The Senate of Rome was called for a meeting by Lucius Licinius Sura, newly elected co-consul and recognized by all as the spokesperson for Emperor Trajan. Sura carried the designated authority of Trajan, and his job was to carry out Trajan's wishes in Rome.

The first business of the day for the Senate was to hear a report from Publius Aelius Hadrianus, whom everyone called Hadrian. The young man was Trajan's royal quaestor. Tall and powerfully built, with a full head of curly hair, he made an imposing physical presence. He did not have the authority or gravitas of Sura, being too young for that, however he was an official representative of Caesar and that alone earned him respect.

Hadrian was also married into Trajan's family. Many expected that he would, one day, likely be named as Trajan's heir and follow him as the next Caesar. He was a man to be taken seriously by the men of wealth and power in Rome.

After being introduced by Sura, Hadrian took command of the center of the chamber floor to address the distinguished assembly. He watched Trajan do this many times before. He knew the correct style and form. It pleased him greatly to stand as Caesar stood, and to speak for Caesar.

"The campaign in Dacia goes well," Hadrian announced in a clear and strong voice. "Our armies led by Caesar won a great victory in the battle of Tapae. We drove the Dacians and their barbarian allies back into the Dacian mountains. We destroyed many of the Dacian forts in the eastern and western parts of Dacia. Decebalus is severely weakened, and his military grows weaker every day."

A senator rose to his feet with a question. "What of the reports of fighting in Moesia?"

"There have been attacks against our forts," Hadrian replied. "We do not yet know how extensive. Caesar will send reinforcements if needed. The major campaign will be in the spring, when Caesar marches on Sarmizegetusa."

Another senator stood. "Given the size and the might of Caesar's army, many of us expected that Decebalus would be crushed by now. Why do we have this delay?"

"There is no delay," Hadrian answered in a voice of authority. "You lack understanding of military matters. We fight a Dacian army that in the past had not only matched but defeated Roman armies, for almost twenty years. They are led by a warrior king who, in the past, bested every Roman general that was sent to defeat him. Any man with military sense knows that this was never expected to be a fast or easy campaign."

The senator sat down, showered with calls of disapproval and scorn from many of the Trajan allies who were seated around him.

"Fathers of the nation, I tell you this now," Hadrian continued. "Decebalus is a strong leader and a wily military commander. He has been a thorn in the paw of the lion of Rome for much too long. Now, at last, he has met his superior in Caesar."

Hadrian paused to allow the senators to applaud and express their support. It always surprised him to see that the support was almost never unanimous. Caesar was Rome's savior, and still they were not satisfied? Why this delay, indeed.

"As I said, fathers of the nation, Caesar will press the military campaign in the spring. He will march on the Dacian's holy city and bring Decebalus to his knees. I shall return to Dacia before spring and assist Caesar in the battles to come. Before I go back," Hadrian paused and turned his body to acknowledge Sura, "I shall remain in Rome for the winter to assist the consuls Lucius Licinius Sura and Julius Ursus Servianus in implementing the many laws that Caesar instructed us to implement."

Sura acknowledged him in return with a nod. Hadrian paused again and looked up at the senators, now accepting his message without dissent. The complainers among them were very few and had little influence. Good. This was Trajan's Senate, and they would do as they were asked by Trajan's representatives.

Mountains of eastern Dacia, February 102 AD

Dochia and her cavalry escort made their way slowly over the narrow mountain roads. The late February weather was still frigid cold. Snow drifts covered sections of the roads. Tree branches bent low under the weight of snow and ice. The mountains of Dacia presented beautiful winter scenery, but also a deadly danger for those not well equipped to deal with it.

Tsiru rode at the head of the column of riders. As chief of scouts he had travelled these roads many times over the years. He planned their schedule so that they would cover as much distance as possible in the daytime, then reach one of the Dacian forts before nightfall. The forts provided shelter and warmth, food, and supplies. They also provided safety against the random patrols of Roman cavalry.

"How long to the next settlement, Tsiru?" Dochia asked, urging her horse forward to ride beside him. The sunlight was growing dim and evening was approaching.

"Not far, My Lady," he answered. "We shall arrive there within the half hour."

"Good. The horses are spent, they need to be watered and fed."

Her comment made Tsiru smile. Dochia was known as a practical woman with a heart of gold. She was a member of Dacian nobility, yet her first thought was for the wellbeing of their horses.

"We shall stay at the fort for two days and give the horses a rest," Tsiru said. "We still have two weeks of riding ahead of us. Spring is almost here and then travel will be easier."

"Very well, two days is fine. I could use a rest as well as the horses." Dochia sounded tired and cold. She enjoyed occasionally going for a ride on her favorite horse, but spending days after day in the saddle brought fatigue to any rider.

"Are you warm enough, My Lady?" Tsiru inquired politely.

"Warm enough," she replied. "But I think some of my toes are starting to go numb!"

"Ah! That is a small matter. An extra pair of socks should remedy that problem."

"If you would kindly lend me a pair of soldier's socks," Dochia said, "I can remedy the problem."

"Of course, My Lady."

They caught sight of the walls of the fort shortly after. This was not a large fort, housing perhaps two hundred defenders. Like almost all Dacian forts it had walls made with stone, and heavy wooden gates reinforced with iron. Wooden ramparts were built on top of the walls to allow for archers and spearmen to fight off attackers. The Roman invasion of Emperor Trajan stalled in part because it took time to assault and overwhelm these well defended forts guarding the mountain roads to Sarmizegetusa.

Tsiru stopped in front of the closed gates and looked up at the sentries on the wall. The gates would remain closed until the visitors were properly identified.

"I am Tsiru!" he shouted to the gate guards. "With me is the Lady Dochia! Open the gates!"

The captain of the guards stepped forward to the edge of the stone rampart. “I’d know your gravelly voice anywhere, Tsiru. Come inside and let us welcome the Lady properly!”

The heavy double gates were slowly swinging open even as he was speaking. They were heavy and massive and required teams of men skilled at their job to be worked efficiently.

The fort was crowded. Besides the two hundred soldiers it also housed another two hundred civilians, the wives and children of the military men. When fighting was expected the civilians were moved to camps and villages deep in the mountains. There had been no fighting during the winter months however, and so the civilians took shelter in the fort to be with their husbands and fathers.

The arrival of the royal visitor stirred a big commotion. Everyone except for the sentries on the walls turned out to greet them, which formed a large crowd in front of the large dining hall. King Decebal had visited the fort a number of times during his tours of the Dacian forts, but none of the local people had ever seen his sister Dochia.

The commander of the fort was a grizzled army veteran past forty years of age. He waited for Dochia and Tsiru in front of the soldiers’ dining hall, which was also the largest building in the fort.

“Welcome, Lady Dochia,” the man said and gave her a bow. “We are honored to be your hosts during your stay here.”

“Thank you,” Dochia replied. She turned to the crowd and raised her voice. “Thank you, everyone! Today I travel far from my home and my family. But I want you all to know that, in my heart, you are all my family! I thank you for this welcome, my Dacian family!”

The crowd cheered and applauded. Children made their way to the front to get a better look. Dochia greeted them with warm smiles. She wished that she had some small gifts to give them, but there were no such items among their supplies.

“Will you come inside the dining hall, My Lady?” the commander suggested. “We would be honored to have you join us.”

"At this moment you would honor me best with a hot bowl of soup," Dochia told him with a smile.

"Immediately, My Lady. Come this way please."

She followed him inside, Tsiru walking beside her. Their cavalry escorts were still busy stabling their horses. In the life of the cavalry the care of their mounts always came before the care of their riders.

Roman province of Moesia, February 102 AD

The Dacian army attacked the Roman fort with field artillery for just half of one day. They would then storm the walls using ladders, and a battering ram to beat down the fort's gate. As with most forts in Moesia this fort was defended by Roman auxiliary infantry. They were strengthened by a centuria of legionnaires, some eighty men to provide the fighting core for the units stationed there. The centurion in charge of the fort's defenses led his men to the walls to put up a desperate fight. The Dacian army was not taking any prisoners. This battle, they all knew, was a fight for their survival.

King Decebal had three main goals in this campaign. He wanted to punish Emperor Trajan for his aggression. He wanted to destroy the Roman forts and camps in Moesia and weaken Trajan militarily. And perhaps most important, he wanted to draw Trajan's army away from southern Dacia. Thus far in this campaign all three goals were being accomplished.

"Sinna, you will direct the horse archers behind the first wave of infantry," Decebal instructed his military council before the morning assault on the walls. Diegis, Buri, and Drilgisa were also there along with the general of cavalry. Tarbus stood beside General Drilgisa.

"Concentrate on killing the defenders on the gates to protect our ram. And, Sinna," Decebal continued, "no excessive heroics like last week."

Sinna gave a casual shrug. "Yes, Sire."

"That is not a suggestion but an order," the King commanded. "You will stay out of range of their archers! I need you to command our cavalry, not put arrows into Roman defenders and risk becoming a casualty yourself."

"I understand, Sire," Sinna replied respectfully. "I will comport myself as appropriate for a commander of troops."

"Meaning," Drilgisa said with a grin, "you won't do anything that stupid again?"

Sinna laughed. "Yes, that too."

Decebal looked around at the men awaiting his orders. "A strong army needs strong leadership. You are that leadership. Keep that in mind and do not risk your lives foolishly."

No one disagreed. The brief silence was broken by Tarbus clearing his throat before he spoke.

"I request to lead the assault on the walls this morning," he said, directing himself to the King. This request took everyone by surprise. Buri, his father, gave him an uneasy look.

"Why do you wish that?" Decebal asked.

"Because I believe that it is my duty," Tarbus said in a serious tone. "Because you are all great leaders, but before you became leaders you were first great warriors. I am told that when you fought in battle you always fought in the front line, Sire. Along with my father. You led from the front."

"Yes, I did," the King agreed. "That was a different time, Tarbus."

Tarbus shook his head. "Forgive me, Sire, but I must disagree. A soldier's duty does not change with the times. You were not a king then, but you were a general when you fought in the front lines. As do you, General Diegis, and you, General Drilgisa. And you, Father."

Decebal smiled at the young man's enthusiasm. "That decision will be made by your commanding officer, Tarbus. Perhaps you should ask General Drilgisa."

Drilgisa shot a quick glance at Buri, then turned to Tarbus. "You have my approval. Your heart is right, Tarbus. Go and kill Romans and help us take this fort."

Buri gave a nod. "You have my blessing also, my son. Keep your shield up and your eyes open."

"Thank you," Tarbus said gratefully. "I won't let you down."

"Now that that is settled," Diegis said, looking around, "can we go and take this bloody fort?"

One tactical advantage for the Dacian army was their very large numbers of archers. Between their foot archers and horse archers, almost half of the army was made up of bowmen. Foot archers could kill effectively at two hundred paces. Horse archers, who used a smaller and lighter bow, were effective from one hundred paces. At a range of fifty paces both were deadly accurate, not only in open field but also when attacking defenders on top of city walls.

When concentrating fire on designated sections of the walls they sent a withering swarm of arrows that either killed defenders or kept them pinned down behind their barriers. This made it easier for the soldiers who manned the battering ram to break down the gates, and for those who used ladders to scale the fort walls. The Roman archers on the walls simply could not match the fire of the Dacian archers on the ground.

Tarbus led a wave of infantry to the wall, carrying his shield raised overhead to protect against arrows, javelins, and spears. Some of the men carried shields on their left arms and with their right arms helped carry the long ladders that reached to the top of the walls.

The soldier walking besides Tarbus at the front end of a ladder stopped when they reached the wall, placed the end of the ladder down into the ground, and held it firmly in place. The men behind raised the ladder so that it stood upright against the wall. A soldier jumped on the ladder and moved to climb it, quickly, one rung at a time. Another followed right behind him.

Tarbus went third, moving as fast as he could but slowed down by the man in front of him. A thrown spear sailed by his helmet and hit an infantryman on the ground. The first man was almost at the top. He shouted out in pain, the side of his neck pierced by a spear point. The man flailed out with his arms for an instant then fell sideways off the ladder and crashed to the ground below. Two Dacian arrows took down the Roman spearman atop the wall.

The man in front of Tarbus reached the top of the wall. Suddenly he saw only blue sky above him, which filled him with a strong and unexpected surge of joy. He raised himself to the top of the wall, stepped to the side to make room for the man climbing behind him, and crouched low as he drew his sica. There were archers on the ground inside the fort, shooting at the Dacians on the wall, but there were not many of them. Tarbus turned to face a spearman coming at him. He parried the spear thrust aside with the sica, then took a quick step forward and smashed his round shield into the man's face. The spearman staggered backwards a step, dazed. Tarbus slashed the sica in a backswing, quick as a viper, and cut cleanly through the soldier's throat. A gush of blood sprayed over them both.

Tarbus fought on. More Dacian soldiers were on top of the walls now, driving more defenders off and making it easier for the Dacians following to climb their ladders. The Romans were outnumbered and overpowered. Tarbus heard shouts from the direction of the gates. He looked down to see Roman defenders backing away hurriedly and forming a defensive line.

The Dacian battering ram had beaten down the main gate into the fort. Dacian infantry surged in through the broken gate. They would immediately be followed by Sarmatian heavy cavalry and Dacian horse archers. As in the previous Dacian attacks on Roman forts, the battle would end in a massacre.

King Decebal knew that Emperor Trajan brought a major part of his army to Moesia. He restored order in some parts of the province and set the local people to work rebuilding destroyed Roman camps.

He still had not caught up with the rampaging Dacian army however. Decebal planned to stay on the move, to destroy and weaken Trajan's military resources. A showdown must come later, but for the time being his plan was working well.

Mountains of eastern Dacia, first week of March 102 AD

In the late afternoon of their last day at the mountain fort Dochia's travelling party gathered the last of their supplies that would see them through another week of travel. Breads, cheeses, and dried fruits and vegetables were the staples of food for the road. Pack mules were loaded down with hay and other forage to feed the horses on the road.

It was the first week in March and the day was very bright, sunny, and unusually warm for the season. The children playing outside did not need to put on their winter clothing. Many of the women and older children went out into the woods around the fort to gather firewood. Some went hunting for mushrooms, winter plants, and flowers. The mood was relaxed and festive because the royal party would not be leaving until the following morning.

"What a beautiful day!" Dochia said to Tsiru. She was wearing her light blue spring cape, a gift from Queen Andrada, which always made her feel cheerful. "A shame it is almost over."

"This time of year sometimes brings good weather, My Lady," Tsiru said.

"I hope it lasts for two more weeks," she said wistfully. "Wouldn't that be wonderful?"

"It would be a blessing from Zamolxis," Tsiru said with a smile.

Dochia looked across the courtyard toward the dining hall. "The people are preparing a large feast for this evening. They are so very kind."

"It is in your honor, My Lady. Your farewell feast."

"I wish that I had some way to repay them." Noises from outside the walls caught her attention. "What is that commotion?"

People were running into the fort through the open gates. They dropped whatever they were carrying, and they looked alarmed.

"Close the gates! Close the gates!" the gate sentry shouted, very loud and also alarmed. Now many hoof beats could be heard in the distance, drawing closer. The gate keepers rushed to push the heavy gates closed, a heavy and slow process.

"We are under attack," Tsiru said. "To the dining hall, My Lady. Quickly!"

Dochia followed him, walking briskly. Men were rushing towards the gates and climbing stairs to join the sentries already on the walls. The fort was caught by surprise and completely unprepared. They made a mistake that they knew must never be made. They let their guard down.

Just before entering the dining hall Tsiru and Dochia stopped to look back towards the gates one more time, their attention drawn by the sounds of shouting and fighting. The gates were only partly closed. Through the opening in the gates enemy cavalry were rushing in and attacking the gate guards. It was an uneven battle and the guards near the gate were overwhelmed and killed.

Dacian warriors on the walls attacked the invaders with bows and spears. The resistance was too late and many more riders galloped into the fort. They were Roman auxiliary cavalry.

"Inside, Dochia! Quickly!" Tsiru took her firmly by the upper arm and pulled her inside the dining hall, then closed the door behind them. The hall was filled with a large number of women and children, preparing food. They all stopped their work and now stood silently, confused and afraid.

Dochia turned to Tsiru. "Can you fight them?"

Tsiru shook his head. "I don't know. Our men are scattered all over the fort, in the stables or gathering supplies. The Romans are inside the walls already and we don't know how many of them there are."

Dochia heard the frustration and resignation in his voice. "What should we do, then?"

"You must run, Dochia. I will stay behind and hold them off for as long as I can."

"Run? Run where?" For the first time in her life Dochia felt lost and helpless.

"Run into the forest and hide. There must be an escape exit here," Tsiru spoke calmly but fast. He looked to the group of women who were standing nearby and raised his voice. "Where is the escape door? An escape tunnel? Every Dacian fort has one!"

A stern looking middle-aged woman stepped up and took charge. "I am Mira. My Lady, you must come with me immediately. There is an escape door in the back of this hall. It leads into the woods and up the mountain side."

Tsiru caught Dochia's eye. "She is right. You must go with her, and immediately. The Romans could be coming through this door any moment now."

Dochia gave a quick nod. "I understand. Will you find us?"

"I will find you when I can," he promised. "Now I must protect your escape. Go, now!"

Dochia turned to the frightened women around her and took command, pushing down her own fear because she had to lead.

"All of you, come with us," she ordered. "Now!"

"To the back wall!" Mira instructed. "Out the escape door, my dears, quickly!"

A slim black-haired young woman holding a baby looked around frantically for a basket to pack her infant's belongings. Mira took her by the upper arm and steered her towards the door.

"We must leave quickly," the older woman said in a calm but firm voice.

"My baby's food! His clothes!" the woman exclaimed, looking around in panic.

Dochia shook her head sadly. "The Romans will be here before you can go and find his things. You will be dead or captured, and so will your baby."

The young woman allowed herself to be led towards the escape door, tears streaming down her cheeks. Every other woman and child did the same, following Mira's lead. To stay would mean being raped, killed, or sold into slavery.

Before going through the escape door Dochia turned back one last time to look at Tsiru. He stood silently by the door, watching them leave. He raised his left arm and gave her a farewell wave. His right hand drew his sword, and he turned to face the door. Dochia followed the other women and their children, streaming out into the forest.

There was no road or path leading from the fort up the mountain side. The forest was unspoiled. Pine trees were plentiful, along with birch, elm, and oaks. The evergreens provided some vegetation and some cover from the fort below. The other trees stood majestically, their branches bare and last year's leaves rotting around them on the forest floor.

Mira came up to walk beside Dochia. She was the wife of the fort's commander, which made her a figure of authority. She was also a natural leader and the others respected her guidance.

"Where are we going?" Dochia asked her. "You seem to know this area well."

"I do, My Lady," she replied. "I grew up in these mountains and have lived here my entire life."

"No formalities here, please," Dochia requested. "You may call me Dochia. We are all in this together, Sister. And it is you who must lead us now, not I."

"Very well, Sister. And thank you for being gracious," Mira replied.

"So, Mira, where are we going?"

"We will walk due east. Around the other side of this mountain is a small village. We shall find shelter and food there."

"Very good," Dochia said. She felt relieved. "How long will it take to walk there?"

"A day, perhaps." Mira looked around her. "With this group with the small children, perhaps a day and a half. There are more than one hundred of us and one third are children."

Dochia gave a nod. "The little ones get tired, they need to stop and rest."

"Yes, they get tired quickly. Also hungry, but there is nothing to eat in these woods except for roots and nuts. No one will starve in two days so do not worry."

"I am not worried about lack of food," Dochia said. "But we have no warm clothes." She looked down at her light blue cape and her deerskin slippers. "Look at me, I'm wearing my spring clothes. The children were playing outside without their coats."

"We enjoyed an early spring day," Mira agreed. "Let us pray the weather stays mild."

Dochia looked up at the sky, growing darker above the tree tops. Night would fall soon.

"Yes, Mira, let us pray that it does."

When the door opened Tsiru raised his sword and braced himself for a fight. The four men who entered were not Romans however, but four of his cavalry soldiers. They all carried bloodied swords and one was limping on an injured leg.

"I am glad to see you!" Tsiru exclaimed. "The others?"

One of the soldiers shook his head. "We are all that are left. The fort is lost. Roman infantry is now marching in."

Tsiru grimaced, then his face hardened. "So we fight here, and we die here, my brothers."

"The Lady Dochia?" one of the men asked.

"She fled into the woods along with many women and children. We will fight a rear guard battle and give them time to get away. Quickly, put up some of those tables against the door. Let's not make it too easy for the Roman bastards."

It did not take long for the Roman soldiers outside to try the door. When they found that it was blocked it did not take them long to break down the door and force aside the flimsy barricade.

The battle inside the dining hall only lasted a few minutes because the Dacians were badly overmatched. The Roman infantry were not auxiliary soldiers but fully armed and armored legionnaires. Tsiru found himself the last one standing, fighting desperately to hold off two legionnaires. A thrown spear pierced his right shoulder, which made him lose strength in his right hand. He groaned with pain and dropped his sica, lacking the strength to hold it any longer. A large burly legionnaire hit him with his shield and knocked him down. He stood over Tsiru and raised his gladius for the killing downward stab.

"Wait!" a voice commanded. "Don't kill him just yet. Bring him over here."

Two soldiers picked Tsiru up from the floor and dragged him to a table, where he was plopped down in a chair. A Roman centurion took a seat opposite him on the other side of the table.

"You look like the officer type," the Roman said. "So tell me, what information can you provide for me that would make me spare your worthless Dacian life?"

Tsiru's shoulder was in searing pain but he kept a straight face and kept his composure. "I have a great deal of information. What would you like to know?"

"Oh, ho!" the centurion laughed. "Look at this one! He thinks he's a general!"

"I'm no general," Tsiru smirked, "but I happen to know more than most generals in the Dacian army."

"Is that so? Then maybe I should have you talk directly to General Quietus himself, eh?"

"Yes," Tsiru said cooly. "You should."

"I don't believe you, Dacian," the Roman scoffed. "I think you are a big liar."

"You ignorant pigeon brained fool!" Tsiru shouted at him. "My name is Tsiru. For twenty years I served as chief of cavalry scouts for King Duras and King Decebal. General Sinna and General Drilgisa are like brothers to me. The family of King Decebal is like family to me. Does the name Vezina mean anything to you?"

"Yes," the centurion replied, taken aback. "He is the High Priest for you Dacians and master of your spies."

"I know half of the information in Vezina's head," Tsiru said. "And do you know why?"

"No. Why?"

"Because I gave him that information! It was gathered over the years by my cavalry scouts, who all reported to me. Now, if you had as much brains as a pigeon, would you say that was worth sparing my worthless life?"

The centurion became quiet for a moment. "All right, I will let you live for now. We will wait for General Quietus to arrive and he can question you himself." The man paused again, and his face darkened. "And I promise you this, Dacian. You will not enjoy the methods by which the General asks questions."

After sunset Dochia, Mira, and the other women escaping from the fort found themselves very tired and, suddenly, very cold. The warm afternoon sun now seemed like a distant memory, replaced by a bone-chilling cold wind blowing in from the northwest. The women and children gathered in small groups, huddled together as best they could, and shivered.

"Is there no way to build a fire?" Dochia asked Mira.

Mira shook her head. "No, we brought no flint to build a fire with. And if we had flint, all the wood around us is wet and soggy and would never light. And if we did manage to build enough fires for one hundred people, they would be able to see us all the way from Rome."

Dochia gave her a grim smile. "So no fires, then."

"No, sister," Mira said. "We must endure through the night. It will be warmer tomorrow."

"We would be warmer if we could walk," Dochia suggested.

"It is too dark to walk in the forest, the clouds are thick and there is no moon. I am sorry to be the bearer of all bad news, Dochia, but that is all I have to offer."

"Tomorrow, then," Dochia said. "We start walking again at first light and that will warm us up."

"Tomorrow, then."

They were approached by a slim figure, shivering so violently that her teeth were chattering. This was the young woman with a baby, now holding the child tight against her bosom. She sat down next to Mira. The older woman wrapped an arm around her and drew her close.

"I am so cold," the young mother said, her voice shaking. "My baby is cold."

Dochia wanted to cry for her but no tears came. No matter, it would do no good anyway. She unwrapped the light blue cape from her shoulders.

"Let me hold the baby for you, my dear," she asked. "I will wrap him in my cape to keep him warm."

"Oh, thank you," the woman said. "Yes, please do that."

Dochia took the infant and gently wrapped him in the folds of her cape. The child murmured but did not cry. Perhaps he too was too cold to cry. Dochia wrapped her arms around the small bundle and pressed him softly to her chest.

She thought only about tomorrow. Tomorrow they would walk, they would leave this forest, and they would be warm. Tomorrow.

Tsiru sat and waited. Night had fallen and General Lusius Quietus was expected to arrive at any time. In the meantime he was watched over by his guards and the centurion who regarded him with pure contempt. They had bandaged his shoulder to stem the bleeding but his sword arm was still useless. They even brought him a cup of water when he asked. If he was who he said he was, then he was a very valuable prisoner.

A soldier entered the dining hall and headed for the centurion. "One of the prisoners talked under torture, sir. It seems there was a woman of the Dacian royal family staying here. Her name is Dochia, sister of Decebalus. Her escort is called Tsiru."

The centurion gave Tsiru a furious look. "Where is she?"

"What is this nonsense?" Tsiru asked. "There was no member of the Dacian royal family here."

The centurion stood up quickly, knocking over his chair. He walked over to stand beside Tsiru and drew his gladius. He placed the tip of the sword against Tsiru's throat, pressing against the skin.

"Tell me where she is right now or you will meet whatever gods you worship in Hades."

"Your prisoner is lying to you," Tsiru said. "There was no sister of Decebal here."

The centurion pressed the gladius tip tighter and drew a drop of blood. "You are stalling. You have been stalling with me all along, to give her time to escape, eh? I am finished listening to your lies, you Dacian scum."

"You are easy to fool, pigeon brain," Tsiru said and spat in his face. "Now kill me then go to Hades!"

The Roman made a savage thrust with the sword and plunged it straight through Tsiru's neck. The Dacian fell sideways, dead before he hit the floor. He died with a smile on his face. Tsiru believed for certain, as all Dacian warriors believed, that in the moment after death he would be in the heaven of Zamolxis for all time along with the countless thousands of Dacians who died before him.

The centurion was enraged. "Find this Dochia! Send out patrols!"

"Sir, we cannot send out patrols now. It is pitch black outside," his aide pointed out. "And besides, she has nowhere to go."

The Roman stopped to gain his composure. "At first light, I want patrols sent out in every direction leading away from the fort! Find her or I'll have your skins!"

The next morning was a bright and sunny day. Search parties fanned out from the fort to the west, north, east, and south. Cavalry covered the mountain roads. Infantry walked through the heavily wooded mountain slopes where cavalry could not go. They all knew that a prisoner of such high status could not be allowed to escape.

Although it was very early in the morning the cold brisk air woke the men up quickly and put a bounce in their step. The search party heading northeast soon found markers that a large group of people had passed through those woods. A series of bugle calls brought more searchers to their area.

"Spread out!" their officer commanded. "We capture as many prisoners as we can find, and I don't want to miss any!"

The walk uphill in the freezing wind was tiring. Men's breaths frosted in the cold air. One of the legionnaires in the front line got an eerie feeling, although he could not say why.

"What are you skittish about?" his companion on the right asked. "You look spooked."

"I don't know. I feel the presence of ghosts."

"There are no such things as ghosts, you ignorant fool," the man said scornfully.

The legionnaires climbed on. One man near the front suddenly cried out, a shout for their officers. A centurion hurriedly walked over to investigate.

"What is it?"

The legionnaire who cried out pointed to a spot a short distance up the wooded mountain side.

"Statues," he said, puzzled.

The officer walked closer. Scattered among the trees he saw a group of figures, women and children of various sizes, dressed in a variety of clothes, all still as statues. But they were not statues.

The figures were frozen in various positions of rest. Some were sitting. Some were lying prone on the ground. Many had their arms wrapped around each other, embracing.

Towards the front of the group, seated close by two other frozen female figures, was a woman with a regal look about her. In silent death she still held pressed close to her bosom the body of an infant, wrapped in a light blue cape. Her long brown hair was lightly frosted with snow. Her eyes were closed, and she looked like she was in a deep and peaceful sleep.

> Chapter 14

We Have No More Bandages

Moesia, first week of March 102 AD

Caesar Trajan was pacing impatiently when two scouts from the auxiliary cavalry approached the command tent. For weeks now he had been chasing the Dacian army across Moesia but could not pin them down. Decebalus attacked Roman forts, killed the troops guarding them, then quickly moved on to his next target. He left destruction and burnt rubble behind.

"Report," the Emperor ordered after the two men bowed to him in greeting. "You saw the Dacian camp? Where?"

"Near the town of Nicopolis, Caesar," one of the scouts replied. "We saw infantry and also Sarmatian cavalry. And many four wheeled wagons."

"How many Sarmatian cavalry?" asked commander of the cavalry Lusius Quietus. He and Laberius Maximus were standing by a table where a large map of Moesia was unfurled.

"I do not know, General," the scout replied, shaking his head. "We only saw the camp from a distance. It is a very large camp."

"You have done well and will be rewarded," Trajan told them. "You are dismissed."

The scouts bowed again, then quickly turned and left. Trajan walked over to join his generals at the map table.

"Nicopolis is one day's march to the east," Maximus said. He glanced up at the sky where the sun was sinking lower in the west. "Night falls in two hours. We cannot march until first light."

"We will not march with infantry, Laberius," the Emperor told him. "By the time we reach Nicopolis at this time tomorrow the Dacians will be gone."

Maximus raised an eyebrow. "I am guessing you have something different in mind?"

"I do," Trajan said, turning to Quietus. "The only way to reach the enemy before they move on is with a cavalry attack. Can you launch a night attack, Lusius?"

Quietus gave an eager nod. "I certainly can, Caesar. My men can leave within the hour. We will ride through the darkness and arrive at their camp in the night."

"Do it," Trajan said. "Get your men ready now."

"Immediately, Caesar," Quietus acknowledged and headed off for his command tent to instruct his cavalry officers.

"A night cavalry attack?" Maximus asked. "That is a daring plan Marcus. Also one that Decebalus will not expect."

"We must surprise him, as he surprised us. In truth, Laberius, I am tired of his surprises," Trajan said. "Now we must put him on the defensive, reacting to us. We spend too much time reacting to him."

"I agree completely. So Lusius will lead this attack?"

Trajan shook his head. "No. I will take the Praetorian cavalry and lead the attack. You will stay here in command of the infantry and march to Nicopolis tomorrow to join us there."

"I understand," Maximus said. "Promise me one thing, Marcus?"

"And what is that?"

"That if you meet Decebalus face to face, you will not personally fight him," Laberius said with an amused smile.

That made Trajan laugh. "Depends on the circumstance, Laberius! I have killed many barbarians in my time."

"I know that," Maximus replied. "And I am not questioning your courage, no one has reason to doubt that."

"Ah ha! You are questioning my fighting skills perhaps? Although I must admit, they are a bit rusty."

"You know perfectly well what I am saying. Caesar cannot engage in hand to hand fighting no matter how great the temptation. It is beneath your position. That is all."

"Do not worry, Maximus. Of course I understand that. Even the Divine Julius gave up fighting once he became Caesar." Trajan paused and gave a frown. "It would however give me great satisfaction to chop off the head of this barbarian king."

"I will chop it off for you, Caesar," Laberius said. "I will do for you what Cornelius Fuscus could not do for Domitian."

"Ah, yes, poor General Fuscus. Decebalus killed him in single combat, we are told."

"So we are told."

"That was sixteen years ago, Laberius. We are no longer in the age of Domitian and Fuscus. Now I must go and catch this barbarian king and show him that I am no Domitian."

"I believe that he already knows that, Marcus. But yes, you must catch him and put him in his place."

Prince Davi was awakened by thundering hoof beats and the shouts and sounds of battle. He was instantly up from the blanket that served as his bed, grabbed his sword and bow, and joined the other men who were making their way towards their horses. They were under surprise attack by fast moving cavalry and would not have time to put on their armor or the armor on their horses. The night sky was very clear and there was just enough moonlight to see where they were going.

"Gather here!" Davi shouted. "Lances and swords!"

It was too dark to see at a distance. The attackers were on horse, marauding between the wagons, killing everyone in their way with lances, spears, and swords. At a distance it was impossible to tell friend from foe, and Davi did not want his men killing each other with their bows.

He urged his horse forward towards a rider who was spearing men and women emerging half-asleep and confused from their tents. The enemy horseman noticed Davi's approach too late to turn his horse to meet the attack. Davi batted away the spear point turning towards him, then closed in and stabbed his sword into the man's side below the ribcage. The rider groaned with pain and slumped low in his saddle. Two women quickly dragged him down from his horse and repeatedly stabbed him with their knives.

Bastarnae spearmen gathered themselves in small groups to fight off the cavalry attackers. The camp was in wild chaos and the Roman auxiliaries seemed to be everywhere. Some of the tents caught fire. The defenders on the ground were overwhelmed by the numbers and the speed of attack of their assailants. The battle was fast turning into a massacre.

Davi's Sarmatian riders were being attacked by multiple Roman cavalry and fighting desperately for survival. They were being killed, one man at a time. Davi saw that almost half his men were already down. He roared with anger and again rallied his men to him. This time he led them away, riding south out of the battle zone. To stay and fight now would invite their annihilation. They would live to fight again, under conditions that were not hopeless.

Adamclisi, Moesia, March 102 AD

The main army of King Decebal was camped further south and east, near the city of Adamclisi. Decebal learned the next morning of the defeat of his army camp at Nicopolis. Roman cavalry numbering in the thousands had attacked in the night and caught his troops by completely surprise. The losses of Bastarnae infantry and Sarmatian cavalry were substantial. Many in the Bastarnae infantry travelled with their wives and children, and it was the wagons of these that slowed the army down. Half of the soldiers and civilians escaped in the dark and make their way south towards Decebal's main army.

"The Roman infantry will catch up with their cavalry in one day, two at most," Diegis said. "Now that Trajan has caught up with us he will be aggressive in stopping our movement."

"Then let's give them the fight they came for," Drilgisa said. "I am tired of attacking one fort at a time."

"You are both right," Decebal said. "Trajan has a large cavalry and now he will cut off our free movement. And I agree with you Drilgisa, we must make a stand here in Moesia before we return to Dacia. We must cripple Trajan further, otherwise he will be chasing us like hounds chasing rabbits."

"They will outnumber us badly," Davi said. His left upper leg was wrapped tightly with a bloody bandage, the wound coming from a Roman spear point suffered while he was furiously fighting off two other attackers.

"The Romans always outnumber us," the King said.

"We were outnumbered at Tapae and held our own," Drilgisa said.

"Tapae is in the past," Diegis growled. "This is a different battle entirely. We will damage Trajan's army, then move back across the Ister into the mountains."

"You are correct, my brother," the King said. "This will be a very different kind of battle. At Tapae we had fifty thousand fighters, here we have one third of that. Trajan will have twice our army if not more. We can match him in cavalry but not in infantry."

"Then we'll have to fight twice as hard," Drilgisa said with a grin. "That never changes in our fight with Rome."

"Prepare your men," Decebal said, looking around at his generals. "We will not be surprised again. Trajan will bring his army here and we will be ready for them."

Emperor Trajan supervised the positioning of his army from behind the lines. He did not have his heavy artillery, but there were enough of the light artillery carrobalistae to inflict damage on the massed Dacian troops. The artillery was positioned in the front and the flanks of his infantry formations.

Adamclisi was located on a flat plain, terrain that favored Roman legions. At last the Roman army had the advantage after almost a year of fighting in the Dacians mountains. Here the Dacians did not have their stone walled forts. Legionnaires would not be ambushed on narrow mountain roads cutting through forests of broadleaf trees. In the woods the Dacians could quickly launch surprise attacks, then vanish and escape. Here they were out in the open.

Trajan had three legions of Roman infantry and another four of auxiliary infantry under his command. In this battle they would fight side by side, with no preferential treatment shown to the Roman soldiers in order to reduce their casualties. Nothing and nobody would be spared or held back, because the Emperor knew that this battle would be decisive in crushing Decebalus and his army.

Trajan watched from horseback as his army moved into position to face the Dacian lines. General Maximus and his aide Titus Lucullus watched with him, sitting tall in the saddle so they could see well. Both were veterans of many battles, critical battles. Each knew the familiar feeling of tension slowly building before a major conflict between two large armies.

"What strategy do you expect Decebalus will use, Titus?" Trajan asked. "You fought against him in two campaigns prior."

Lucullus took only a moment to think about his answer. "Caesar has Decebalus at a disadvantage in men, so their initial stance is a defensive posture. Decebalus will take advantage of his large units of archers, both foot and horse, to blunt our initial attack."

"And then?" Maximus asked.

"Then he will react and adjust to situations as they develop."

Trajan laughed. "In other words, Titus, you are telling me that he will follow the exact same strategy that we would follow."

"Yes, Caesar," Lucullus answered. "Decebalus is no ignorant and hotheaded barbarian, and he is certainly no fool."

"No, he is not," the Emperor agreed.

"Fool or no fool, we will crush him," Maximus declared.

"In due time, Laberius. In due time and never in haste."

In years past Titus Lucullus witnessed other Roman commanders take Decebalus lightly, much to their later regret. Trajan would never do so. This explained why Trajan never lost a major battle in his long military career. In past wars Roman arrogance cost Rome dearly in horrific losses, and so Roman armies lost battles and lost wars. This Roman army, led by this Caesar, was in no danger of doing that.

The Dacian command post was located behind a tree lined hill that offered some protection from the Roman artillery. Arrows and bolts from the carrobalistae positioned at the front of the Roman lines flew overhead. Dacian and Bastarnae infantry in front positions took casualties and silently endured. Shields provided no protection against artillery, and neither did the body armor that some of the men wore. Aside from some officers, few of the infantry soldiers wore any kind of armor in any case.

King Decebal was surrounded by his Royal Guards and a group of high ranking officers making last minute preparations. Chief Fynn of the Bastarnae and Davi of the Roxolani joined him. Davi had his wounded leg heavily bandaged, and would not allow his wounds to stop him from fighting on horseback.

"General Drilgisa, as usual you will command the center," Decebal addressed the group. "Chief Fynn commands the right flank. General Diegis, you have the left. Davi will support you with his cavalry. Fynn, Sinna will support your flank with the Dacian cavalry."

"That sounds good," Fynn said. "My men are ready."

"So are mine," said Davi. "We lost too many of our brothers at Nicopolis. My men are thirsting to make the Romans pay for it."

"See to your men now," Decebal said to them. "Prepare them for the attack that will come very soon. Your men will not need to wait for long, Davi."

The high officers left except for Drilgisa and Diegis. Along with Buri they formed Decebal's inner core of leadership.

"Trajan will want to overwhelm and break us," Diegis said. "Hold the center, Drilgisa. The battle will be won or lost there."

"I agree," the King said. "There is no commander more capable than you, Drilgisa. Stand firm and I will send our reserve troops to reinforce you as needed."

"We have reserve troops? Nobody tells me these things," Drilgisa said with a grin.

Decebal returned his grin with a smile. "Take your field positions, men. We have a long day ahead of us."

Tarbus waited for Drilgisa at the very center of the Dacian line. The general clasped his shoulder and gave him last minute instructions.

"Tarbus, you will position your unit directly behind my men," Drilgisa commanded. "You will reinforce the line where it is most threatened. Can I trust you with making that decision on your own?"

"Yes, General," Tarbus replied. He was now a veteran of two dozen fights and learning quickly under Drilgisa's guidance.

"Good. When the Romans come at us they will want to break through our lines at certain points. Your men will be needed most at those attack points."

"Yes, sir," Tarbus said firmly. "You can count on me, sir."

"This is a large Roman army and they outnumber us, so they will use standard infantry tactics," Drilgisa continued. "The legionnaire units will first approach in the testudo formation to protect against our archers. Once they close in they sometimes form into the cuneus formation, the wedge formation used for breaking through enemy lines."

"I understand, General," Tarbus said with a nod.

"Our job is to blunt that wedge and shove it back down their throats."

"Yes, sir!"

"Good man. Now get your men in position, Tarbus. The enemy is preparing to advance."

Emperor Trajan launched his attack with three legions of infantry. The fifteen thousand foot soldiers closed in on nine thousand men in the Dacian lines. Trajan's decisive advantage was that he had another fifteen thousand men in reserve. Kind Decebalus had at most another five thousand soldiers in reserve in the Dacian army. Soldiers grew tired quickly in battle, and the Emperor knew that his advantage in numbers would wear down and ultimately beat down the enemy.

Trajan also knew that the Roman legionnaires were better armed and better trained than the Dacian and Bastarnae infantry opposing them. They wore metal armor and each carried a scutum, the large rectangular Roman shield made of laminated wood and covered with leather. The scutum protected a man from below the knee to eye level. When the shields were overlapped in the defensive testudo formation it made the men under them nearly invincible to enemy archers.

Trajan's auxiliary infantry were not nearly as well armed or trained as the legionnaires, but they were fierce fighters brought in from Germania, Gaul, and as far away as Spain and Brittania. In the heat of battle they matched the soldiers in the Dacian army in daring and aggression.

"Let them get bloodied, then we send in the reserves," General Maximus said. He was watching from horseback from behind the Roman lines, along with Trajan and Titus Lucullus.

"I leave you in charge of troop movements, Laberius," the Emperor said. "I want the Dacians worn down by the afternoon. I want King Decebalus captured before nightfall."

"Yes, Caesar," Maximus said. He shot a glance at Lucullus. "Will Decebalus allow himself to be captured, Titus? In your opinion."

"I do not know, General," Lucullus replied in an even tone. "His pride might not allow it."

"Damn his pride!" the Emperor said hotly. "The man will answer to Roman justice."

"Yes, Caesar," Titus replied. "Decebalus will face Roman justice, perhaps even today."

"Perhaps, Titus? Do you doubt our army, or do you think this man is some type of magician?"

"Of course not, Caesar. I have no doubts about our army. I am simply saying that Decebalus is a hard prey to catch."

Maximus snorted. "Even a greased pig gets cornered and caught. I will catch him."

King Decebal also watched the unfolding battle from horseback, well behind the Dacian lines. Buri watched alongside him. The cavalry of the Royal Guard surrounded their command post.

"They are massing against our center," Buri observed.

"As we expected, Buri," Decebal said. "Emperor Trajan expects that he will cut through us and we can't stop him."

"Another arrogant Roman, eh?"

Decebal shook his head. "No, this one is not arrogant. He is very careful in his strategy and confident in his army. His soldiers trust him and fight hard for him."

"Even the ones from Brittania? They don't know him," Buri said skeptically.

"He pays them well. And you know soldiers as well as I do, Buri. They trust what their fellow soldiers tell them."

They watched the troop movements in silence. The Roman cohort in the very front of the advancing line weathered a barrage of arrows and thrown javelins, then formed into a wedge formation. The wedge closed in quickly on the Dacian front line.

"Hold firm, Drilgisa," Buri said. "And fight well, Tarbus, my son."

"We attack the left flank of their wedge!" Tarbus shouted to his men. "Follow me! Kill the Romans!" He turned and moved swiftly at a run towards the advancing enemy.

The two hundred men under his command yelled war cries and followed Tarbus. They moved swiftly around the right edge of Drilgisa's troops and smashed at an angle against the Roman wedge formation. On the other side of the wedge another Dacian unit did the same. The legionnaires on the outside of the Roman formation had to stop and fight off the attacking Dacian infantry, and the forward momentum of the wedge was slowed.

The Dacian soldiers did not budge when the lead Romans reached their line. They faced the enemy with a wall of falxes and spears. The falx had a great reach advantage over the legionnaires' swords, and the lead Roman soldiers were quickly cut down.

Drilgisa fought with the two-handed falx. Trajan's modifications of the Roman armor, to better protect sword arms and necks against the dreaded falx, increased a soldier's protection but did not make him invincible. Drilgisa swept the sharp curved blade low, under the legionnaire's shield, and sliced halfway through the man's leg above the ankle. The soldier groaned with pain, tried to step back, and fell on his side as his leg gave away. A Dacian soldier took a step forward and plunged his falx into the man's now exposed face.

"Hold steady!" Drilgisa shouted. "Hold the line!"

No Dacian had yet retreated a single step, but Drilgisa knew that could not last. Large formations of mixed legionnaire and auxiliary infantry were moving in slowly and steadily. As more Roman soldiers closed in they drove back the Dacian attackers on the failed wedge formation. Tarbus pulled his troops back to fight alongside Drilgisa's men.

"Well done!" Drilgisa told Tarbus, now fighting close by. "That is how you attack a wedge!"

Tarbus grinned in reply. The front of his trousers was soaked red with blood, but apparently not his own blood because he still moved swiftly and steadily on his feet. He was fighting off the attack of a broad chested Roman trying to use his shield to push him back.

"Attack the legs!" Drilgisa shouted.

The Roman must have heard him and understood because he took a step backwards, just out of reach of Drilgisa's falx. Tarbus was fighting with the shorter Dacian sword, the sica. It was very effective in close combat with Roman auxiliaries, but much less effective against well armored legionnaires. The weapon all legionnaires feared most was the falx.

Davi gritted his teeth against the pain in his wounded leg as he rode along the left flank of the Dacian army. This was the section commanded by Diegis. The troops here were still under attack by Roman artillery fire but no infantry yet approached. The Romans were trying to break through the center of the Dacian line and divide the army in two. Thus far they were failing.

"Davi!"

He turned towards the familiar voice of Diegis. The brother of King Decebal was famous for wandering up and down the line, checking on the men and encouraging them to great effort. He was liked and respected by the men because he always fought at their side. Decebal had done the same before he took the crown.

"Davi, get your fool self to a medical tent!" Diegis told him.

"Not yet," Davi replied. "After I've killed some Romans, brother."

Diegis looked towards the Roman formations moving towards his location. "Here they come now. Don't get too greedy and try to kill them all, brother. There will still be plenty of Romans to kill after your leg heals, you know."

"I know."

Davi's horse reared, spooked as an artillery bolt flew by within an arm's length. Davi cursed very loudly and grimaced at the sharp pain in his leg as his horse settled on its feet again.

"Good hunting!" Diegis yelled to him, then turned quickly to move back up the line. Now the battle was fully engaged.

"Press the attack, Maximus," Trajan commanded. "The Dacians will not break and they will not run."

"Yes, Caesar," Maximus acknowledged. "I shall send one legion supported by cavalry around their left flank. We have sufficient troops to outflank them."

"Give the commands, Laberius."

"Immediately." Maximus urged his horse forward towards the front. "I will go down and have a word with Quietus."

"Very well," Trajan said. "Lucullus? Remain here."

Titus watched Maximus ride off. "Yes, Caesar?"

"I want Decebalus brought before me, alive."

"Of course, Ceasar. What do you wish from me?"

"I need an envoy to the King, Titus. Will he listen to you? He will not listen to Laberius, for certain."

That caught Titus by surprise. He was unsure how to answer.

"He refused to meet with Sura," Trajan explained. "But he knows you, Titus."

"Perhaps he will see me, Cesar," Lucullus said. "Not now while the battle rages, of course."

"No, not now," Trajan agreed. "Unless we kill or capture him today he will withdraw with what is left of his army. You will approach the King later, as my envoy, and ask for his surrender."

"I understand, Caesar. I will do as you command."

"Good. Stay by my side, Titus. You are my only link to Decebalus."

By the early afternoon the casualties on both sides were piling up. The Romans attacked in waves, reserves coming in to relieve the front line troops when these thinned out or became too tired to fight effectively. The Dacian army and their allies gave ground but never broke. The battleground was covered with bodies, blood, and bodily fluids of men pushed beyond their limits of strength and courage. The injured were dragged to the back of the lines where the surgeons waited. The injured who were within reach of the enemy were killed without mercy by both sides.

Decebal used his reserves sparingly and then only when they were tactically essential. Men fought in the front lines to the point of near exhaustion, then backed away to let others take their place for a brief time. One fourth of his army was dead or wounded, and still the men did not break. The Roman losses looked to be just as heavy.

Prince Davi of the Roxolani cavalry approached with two of his men providing an escort. A large group of Roxolani riders followed them. All their horses looked spent. As Davi pulled up the King could see that the bandage on his left leg was soaked red. Davi's face looked white and pale.

"You have done enough, Davi," Decebal told him. "Go see the surgeon now or you will die on that horse from loss of blood."

"I will do that," he replied. "We must rest our horses in any case. We are pushing them too hard."

"How are my brother's men holding up on the flank?"

"I am here with a message from Diegis for you. The men are fighting hard but cannot sustain for long," Davi answered. "Trajan sends in fresh troops while our men grow more tired."

"I understand. Go, Davi, the surgeon awaits. See to your leg."

Davi gave a nod, then veered his horse towards the rear and rode off. His two guards accompanied him, more concerned about him not falling off his horse due to loss of blood than about any Roman attackers.

"Do we send Diegis reinforcements?" Buri asked. "He is now without cavalry support."

Decebal shook his head. "We do not have the men to send. Diegis will know when to pull back if he must."

Buri stood up taller in the saddle to look over the battlefield. "That time may come sooner than we wish. I see two legions plus cavalry moving against our left flank."

"I see them too, Buri," the King said. "The Romans will try to flank us there. Diegis must hold firm."

"Hold the line!" General Diegis shouted to his men. "The bastards outnumber us but they will not out-fight us!"

Holding the line for a while longer was the best that he could hope for at that moment. Many of his men were bleeding from wounds inflected by Roman spears, swords, and arrows. All were near exhaustion but driven by sheer ferocious determination not to give in to their relentless enemy. They would rather accept death before defeat.

The Roman reserve legions were made up mostly of legionnaires. They were protected by their armor, and they fought as well trained and disciplined units. A row of legionnaires advancing behind a wall of interlocked shields was well protected against the many Dacian foot archers positioned among their infantry. When they closed in within sword range the legionaries had the advantage.

Diegis was facing off against a sturdy built, blue-eyed Roman. The man crouched behind his large rectangular shield, his gladius held low and poised to attack. Legionnaires were trained for close hand to hand fighting. Diegis was also fighting with a sword, the Dacian sica with the razor sharp curved tip, and holding his round Dacian shield on his left arm. Neither man could get past the other's defenses.

The legionnaire crouched lower and pushed forward with his shield to knock Diegis off balance. Diegis went backwards half a step but kept his feet. He dropped his shield a foot lower because, as expected, the Roman's gladius came up in a swift motion aimed towards his lower stomach to deliver a blow that would cut deeply into his guts. As his shield blocked the gladius Diegis took a step forward to swing his sword at the legionnaire's head. The Roman leaned away backwards and the sica's blade glanced off the side of his helmet with a loud clang. The legionnaire was mildly dazed but unhurt.

Both men took a step back to gather themselves. A Roman whistle on the line blew shrilly, a signal to re-deploy. The legionnaires on the front line stepped back and were replaced by the line of infantry waiting behind them. Diegis faced a new man, a rested opponent whose clean uniform indicated that his unit just now joined the battle.

The new legionnaire was younger and eager for battle. He looked at Diegis' bloodied clothes, at the blood splattered on his shield and his legs, then looked the Dacian in the eye and gave him a grin.

"Aren't you tired yet, grandpa?" he taunted.

Diegis did not reply. He was too tired to talk and he had no patience for fools. And yes, he was forty years old, but his daughter Ana was only eleven and he was not old enough to be a grandpa. He stood his ground and waited for the young fool to make the first move.

The Roman gave a shout as he raised up his shield and gave Diegis a bull rush. He was counting on the extra weight of his armor and shield to give him enough force to knock down the tired Dacian old man. Diegis took a quick step back and to his right, away from the Roman's sword hand. He crouched low at the knees and swept the sica towards the soldier's left leg, the sharp curved tip slicing across the Roman's calf as he pulled the sica back. The sica sliced through muscle and sinew and cut to the bone. The legionnaire groaned and stumbled, then fell to his knees. A Dacian soldier swung his war axe and hit the Roman across the back of the neck, nearly taking the man's head off.

Diegis turned towards the Roman line just in time to raise his shield to deflect the spear aiming for his head. The spear point scraped over the copper facing of the shield and glanced off Diegis' right forehead. He took a step back, then another. Blood streamed into his right eye and he could not see.

A pair of hands pulled him further back into the Dacian lines. "That's enough, sir! Let's get you to the rear!"

Diegis used the back of his hand to try and wipe the blood out of his eye. He had no vision there. "Did I lose the eye?" he asked the man walking beside him, still guiding him away from the battle front.

"No, sir! Your eye is still there!" the man replied, shouting to be heard over the noise of battle. "But you have a deep cut above the eye that is bleeding heavily. You need to see the surgeon and get that patched up, sir!"

Diegis groaned, feeling disgusted. His part in the battle was over. He was not concerned about his wound or his eye. He was concerned about his men still on the line.

"How many wounded?" Emperor Trajan asked the chief of the field surgeons. He was touring the field stations behind the Roman lines accompanied by Titus Lucullus and a unit of the Praetorian Guard. The battle casualties were high and Trajan checked to make certain that his wounded were being taken care of.

The surgeon's face was shiny with sweat even though the temperature was cool. Each legion was staffed with twenty-four surgeons and assistants, but on this day that was not enough. The surgeons had been working without a pause since late morning, and the large field-dressing station was covered with wounded soldiers. They were laid out on the open ground, arranged in long rows that stretched out into the distance.

"Over two thousand wounded, Caesar," the chief surgeon answered, wiping the perspiration from his brow with his sleeve. "Many were felled by archers but the most serious lose hands, arms, and legs to falxes."

"I see," Trajan said. He looked at the bleeding men on the ground and frowned. His soldiers were like sons to him and it bothered him greatly to see them suffer. The casualties thus far in the battle were three thousand dead and these two thousand wounded. Many who were severely wounded would not live long. The most severe wounds were fatal within two or three days, and many of the rest would die from infections.

Titus Lucullus noticed that a legionnaire on the ground was bleeding profusely from a cut on his leg. Another was bleeding from a head wound. And yet nobody was paying attention to them.

"Why are these men not attended?" Titus asked the surgeon.

"We have no more bandages," the man replied with a pained look on his face.

Trajan gave him a hard look. "What?"

"We have no more bandages, Caesar," the chief surgeon repeated. "There are simply too many wounded."

Trajan took a quick look at the men on the ground and shook his head with displeasure. He reached up to his neck, unclasped his cape, and handed the red garment made from rich cloth to the surgeon.

"Here, cut this into strips and make bandages from it," Trajan commanded. He looked around at the eight Praetorian Guards who came with him. "All of you, give him your capes."

Lucullus had already taken off and given his cape to one of the other surgeons, and the Praetorians followed. The surgeons and their assistants eagerly began to tear and cut the capes into narrow strips.

Trajan turned to the chief surgeon again. "If you need more cloth send men to my tent and take more of my garments."

"Yes, Caesar," the surgeon answered, sounding very surprised and also profoundly thankful.

"Good. Be resourceful, man!"

The chief surgeon gave a silent nod to acknowledge the order, then moved to tend to the soldier with the head wound.

The Emperor walked away, with Lucullus at his side and the guards following. Trajan's face was hard and grim.

"Another very costly battle, Titus," Trajan said. "We are losing too many men."

"Yes, Caesar," Lucullus agreed. "It would be better to convince King Decebalus to surrender. Do you wish for me to go and try to reason with him?"

"Do that," Trajan said. "We have five thousand casualties. He no doubt has many more. If the man has any sense he will know when to give up."

"I do not believe that lack of sense is what guides his decisions, Caesar," Titus said. "Most of all, Decebalus is driven by pride."

"So am I," Trajan said. "So am I. But pride has its limits."

King Decebal ordered a retreat in late afternoon. Units moved back slowly and gradually, an orderly retreat and not a mob running away. Some Roman units followed but much less aggressively, because they were all bloodied and tired. The battlefield was covered with corpses and blood. The air was filled with screams of the wounded men who were in great agony and wished only for a quick death.

Chief Fynn of the Bastarnae approached Decebal's command post looking like an apparition from a nightmare. His clothes, shield, and sword were stained red. There were streaks of blood on his face and in his hair. He looked exhausted, and his face was drawn and grim. He lost far too many of his men today.

One of the Dacian soldiers handed Fynn a pitcher of water. He drank half of it thirstily, then poured the rest over his head. The water ran down his face, neck, and chest stained red.

"We sent many Romans to hell today," Fynn said when he reached the King's side. He was not bragging but simply stating what both of them knew was true.

Decebal gave him a nod. " Your men fought well," he said. "You did all that could be done."

"What now?" Fynn asked. "I lost near half my men, and the others cannot continue the fight."

"Now we head north across the Ister and find the roads home," Decebal replied. "We lost half the army, Fynn. We must save the other half and fight another day."

"I agree, Decebal. The Bastarnae are done fighting for this season unless Trajan pursues us to our homes."

"No, he won't do that. Trajan will pursue me, for certain. He will not split his army and come after you as well. That would be foolish of him, and the man is no fool."

Diegis approached, flanked by two guards. He also looked like a bloody horror. A thick bandage was wrapped around his forehead, and another around his right shoulder.

"I am happy to see you, Brother," Decebal said with a smile. "You will travel with my Royal Guards during the retreat."

Diegis shook his head. "No, I will march with my men. My loyalty to them must match their loyalty to me."

"Spoken like a true commander," Fynn said with a grim smile. "Now I must do the same."

"To your men, then," said King Decebal. "We must stay ahead of Trajan and cross the Ister before his army gets there."

And so the wounded army of Dacia and her allies left that great battlefield and moved north towards the great river Ister, known to the Romans as the Danubius.

> Chapter 15

The Lost Standards

Sarmizegetusa, April 102 AD

Reports of Dochia's journey to Scythia stopped coming in March. Queen Andrada saw no reason for concern then. Dochia was in good hands with Tsiru and was travelling swiftly with a good sized cavalry escort. She was concerned now that there was still no news from Scythia about Dochia's arrival. Vezina sent out messengers and interviewed merchants and other travelers coming through Dacia from the east.

What worried Andrada and Vezina more was news from eastern Dacia coming from King Decebal. After a terrible battle in Moesia the army was again fighting in the mountains of Dacia. The Bastarnae and Sarmatians had returned to their home lands because they also suffered terrible losses in Moesia.

Decebal and the Dacian army were fighting a retreating battle and slowly moving farther and farther to the west. They were returning home to Sarmizegetusa.

"When will Tata and the army be here, do you think?" Zia asked her mother at the supper table. As usual she, Adila, Dorin, and Ana joined the Queen for the evening meal.

Andrada paused between spoonfuls of hot and savory vegetable soup. "Another month. Perhaps two."

"I wish he was here now," Zia said. "I hate this war."

“I hate it too,” Ana agreed. “I wish my father was here.” She had not seen her father Diegis since December.

Adila turned to her older sister with a frown. “Do you know what you are saying, Zia? If Tata was here right now it would mean that our army was beaten. The Romans would be right behind them!”

“Let them come,” Dorin said defiantly. “If they come here we will kill them.”

“It won’t be as easy as you think,” Adila retorted.

“My children, do not argue,” Andrada said calmly. “Our army is still fighting. We are not beaten. Your father always finds a way to keep our enemies away.”

“Yes, Mama,” Adila said. She tore off a piece of bread and chewed on it slowly, but her mind was far away. She thought of her father and the army in the mountains, fighting a battle against a much larger Roman army. There was a restless part of her that wished she was with them again.

Vezina entered the Queen’s dining room and approached them, walking slowly. Andrada saw the downcast look on his face and felt cold chills going down her spine. She could tell that the High Priest of Zamolxis had very bad news.

“Decebal?” she asked, struggling to keep her voice calm.

Vezina shook his head no as he took a chair beside her. He looked around the table at each of the children, then back to the Queen.

“I have very sad news about Dochia.”

“What happened?” Andrada asked, but in her heart she already knew. It was her worst fear.

Everyone stopped eating and stared at Vezina.

“I just spoke with a scout returning from the east. Dochia and her cavalry escort stopped at a fort on their way to Scythia. The Romans attacked and defeated the fort.” He paused to find the right words. “Dochia fled and escaped into the forest along with a large group of women and children. The weather turned bitter cold during the night. They could not find shelter.”

Zia gasped and put her hand over her mouth. Ana's eyes filled with tears. Dorin went very still.

"Is Aunt Dochia dead?" Ana asked.

"Yes, child," Vezina told her in a gentle voice. "She died from the cold, in the forest."

"Poor Dochia," Andrada said. "She wanted so much to help and it led her to her death."

"The cold did not kill her," Adila said with bitterness. "The Romans killed her."

Ana started to cry with loud heaving sobs. She walked over to the Queen, who took her in her arms and held her. Ever since her mother died, when Ana was very young, Dochia and Andrada had been like mothers to her.

"What was done with them?" Andrada asked Vezina. "I mean Dochia and the women and children."

"They were buried by the local people, after the Romans left," Vezina replied. "Dochia was buried in the forest on the mountainside alongside the others who died there."

"May she rest in peace then," Andrada said. "We shall see her again in the kingdom of Zamolxis."

"Yes, My Queen," Vezina agreed in a solemn voice. "We shall see her again."

Mountains of Dacia, April 102 AD

The Dacian army travelled lighter and faster over the mountain roads than the Roman army. They gathered supplies waiting in storage in their forts while the Romans had to carry their food and supplies in supply wagons. The large artillery and siege engines of the Roman army had to be pulled by oxen, slow and ponderous beasts of burden. Dacian wagons were pulled by horses and mules.

The army of Emperor Trajan had to stop to attack every Dacian fort along the way on the mountain roads. Trajan had a big advantage in siege machines and men, and every fort fell after putting up a fight. Each of these battles took several days of time however, and also inflicted more casualties on the Roman troops.

As the army of King Decebal retreated they resumed their tactics of mountain warfare. They were very skillful at surprise attacks, quick strikes, and swift strategic withdrawals. Small units of one hundred to two hundred warriors ambushed Roman supply trains and hit marching units of infantry. Dacian horse archers made hit and run raids all along the Roman lines. There would be no more large battles because the Dacian army was now severely depleted and badly outnumbered.

King Decebal met with his generals of infantry, Diegis and Drilgisa, in the courtyard of the fort. Buri, who was seldom far from the side of the King, joined them at the table. It was a bright and sunshiny day and Decebal preferred to be outdoors in the fresh air and sun when he could.

A sentry on the wall called down to them. "Riders approaching! Three Romans! They carry a flag of truce!"

"Flag of truce?" Buri asked. "What do you suppose they want?"

"Maybe Trajan wishes to surrender?" Drilgisa wondered.

"I don't know, Buri," Decebal said. "Would you go and ask them?"

"Of course," Buri answered. He walked out through the gates that were partly open and faced the three Roman messengers. The rider on the right carried the flag of truce. The rider in the middle was a familiar face.

"Hello, Titus," Buri greeted him in a friendly voice. "What can I do for you?"

"Hello, Buri," Lucullus said. "It is good to see you again. You are still looking fit for the battlefield, I see. A little older than when I last saw you in Rome, eh?"

"I will say the same for you, Titus. So is this a social call?"

Lucullus smiled. "I wish that was so, but no. I come to talk with King Decebal if he would receive me."

"That is what I figured," Buri said. "You can come with me, alone. Leave your horse and your weapons with your friends here."

"Certainly," Titus agreed. He dismounted, then handed his gladius to one of the other riders. "You will wait for me here. This man is a friend and I am in no danger."

"Yes, sir," the man acknowledged, still looking warily at Buri. The huge warrior with the big bushy beard looked exactly like the fierce barbarians he imagined in his boyhood nightmares.

Buri walked Lucullus through the gates and to Decebal's table. All the Dacians seated there were familiar with this Roman. Diegis, Drilgisa, and Buri had been guests of Emperor Domitian in Rome, and Lucullus was their guide on that visit. King Decebal knew him less well, but saw him once in Sarmizegetusa when Titus came as part of a Roman diplomatic mission.

"Look who comes before us now! An honest Roman," Diegis said.

"Welcome, Titus," Drilgisa said in greeting. "I am glad that we meet here and not on the battlefield."

Lucullus greeted Diegis and Drilgisa with a nod, then made a small bow before the King. "King Decebal, greetings. I am sent by Caesar to discuss terms of peace with you."

Decebal was in a somber mood. He gestured towards the bench on the other side of the table. "You are our guest, Lucullus, so sit with us. Then we will talk on friendly terms."

"Thank you. I am honored to join your table," Titus said, taking a seat between Drilgisa and Diegis. Buri went to stand besides Decebal.

"What terms does Emperor Trajan offer?" Decebal asked.

Lucullus cleared his throat. "Before we talk about a treaty, King Decebal and General Diegis, I wish to say that I am saddened to learn about the death of your sister Dochia."

Decebal gave him a nod. "Thank you for your kind words. She was a very good woman. She did not deserve such a death."

"She died while fleeing a Roman attack," Diegis added, holding his anger down.

"Diegis, I grieve with you," Lucullus said. "Her death was not wished for nor welcomed by Rome."

Diegis waved the comment away. "The intentions of Rome do not matter. But there is nothing to be done now."

"No, nothing to be done," Decebal said. "What message do you bring from Trajan, Lucullus?"

Titus paused for a breath to compose himself. He turned to face the King squarely.

"First, Caesar asks that you surrender to him. In person."

Drilgisa laughed. Diegis slowly shook his head.

"What else?" Decebal asked.

"Caesar orders that after you capitulate you will swear loyalty to Rome," Titus continued. "You will serve as a true client king, not a sham one as you did with Emperor Domitian."

"I do not serve as a puppet king, Lucullus," Decebal said. "You have a reputation for thinking with a clear head, so you know this."

"Kings of Dacia do not capitulate," Diegis cut in.

"I understand," Lucullus said. "These however are Caesar's terms for peace."

"My brother is right," Decebal said. "No king of Dacia has ever bent a knee to a foreign ruler. Nor will I be the first."

Titus glanced around him at the face of each man. He saw only calm and firm resolve.

"King Decebal, you are known to all as a man of great honor and courage. I must however plead with you to accept Caesar's terms. If you do not agree to the terms Caesar must then pursue you and seek your destruction."

"Caesar will do what he must," Decebal said. "And I will do what I must. At times the choices are difficult, Lucullus."

The men grew quiet. The negotiations were over.

"Very well," Titus said evenly. "I shall give Caesar your message, King Decebal."

Drilgisa shot him a smile. "Will you also give Caesar my message?"

Titus could not help but smile back. "No, Drilgisa, I will not. And it would be best for all if you kept your message private."

"Well then, since we are done with business, will you have some wine before you leave?" Diegis asked him, a peace offering. "It is not the quality of your Falernian grapes but it will quench your thirst."

"Thank you, I will," Titus said. Although he was not a big wine drinker, he knew that Diegis made the offer out of friendship and it would have been impolite to refuse.

"Good," Diegis said, and gestured to a servant who ran to bring the wine. "And the next time we drink wine, Titus, may it be under more happy circumstances."

"Yes, my friend," the Roman agreed. "I pray that is so."

Mountain valley near Costesti, Dacia, June 102 AD

The river crossing was slow going for the Roman army, as were all river crossings. A number of boats had to be lined up side by side so that the timber frame for a boat bridge could be built on top of them. Wide boards were nailed and tied to the wooden frame to provide a floor. Guard rails had to be erected so that men and animals did not fall over the side.

Roman engineers were the best in the world but still the work was very time consuming. Trajan watched a scorpion go by, mounted on a cart drawn by mules. The carrobalistae were easy. The siege engines such as the catapults were bigger, heavier, and more difficult to move.

"We must find an easier way to cross rivers," Trajan said. "It slows the army down to a snail's pace."

"It would help if we could make oxen float," Laberius Maximus joked. He was mounted on a big warhorse next to Trajan, watching the army march by. The Emperor supervised all things including the crossing of rivers.

Trajan was not amused. "The answer is stone."

"Stone, Marcus?"

"Stone bridges, Laberius. Build a solid stone bridge and it will last for a hundred years."

"Ah, I see. This country has no shortage of stone, that is certain, but unfortunately they use it to build forts and not bridges."

"We will change that," the Emperor said. "We need Dacia's gold and silver, and we need her grains and livestock. We need good transportation, and that requires roads and bridges, not forts."

"Tell that to the barbarians, Marcus. Here comes a gaggle of them now," Maximus said, gesturing towards the river bank.

Trajan turned his head to watch Hadrian approaching at the head of a small group of men. A number of them were Dacians, dressed in the rich clothes of the nobility. The pileati, they called themselves, after the lambs-fur caps they wore as a symbol of their noble status. These men were Hadrian's helpers, not his prisoners.

The group was stopped by the Praetorian Guard before they got too close to Caesar. The Dacians all bowed low before the Emperor. Trajan gave them little notice. Such men were not important to his goals and were rarely worth his time.

"Caesar, these men are friends of Rome," Hadrian announced. "They bring grain and livestock for our troops. They provided these boats to make our boat bridge, and they have information that Caesar would be pleased to hear."

"Yes?" Trajan asked.

One of the Dacians took a step forward amd bowed again. "Hail, Caesar! We are thankful for this opportunity to be of service to Rome and Caesar."

"You are not loyal to your king?" Trajan asked.

"No longer," the pileati replied. "He takes our wealth via taxes and takes our men to serve in his armies. He is a tyrant who leaves us poor and destitute, Caesar."

Trajan gave him an amused smile. "And also, he is losing the war."

The Dacian maintained his tone of bravado. "Yes, Caesar. A foolish war, as we tried to tell him, but Decebal is too stubborn to listen."

"Enough," Trajan said impatiently. "What information do you have for me?"

"We are here to guide Caesar to treasures of great value, if Caesar would do us the honor of accepting our assistance."

"Dacian treasure?"

"No, Caesar," the pileati said. "Roman treasures. The treasures of General Fuscus."

The Dacian fort of Costesti put up a fierce fight for two days. Archers and spearmen crowded on the parapets and beat back all efforts to attack the walls directly. The valley soil here was soft and grassy, and Roman infantry storming the walls found themselves falling into concealed pits and being impaled on sharp wooden stakes. Twenty pieces of artillery on top of the walls, mostly the light carrobalistae, fired arrows and bolts at the attackers.

Roman artillery gave the Dacian defenders on the walls a beating and destroyed buildings inside the fort. Artillery caused damage to the fort walls but could not bring them down. The walls were built thick, stone blocks on the outside and filled with rubble and earth in the middle to absorb the impact of battering rams and the large boulders hurled by catapults. The defenders on the walls were getting thinned out and would eventually be overwhelmed by sheer numbers.

In the early morning of the third day, just after daybreak, Hadrian came to Emperor Trajan with welcome news. The siege of the fort was over.

"All left?" Trajan asked with mild surprise.

"There are no defenders to be seen, Marcus. Only smoke rising from inside the fort. Our men are inside now and have opened the gates," Hadrian reported.

"Search the fort for hidden gates or tunnels and you will find them," said Titus Lucullus, there alongside Laberius Maximus. "That is how they escape into the forests."

"No doubt, Titus," said Trajan. "They did not wish to sacrifice themselves for the sake of killing a few more Romans."

"By now they are moving through the forest and heading west to join Decebalus," Maximus said. "No matter. We shall catch up with them again and finish them."

Trajan turned to Hadrian. "Form search parties and search the fort thoroughly, Hadrianus. Every building, shed, every hole in the ground. Thoroughly."

"Yes, Marcus. Immediately," Hadrian replied, and quickly left to see to his task.

"The boy is good with administrative tasks," Maximus said wryly after Hadrian departed. "You trust him with those more than with military tasks, I think."

"You think correctly," the Emperor replied. "Hadrian has a better administrative mind than a military mind."

"All that training in philosophy and mathematics, eh?"

"Exactly. They have their uses but not for a military man," Trajan said. "Hadrian lacks enthusiasm for military matters in any case. Now let's go and examine this fort."

"Very well," Maximus replied. He gestured to Lucullus. "Join us, Titus. You are more familiar with Dacian forts than anyone else here."

"Yes, sir," Titus replied. "They are all built in a like manner, very sturdy and efficient. That seems to fit the Dacian character."

As they walked the grassy turf, wet with morning dew, Maximus turned to Trajan and spoke casually. "Hadrian is family to you. One day he might resent the treatment you give him. I mean given the role of an administrative aide. He has pride."

"Laberius, you surprise me," Trajan answered just as casually. "I only appoint the best men for the most important jobs, you know this. That is why you lead my infantry and not another man. I do not favor family."

"Of course not, Caesar," Maximus agreed. "I would not question your judgment and certainly not how you rule your family."

"Good. Hadrian enjoys many favors being married to the daughter of my niece. I trust that he is grateful enough."

They entered the fort through the open gates. The air was thick with a smoky haze. A large pile of wood and timbers burned in the courtyard. These included the charred remains of what had been the Dacians' artillery. The fort's defenders were in a hurry to leave and did not fire the buildings.

"They destroyed what weapons they could not carry," Maximus observed. "They did not want to leave us their artillery."

"I do not care about their artillery," Trajan said. "We can build more artillery. But if those Dacian pileati are wrong I will have them skinned alive."

"They were not wrong, Caesar," Titus Lucullus said. "Look, here comes Hadrian now."

It did not take long to find the treasures that Hadrian went searching for. The Dacian soldiers did not consider them treasures but rather objects of curiosity, and made no effort to either hide them or destroy them. Walking in front of his men, many of whom were carrying the flags and banners of Roman legions and flags of the Senate and People of Rome, Hadrian was proudly carrying a large flag bearing the emblem of the legion of the Praetorian Guard.

Hadrian stopped in front of the Emperor, sporting a grin from ear to ear. "Caesar, it gives me great pride and satisfaction to present you with the recovered standards of Legio V Alaudae."

Trajan took the flag, made from rich and thick cloth. He ran his fingers over the letters on the front.

“Sixteen years ago General Cornelius Fuscus was defeated by General Decebalus and lost this standard, along with his legion.” The Emperor stopped and took a deep breath. This moment was history being made. “Rome has lived with that loss, that humiliation, ever since. Now the standards are recovered and that shame can finally be washed away.”

“Hail, Caesar!” Hadrian said. “Caesar restores the dignity and the glory of Rome.”

Maximus clasped Hadrian on the shoulder. “Well said, Hadrian. Now we must complete this campaign and bring Decebalus to his knees. Then Rome will be avenged and Mars Ultor will rejoice.”

Trajan handed the standard back to Hadrian. “See to it that this is well protected. Treat it with reverence! It will be transported with my personal belongings. I will carry it back to Rome and fly it during my Triumph parade.”

“As you wish, Caesar. The people of Rome will celebrate to see the standards again.”

“Did you find the escape gates, Hadrian?” Maximus asked.

“We found one gate in the wall, disguised. No doubt there are more. They left very quickly in the night.“

“Do not waste your time looking for hidden gates and tunells,” Trajan ordered. He gestured around at the fort. “Burn it all down. I want no more Dacian forts in Dacia.”

> Chapter 16

Barbarians At The Gates

Sarmizegetusa, July 102 AD

Company after company of the Dacian infantry marched into the city through the gates of Sarmizegetusa. Their return was greeted joyously by their families, however the joy was tempered by the knowledge that even a strategic retreat in many ways felt like defeat. Usually the soldiers returned home through these gates as conquering heroes. This time they expected to have to defend this massive fortress that was the holy city of Dacia. This was the first time that a Roman army would reach Sarmizegetusa. What would happen next no one knew for certain.

Decebal and Diegis rode their horses to the entrance of the royal palace. As soon as Diegis dismounted Ana flew to him and jumped into his arms. He picked her up with a delighted laugh. Andrada, Zia, Adila, and Dorin waited for Decebal by the entrance. He embraced each in turn, gratified to see that they looked healthy and well. The reunion was warm, but something felt missing. For the first time in his life Decebal's two sisters were not there to welcome him home.

"The people need a message about what will happen now," Andrada said when the royal couple could finally talk in private. "Everything feels uncertain now."

"I understand," Decebal replied. "I called for a general and public council meeting tomorrow. The nobles and priests are all asked to attend, and every one of them will be there. We will speak with them, and they will spread our message to the people."

"So," the Queen wondered, "what will happen now?"

"That remains to be seen, my dear. Trajan will approach the city within two weeks. We may then have talks and negotiate. Or we may have to fight and defend the city."

"Will he attack the city?"

Decebal gave a small shrug. "Depends on how the talks go. If we cannot reach agreement, then yes he will attack."

Andrada shook her head slowly, doubtfully. "What will Emperor Trajan want that would convince him not to attack?"

Decebal gave her a grim smile. "My neck, perhaps?"

"Do not jest about that!"

He reached out and gently touched her cheek. "Don't worry about me. Many have wanted me dead, and yet here I still am."

Andrada was silent for a few moments, lost in thought. "I miss Tanidela and Dochia. My heart aches when I think of losing them."

"Yes. I mourn for Dochia also. Tanidela lives, I am told. She was taken prisoner to Rome but she lives, and so does little Tyra."

"That is good news," Andrada said with a sigh. "I worry also about our children. And the people of the city."

"The soldiers will fight to the last," Decebal said. "So will I. You and the children, on the other hand, will not."

"I don't want to run away. I will not run."

"No one is running, Andrada," the King said in a calm tone. "For now patience and courage are required. The people need to see that from their Queen."

"Yes, I know that! For all these months when you were gone, my daily message has been one of courage and patience. I am not lacking courage, Husband, but my patience is frayed very thin with this war with Rome that never ends."

"Display the courage then, Andrada. It is much more important than patience. A cow in the field may display patience, but what good comes from that?"

Andrada rolled her eyes. "If you compare me to a cow I will kill you myself and save Trajan the trouble."

"Ha! Don't jest, she said."

"I am not jesting," she replied, then relaxed and gave him a smile. "All right, I am jesting. Now let's discuss what our message will be at the council meeting tomorrow."

The council meeting was held in the throne room. King Decebal and Queen Andrada sat side by side on identical thrones. The High Priest Vezina stood by the side of the King. Generals Diegis and Drilgisa stood on the other side, next to the Queen.

Over one hundred nobles of Dacia and priests of Zamolxis stood in the audience. All were in a high state of tension. They waited to hear news and instructions from their monarchs.

King Decebal opened the discussion. "Our scouts tell us that the army of Emperor Trajan is marching towards Sarmizegetusa at a slow pace. They are perhaps ten days away. We shall use that time to strengthen the city defenses and prepare the army for a siege against the city."

A distinguished looking elderly man with silver hair raised his arm to be heard. He was Sorin, the grandfather of Ana and father in law of Diegis. He was respected by all for his honesty, fairness, and sound judgment.

"Are the Romans so aggressive that they will immediately launch an attack? Or will they be willing to parlay?"

"That is my question also, Sorin," Decebal answered. "We will not know Emperor Trajan's intentions until Emperor Trajan arrives."

Another nobleman raised his hand to be heard. He was a man of average height and stocky build, with graying brown hair and brown eyes. His bushy eyebrows made his face look almost fierce.

"Yes, Bicilis?" the King acknowledged him.

"Would it not be better to reach an agreement than to be subject to a long and destructive siege?" Bicilis asked.

Vezina gave him a patient look. "It all depends on terms, Bicilis. Would you surrender the city to keep the peace?"

"No, I would not, Your Holiness," Bicilis said. "But there may be terms short of surrender that the Romans would accept."

"What do the Romans want?" another nobleman asked.

Vezina turned to Decebal. "Sire, you know them best."

Decebal leaned back on his throne and addressed the crowd. "The Romans want many things. They want revenge for the wars Dacia has won against their armies, because that is a deep injury to Rome's pride. They want Dacia's gold and silver, because they know that our wealth will cure Rome's financial problems. And, perhaps, they want my neck."

The crowd became quiet.

"Which of those would you concede to the Romans, Lord Bicilis?" Queen Andrada asked.

The nobleman colored, not sure how to answer her question. "Not the King's neck, surely, My Queen."

"Good," Andrada said. "Because the King's neck is not an item for negotiation."

"Many sieges have been ended by payment in gold," Vezina said.

"Not in our case," Decebal said. "Emperor Trajan will not simply want payment in gold, he wants all our gold. And not only the gold in our treasury but also the gold in our mountains."

The nobles and priests murmured unhappily. Paying that high a price would mean surrendering Dacia to the Romans.

"What we must do for now," the King declared in a firm voice, "is to prepare for battle. Sarmizegetusa can withstand a siege for many months. Our walls have never been breached. A great many Romans will die trying to breach them."

"That is the message to our people," the Queen added. "Prepare for a battle, if we must have a battle."

"Our people have always paid a high price for our freedom," King Decebal added. "We must continue doing so. No price is too high, and no sacrifice is too great, to preserve our freedom."

There were no voices of dissent.

Decebal and Buri toured the army camps inside the city walls and spoke with many of the soldiers preparing themselves for battle. Their spirits were high. The Romans had conquered the mountain forts. However, comparing a Dacian mountain fort to the walls of Sarmizegetusa was like comparing a house cat to a lion. The soldiers did not believe that Sarmizegetusa could be conquered.

The sprawling city was built into the side of a mountain. One side faced a high and towering cliff, and another side was protected by a cliff that dropped sharply and could not be climbed. The rest was surrounded by walls thirty feet high and nine feet thick. Blocks of stone lined the outer sections of the wall. Battlements on top of the walls, made of andesite and limestone, provided platforms for archers, spearmen, and artillery to fight off attacking forces. Massive gates made of thick wood reinforced with iron guarded the main entrance.

A large group of young infantry soldiers were being trained by former legionnaires, the Romans soldiers who deserted from their units and joined the Dacian side almost two decades ago. Many of them had married Dacian women, raised Dacian children, and now considered Dacia their home.

"Never rush a legionnaire!" Cassius Danillo instructed in a very loud voice of authority. "He is better armored than you! His Roman shield gives him more protection than your Dacian shield! He will crouch behind his scutum, wait for you to get close enough, then stab up with his gladius and gut you!"

The young Dacian soldiers listened with rapt attention. Cassius Danillo was somewhat of a legend among the young men of Dacia.

Their fathers and older brothers told them of the many occasions when Danillo's training helped to save their lives.

King Decebal and Buri paused to watch the lesson that Cassius knew by heart and repeated with precision, because he had taught it thousands of times to thousands of other young men.

"Pick your spots to attack!" Danillo continued. "Work your way around to their sides or their backs! Those of you fighting with falxes, use the reach advantage and power advantage that the falx provides for you! Attack where they are least protected, on their limbs and their necks! The weapon most feared by the Roman legionnaire is the Dacian falx! Use it to your advantage!"

Danillo paused. He turned to the King and Buri with a grin on his face. "Do you think they believe me?"

Decebal nodded. "By the looks on their faces, Cassius, every single one of them believes you."

"They would be foolish not to believe you," Buri said, "and Dacian mothers do not raise foolish boys."

"Ah! You are exactly right, Buri. And here comes another one of those boys now."

A gangly fifteen year old approached them. His hair, eyes, and nose made it obvious that he was Danillo's son. The boy was not shy in the presence of the King and gave Decebal a small bow.

"Sire, this is my oldest son, Marcu," Danillo said. "He will join the army next year after he grows a bit taller, and after his mother's good cooking puts a bit more muscle on him."

"I am eager to serve this year, Sire," Marcu said. "But Father tells me to wait."

"Listen to your father, boy," Buri told him in a stern tone.

"Yes, sir," the boy said respectfully.

"Your name is Marcu?" the King asked. "Not Marcus?"

"He has a foot in both camps, Sire," Danillo said with a half smile. "In Dacia he is Marcu. If he ever goes to Rome then he is Marcus.

Some day he might want to see his grandparents, uncles, aunts, and cousins. We will not be at war with Rome forever."

"That is a prudent strategy, Cassius." Decebal looked at the boy. "Are you happy here in Dacia, Marcu?"

"Yes, Sire," he answered in a serious tone. "Dacia is my home and I have no wish to be anywhere else."

"Good," Decebal said, giving the boy a pat on the shoulder. "I will welcome you into my army next year, Marcu."

"Thank you, Sire!" Marcu replied with a big grin.

"Keep in mind what I told you, boy," Buri reminded him. "This man is your father, and he is also a master trainer of soldiers. You are very fortunate to have him for a father."

"Yes, sir," Marcu replied in a serious tone. "I shall remember."

The elder Danillo gave Buri a grateful nod. His son was at an age when boys often thought they knew everything there was to know, and knew what was best for them.

"Carry on the good work, Cassius," the King said. "We will need every soldier we have in the coming weeks and months."

Aquae, south of Sarmizegetusa, June 102 AD

All the units of Emperor Trajan's army assembled at the hot springs resort of Aquae, within an easy march of Sarmizegetusa. They made plans there for the assault on the Dacian holy city. General Lusius Quietus brought in his Moorish cavalry from their raids in western Dacia. He was supported by Iazygi cavalry and some small units of Roman cavalry. General Laberius Maximus had overall command over heavy infantry, which was made up exclusively of legionnaires. General Gnaeus Pompeius had command of the light infantry, which was made up of auxiliary infantry including large units from Gaul, Germania, Pannonia, and Spain.

Emperor Trajan had over seventy thousand fighting men to send against Sarmizegetusa. By his best estimates, after questioning a number of Dacian prisoners under torture, he knew that Decebalus had less than twenty thousand warriors with which to defend the city. Friendly Dacians, most often the wealthy pileati, confirmed the information gotten from the prisoners. There were additional Dacian troops scattered in northern and western Dacia, however they had no way to reach Decebalus in the city.

Caesar was not worried about winning this final battle. Yes, he wanted to crush Decebalus, but he also wanted to limit the loss of his own troops. There was a smart way to win wars and a reckless way, and Trajan always preferred the smart way.

"When do we attack?" General Quietus wondered. "My men were taking a great deal of plunder in our raids, until we were ordered here. They do not like to sit idly and waste time."

Trajan looked up from his map. "You are always eager to attack. Patience, Lusius. Sarmizegetusa has stone walls thirty feet high. If you go against them with your cavalry the Dacian archers on the walls will turn your men and your horses into food for crows."

Quietus bristled. "I will not attack the walls, Caesar. Open the gates for me and my men will do the rest."

"You are asking for the easy job!" Gnaeus Pompeius said with a laugh. "The hard part will be breaching the walls. If they can be breached, that is."

Trajan turned to Titus Lucullus. "Titus, you are the only man here who has been inside the city. What are your thoughts?"

Lucullus cleared his throat. "Any defense can be breached, Caesar. It is a matter of how much time time and how many casualties."

"I agree, Lucullus. But explain how that applies to Sarmizegetusa."

"When I was here last, with Senator Paulus, I made observations from the viewpoint of a military scout. I knew that someday I would be back in exactly this type of situation."

"Smart lad!" said Maximus. "Continue."

"We should understand that this is not a fort but a very large city. They are self-sufficient for food and water. They have many large granaries stored with food that will not perish. They have orchards, and herds of cattle and sheep with enough pasture land to sustain them. They can resist a siege for months, and perhaps for years."

"I will not spend years on this campaign," Trajan said evenly. "It has been one year now and that is long enough. I want to be back in Rome before winter."

"Of course, Caesar," Titus agreed. "I do not suggest that we press a siege for a number of years, simply that it might require a number of years to starve them out."

"What of the military attack option?" Lusius Quietus asked. "That would not take years."

"No, but it would cost a great number of casualties, General," Titus continued. "As Caesar has said the stone walls are thirty feet high. They are also nine feet thick. The walls cannot be breached by our artillery or by battering rams. They are built with towers that jut out, which allows their archers and artillery to attack our men with crossfire as they try to scale the walls. Our casualties would be very high."

"How high?" Maximus wondered.

Lucullus paused to give it thought. "If Decebalus has ten thousand fighting men on the walls, our casualties would be fifteen thousand or perhaps higher."

Trajan gave a nod. "In a direct assault on a walled city attackers have higher casualties than defenders."

Gnaeus Pompeius frowned. "Unfortunately I think that you are both right. We have never attacked a fortress this strong before."

"Can we dig under the walls?" Maximus asked.

Lucullus shook his head. "The ground is mountain rock in most areas. It would take months to dig through it, if it can even be done."

Trajan waved his hand dismissively, growing impatient with the tone of the discussion. "We will not dig tunnels through rock, and we will not press a siege that takes years. We came here on a mission to punish Dacia and bring Decebalus to his knees. We will be successful in our mission."

"So we attack, then?" Quietus asked.

"We attack if necessary, Lusius," Trajan said and brought his fist down hard on the table, making the maps jump. "We do whatever is necessary to win this war. We are Rome! Only victory is acceptable."

Mountains of Dacia, July 102 AD

Tarbus could not make out the language of the men marching and talking casually on the slope below his ambush position. They were clearly auxiliary infantry, based on their uniforms, weapons, and their long hair and beards. It was a good sized group. The auxilia were organized similarly to the legions, so if this unit was formed to be the equivalent of a centuria it would be approximately eighty men.

Tarbus had thirty archers and forty spearmen. An ambush attack however relied on surprise, not numbers. Tarbus and his men were hidden behind thick shrubbery that grew among a copse of oak trees. He had complete surprise and was simply waiting for more of the enemy to come into view. He was tempted to ask the man on his left about the marchers' unrecognizable language, but did not wish to break silence and risk giving away their position.

"Germans," said the man to the right of Tarbus.

Tarbus grimaced and put a finger to his lips for silence. The man gave a small shrug, only mildly embarrassed over his momentary lapse in judgment. He turned his attention back to the Germans. The enemy was now in attack range.

"Kill them!" Tarbus shouted as he stood up, his falx pointed at the enemy. The infantry below was hit with a barrage of seventy arrows and javelins. Thirty men fell, dead or wounded. At close range the archers were very accurate and very deadly. They loosed another round of arrows, then the spearmen rushed down the slope and hit the remaining auxiliaries before many of the Germans could even position themselves for battle. This enemy was unprepared and now very confused, and that made them easier to kill.

Tarbus rushed downhill towards a young warrior wielding a spear and a small round shield. The soldier saw Tarbus out of the corner of his eye and turned towards him in a panic, starting to raise his spear to meet the onrushing Dacian. Tarbus knocked the spear away easily with the longer and heavier two handed falx. He made a backhand cut with the falx that slashed through the panicked German's throat. The man fell heavily, blood spurting from a severed artery.

Another spearman moved towards Tarbus, his face a mask of rage. He was stopped by an arrow that hit him in the stomach and another in his chest, and fell forward clutching at his chest. Dacian archers were shooting at close range and could not miss. Someone at the back of the German column blew a shrill whistle. It was the signal that they were under attack. Reinforcements would arrive within minutes.

Tarbus saw that four Dacians were down. He did not want to lose any more men. Quick strike, kill the enemy, rapid retreat, General Drilgisa had ordered.

"Back!" Tarbus shouted loudly to his men. "Back!"

The Dacians turned immediately and ran back up the mountain slope. One caught an arrow in the back from a German archer. The man gave out a shout of pain, then staggered and fell. The rest of the Dacians vanished among the shrubbery and trees within seconds. They would all meet at a prearranged spot in the forest some distance away, then return to Sarmizegetusa.

Sarmizegetusa, July 102 AD

The King walked down the long hallway between the royal living quarters and the throne room. He was distracted and deep in thought, and did not even notice the servant walking the other way until he almost bumped into her.

“Oh, forgive me, Sire!” the young woman apologized. “I should be more attentive to where I am going!”

He gave her a forgiving smile. “Do not apologize, the fault is mine. My mind was elsewhere.”

“Of course, Sire,” she replied. “I understand.”

The young woman was tall, with long strawberry-blond hair. She looked at Decebal as if she wanted to say something more.

“You work in the palace kitchen, as a baker. What is your name?” Decebal asked.

“Salia,” she replied with a smile, pleased that he recognized her.

“Ah, yes, of course. Salia.”

“You surely will not remember, Sire, but you made a promise to me once. Well, to me and to the other children in High Priest Vezina’s class. I was only six years old, but I always remember what you said to me then.”

“What promise did I make?”

“You promised that you would always keep the Romans away, and that you would keep us safe.”

Decebal’s expression turned somber. The trust this young woman placed in him felt in part like a burden, and also a sacred obligation. This was the burden of kings. It was inexorable, inescapable.

“And do you think I have kept my promise, Salia?”

“Yes, Sire. You have,” she replied in a serious tone.

“Do you mean to say, I have kept my promise so far?” the King asked with a wry smile.

The question took Salia by surprise. “Yes, Sire. You have kept your promise so far. You always keep your promises.”

“Very well, then,” Decebal said, also in a serious tone. “I shall do my best, Salia, to keep my promise to you for as long as I am able.”

She gave him a respectful bow. “I know that you will, Sire. Thank you, Sire.”

Decebal left her and resumed his walk to the throne room. He had much to think about and his thoughts jumped between the past, the present, and the future. How easily promises are made, he thought to himself, and how eagerly we make them with the best of intentions. And how difficult it is sometimes to keep them. And yet a king who did not keep his promises was no king at all. And a promise made long ago to a six year old girl might change not only her life but also the life of a nation.

"The barbarians are at our gates," Queen Andrada said. "Now we need to make decisions to protect the lives and freedom of our people."

The King's council was meeting in the throne room. The King, the Queen, Drilgisa, and Diegis were seated around the big round table used for council meetings. They were joined by Vezina, chief advisor to the royal couple. The King also invited the two noblemen Sorin and Bicilis, leaders of the Dacian nobility.

"The barbarians are here, My Queen, and we don't yet know what they want," Vezina said. "Our first task is to find out. Following that we can decide how best to make them go away."

"I agree," Decebal agreed. "But first, before we discuss what they want let's discuss what we want." He paused for a moment and looked around the table. "First and most important Dacia does not surrender independence, not for any reason. We do not open our gates to Rome for any reason. The barbarians at our gates, Queen Andrada, will remain outside the gates."

"Good," said the Queen. "I like the plan so far."

"Trajan might not like this plan, I would guess," Vezina said.

Decebal waved the comment away. "That does not matter. If the Emperor wants to enter Sarmizegetusa then let him kill his army by smashing it against our walls."

"I agree!" Diegis said, pounding his fist down on the table top.

"I agree also," said Drilgisa. "If they want a fight, let it be a very bloody fight."

"Very well," Vezina said. "The Romans will not enter the city."

Decebal continued. “Second, Dacia is not for sale. We will make concessions to Rome for a peace agreement but we will not pay any outrageous ransoms to Rome. They do not get the gold and silver in our treasury. And they most certainly do not get the gold and silver and all the other wealth in our mountains.”

“So be it,” Vezina said. “Dacia’s freedom and wealth are not items for negotiation.”

“And third,” Queen Andrada added, “King Decebal’s neck, and the royal head attached to it, are not items for negotiation.”

“They never were, My Queen,” Vezina said with a smile.

“That settles what we want,” the King said. “Now let us return to your question, Vezina. We need to talk with Trajan and find out what Rome wants.”

“Who will be our envoys?” Andrada asked.

Sorin looked around at the men sitting at the table and laughed. “Now I understand why Bicilis and I were invited to this council meeting.”

Bicilis raised his bushy eyebrows, surprised. “Us?”

“I cannot send my generals, Bicilis,” the King explained. “And not our High Priest either. Yet the envoys must be someone of high rank that the Romans will treat with regard. You and Lord Sorin are the best choices to represent Dacia.”

“I will be proud and honored to serve as your envoy, My King,” Sorin announced.

“I as well, Sire,” Bicilis agreed.

The two envoys listened with a serious purpose as King Decebal and Vezina briefed them on the details of their mission.

> Chapter 17

The Price Of Peace

Aquae, Dacia, July 102 AD

Next to the hot springs of Aquae was an elegant villa that was the equal of some of the finest mansions in Rome. The floors were marble, the walls richly decorated with art and tapestries, and the grounds were beautifully landscaped with marble fountains and large gardens. The nobility of Dacia made annual trips there for the health benefits of the hot springs and also for relaxation and socializing with other wealthy nobles.

Emperor Trajan immediately made this villa his headquarters. After many months of living in tents, pitched in mountain valleys that were wet in spring and dusty in summer, he craved some of the luxury that Caesar enjoyed in Rome. The villa was very comfortable, and for the time being Caesar was in a better mood about being in Dacia. Several amphorae of the finest wines arrived there from Rome, which also improved his mood.

Sorin and Bicilis were both very familiar with Aquae from their many trips to the hot springs. They knew the roads and the grounds, however it was jarring for both of them to see the area occupied by Roman troops. They presented themselves as envoys of King Decebal and were escorted by Praetorian Guards to meet with the Emperor.

Trajan received the Dacian nobles while seated on a marble patio in front of the villa. It was a warm and sunny summer morning, a clear blue sky with dashes of white, and Caesar was in a happy mood. He shared some of the newly arrived Caecuban wine with Tiberius Livianus, the Prefect of the Praetorian Guard. Although Falernian red wines were all the rage in Rome, true experts of the vine such as Sura and Trajan considered that Caecuban wines were just as good.

Sorin and Bicilis approached to within ten paces, then bowed low before Caesar and waited for him to speak. The Emperor remained seated in his cushioned chair, holding his elegant silver wine goblet in his right hand.

"Tell me plainly what your King Decebalus told you to say," Trajan ordered them.

Sorin took the lead and explained, in a general and diplomatic way, what King Decebal laid out at the council meeting. He spoke like a polished and well-mannered man of the nobility, and also looked the part. Trajan liked to portray himself as a man of the people and was not impressed by polished and genteel behavior.

"I do not wish King Decebalus dead, and you may tell him so," the Emperor said. "However I require him to accept the rule of Rome and to serve Rome as a true client king. Will your King accept this?"

Sorin gave him a small bow. "Yes, Caesar."

Trajan turned to Bicilis. "Do you agree?"

"Yes, Caesar. King Decebalus will accept the rule of Rome," Bicilis replied in a deferential and somewhat shaky voice.

Trajan leaned back in his chair. He was relaxed and confident, the ruler of the world. His very next words would determine the fate of a nation. He let the Dacian messengers stand and squirm for a while longer. The one with the bushy eyebrows was looking nervous.

"You will tell King Decebalus that I accept his terms for peace, however he will also agree to my terms. Three days from now he will come here, along with his family, and present himself before Caesar. As client king of Rome he will vow an oath of loyalty to Caesar and to the Senate and People of Rome."

"I shall give the King your message, Caesar," Sorin replied with another bow. Bicilis also bowed, looking relieved.

"Three days from now," Trajan repeated. "Caesar and Decebalus shall talk directly then. Your King will then hear Caesar's additional terms and demands."

"Yes, Caesar," Sorin and Bicilis said together.

"You may go now," the Emperor said. He watched them being led away to their horses. Laberius Maximus and Titus Lucullus, who had been standing nearby, walked over to join Trajan.

"Will Decebalus come?" Maximus wondered.

"He will come," Trajan replied.

Titus gave a nod. "Yes, I agree, Caesar. Decebalus is a proud man but it would be reckless of him to refuse your terms."

Trajan held up his wine goblet for a servant to re-fill. "The price for his recklessness, gentlemen, if he behaves in a reckless manner, is that we will tear down Sarmizegetusa until nothing remains but pasture for sheep."

Sarmizegetusa, July 102 AD

"Vezina is asking one hundred of our people to come along to Aquae," Queen Andrada said. "Women and children and a few older men. They will represent the people of Dacia."

"Good," the King said. "Let the Romans see that we are not the savage barbarians they fear. Are our children prepared to leave?"

"They are," Andrada replied. "Dorin wants to bring his dog. He goes nowhere without Toma in tow."

Decebal shook his head. "That would be unwise. If Toma feels threatened for some reason and gets aggressive, a Roman spearman will make the end of him."

"I don't think Toma will be aggressive. On the other hand," the Queen said with a sigh, "I can make no such promises for Adila."

"Yes, I know. She still carries a deep anger ever since Tapae."

"Dochia's death made her anger worse," the Queen said. "She blames the Romans for her death."

"Of course she does. Dochia would still be alive if she was not forced into the forest to escape the Roman attack."

"Yes," Andrada said. "Too many have died. I shall be glad when we make peace."

Diegis came into the room with Ana at his side. The girl had a tense and worried look on her face.

"The travelling party is ready," Diegis told them. "I wish that I was coming with you."

"Me too," Ana echoed her father.

Andrada leaned down and kissed the top of her head. "You will stay here with your Tata. Do not worry about us, we will not be in danger."

"But the Romans!" Ana protested. "They hate us, like we hate them. When they see you they will hate you, I just know it."

"Ana, quit worrying," Diegis said. He gave her a quick smile. "No one hates your Aunt Andrada, you know that."

Decebal turned to his brother. "While we are travelling, the city is yours. Drilgisa will assist you. Mircea will stand in for Vezina and supervise the priests. There should be no problems."

"Oh, I expect no problems in the city, Brother," Diegis said. "If problems arise they will happen in Aquae."

"There will be no problems in Aquae," Decebal declared. "We will talk, make the peace, and that will be it."

"I remember a time," Diegis continued, "when you were wary about going to Rome to meet with Emperor Domitian."

"This is not the same, Diegis," Decebal said. "Trajan is a man of character and honor. Domitian utterly lacked those qualities."

"We should go," the Queen interjected. "The women and children have been placed in wagons for the trip. We keep them waiting."

"Goodbye," Ana said to them. She was close to tears.

Andrada crouched down and looked her in the eye. "While we are gone I have an important job for you to do, Ana."

"What job?"

"We cannot take Toma with us, so he must stay here. Will you take care of him until we return? You father will help, I'm sure."

The girl's face brightened. "Yes, Aunt Andrada. I will watch Toma until Dorin comes back."

"Good! Dorin will thank you too. Now give your auntie a hug, and we'll see you again in a few days."

"Have a good trip," Diegis said. "I will be waiting for scouts daily to report your progress."

"It will be a short trip," Decebal replied. "We'll be back within a week. I am looking forward to finally seeing this Trajan, our most capable enemy."

Aquae, July 102 AD

The Emperor received the Dacian party in front of his villa again, this time with the legions assembled in formation to witness the historic ceremonies. Trajan wanted to impress the visitors with a show of Rome's military might. He also wanted his legions to witness the power and glory of Caesar in dealing with the enemies of Rome.

Sorin and Bicilis led a group of twenty Dacian nobles dressed in their finest formal attire. King Decebal and Queen Andrada followed, flanked by Vezina and Buri. Zia, Adila, and Dorin walked behind them. Bringing up the rear of the Dacian delegation was a group of women, children, and older men, the common people of Dacia.

Trajan waited for them seated on a throne. His generals gathered around him. The flags and standards of the Praetorian Guard and the Senate of Rome were raised on tall poles behind them, flying in the mild mid-day breeze. This was the pomp and glory of Rome on full display, and it always had the desired impressive effect on those who were witnessing it for the first time.

Sorin and the noblemen paused ten paces in front of Trajan's throne and kneeled down before Caesar. The Dacian citizens in the rear also kneeled before Caesar, all except the children who were not expected to understand the solemn occasion of this ceremony. King Decebal and the Dacian royal family did not kneel, because Dacian royalty did not bend a knee to any foreign power. Vezina and Buri stood beside their King and Queen.

"Caesar," prefect Tiberius Livianus announced in a voice loud enough even for the legions to hear, "here stands King Decebalus of Dacia, with his family and his advisors!"

Trajan paused for a moment for effect. He was in charge of these proceedings, and he took time in the moment for a close look at his adversary. Decebalus, the Dacian king who had been such a painful thorn in Rome's side for so many years. The adversary he had been chasing across Dacia and Moesia for a year now. This was a man of character, built like a warrior but with the regal bearing of a born leader. We are not unlike, Trajan thought. The gods and the goddess Fate has placed us on opposing sides.

"Welcome, King Decebalus and Queen Andrada. What do you ask of Rome?"

Decebal held out his arms towards Trajan, an appeal for peace and conciliation. He spoke in a loud and clear voice. "Dacia wishes to end the war between us. Let us end these hostilities, Caesar. Too many Dacians and Romans have died. Dacia wishes to form an alliance with Rome and to pledge loyalty to Rome."

Trajan paused to allow the words of Decebal to be repeated for those in the back of their very large audience.

"Do you pledge to serve as client king of Rome, and vow that you will be loyal to Caesar and to the Senate and People of Rome?"

"Yes, Caesar. I make that pledge."

Trajan addressed Decebal in a lower tone of voice. "You once made such a vow to Emperor Domitian."

Decebal answered also in a lowered tone. "I made no vows to the Emperor Domitian."

The Emperor had no wish to debate the matter. This was not a Senate discussion. He cleared his throat and continued.

"King Decebalus, Rome grants you the title of client king to Rome. You will agree to the following conditions." Trajan paused again for a moment. He had everyone's attention and now Caesar would show his authority.

"First, Rome will no longer make annual payments to Dacia per the former treaty with Emperor Domitian."

"I agree," Decebal replied. This was entirely expected. The large sums of money that Domitian agreed to pay to Dacia to keep the peace were a source of embarrassment to Rome and a drain on the state treasury.

"Second," Trajan continued, "you will surrender to Rome all the lands occupied by Dacia in Moesia and Banat. Dacia will not occupy any lands beyond your side of the Danubius River."

"Agreed," Decebal said. He did not have enough military troops to defend those lands in any case.

"Third, you will surrender all of your siege weapons, artillery, and other weapons of war. You will have no need to wage war again on Rome or on any allies of Rome."

"I agree, Caesar," Decebal said. More artillery could be built and this was no time to maintain an aggressive posture.

"Fourth, you will tear down the walls of your forts in Dacia. As an ally of Rome you need no longer fear any attacks from the armies of Rome or her allies."

Decebal shot a sideways glance at Vezina. The High Priest gave him a very small nod. They had no choice in the matter at this time.

"I agree, Caesar," Decebal told him.

"Fifth, you will surrender to Rome all the men who deserted the armies of Rome and joined the armies of Dacia."

Andrada cringed inside, but kept her facial expression neutral. Those hundreds of Roman deserters now had homes and families in Dacia. She considered them to be a part of Dacia, but clearly Trajan had other views on the matter. She noticed that Buri, standing by her side, showed a similar discomfort.

"I agree," Decebal said reluctantly. It was a matter of honor for Trajan to dispense Roman justice to the deserters, and Decebal knew what fate awaited those men. And yet he had no choice now to defy Rome on dealing with Roman deserters. This was a matter of pride for Trajan and he would not back down.

"Sixth," Trajan continued, "Rome will not station troops in Dacia, with one exception. Rome will keep a small military garrison inside the walls of Sarmizegetusa so that we may monitor how well Dacia fulfills the terms of this treaty."

"I agree," Decebal said. Those men would be observers and not a military threat to Dacia.

"Very well. Our negotiations are concluded," Trajan declared. His generals looked pleased with Caesar's terms for peace. They knew that the Senate in Rome would also be satisfied.

Trajan sat up from his throne and, accompanied by the prefect Tiberius Livianus, approached the Dacian royal party with a smile on his face. The conqueror would now play the gracious host.

"King Decebalus, Queen Adrada, and High Priest Vezina. I am happy that we can be friends," Trajan said.

"I am happy also, Caesar," Decebal replied. "Rome and Dacia make terrible enemies. It is time to stop the fighting."

Trajan gave him a nod. "You have been a fierce enemy to Rome for many years. Yet you do not fight for wealth or personal glory, I am told. What, then?"

"Dacia has enough wealth," Decebal said, "and I have no hunger for glory. We Dacians fight for one thing. One of your countrymen described it best. He was called Cicero, Vezina tells me."

"Ah! Cicero said many wise things. Which do you have in mind?"

"I believe that the saying is, freedom is a possession of inestimable value," Decebal replied.

Trajan gave him a solemn nod. "So it is. And freedom is not denied nor begrudged among friends."

Decebal returned the nod. They had taken the measure of each other, and they understood each other on this vital matter at least.

"I am happy to be friends as well, Caesar," Andrada said. "I wish for my children to live in peace, and to grow older and have their own children."

"And these three surely are your children, Queen Andrada? Both your daughters look so much like you they could not be otherwise." Zia and Adila inherited their mother's big blue eyes and general facial features, along with her lustrous black hair.

"Yes, Caesar. These are our children, Zia, Adila, and Dorin," the Queen introduced them with pride. Each of them gave the Emperor a small respectful bow. They knew not to speak unless first spoken to.

Trajan turned to Vezina, looking regal in the blue robes trimmed with gold and silver that signified his status as the High Priest of Zamolxis. "I have heard much about you, High Priest Vezina. You have been a strong force in the military success of Dacia. Will you be an equally strong force in keeping the peace with Rome?"

Vezina gave an easy laugh. "You credit this old man too highly, Caesar. But yes, of course I shall strive to help my King and Queen keep the peace."

"I am gratified to hear that," Trajan said, although he knew very well that Vezina was saying what he was expected to say. Only time would tell how things would work out with these Dacians. They were a proud and stubborn people, and those kinds of people always made poor subjects under the rule of Rome.

Trajan and the Dacian royal couple bid their farewells. The Dacian party walked back towards their horses and their wagons. The adults seemed happy with what transpired, which in turn put the children in a playful mood. These Romans no longer seemed so scary.

For a short while Trajan stood and watched them walk away, lost in thought. All in all, the Emperor felt satisfied. Dacia was subdued. Decebalus was humbled. He had saved himself months of further trouble and also spared the lives of many thousands of Roman troops.

The Emperor turned and headed to a raised wooden platform from where he would address the assembled legions and speak to them of the end of the Dacian war. After a difficult war soldiers were always relieved to hear that the fighting was over. Later in the day he would sacrifice to the goddess Victory. When he returned to Rome later in the year the Senate would grant him a Triumph. Rome would celebrate with a great parade and feast to mark his victory over Dacia. The campaign he began a year ago, the mission of Mars Ultor, was finally accomplished.

Sarmizegetusa, August 102 AD

King Decebal and Buri approached the house of Cassius Danillo, but stopped to watch from a respectful distance as the former Roman legionnaire bid farewell to his wife and three children. The youngest boy was four years old and did not understand the reason for all the tears. His father sometimes went away, and he always came back. Sometimes he brought back little prizes for the children.

Decebal and Buri waited for Danillo to finish his goodbyes. As Cassius walked away, heading for the city gates, he noticed the two men waiting for him. He returned their greeting with a nod and they joined him on his walk.

Outside the city gates a cohort of Roman soldiers waited to escort the Roman deserters to the Roman camp in Aquae. Five hundred armed legionnaires would be guarding almost two hundred former legionnaires, stripped down to their tunics and sandals, over the one day march to Trajan's villa at the hot springs.

"You understand what was done, Cassius?" Decebal asked.

Danillo gave him a grim smile. "Dacia needed to make peace with Rome. Yes, I understand. The fates of little piss-ants like me are a small matter compared to the fates of nations."

"That sounds about right," Buri agreed. "Speaking from one piss-ant to another, Danillo."

That made Cassius smile. "I have faced death hundreds of times in my life. I am not afraid of death." He turned his head to look at the King. "Ever since the day I left Legio VI Victrix and came to your camp in the mountains, King Decebal, I knew that someday this day might come. I knew how Rome deals with deserters, and still I made the decision and took the risk."

"Yes, I understand," Decebal said.

"Now it seems like a lifetime ago," Danillo continued. "In truth, it was a lifetime ago. I found a new life here. I have no regrets. I found happiness here that I never would have found serving in a Roman legion."

The tall and massive city gates came into sight. The three men grew silent as they walked. When they reached the gates Danillo paused and turned to face Decebal and Buri.

"I thank you for the respect you have shown me," he said in a firm tone. "Buri, it would mean a great deal if you looked after my family when I am gone. Look in on them once in a while."

"I will do that, my friend," Buri promised. "You have my word."

"They will be taken care of, Cassius," Decebal said.

Danillo bid them both farewell and walked towards the group of waiting men, stripped down to their tunics and sandals, who were being guarded by the legionnaires. Decebal and Buri stood to watch them for a short while.

A silent figure moved by them, walking very briskly, his head turned away. Buri saw him in the corner of his eye and reached out a quick hand to grab the boy by the upper arm.

"Whoa, there! Where do you think you're going?"

"Let go!" the boy protested and struggled to break free but he was no match for Buri's size and strength. Decebal recognized Marcu, Danillo's son.

"Let me go!" Marcu said again, his eyes blazing.

"Marcu, stop," Decebal commanded. "You cannot join your father. You cannot help him, and you will only get hurt."

Marcu ceased his struggles and Buri let go of his arm. He did not wish to disobey the King. He would need to make another plan.

"Son, listen to me," Buri said, looking him in the eye. "You must do what your father would want of you. That means you stay here and help your mother take care of your family. Do you understand?"

"Yes, sir," Marcu said, looking at the ground.

"Go home," the King told him. "Your mother needs you there."

"Yes, Sire," Marcu replied. He turned and walked away. His mind was racing ahead, to later in the day after the group of legionnaires and their prisoners left on their march to Aquae. There would be few people crowding around the gates then, and the King and Buri would no longer be standing there. It was always a simpler thing to leave the city than to try to enter the city.

Aquae, August 102 AD

Titus Lucullus was surprised to be summoned from the staff tent of General Maximus to Trajan's headquarters in the villa. Not that he minded in the least. Being in the villa reminded him of being in Rome, and the accommodations were far superior to any army camp. Also it was always a positive thing to catch the Emperor's attention. Careers and fortunes were made by those who gained Caesar's favor.

Trajan was enjoying the lively company of Gnaeus Pompeius and Hadrian. Their mood was light, the easy banter helped once again by several cups of a good wine. Wine was a daily passion for Caesar.

"Lucullus! Come join us," the Emperor invited, pleased to see him. "Have some wine."

"Thank you, Caesar," Titus said. "You honor me."

"Don't be so quick to feel honored, Titus," Trajan said, a wry smile on his lips. "You do not yet know why you are summoned here."

Pompeius laughed. Hadrian giggled. Titus poured himself a cup of wine. Caesar would tell him what he wanted from him in due time. One did not rush Caesar.

"We were discussing bridges, Lucullus," Trajan continued. "What do you know of bridges?"

"In truth, Caesar, I know nothing about bridges."

"Ah! No matter. Hadrian does. He has an interest in architecture."

Titus gave Hadrian an admiring nod. "Architecture is a noble art, certainly, and one that requires a great deal of talent and training."

Trajan waved his hand dismissively. "It is one of his many Greek pursuits. Hadrianus has a grand idea, however. If it can be made to work it will astound all men. Tell him!"

Hadrian was so used to Trajan's teasing that he no longer reacted to it. He turned to Lucullus, eager to express his idea.

"I believe that it is possible to build a very long bridge made of timber and stone," he explained, his eyes shining. "A bridge long enough to cross the Danubius."

"Ah, the foolishness of youth!" Gnaeus Pompeius exclaimed with a good-natured laugh.

Titus could not quite picture it. "The Danubius River is too wide and too wild for any standing bridge. A temporary bridge built over the tops of boats, perhaps, but those don't last very long."

"Do you think the idea impossible?" Trajan challenged him.

Titus paused. "I am no architect, Caesar. No one has accomplished the feat, yet who is to say what is impossible?"

Hadrian grinned. "Exactly, Titus. We do not know until we try."

"When we are back in Rome, Hadrian will talk to Apollodorus and make plans for such a bridge across the Danubius," the Emperor said. "That is Hadrian's mission."

"I wish you good fortune in your mission," Titus said to Hadrian, feeling impressed. Apollodorus of Damascus, Trajan's architect, was the most famous engineer in the world. Perhaps a bridge over the Danubius could be built?

"On the other hand, Lucullus," Trajan continued, "your mission is very far from Rome. I am appointing you to command the garrison at Sarmizegetusa that keeps watch over Decebalus."

The announcement took Titus completely by surprise. “I will do as you command, Caesar. But might I ask, why me?”

“Can you think of anyone better? You know the Dacians best, and they seem to trust you.”

“I see. Then it will be my honor to command the Roman garrison in Sarmizegetusa,” Lucullus said. “Might I ask, how large a garrison will it be?”

“It need not be a large garrison, Titus. It is not a fighting garrison. Just large enough to make a presence," the Emperor replied. “Half a cohort, let us say.”

“Yes, Caesar,” Titus said, hiding his disappointment. Half a cohort was roughly two hundred and fifty men, not a large command.

Trajan seemed to know his mind. “It is a small garrison but a very important mission, Titus. Decebalus is stubborn and independent minded. I need to know his intentions. Manage this well for me and you will be well rewarded.”

“I understand, Caesar,” Lucullus said. “I will be your watchdog.”

The two hundred deserters from the Roman army being marched from Sarmizegetusa to Aquae received brutal treatment. Soldiers hated traitors, and deserters were considered to be the worst kind of traitors. The prisoners were given no food and very little water. They were beaten with clubs and prodded with spears as if they were beasts of burden. Those too sick or injured to travel were executed on the spot and left to rot by the roadside.

When they reached Aquae the prisoners were herded into a cattle pen. There they awaited their fate, which all knew would not be long in coming. They all were resigned to being executed and some even welcomed it. The sooner their humiliation would end the better.

The next morning Trajan assembled the legions on a large open field outside the city of Aquae. Ten chopping blocks cut from thick logs were lined up in the middle of the field. An executioner with a sharpened battle axe stood by each chopping block. The two hundred prisoners were brought to the field, herded like cattle, each with his hands tied behind his back. The assembled legionnaires jeered them and laughed at them.

At Caesar's command the first ten prisoners were walked to the chopping blocks. They were forced to kneel and place their necks on top of the blocks. When all were in place, on command ten battle axes fell and ten heads rolled away completely severed from their bodies.

The corpses were quickly dragged away and another ten prisoners were brought to the blocks. Then another ten. Then another ten. The ground in the execution area became wet and slick with blood, and the executions continued. This was Caesar's justice for deserters. Not a single man present would ever forget it.

Some distance away, from between the branches of a tall elm tree growing on a hill, a fifteen year old boy looked out on the assembled legions and the execution grounds in the middle of the field. He was too far away to recognize individual faces or other body features. He could clearly see the prisoners being walked forward to the row of blocks and then beheaded. Once he thought he saw a prisoner who looked and walked like his father, but he could not be sure.

Marcu Danillo found that he could no longer cry. He felt numb and cold, except for a burning anger in the pit of his stomach. He hated legionnaires. He hated Romans. Most of all he hated Emperor Trajan, who was responsible for it all. As his anger grew hotter Marcu dreamed of revenge. One day he would have his revenge. He prayed to Zamolxis to make it so.

Sarmizegetusa, September 102 AD

"Emperor Trajan is not returning to Rome quite yet," Vezina reported to the King and Queen. "He is inspecting and strengthening the forts along the Ister River on the Roman side, and rebuilding the forts in Moesia that we destroyed."

"He doesn't trust the peace," Decebal said.

"No, he does not," said the Queen. "Do you?"

The King shook his head. "I take nothing for granted when the fate of the nation is at stake."

"A wise decision, Sire," Vezina said. "We must rebuild our army. Rome is Dacia's greatest enemy but not our only enemy."

"Yes, we must," Decebal agreed. "And we will. It will take us two years to replace the men we lost at Tapae and in Moesia."

"We should also send envoys to all our allies," Vezina said. "We need to re-build our alliances."

"Will this ever end?" Andrada wondered. "Are we heading for war again soon? We must have time to rebuild the nation."

Decebal shook his head. "No, we are not heading for war. But we must be prepared for war. When we stop being prepared is when we face destruction."

"Pray to Zamolxis that day never comes," Vezina said.

"Oh, I do pray to Zamolxis," Andrada said. "I also pray to Trajan and to Decebal. War and peace are not determined only by the gods."

> Chapter 18

Dacicus

Sarmizegetusa, November 102 AD

Rome was formally asking Dacia for symbols of surrender. Human ones worked best, preferably royalty, but if none were to be had then high nobles would suffice. The Senate of Rome planned a grand celebration of the Emperor's military victory over Dacia. The many public ceremonies needed representatives from Dacia to bow before Caesar and show Dacia's acceptance of Rome's authority.

"They would prefer your presence of course, Sire," Vezina said to Decebal in the King's council meeting. "You would bow before the Senate and be marched in Trajan's triumphal parade."

The thought of it made Queen Andrada chuckle. "It would make quite a spectacle, no doubt. The great barbarian king, enemy and scourge of Rome! Humbled at last!"

"That will never happen," Decebal said. He looked at the other people sitting around him. Besides Andrada and Vezina the council table also held Diegis, Drilgisa, Bicilis, and Sorin. "So who wants to go to see Rome and march in a Triumph?"

"I would find it interesting," Vezina said. "Sadly, I am too old for such a trip. Also I would never debase myself by kneeling before the Senate or before Trajan."

"Nor would I ever allow you to do that, Vezina. However we are asked to send representatives. It would be poor diplomacy to refuse."

"I spent enough time in Rome," Drilgisa said. "I have no wish to go back, and neither will I bow to any Roman."

"Your last trip there ended with a dead Roman, as I recall," Diegis said with a laugh. "You make a poor guest."

Drilgisa gave an indifferent shrug. "Justice was served. I make no apologies."

"What about you, Diegis?" Vezina asked.

"Not me!" Diegis cried. "One trip was enough. And also, like Drilgisa, I will bow to no Roman."

Vezina paused in thought. "I will ask Mircea to go to represent the priests of Zamolxis. He will be happy to do so. He enjoyed the last trip, and in fact he still talks about it."

"Mircea is a good choice," Decebal said. "Now we need two or three others besides him."

"I assume that leaves us, again?" Sorin asked, raising an eyebrow.

"You would represent Dacia well and are sufficiently high placed to placate the Senate," Queen Andrada said. "You also, Bicilis."

Bicilis was pleased with the compliment. "Thank you, My Queen. I will be happy to represent Dacia. And like His Holiness Vezina, I also am curious to see Rome."

"Very well," the King said. "Three representatives will be enough. You will be polite and diplomatic, and nothing more. There will be no more discussions or negotiations on behalf of Dacia."

"Yes, Sire," Sorin agreed.

"This will be your diplomatic mission, Lords Sorin and Bicilis," Andrada added. "However we also have a personal mission for you."

"Yes, My Queen?"

"We understand that Tanidela is now residing in Rome," Andrada continued. "If you are able to, you will find her and talk with her."

"Yes, of course," Sorin said. "We shall make every effort to find the Lady Tanidela."

"Tanidela will be just as eager to talk with you," Decebal said, "and she may find you first. She is treated as a guest in Rome, not as a prisoner. This is what we hear from Vezina's contacts in Rome."

Vezina nodded. "A guest, but under observation. We don't know how free she will be to talk with you."

"I understand, Sire," Bicilis said to the King. "I will deliver any messages you have for her. And bring back any messages she has for you and the Queen."

Decebal addressed both noblemen. "Find my sister. Talk with her. Consider this the most important of your two missions."

Rome, December 102 AD

The Empress Pompeia Plotina was mildly exasperated. "Who gives a Triumph in late December? Sometimes the Senate acts without any sense at all. People will be cold and the crowds will be smaller."

Trajan casually waved away her complaint. "The fault is mine I am afraid, my dear. I had work to do in the north until now. The Senate could not give a Triumph for Caesar without Caesar."

"I suppose not," Plotina agreed. "We shall have to dress warmly in our winter clothes. And keep the parade shorter, perhaps? We can't have people standing out there for hours on end."

"Stop your worrying," Trajan chided her with a smile. "The people will be excited for the celebration. They will come out. And they know how to stay warm in winter."

"The people already celebrated in the streets when you arrived back in Rome, Brother," said Ulpia Marciana. "Still, you deserve a proper Triumph for Dacia. It is an honor richly earned."

"Thank you, Marciana," the Emperor replied. "It is traditional and we must respect tradition. Never in the history of Rome has anyone refused a Triumph voted by the Senate because the weather was too cold!"

"All right, I yield," said Plotina. "We must make plans for the guests to invite to the palace after the public feast."

"That, my dears, I leave entirely to the two of you."

"Not too many guests, I don't think," said Marciana. "We don't want to appear ostentatious."

Trajan raised an eyebrow. "Speaking of guests, how is our Dacian guest?"

"She is well, Brother," Marciana said. "When she was delivered here by Hadrian we placed her under my wing. She has quarters close by Salonia and the girls. She and Salonia are now friends, actually."

"Oh? That is interesting," Trajan said.

"They are close in age, and also in temperament," Plotina said. "They all dote on the baby girl Tyra and treat her like a little princess."

"I should speak with her," Trajan said.

"Shall I have her summoned here, Brother?"

"No, no," the Emperor decided. "I want to see her in her quarters, to see how comfortably she is adjusting to life in Rome."

"I would say that Tanidela is adjusting very well," Plotina said. "Because the royal family accepted her so warmly, so have the people. They treat like a foreign celebrity."

Trajan laughed. "Well, that is a good thing. She bears no blame for the actions of her brother Decebalus."

Trajan found Tanidela teaching the fine art of Dacian embroidery to Salonia and her daughter Mindia Matidia. Different colored threads in green, yellow, red, and brown formed patterns of delicate flowers on white cloth that would be made into blouses. Vibia Sabina was off to the side, playing with Tyra. A Roman wet-nurse stood by in case Tyra needed personal attention.

"Hello, Uncle," Salonia greeted Trajan and stood up to give him a kiss on the cheek. Vibia and Mindia walked over and did the same. Tanidela stood up and waited respectfully.

"Hello, my lovelies," the Emperor greeted them. "Hello, Tanidela. You are well, I trust?"

Tanidela gave him a bow. "Yes, Caesar. I am well."

Trajan glanced at the baby, now in the arms of the wet-nurse. "And your daughter?"

"Tyra is well also. Thank you for your kindness, Caesar. To me and to my daughter."

"Tyra is a wonderful little girl. I want to adopt her!" Vibia said with a laugh.

"Oh? But she already has a mother, Vibia. Perhaps you should talk to Hadrian about having one of your own?"

Vibia frowned. "Let's not discuss that right now. Hadrian and I are not on speaking terms."

Trajan gave Salonia a quizzical look. She shook her head slowly, a signal not to pursue the subject.

"Perhaps I should excuse myself," Tanidela said, embarrassed. "I have no place in family discussions."

"Nonsense," Salonia said to her. "We have no secrets, and we have talked about these things before."

"Ah!" Trajan said with a laugh. "Perhaps I am the one who has no place in family discussions, eh?"

"Not true, Uncle," Salonia said lightly. "Vibia can talk to you about this later if she wishes to."

"I don't wish to," Vibia said, just as lightly.

Trajan smiled and shook his head. "We can discuss that later. Would you excuse us now, my dears, so that I may speak with Lady Tanidela?"

"Of course, Uncle." Salonia turned and left the room, followed by her daughters. The wet-nurse holding Tyra retreated to the far side of the room. In Rome servants were expected to not pay attention, no different from a piece of furniture. Gossip could be punished by death.

"You are no doubt aware of the peace treaty between Rome and Dacia," Trajan said.

"Yes, Caesar," Tanidela replied with a nod. "I am happy to see that the war is over."

"I met and talked with your brother the King. He is fierce in the defense of your people. I trust that he is also reasonable in honoring his agreements?"

"He can be reasonable," Tanidela replied. "But please remember, Caesar, why the symbol of Dacia is the wolf. When a wolf is cornered or threatened it becomes anything but reasonable."

Trajan gave her a nod. "That is a diplomatic answer but also an honest one. Very well. I will ask you, Tanidela, to communicate to your brother the wisdom of being reasonable."

Tanidela paused to consider this message to her. "Is that why I am being held here and treated well, Caesar?"

"In part," Trajan said. "You are also treated well because I wish it, and because you are deserving of it."

She gave him another small bow. "Thank you, Caesar."

"I hear that you and Salonia have become friends. I am pleased to see that. Is there anything more you wish for?"

Tanidela paused for a heartbeat. "Only my freedom, Caesar."

Trajan gave her a sympathetic look. "You are free to live in Rome. You have the freedom to be a Roman."

"I am not a Roman, Caesar. I am a prize, a symbol of your victory over Dacia."

"True, you are a symbol, Tanidela. And when you march in my Triumph parade the people will see you as a representative of your royal family and King Decebalus. And yet, I am told that the people admire you and treat you with affection."

"The people of Rome have been kind to me, Caesar."

"Good. My family has been kind to you, and you have returned the kindness." Trajan gave her a half smile. "Perhaps it is possible for Romans and Dacians to get along."

"I pray that is so, Caesar," Tanidela said, and meant it. "The wars between our nations have been terrible."

"There need not be more wars in the future. Play a small part in that if you are able, Lady Tanidela."

She nodded amicably. "I will do what I can, Caesar."

The Senate of Rome met to celebrate the end of the Dacian war and the victories of Caesar. Consul Licinius Sura welcomed the Dacian delegation of the noblemen Sorin and Bicilis, and the priest Mircea. They were told to stand by the doors in the Senate House and watch the proceedings. Trajan sat on the throne in front of the assembled senators. Sura held up his arm for silence, then began his oration.

"Fathers of the nation! Two years ago Caesar stood before us on this very spot on the Senate floor. Caesar promised us that the savage wolf to the north would be tamed and beaten back. He promised us that the outrages and humiliations against the dignity and honor of Rome would be avenged. He promised us that Rome would no longer pay treasure to a greedy and over-proud barbarian king. Caesar promised to wage war on the pride and arrogance of Dacia."

Sura paused briefly. Every Senator in the assembly was hanging on his every word. They knew what was yet to come.

"Fathers of the nation! Here is Caesar now, before us, with every promise kept and every victory achieved! Victory over the armies of Dacia, which are now greatly diminished! Victory over the traitors and deserters, who all met Caesar's justice and the executioner's axe! Victory over the aggression of Dacia, which now seeks peace on terms dictated by Rome! Victory over the arrogance of Decebalus, who is now humbled and pledged to serve as client king to Rome!"

The Senators erupted with shouts and cheers. Many stood up and applauded, some remained seated and stamped their feet on the floor. Sura walked slowly in front of the assembly and let the cheers fill the Senate House and wash over him. This was a moment that Rome had longed for, for almost twenty years.

"Fathers of the nation!" Sura continued. "Before us come three Dacians, who represent King Decebalus and the nation of Dacia. They come now before Caesar and the Senate and People of Rome to show their submission to Caesar and vow their allegiance to Rome!"

Sorin, Bicilis, and Mircea were guided by two lictors to a spot in front of the Emperor. They allowed themselves to be led, silent and compliant.

"Kneel before Caesar," Sura commanded in a low voice. All three men obeyed and got down on their knees.

"Bow down to Caesar."

The Dacians put out their arms in front of them and prostrated themselves before Trajan, their foreheads almost touching the floor. They remained prostrated as Senators cheered and applauded again.

"You may rise," Trajan told them. Forcing too much humiliation on them would be in bad taste.

When the Dacians rose to their feet Sura addressed them again. "Now face the Senate of Rome, and repeat the same steps again."

Sorin's face reddened. Was one humiliation not enough? He turned to face the assembled Senators, along with Bicilis and Mircea. They kneeled again. They prostrated themselves again. The Senators cheered and shouted again. This was a moment of pride for all Rome to celebrate.

"You may rise," Sura finally told them. "Well done, gentlemen. You represent Dacia well with your grace and humility." He gave them a few moments to walk back to their spot by the doors, then turned to face the Senate assembly again.

"Fathers of the nation! I propose that the Senate and People of Rome honor Caesar for these victories over Dacia by granting Caesar the title of Dacicus! Dacicus, the conqueror of Dacia! Stand now if you vote in the affirmative!"

Every single Senator in the assembly rose to their feet once again to approve this acclamation. Their roars of enthusiasm and joy filled the Senate House until it hurt their ears, and still they stood and shouted and applauded.

Sura turned to Trajan and held out his arms. "Hail, Dacicus!"

The Emperor stood up from his throne and acknowledged their acclaim. He was gratified by the honor, and also confident in his knowledge that it was well earned. Many years ago Domitian had demanded the title of Dacicus and the Senate denied it to him. Trajan on the other hand earned it. He earned it completely.

After the Senate ceremonies concluded Sura approached the three Dacians. Their diplomatic mission was over. They had shown up and humbled themselves, and expected that was all that was required of them. Sura surprised them with additional plans.

"You will be my dinner guests tonight," he told them, a gracious smile on his face. "I will send a slave to your inn to fetch you and guide you to my villa."

"We are honored," said Mircea. Sorin and Bicilis looked uncertain so he gave them a reassuring smile. "It will be an experience that none of us will forget, my friends."

"I promise you that you will not forget it!" Sura chuckled. "Caesar will be attending, as will the Empress Pompeia Plotina, as will the sister of Caesar, Ulpia Marciana."

"They honor you as well, Consul Sura," Sorin acknowledged. "There is however one other person in Rome whom we wish to see and speak to. Perhaps you can assist us in this matter?"

"Who is this person?"

Sorin was almost reluctant to say. "She is Tanidela. The sister of King Decebal."

Sura gave a hearty laugh. "Then your problem is solved! Tanidela will also be attending my dinner tonight."

Bicilis' bushy eyebrows shot up in surprise. "Will Caesar not mind if we talk to the Lady Tanidela there?"

"Not at all," Sura answered. "Why would he mind? Caesar insisted that you be invited to my dinner, so that you may talk with Tanidela."

Sorin cleared his throat. "We will be happy to attend your dinner, Consul Sura."

"Very good," Sura declared. "My man will fetch you at your inn. No formal dress is required, come as yourselves in your normal Dacian clothes. We so rarely have Dacian dinner guests in Rome."

Horse-drawn carriages were not allowed on the narrow and crowded streets of Rome, so Sura's man came with two litters and their litter bearers. Each litter would carry two men to the house of Sura. His Dacian guests would travel in comfort.

Mircea was enjoying himself more than his two companions. He had a strong curiosity and a love for learning. This was his second visit to Rome, the first being a part of the delegation that included Diegis, Drilgisa, and Buri, some thirteen years ago. He pointed out some of the historical sites to Bicilis, seated across from him in the litter. There is the Arch of Titus! There is the Temple of Venus!

Bicilis showed little interest. He was already thinking about what he would say to Tanidela. This vast and foreign city felt oppressive to him. The sights, sounds, and smells of Rome were bewildering to him. He missed the large open spaces and the clean mountain air of Sarmizegetusa.

They were ushered into the house of Sura by a door slave, then led to the large dining room by another house slave. Dining couches were arranged in groups of three around the room. Diners would be seated nine to a group, three diners on each couch. This allowed for a varied and interesting mix of people that produced lively conversation but also maintained a sense of small group intimacy. Roman dinners were planned in detail on all levels.

Sorin spotted Tanidela first, sitting on a couch on one side of the room. She was seated between a beautiful and elegant woman with a look of nobility about her, and an elderly gray-haired man of medium height and built. Sorin nodded in her direction for the benefit of his companions.

Tanidela looked excited to see her fellow Dacian countrymen. She recognized all three men and stood up to greet them eagerly as they approached, a big smile on her face.

"Lady Tanidela, we are overjoyed to see you again," said Sorin. He gave her a small respectful bow, and Bicilis and Mircea did the same.

"I am very happy to see you Lord Sorin, Lord Bicilis, and Mircea," Tanidela replied. "Do join us, please," she invited, gesturing to the couch opposite her.

The elderly man smiled pleasantly at the Dacian men, then turned to Tanidela. "Would you do us the honor of introductions, my dear?"

"Of course, Marcus," Tanidela agreed. "These men are Lord Sorin and Lord Bicilis, noblemen of Dacia. And this is Mircea, who is a priest of Zamolxis."

She waited for pleasant nods to be exchanged, then turned to the woman seated beside her. "This is Salonia Matidia, niece to Emperor Trajan, and this is Marcus Valerius Martialis, also called Martial, who is royal poet to Emperor Trajan."

The Dacians each gave a respectful bow to Salonia and nod of the head to Martial. Sorin glanced around the room and saw that Trajan was not yet present. He would likely be the last guest to arrive.

"How are you enjoying your stay in Rome?" Salonia asked them, making polite conversation.

"Very well, thank you," Mircea answered with sincerity. "There is so much to see and so much to learn here."

"Indeed," Martial agreed. "I have lived here most of my life and still only know a few parts of the city."

Salonia grinned. "Marcus only knows the best mansions in Rome, where the best dinners are served."

"I plead guilty, my lady!" Martial said with a laugh. "And who can blame me? The food in Rome can be exquisite, and sometimes it can be horrid. I am invited for dinner by the best hosts and I'm happy to share their company as they are happy to share mine."

"Did you ever eat a fish caught in the Tiber?" Mircea asked him with an amused smile.

"Say again? Ah, you mean that old joke about never eat a fish caught in the Tiber," Martial replied. "Do they tell that joke in Dacia, Mircea? The waters of the Tiber River are certainly polluted but not so bad as to cause a worldwide scandal I hope."

Mircea shook his head. "No, not in Dacia. I heard the joke here in Rome, at the house of Senator Marcus Paullus."

Tanidela noticed Sorin and Bicilis looking uncomfortable, getting impatient with the small talk. She felt the same. There were many more important things to talk about than fish in the Tiber.

"Lords Bicilis and Sorin, would you care to take a walk outside in the gardens? The air is still a bit chilly but the winter gardens are beautiful to see."

"Yes, my lady," Sorin agreed. "That is a wonderful idea." Bicilis also nodded in agreement.

The three excused themselves and Tanidela led them outside to a marble patio. There was a spacious garden decorated with winter plants, marble fountains, and fine statuary. Tanidela set the pace with a slow and leisurely walk. Here they could talk in privacy.

"What message do you bring from my husband and my brother?" Tanidela asked.

"That you are not forgotten, and that you are loved by all, my lady," Sorin replied. "Prince Davi, King Decebal, Queen Andrada, Diegis, and Vezina pursue every effort to gain your freedom."

Tanidela shook her head sadly. "Trajan will never allow me to go free. I am too big a prize for him."

"You are not a prize!" Bicilis blurted, offended. "You are a princess of Dacia and someday a queen of the Roxolani!"

"Trajan is playing a political game, Lord Bicilis. I am a political prize for Rome. There is no sense calling it something else."

They walked in silence for a bit. The marble fountains, although drained of water for the winter, were still beautiful. The green branches of the evergreens were still dusted with snow from the night before.

"Are you treated well, my lady?" Sorin asked.

"Yes, very well. That surprised me most of all," Tanidela said. "I am almost a part of Trajan's family, they have accepted me and Tyra so warmly. Salonia is a friend and treats me like a sister." A dark cloud seemed to pass over Tanidela's face and she fell silent. "I heard about the death of Dochia. I cannot bear the loss of her."

Bicilis gave a silent nod. "This has been a year of heavy losses, my lady. Now we must take time to heal."

"Yes," Tanidela said. "I am glad the war is over. Too many have died, including Dochia and Cotiso. But is that not always the case? Too many always die."

"Indeed so," Sorin agreed. "We must keep the peace, at least for a while."

Tanidela gave him a half smile. "And that, Lord Sorin, is exactly Emperor Trajan's message to Decebal."

"What message is that, my lady?"

"To keep the peace. He does not trust that Decebal will honor the treaty."

"Ah, I see. Trust is fragile, on both sides," Sorin pointed out.

Bicilis frowned. "The history of treaties is that they are broken when it suits someone to break them."

There was commotion inside the house, loud voices cheering and rising in greeting. It made Bicilis cringe as he thought back to Roman cheers while he was prostrating himself on the floor of the Senate House.

"Emperor Trajan has arrived," Tanidela said. "We should go back inside, I think."

Sorin paused and caught her eye. "Do you have a message for us to carry to those you love, my lady?"

"Yes," Tanidela replied. "Tell them that Tyra and I are well and healthy. Tell them that although I now live in this golden cage, my mind and my heart will forever remain free. Tyra will grow up with Roman friends and a Roman family, and she may choose to live as a Roman if she so wishes. As for me, I shall never stop being who I am. I shall always be Dacian."

Rome, December 28, 102 AD

To be given a Triumph, and the right to March through Rome as a triumphator, was the greatest honor any Roman could receive. Once it was given most frequently to conquering generals, however in more recent times it became more restricted and bestowed only on Caesar.

Each Triumph was an exercise in excessive opulence and a grand celebration of glory. They began with religious sacrifices, followed by a march through the city, followed by more sacrifices and a public feast, and ending with public games over several days at the Circus Maximus.

Emperor Trajan began his preparations on the morning of his Triumph by having his face painted red, the color of Jupiter. This was the same sacred paint that was used to paint the statue of Jupiter on the Capitoline. For this one day and this day only, Caesar would take on the qualities of Jupiter, the supreme god. For this one day Trajan would become a god.

The Emperor was then dressed in a white tunic embroidered with green palm leaves, which were a symbol of his victories. Over this tunic he wore a purple toga. Purple was the color of royalty and could only be worn by Caesar. He then accepted a golden scepter, which he would carry with him throughout the day. The golden scepter was the symbol of the triumphator.

The day's events began in the vast Field of Mars outside the city. Trajan ascended the steps to the front of a wooden stage. He gave a stirring patriotic speech before the assembled Senate of Rome, the priests of Jupiter, soldiers assembled in their legions, and a large crowd of spectators. Excitement surged through the crowd and few even noticed the cold.

Trumpets sounded and two perfectly white oxen were led before Trajan's stage. Each beast was led by a man holding a rope in front, and followed by a large man carrying a very sharp axe in back. The oxen were drugged to make them sleepy and docile. At a signal from Trajan the axe men chopped down with their axes and severed the oxen's spines. The sacrificial animals fell heavily to the ground, their blood gushing out to turn the ground red.

The Emperor then took his place in a gilded quadriga, the chariot reserved for the triumphator. The quadriga was drawn by a team of four perfectly white stallions, arranged abreast. A slave stood at the side of Caesar and held a golden crown over his head. He would do so throughout the entire parade.

Lined up behind Caesar's chariot was a row of other chariots and wagons, some carrying people and some carrying large paintings that depicted key events in the Dacian war. The chariot right behind the Emperor carried his top generals, including Maximus, Pompeius, Quietus, and also Hadrian. The chariot behind them, also considered a position of honor, held the Dacian party of Tanidela, Sorin, Bicilis, and Mircea. They were a prominent symbol of Trajan's victory.

Consul Licinius Sura, other magistrates, and Senators lined up in front of Caesar's quadriga. They would lead the parade through the city gates and through the streets of Rome. They started the march at a leisurely pace. They had plenty of time, and such a sacred occasion could never be rushed.

The procession passed the Circus Flaminius, then winded its way past the Porta Triumphalis. It went around the Circus Maximus and took the Via Sacra to head towards the Roman Forum.

The Dacians pulled their clothing tight against the cold and took in the sights. Large and enthusiastic crowds lined the parade route cheering for Caesar and the other marchers. To her pleasant surprise Tanidela found that some in the crowd were cheering for her.

"Tanidela! Over here!"

"Marry me, Tanidela!" one man shouted with a laugh.

"It appears that you are a celebrity in Rome, my lady," Sorin said with a smile, amused.

"It appears so," Tanidela said calmly. "Not that I did anything to invite it or deserve it for that matter."

"They admire your beauty and your grace, my lady," said Bicilis. "That requires no effort on your part."

Tanidela shook her head. "You compliment too easily, Bicilis."

Sorin was looking ahead, at Caesar's quadriga. "Why is that slave holding the crown talking to Trajan? He never seems to stop."

"That is a Roman custom," Tanidela answered. "On the day of the Triumph the triumphator is considered to be a god. So that it does not make him arrogant, the slave holding the crown over his head always whispers in his ear to remind him."

"Whispers what?"

"He whispers, remember thou art but mortal."

Bicilis chuckled. "And does Trajan believe him, do you suppose?"

"That we shall never know for certain, Lord Bicilis," Tanidela told him. "We should however be gracious towards our host on the day of his Triumph."

"Yes, my lady," Bicilis said. "On this day Trajan is free to believe whatever he wishes to believe, I suppose."

Mircea gestured at the crowds shouting greetings and praise for Caesar. "When so many people adore you, even worship you, it might not be difficult to think of yourself as a god for one day."

Sorin raised an eyebrow. "That is an interesting thought coming from a priest of Zamolxis."

"Zamolxis was a man who later became a god," Mircea explained. "He is a true god. I care nothing for statues of Jupiter nor any of the other Roman gods. They are nothing but clay and paint."

"Mind your tongue, Mircea," Tanidela chastised him. "In Rome such talk is blasphemy. It will get you crucified."

Mircea gave a nod, looking slightly embarrassed. "I understand, Lady Tanidela. I spoke too harshly."

The parade reached its end near the Temple of Jupiter. The crowd gathered once again to watch the sacrifice of more oxen to Jupiter. The sacrificial animals died cleanly, and Jupiter was pleased. Caesar was ushered inside the temple where the banquet would be held. The generals, senators, magistrates, and other guests followed him.

The temple had limited room for dining but was adequate to fit in Caesar's important guests. Tanidela joined the table of Marciana and Salonia and brought the other Dacians with her. Emperor Trajan and Empress Plotina finished talking with the group of generals, then stopped by to talk with family members at Marciana's table.

"A magnificent Triumph, Caesar," Marciana said to her brother. "All Rome worships you today."

"And rightfully so," Trajan said. "Today of all days I deserve to be worshiped, my dear. Today I am Jupiter come to life."

"So god-like," Plotina said with a smile, "and yet still so humble."

"Do you see?" Trajan asked Tanidela, an amused smile on his face. "I need no slave whispering in my ear to remind me that I am mortal. My family reminds me every day."

"Oh, hush," Plotina teased her husband. "We treat you like a god every day and you know it."

Salonia turned to the Dacian men. "Will you be coming to the games at the Circus Maximus tomorrow?"

Sorin glanced from Bicilis to Mircea. Bicilis looked doubtful, but Mircea looked eager. "In truth, we had not planned to stay in Rome past today, my lady."

Trajan waved the comment away. "That is no matter, you will stay a few days longer. I had the Circus Maximus enlarged specifically to celebrate this Triumph so it will be a spectacle to see. You will attend tomorrow as guests of Caesar."

"Of course, Caesar," Sorin conceded with a small bow. "We will be honored to attend the games."

"I am glad," Tanidela said to him with a smile. "It may be a while before I have the company of fellow Dacians again."

"It is our pleasure to have your company, my lady," Mircea said.

"The company of Dacians need not be so scarce, Tanidela," Trajan said. He turned his gaze to the Dacian envoys. "When you return to Dacia tell King Decebalus that Rome has no wish for further conflicts with Dacia as long as Dacia honors the terms of our treaty. Tell him that his sister is treated in the most kind and honorable manner in Rome. Tell him that this is how Caesar wishes for Rome and Dacia to treat with each other."

"Yes, Caesar," Sorin replied with a respectful nod.

And thus Emperor Trajan made known his wishes that Rome and Dacia would be at peace. As Emperor of Rome he had other plans to make, other things to do, other matters to attend to. Whether or not Decebalus would allow him to attend to those plans, only time would tell. Not even Jupiter could foresee the actions of the Dacian king.

> Chapter 19

The Winter Wedding

Sarmizegetusa, December 102 AD

Princess Zia of Dacia was planning her wedding. A royal wedding always became a very large scale operation that went beyond the royal family itself. Queen Andrada, Zia, Adila, and Zelma took the lead. The young girls Ana and Lia were very interested, but they were inexperienced and thus only given simple tasks that they could handle.

Tarbus was the groom but he knew enough to stay out of the way. So did the male heads of the household, King Decebal and Buri. Wedding planning was traditionally women's work. For this wedding the only exceptions made were for Vezina and Dadas. Hundreds of foreign dignitaries were invited to the wedding, including kings, chiefs, and nobles of all of Dacia's allies. Vezina was in charge of sending out the invitations, and Dadas was needed to manage the many cavalry scouts who would serve as messengers to deliver them.

"People will not want to travel far in winter weather, Mother," Zia fretted as they went over the invitation lists. "The wedding is one week away and we only have two hundred replies!"

Andrada saw nothing to worry about. "They will come, Zia. Some replies will come late, and some guests will arrive even when we get no reply."

"Yes, be calm. Don't behave like such a typical bride," Adila teased.

Zia did not find her sister's teasing amusing. "I am not acting like a typical bride! I am worried about bad weather that will prevent my guests from arriving on time."

Zelma gave her a smile. "I was a bride once, too. And do you know, I was also worried about this same thing before my wedding."

"Did the guests arrive on time, Mama?" Lia asked.

"Yes, my dear, they arrived. All eight of them!" Zelma answered with a laugh. "But a royal wedding is different. Zia is not expecting only eight guests, she is expecting eight hundred."

"No, not so many," Zia said. "Six hundred would be fine."

"Zia, we'll have five or six hundred guests from the local people alone," said Andrada. "We'll have at least two hundred foreign guests, and more likely closer to three hundred." She paused and gave a sigh. "I am not concerned about the guests not arriving, I am much more concerned about feeding them all when they do arrive."

"You are right," Zia admitted. "Let's go over the menu and food supplies again. We have plenty of grain and cheese. We don't have enough poultry or venison."

"Poultry is not a problem," Zelma said. "We can get more poultry from people in the city, there is plenty to go around."

"Good. What about the venison?" Zia turned to her sister and gave her a wicked smile. "Venison!"

Adila laughed. "All right, all right. I will get Dorin and Toma and some archers. We'll organize a deer hunting party."

"Thank you, Sister," Zia said. "Would you also take Tarbus with you? I think he's bored silly sitting around the palace."

"Of course. Tarbus must do his part in feeding his guests."

"Can I come along?" Ana asked.

"Me too!" Lia said.

Adila glanced at the Queen. Andrada shook her head slowly. A deer hunt in the forest was no place for young girls.

"No, you are not old enough for a deer hunt," Adila said, getting up to leave. "But there is something very important that the two of you can hunt."

"What?" Ana asked, looking doubtful.

"Chickens!" Adila said with a grin and headed out the door.

"What a great idea!" Zia said. "Let's go and find some servants who can go out in the city and gather more chickens. You girls can both help them. Will you do that for me?"

Ana and Lia were eager to say yes. They very much wanted to be helpful, and no one ever said no to a bride preparing for her wedding.

On the day before the wedding King Decebal called for a summit meeting of Dacia's closest allies. Royal weddings were always a good opportunity for such meetings with so many leaders gathered at one location. The allies gathered in the throne room.

In addition to Davi of the Roxolani, Fynn of the Bastarnae, and Ailen of the Celts, the King also welcomed young Prince Oskel of the Scythians and Chief Attalu of the Marcomanni German tribes. Oskel was the youngest son of Queen Orica and eager to prove himself as a warrior. That kind of man made a strong ally in battle. Chief Attalu was back in a position of leadership with his tribe. Although getting up in age, now nearing fifty years old, the German was still a force as a leader and a warrior.

The Dacians were represented by King Decebal, the High Priest Vezina, General Drilgisa, General Diegis, General Sinna, and Buri. Over time Buri was taking on a more prominent role as the King's advisor and confidant while also serving as bodyguard.

"Welcome, friends," King Decebal greeted them. "I am happy to see you all gathered around my table. The war with Rome is over so let us now look towards the future."

Chief Attalu spoke first. "It is not like Trajan to back down from a fight before he has complete victory. Tell us about your treaty with Rome, King Decebal. What do you get, and what does Rome get?"

"You are right, Chief Attalu. Trajan backed down before achieving complete military victory. He might have destroyed Sarmizegetusa in time, but at what cost? He would have lost a large part of his army by doing so. And both he and we already suffered severe losses in our battles at Tapae and in Moesia."

"So then, was your battle with Trajan a draw?" Prince Oskel asked.

"No, it is not a draw," Decebal said in a firm voice. "Rome received major concessions from Dacia, some of which I was reluctant to agree to. Trajan considers it a win and I do not begrudge him that."

Decebal paused to gage the reactions of his allies around the table. These were tough men, hard men, and they expected truth from him. He would never give them anything less.

Decebal continued. "Trajan got what he wanted, and he did not have to destroy Dacia or destroy his army in doing so. I saved Dacia from destruction against a very superior enemy, and I gave us time to rebuild again. Dacia is free, not occupied by Rome, and Dacia shall remain free. In the end, both of us got part of what we wanted."

Chief Fynn gave a nod, his face grim. "It is a good treaty, Decebal. After the slaughter we put on them, and the slaughter they put on us, it was wise to end the war."

"I agree, Fynn," said Prince Davi. "I was there with you in the thick of it. It would have been madness to go on fighting."

"I noticed some Roman troops camped outside, in the middle of Sarmizegetusa," Ailen said with some surprise. "Now there is a sight I never expected to see! What are they doing here?"

"Emperor Trajan asked to post them here as observers," Vezina replied. "There are fewer than two hundred men and they are no threat. They sit there with nothing to do."

"Ha!" Ailen laughed. "Trajan does not trust you so he leaves a watchdog, eh?"

The King agreed with a nod. "Trust between Dacia and Rome is on thin ice these days, Chief Ailen."

"The job of these men," the Scythian prince wondered, "is to spy on you?"

"No," said Drilgisa with a growl. "The job of these men is to sit around until they get their throats cut."

Chief Attalu laughed. "If you do that, Drilgisa, you will certainly re-ignite the war with Rome."

Drilgisa shook his head. "I have no wish to start a war. But if war comes those poor souls out there will be the first to die."

"We are at peace now," Decebal said evenly. "There will be no throats cut."

"What I wonder, King Decebal, is which loyalties are stronger," said Chief Ailen. "Your treaty with Rome? Or your loyalty to us? If one of us ends up in a war with Rome, which side will Dacia choose?"

"I am glad you asked that question, Chief Ailen," Decebal replied, "because I want everyone here to hear my answer and have no doubts about where my loyalties are. The alliances between all of us at this table have been forged in fire and blood over many years of time. Strengthened in times both good and bad, after victory and defeat. Dacia will never betray, just as I will never betray, the alliances we have between us."

"And what of Rome?" Attalu asked.

"My treaty with Rome is a treaty of convenience." Decebal paused to let the message sink in. "There is one thing I know for certain. Rome will honor this treaty for as long as it is in Rome's interests to honor it. And Dacia will honor the treaty for as long as it is in Dacia's interest to do so. That is the situation, gentlemen. Beyond that there are no promises and nothing is guaranteed."

"A very clear answer, King Decebal, and honest," Ailen replied. "And what if Rome attacks one of us?"

"If Rome attacks any one of you Dacia will come to your aid as we always have," the King said. "Nothing has changed."

The men sat in silence for a moment. Then Chief Ailen brought his hands together and began to applaud. Davi joined him, then Fynn,

Attalu, and Oskel. Vezina joined in, then Diegis, Drilgisa, Sinna, and Buri. They applauded King Decebal and his commitment to them, but also they applauded themselves. All knew who the real enemy was. All knew they had to stand together.

Titus Lucullus was reviewing a scroll of expense reports when his sentry alerted him that visitors were approaching. He frowned at the thought of being interrupted. Even here, in a godforsaken outpost sitting inside a tent in the middle of Sarmizegetusa, he had to report to Rome an account of every denarius spent, every soldier's boot that was broken and replaced, every missing piece of weaponry broken or stolen. No nation kept records as detailed as the Romans.

Titus cursed these record keeping tasks that should have been done by a clerk. If he was a legate, in command of a legion, he would have clerks to assign clerk duties to. Unfortunately Titus did not have the wealth required to rise to the senatorial ranks, which made it not possible for him to ever be appointed legate or to command a legion. His only chance was to impress Emperor Trajan sufficiently to be promoted to the higher ranks. Caesar could appoint anyone to any military rank he chose.

"More inkstains for your fingers, Titus?" Diegis joked as he and Buri entered the tent.

"It is wretched work but it must be done," Titus said as he stood up to greet them. He turned to Buri and gave him a grin. "I must congratulate you, Buri, on your son's coming wedding. It is not often that a son marries into royalty, eh?"

Buri gave a shrug. "I take no credit for that whatsoever. They did it entirely on their own."

"In Rome you would be the one arranging the marriage, my friend. That is the responsibility of a paterfamilias," Lucullus said. "But why are you here now? Tomorrow is a big day for you."

"That is why we are here," Diegis said. "Have you ever been to a Dacian wedding?"

"No, I have not had that pleasure."

"I am here to invite you, Titus," Buri said. "Come as my guest to my son's wedding."

"I would be honored to attend, Buri," Lucullus said with genuine appreciation. "Truly, you honor me greatly."

"It is a very big wedding," Diegis said, "but there is room for one Roman. Trajan is not here, so we picked you."

Titus laughed. "I hear that Caesar enjoys a good wedding, as long as the wine flows freely and is of good quality."

"That is scandalous!" Diegis cried, also laughing. "But alas, Dacian weddings are not known for the wine flowing like a mountain stream. We drink sparingly, but there will be some made available for those who want it."

"I will find a bottle or two," Buri said with a smile. "The wedding is a full day affair, Titus. Can you find someone else to put in charge of this, uhhh, citadel and join us in the morning?"

Titus grimaced. "Do not add insult to injury please. This post was not my idea, I am simply its caretaker. But yes, I will assign my duties to an aide tomorrow."

"Good," Diegis said. "Wear your tunic and sandals, and I will lend you a good Dacian cloak. Leave your armor and gladius at home so you don't scare the women and children."

"Of course," Titus said. "However I do know already what Dacian women do with sharp sticks and spears and Roman prisoners. But I shall try to keep my fear in check, eh."

"Well, then," Buri said, "it is a good thing that we are not enemies and you are not our prisoner."

"Good thing indeed, Buri. I look forward to see you tomorrow to celebrate your son's wedding. And also your niece's wedding, Diegis."

"Sleep well," Diegis said. "Tomorrow will be a long day."

The religious ceremonies began in the morning. It was a sunny but cold day, and the ceremonies had to be held outdoors to make room for the very large crowds gathered to watch them. Dignitaries, local people, and other guests gathered on the grassy field in front of the Temple of Zamolxis. The eight great pillars of the temple, covered from top to bottom in sheets of gold, reflected the morning sun brightly and dazzled everyone within sight.

The High Priest Vezina conducted the ceremony to ensure that Zamolxis would bless the wedding. His strong and clear voice carried well in the crisp morning air. Zia and Tarbus each wore the richly embroidered Dacian wedding clothes, made with threads in a variety of colors stitched onto white woolen cloth. Over these ceremonial garments each wore a thick woolen mantle.

The wedding couple kneeled before the temple on a thick blanket laid out over the frozen ground. After a short while Vezina noticed that Zia's cheeks were turning red. In consideration of the bride and the many people standing in the cold, the High Priest went through the ceremony a bit faster than usual. This was a traditional ceremony he had performed hundreds of times over the years and it came to him as naturally as breathing.

Vezina completed the final chant and leaned down slightly towards the kneeling couple. "You may stand now, my dears. It is time for the bread ceremony."

Tarbus took Zia's arm as she stood. She gave him a warm smile of appreciation, her eyes shining. She was excited by the moment and hardly felt the cold. "Don't rush the bread ceremony, let's make it slow and elegant," she told him. "It always looks most romantic that way."

"Your wish is my command," he replied. "Also you have excellent ideas so I'm happy to do it your way."

A children's choir sang a traditional wedding song as they walked to the long table that held the wedding bread. This was a thick and long loaf of bread specially baked for the wedding, made rich with spices and nuts. While the children continued with their singing Zia and Tarbus each tore off a small piece of the bread. They mimicked each other in bringing the bread up to their mouths, as if moving in a dance, then chewed the food slowly. They savored both the delicious taste and the symbolic meaning of the ritual.

The bread ceremony was to ensure that the marriage would be prosperous and fertile. When their part of the ceremony was finished the couple stepped back and gestured to four servants standing by, wielding bread knives. The servants proceeded to cut the wedding bread into small bite sized pieces. These would be shared with people in the crowd who wished to share in the couple's happiness. At the front of the line, Zia noted happily, was her sister Adila leading Ana and Lia by the hand.

After the bread ceremony the wedding party and the crowd moved to a large open space in front of the royal palace where a large bonfire was burning. This was the time for songs and dances, which almost everyone joined in. The dances were lively and joyful and warded off the cold. In good weather the wedding feast would also be held out here. In winter weather the feast was moved indoors.

The largest feast venue was the dining hall in the royal palace. Tables for the wedding couple and the royal family were placed on a slightly raised platform against a wall. Zia and Tarbus held the center table, where they could most easily greet well-wishers. A stream of guests made their way to their table, some to wish them happiness and some to also bring them gifts. There would be a gift ceremony later in the day, but some of the wedding guests preferred to deliver their gifts early to avoid the lines later on.

King Decebal and Queen Andrada, parents of the bride, shared a table with Buri, the father of the groom. Buri's wife, the mother of Tarbus, died when Tarbus was a young child. Buri never wished to marry again and raised Tarbus by himself. To his great surprise the motherless boy Tarbus was now becoming a part of the royal family of Dacia. He did not care about status and neither did Tarbus, but the marriage made Tarbus happy so it made Buri happy.

Zia and Tarbus stopped by their parents' table. Tarbus was not used to so much attention and was starting to find it tiresome. Zia grew up with public attention since she was an infant, and managed even this level of attention in a poised and calm manner.

"Do you feel as happy as you look?" Queen Andrada asked her daughter with a smile. Zia was looking every part the radiant bride.

"Yes, Mother, I do," Zia replied and leaned down to give her seated mother a kiss on the cheek. "Everything is going so well, I wanted to thank you."

"You are welcome, my daughter," Andrada replied. "There are many people to thank, but you will have time for that later. Today is a time to simply enjoy your wedding."

"We are enjoying it very much," Tarbus said. "But there are so many people, how do you remember all their names?"

The Queen shook her head. "You are not expected to remember all their names. Just be friendly and polite and people will react kindly."

"They do," Zia agreed. "Come, Husband, we have so many more guests to greet."

Buri watched them walk away. "Zia will teach him social graces I never even thought about. But it is good for him, I suppose."

"Tarbus will always be a warrior first," said Decebal. "At times he will also need to be a diplomat so those social graces will be useful."

"Ah, here comes Diegis with my Roman guest," Buri said.

Diegis and Titus approached the royal table. Lucullus was dressed casually in his Dacian cloak borrowed from Diegis. His clean shaved face and very short haircut gave him away as a Roman, however.

Titus gave a small polite bow to the royal couple and a friendly nod in greeting to Buri. He was greeted in return with polite friendliness.

"Titus Lucullus, you have the honor of being the first Roman to be a guest at a Dacian royal wedding," Decebal told him. "Well, certainly the first since your Emperor Augustus was friendly with some of our Dacian kings."

"I was not aware that is had been so long, King Decebal," Titus said. "I am honored indeed."

"Is your garrison comfortable with your accommodations in our city?" Andrada asked the question politely but she was clearly not happy with the situation.

Lucullus took the question in stride. He could not expect the Queen of Dacia, and particularly not this queen, to be pleased about Roman troops camped in the middle of Sarmizegetusa.

"No, Queen Andrada, we are not," Titus replied truthfully. "The army tents are drafty and cold. The soldiers will bear it because that is what soldiers do."

"They would be more comfortable camped in Moesia, or even in Rome," the Queen said. She paused and gave Titus a polite smile. "But I do not mean to sound peevish. You are our guest, let us put politics aside. I hope that you enjoy the wedding, Titus."

"Thank you, Queen Andrada," Titus said.

"A wise decision," Diegis said to Andrada. "There are times when we must put politics aside or else they spoil the occasion."

"Politics spoil most happy occasions," Vezina said with a smile as he took a seat at the royal table. The High Priest of Zamolxis had a standing invitation to join the King and Queen at their table.

"Yes, Vezina," Andrada said. "So let us talk of happier things."

"Come this way, Titus," Diegis said. "We'll sit with the generals. They like to drink at weddings and only talk about their old glories."

"Of course," Lucullus said. He gave a bow to the royal couple and followed Diegis down the floor.

"I overheard some of your conversation, My Queen," Vezina said. "I don't like seeing Roman soldiers in Sarmizegetusa either, but Titus there seems like a decent sort."

"I got to know him when we were in Rome," Buri added. "He is a decent sort even if he is Roman."

"I understand," Andrada said. "Perhaps I was impolite, this is my daughter's wedding after all."

"Lucullus does not wish to be here but he has no choice about it," Decebal said. "He also knows that he is in a dangerous position."

"Enough politics!" Andrada cried with a laugh. "Let us enjoy the wedding, shall we. Where is Dorin? I don't see him."

"I saw him outside, playing with his dog Toma," Vezina said.

"Oh, let him be for a little while," said Decebal. "That boy would sleep outside with that dog if we let him."

"He would," Andrada said. She paused in thought for a moment. "It makes me sad for some reason that he is not here. This wedding feels small somehow."

"It feels smaller because it is smaller," Decebal agreed. "We are missing Cotiso. And Dochia."

"And Tanidela, captive in Rome," Andrada said with sadness. "So many painful losses in the past year."

"At least Tanidela is being treated well," the King said.

"Do we know that for certain?" Andrada asked.

"Yes, My Queen, I am told that for certain," Vezina assured her. "If there is one thing Romans hold in high regard it is royalty. Also Tanidela is admired by the common people there for her beauty and grace. She is treated as someone famous, it appears."

"My younger sister has a talent for charming people," Decebal said with a smile.

"She does indeed, Sire," Vezina agreed.

"We shall probably never see her again," Andrada said wistfully. "I shall never see little Tyra again."

Adila walked by, Ana and Lia at her side. The little girls were in a very happy mood.

"Why the sad look, Mama?" Adila asked.

"Oh, I was thinking about those who are no longer here with us. Cotiso and Dochia and Tanidela."

Adila's face went tight. "Yes, I was thinking the same. Which makes me wonder," she said, nodding towards the table where Titus and Diegis were seating, "what is that Roman doing here?"

"He is a guest," Buri replied.

"A guest?" Adila asked. "Dochia and Cotiso would still be alive if not for the Romans. Tanidela and Tyra would be here now, sitting at the table with Davi. I would not be inviting Romans as guests."

Decebal gave her a patient look. "You anger towards the Romans is justified, Adila. However I also ask you to respect Buri's wishes to invite this man to his son's wedding."

Adila sighed, then turned to Buri with an apologetic look. "Forgive my words of anger, I meant no disrespect to you, sir."

"No offense taken, Adila," Buri replied. "We are now in a time of peace, and as long as the peace lasts we sometimes make allowances for certain people. Today Titus Lucullus is my friend. Tomorrow he might be my enemy, but if that time comes then I will deal with it when the time comes. Do you understand, Adila?"

She gave a respectful nod. "Yes, sir. I understand."

"Auntie, where is Dorin?" Ana asked the Queen. "I looked for him everywhere but I didn't see him."

"Ah, I know where you can find him," Andrada said. "Would you girls do something for me?"

"Yes," Ana and Lia replied.

"Go to the kitchen and ask one of the cooks for a big, juicy mutton bone for Toma. Then go outside and that's where you will find both Toma and Dorin."

"Of course," Ana said. "Why didn't I think of that?"

"Yes, I should have known," Lia agreed.

Andrada continued. "Give the mutton bone to Toma and ask Dorin to come inside and join us. Tell him that I said so."

"Yes, Auntie," Ana replied, then hurried towards the kitchen with Lia at her side.

King Decebal caught Adila's eye and motioned to a chair close by him. She walked over and took the seat.

"I know that anger burns deep, my daughter," he said to her. "It is a fierce anger born of pain."

"Yes," she agreed. "I am angry."

"Listen to me now, Adila. You must not let this anger consume you. There is a time for anger, and there is a time to put anger aside. Do you understand?"

She thought for a moment. "Yes, I think so."

"Do not hate all Romans," Decebal said. "If we become enemies again, then hate those who become our enemies. Unleash your anger on them then."

"Yes, Tata," Adila said in a serious tone. "I do understand."

"Good," Andrada said. "This is a lovely wedding, and look at Zia. She looks so happy."

"I think I'll go over there and tell her that right now," Adila said.

"Yes, do," Andrada said. She watched Adila leave, then turned to Decebal. "I hope the day will never come when she needs to unleash her anger on Roman soldiers."

"That is not my wish, either," Decebal replied. "Even so, in life we don't always get what we wish for."

"No, we do not," Buri agreed. He gestured towards the wedding couple. "Then again, look at them. Sometimes wishes come true."

Andrada smiled at the sight. "Yes, Buri, sometimes they do."

Vezina joined in. "Buri is a philosopher with his feet always on the ground. It probably comes from tending the apple and pear orchards. Is that not so, Buri?"

"Of course it is," Buri said gruffly. "A farmer understands seasons. When one understands seasons one understands life. Spring follows winter, and the summer and fall harvests follow that. A bad crop is most often followed by a good crop. We live through floods and droughts and plagues of locusts. Come what may, we endure and we move on."

"Very well said, my friend," Vezina replied.

"And what season is Dacia in right now?" Andrada wondered.

"We are in a dark winter season," Buri said after a brief moment's reflection. "But I know that spring will follow."

"Spring will indeed follow," said King Decebal. "Then will come the summer and fall harvests. It may take us two years or perhaps three, but I promise you this. We will work hard and do whatever is necessary. By the grace of Zamolxis, Dacia will be strong again."

Early in the morning after the royal wedding, while the guests slept, Princess Adila walked in the forest below Sarmizegetusa. The sky was clear and bright and the brisk cold air cleared her mind. She was dressed against the cold in thick woolen trousers, woolen shirt, and a green winter cape. She wore fur lined boots and soft leather gloves.

Adila's soldier's bow, a gift from Cotiso, was strapped across her back. A beautifully crafted bow, made from the wood of a yew tree so that it was light, supple, and strong. A leather quiver full of arrows was slung over her shoulder. She carried a second full quiver in her right hand. Never be unprepared. Never fall short.

Adila came to the forest not to hunt, but to practice. She dropped the quiver in her hand on the ground and went into swift motion. With her left hand she brought down the yew bow from her back. With her right she plucked an arrow from the quiver on her shoulder, set her sight on a thin maple sapling thirty paces away, notched the arrow, pulled the bowstring back, and loosed. The arrow hit the tree with a thud, filling the air around it with a shower of snow that had been resting on the thin branches. The entire sequence of motion took less than four heartbeats.

She fixed her eye on a low branch twenty paces away, notched an arrow, pulled the string back to her ear, and loosed. The arrow flew straight to the target and set off another flurry of snowflakes from the tree's branches. She fixed her eye on another branch close by, notched, pulled, loosed, and got the same results. Three heartbeats, but Cotiso had been able to do it in two.

Shoot again. All in one smooth motion. Don't aim by looking at the arrow tip, aim with your mind. Look at the target and your mind and your arms will guide the arrow there. Don't think about the steps, just follow the motion. The same smooth motion, every single time. Target, notch, pull, loose. Shoot again.

She had vowed to become an archer. She was becoming an archer but still needed to get stronger, faster, more accurate. Be better than the enemy, or the enemy will kill you. It was not a contest of sport but a contest of life and death.

Adila felt at home in the forest. She loved the smell of the pine trees on the mountain slopes, the open sunny patches where grass and flowers grew, the crystal clear water in the streams. This was her home and she would defend it at any cost. She would defend her land and her people even with her life.

Adila did not have the wisdom of Vezina, or the practical mind of Buri, or the regal authority of her parents. She still had much to learn about life. There were only two things that she knew for certain.

The Romans would return. And she would be ready.

Historical Note

Decebal And Trajan is a novel. Even so the author strives to present events and historical figures from that ancient era as faithfully and fairly as possible. Ancient sources were consulted as well as modern historical reviews.

Historical accounts from that era are scant, fragmented, and at times contradictory. When historians have limited facts to work with they often speculate to fill in the blanks. They make educated guesses. Historical novelists do the same, albeit with much more color and imagination and more allowance for poetic license.

On the Dacian side Decebal, Diegis, Vezina, and Bicilis were known historical figures. Most of the major Roman characters were known historical figures. The colorful array of supporting and minor characters in the novel is the author's invention. Their depiction is portrayed as faithfully as possible to describe the people and the events of that ancient time.

Very little is known about Decebal's family or personal life. We know that he had children. Roman history records that his brother Diegis travelled to Rome to meet with Emperor Domitian in 89 AD. History also records that Decebal's sister was captured by General Maximus in the war of 101-102, that she was interviewed by Emperor Trajan, and that she was taken to Rome where she was treated as a celebrity ("a beautiful rose, but with thorns").

The name Andrada has been associated in a variety of places with Decebal's wife, his daughter, and his sister. There are no objective historical records to establish any of those connections as fact. For the purposes of this novel she is Queen Andrada, wife of Decebal.

The great lightning storm that was taken as a terrible omen from Zamolxis at the Battle of Tapae is a historical fact, as is the Dacian army leaving the battle in the aftermath of the storm. It was said that the only thing that Dacian warriors feared was the displeasure of the gods, and this incident appears to support that belief.

The story of Dochia and the "ice statues" is an ancient legend in Romanian culture. The story is told as oral history, as is much of the history of ancient Dacia. The version presented in this novel is based on the oral history of those folk legends.

The story of Emperor Trajan giving up his cape to be made into bandages for the Roman field surgeons is historical fact. Although the event is recounted by Cassius Dio and also depicted on Trajan's Column, it is not known exactly which battle with Dacia required Caesar's wardrobe to be made into bandages. The battles at Tapae and near Adamclisi were both brutal affairs with heavy casualties on both sides, and are the most likely candidates for that event which became part of Roman legend.

The war of 101-102 is often referred to as Trajan's First Dacian War. It was certainly not the first Roman-Dacian war, as is described in the first novel in this series, *Decebal Triumphant*.

The story of Decebal, Trajan, Dacia, and Rome continues to its momentous conclusion in the third book in this series, titled *Decebal Defiant: Siege At Sarmizegetusa*.

ABOUT THE AUTHOR

Peter Jaksa, Ph.D. is an author living in Chicago, Illinois. He is a lifetime student of European history during the era of the Roman Empire. In particular he is a student of the history and culture of ancient Dacia.

Books by Peter Jaksa

Historical Fiction:
Decebal Triumphant
Decebal and Trajan
Decebal Defiant: Siege At Sarmizegetusa

Psychology and Self-Help:
Life With ADHD
Real People, Real ADHD

www.addcenters.com

Made in the USA
Monee, IL
23 July 2021

74170302R00173